THE
FOUNTAIN

THE FOUNTAIN

A SEAN O'BRIEN NOVEL

BY

TOM LOWE

K

Kingsbridge Entertainment

ALSO BY TOM LOWE

ACKNOWLEDGMENTS

I always enjoy writing this page because if it were not for the help of the people listed, the novel would never become published.

To my talented and marvelous wife, Keri, who is my very first reader and editor. Thank you for your vision, continued support, and insight. You always amaze me. To Helen Ristuccia-Christensen. Your beta reading skills are wonderful. My deep appreciation for your time and stunning talent.

I toast the very brilliant and creative people at Ebook Launch. Your team exceeds expectations time after time.

To the artists and designers with Damonza. When you create a book cover you make art.

And now to you, the reader. You make the storytelling circle complete. Thank you for reading and supporting my work. I hope you enjoy *THE FOUNTAIN.*

-Tom

"No one is as old as those who have outlived enthusiasm."

– Henry David Thoreau

"The longer I live, the more beautiful life becomes."

-Frank Lloyd Wright

The novel, the 15th in the Sean O'Brien series, is dedicated to you, the reader.

ONE

Off the Coast of Florida - 1513

They were lost, but what they were about to find would be perhaps the greatest discovery in history. Juan Ponce de Leon stood on the quarterdeck of his ship, *Santiago*, in the Atlantic Ocean, less than three miles offshore, and wondered if the strange land was yet another island.

Earlier, in his voyage from Puerto Rico, Ponce and his men sailed to what would become known as the island of Bimini. They had discovered a dozen islands before sailing further west. They now were looking at land that appeared to be much larger than any island. It was a new world.

Ponce de Leon, face darkened from sun and sea, and with a trimmed, graying beard, stepped up to the gunnel and stared at the shore in the distance. His galleon, *Santiago*, was one of three ships in his caravan. It was near lunchtime, and on deck, there was the smell of rice and beans cooking in fatback, mixing with the salty air.

His chief pilot, Antón de Alaminos, a barrel-chested man, came up beside Ponce, and in Spanish said, "I do not think it is an island. We've sailed off the coast for eight hours. It is too large, and from here I see no signs of mountains or hills like we found on some of the islands."

Ponce rested both hands on the wooden gunwale. He looked at the two ships behind his, each carrying more than 100 men awaiting his orders. "Let us go ashore and claim this land for Spain."

Alaminos took a deep breath, studying his captain's face. "You think you will find it here?"

"Gold?"

"That, and what every man and woman desires. Will this be the place that holds the sacred water for eternal youth? We were told it exists in this strange land, but where?"

1

"If it is here, we shall find it. Let's sail closer and see what this new world offers."

"Aye, Captain. When we get in shallow water, we'll lower the rowboats."

***

An hour later, Ponce and his men came ashore in dinghies, the keel of the boats scraping the hard sand as waves crashed and gulls squawked overhead. Ponce stood in the bow before easing over the side and trudging onto the shore. At that moment in time, he was the first European to step on the land that later would become known as America.

They strolled through white sand so fine the dunes looked like snowbanks. Wading birds eyed the men as if they were a new species. As Ponce walked, he reached out and touched the stalks of golden sea oats, the seed heads caressing his palm. Less than a hundred yards inland, they found tall oaks heavy with hanging moss. The air was filled with the sweet scent of blooming jasmine. Birds chortled from the trees.

The men, some wearing metal breastplates of the conquistadors, converged in the shade and studied the strange flora and fauna, a bald eagle's nest high in a bald cypress tree near them. Ponce motioned for his men to gather around him. They formed a large circle. He pulled a sword from the sheath on his side and held the blade high above his head.

He looked at the faces of his men, and in Spanish said, "Behold! We have landed in a new world that offers many opportunities for Spain. I can feel that there is something very special about this land. It is in the air. Maybe what we sense is in the water, too. As we search for gold, we will hunt for a fountain that is said to flow freely, hidden somewhere in the forests. I am told it is in a beautiful garden, perhaps like the Garden of Eden. One sip from the cool waters is said to increase a man's virility. Beyond that, it will restore his soul because he will stop aging. Imagine living more than two hundred years." He grinned.

His men nodded, exchanging glances, eager to find the legendary fountain. Ponce continued. "The scent of wildflowers welcomes us. As this is the Easter season and we are surrounded by flowers, this land shall be called La Florida. I claim La Florida for Spain and for our King Ferdinand. From now till forever!" He shoved the sword into the ground. Ponce removed his hand from the handle.

The men cheered, some breaking into applause. "What is your plan, Captain?" asked one of the senior officers.

"Our plan is to find gold for Spain's treasury, collect our share, and locate this celebrated Fountain of Youth. When we return to Spain with kegs of this unique water, King Ferdinand may have a very long life on the throne and more children." He smiled and his men laughed.

"We will enter the heart of this place and begin our search. We shall take enough provisions for a week. That ought to give us time to learn the lay of the land. We do not know if there are native people here. But should we find any, our goal is to convince them to lead us to gold and the fountain. I want thirty men to remain with our ships. They rest will follow me."

***

On the sixth day, deep within the interior of the territory that Ponce had christened La Florida, the land of flowers, there were thorns literally in the flesh of his men. They marched through thick, jungle-like terrain and swamps, the men often waist-deep in tannin water. They had managed to dodge poisonous snakes, of which the most aggressive were the dark olive-colored moccasins.

As they made camp on the bank of a broad river at dusk, the men were bloodied, sore, and tired from marching through the most inhospitable terrain they'd ever experienced. The heat bore down on them like an oven, humidity causing their sweat-soaked clothes to cling to their bodies, mosquitoes circling their heads, alighting on faces and ears. Some of the men were allergic to the bug bites, causing lumps the size of walnuts on their swollen faces.

Ponce looked at his exhausted men, their spirits dwindling. Most had removed their armor. He spoke loudly and with vigor. "We are Spanish conquistadors, the toughest warriors in the world. We sail around the globe to conquer places and people. Already, we have found gold for Spain, making it one of the most prosperous nations in Europe, envied by all the rest, especially England. Conquistadors are unrivaled in their bravery and conquest. That said, we will do more heroic acts for Spain."

His men said nothing, the buzzing of deerflies and cicadas in the thick scrub bush. The insects weren't all that was in undergrowth. A dozen

3

warriors, Timucuan natives, watched the new arrivals. They kept their distance, observing the men with the shiny clothes and sunburned skin.

Ponce glanced around the natural clearing near a broad river. "We will make camp here. We can bathe in the river. Maybe we will be fortunate and wash our bodies in the waters of eternal youth. When we come out, maybe there will be no more wrinkles and our skin will be whole and healed again."

His exhausted men sat against the trunks of the oaks, the evening breeze barely moving the hanging moss. Chief pilot Alaminos, eyes red and puffy, looked at Ponce and said, "If the roots of these trees take water from the river, the water must not carry the magic elixir of youth. Why else would the trees grow long beards that are gray?"

Ponce chuckled, waving a mosquito from his face. "Maybe the magic water only works on animals and humans, not trees." He looked at the river as a dozen of his men were disrobing to bathe. One man, his face and arms beet red from the sun, welts on his arms, stood naked in three feet of water and scooped mud from the river. He spread the muck over his insect bites. Seconds later, the man screamed and disappeared under the water.

The rest of the men ran to the riverbank where a massive alligator had grabbed the terrified man by his leg, dragging him into deeper water. Ponce and two others pulled out their swords and axes, charging into the river. Three more alligators were coming fast toward them, the knotty eyes above the dark surface, tails fanning the water, gaining speed.

The men backed up as the alligator with the sailor in its toothy mouth pulled him underwater, a frothy mix of blood and spray boiling up to the river's surface.

TWO

PRESENT DAY

Gideon Wright was floating on his back in a crystal-clear spring when he heard an odd sound. His ears were just under the surface of the water. It wasn't a natural sound in a land of birdsong and palm fronds whispering in the warm breeze. He was in the center of a spring deep within a Florida forest. The surface area was more than a hundred feet across, the diameter almost a perfect circle. Cool water flowed from the springhead, meandering through the verdant forest until it merged with the St. Johns River on a journey to the sea.

Gideon lay motionless, defying gravity, his shadow cast against the white sand bottom twenty feet below him. He opened his eyes, lifted his head from the water, and listened. Dappled morning sunlight streamed through tall cypress trees with gangly limbs swathed in Spanish moss. The air was filled with the scent of wet grass, honeysuckles, and damp moss. A limpkin called out from the top of a bald cypress. The bird's cry was like that of a baby elephant who'd lost its mother in the Serengeti.

Gideon listened for a few seconds for a repeat of the strange sound before lowering the back of his head into the water. His beard and hair floated like silvery eelgrass on the water. His look resembled paintings of Poseidon from the annals of time and Greek mythology. There were wrinkles at the corners of Gideon's blue eyes, which reflected a serenity and wisdom gained through the ages. With snowy white chest hair and tanned, smooth skin, he wore cut-off blue jeans and had rubber diving fins on his feet.

He turned over and dove to the spring bottom, using his fins to cut through the current coming from an aquifer, which flowed with ancient water that had passed through layers of earth, limestone, and quartz. The boil, or *mouth,* of the spring came from a dark, wide hole just below a large outcropping of limestone some twenty feet beneath the surface. Gideon gazed at the dim cave opening as if he were staring into a mystical and forbidden gate to another world—a threshold that he wasn't supposed to cross. Not now.

The current pressed against Gideon's body, his eyes open, his hair and beard pushed back, as if he were flying in a prone position. When he swam to a specific point, about twenty feet from the boil, he opened his mouth and swallowed water. Then he pushed off the sand bottom, swimming to the surface. He inhaled the warm air, his mind clear, his senses sharp, and his body revitalized.

He would float on his back for a minute before swimming to shore and walking through a dirt and pine straw trail fifty yards east to a cypress-planked cabin that was his home. Gideon moved his arms and legs with very little effort, like a da Vinci image of the Vitruvian Man floating in the center of a blue-green goblet hole sculpted out of the earth by the hands of God.

A motion on the left side of the spring caught his attention. He turned his head, watching a great egret stalk the shoreline. The tall egret, with its snowy feathers in a land filled with shades of green, stopped moving. The bird watched him for a few seconds before taking a step on its spindly yellow legs. Gideon took a deep breath, slowly exhaling as he rested his head in the water.

The sound returned.

The birdsong stopped.

The noise was a dull thud, as if someone had struck two steel rods together underwater. Gideon knew the sound wasn't from the spring. He lifted his head and slowly swam to the grassy shore. He got out of the spring and stood there a moment, the water dripping from his body, the sun warm against his skin.

The sound came again. This time, Gideon knew what was making the noise. It was the slamming—the opening and closing of doors on a car or truck, and it was coming from somewhere downstream, just beyond a grove of old oaks that grew near the spring run. He used his fingers to push his wet white hair back and out of his face. He placed a towel over his shoulders, put on sandals, and started walking near the spring run toward the strand of trees. An osprey circled high overhead, issuing a long cry as if trying to warn the man who'd just stepped from the spring.

Through gaps in the trees, Gideon could see the glint of sunlight from the front window of a parked black pickup truck. And he could see two men unloading equipment. As a former geologist, Gideon knew the equipment was used for testing water quality and pollution levels. It also was used for assessing lakes and rivers for their potential as sources of municipal drinking water.

But not here. This land had been in his family since the end of the Civil War. It was private property and not for sale. There were *no trespassing* signs on the gate leading from the county road to his secluded driveway, to the spring, and to Gideon's home under the oaks.

As he got closer, Gideon recognized the truck and the two men who were next to the spring with their equipment. Two black cases, resembling fishing tackle boxes, lay open on the ground. Gideon knew there were no fishing lures in the boxes, only test equipment. One man was bent over, taking water samples from the spring run. The taller of the two, a sandy haired man in khaki pants and a black polo shirt, was pulling a digital water testing meter from a case when Gideon approached. "Good morning. May I ask you fellas what you're doing back out here?"

The tall man stepped from the shoreline, a digital test gauge in one hand, squinting from the sunlight. He grinned, nodding his head. "Good to see you again, Mr. Wright."

"I never told you my name."

"I'm Darnell Reid. This fine fella next to me is Lamar Dunn."

The other man was shorter, his round belly stretching the fabric of his shirt. He had a double chin and thin hair that spread like a spider's web over his balding head. He said nothing, looking back at the spring and the two water samples in glass containers, his face impassive.

Gideon stepped closer. "Last time you came here, almost a month ago, I asked you not to drive your truck onto my property. Shouldn't have to ask again. There are two *private property* and *no trespassing signs* on my gate. And the gate is closed. Last time I was cordial because you'd made a mistake, getting my land confused with another parcel. That excuse won't work now."

Reid set the scope back inside the plastic case. "Wasn't closed this morning."

"It was closed last night."

"Maybe somebody opened it while you were in bed. Older folks need their rest."

"You can read the signs. What are you doing here?"

"Just wanting to test the water quality of the spring. We're testing for things like phosphorus, nitrates, total solids, alkalinity, minerals, and bacteria levels. It's routine. Keeping tabs on Florida's springs. That's all. Everybody is interested in keeping the springs healthy."

"Testing for whom? It's not the state of Florida. You have no legitimate business here."

"We're field lab techs working for a private company that has an interest in springs. Mostly in the southeast. Tennessee is about as far north as they go."

"What company?"

"I'm not at liberty to say."

"Then leave. Your employer wants to pump water out of this spring. That isn't going to happen. Water bottling companies are one of the reasons the Florida aquifers are depleting."

"That's not the science, and it's not necessarily true."

"Science? I was a hydrogeologist for thirty-five years. It is true. Get this gear in your truck and leave, or I'll call the sheriff and have you escorted off the property."

The shorter man cleared his throat. "Sir, we apologize for not notifying you that we were here. Darnell is telling the truth about the gate. It was unlocked."

"Unlocked doesn't mean it's open."

"I understand. We just wanted to spot check this lower section of the spring and then leave. We understand that your cabin is near the springhead. We don't mean to interfere with your privacy."

"Who hired you two?"

He glanced at the man named Darnell. "A company called Enviro Resources. They're out of Tallahassee. They aren't in the spring water bottling business. They are only technical consultants for bottling companies, mostly in the Southeast part of the country."

"Your consultants should consult me before sending you two here. Get your stuff and go. Tell whoever you're working for inside Enviro Resources not to come on my land again."

Reid shrugged his narrow shoulders. "Suit yourself. But remember this: It's just a matter of time before the state comes in here and declares eminent domain. That is, they will seize this land and the spring from you for the public good. It'll become a state park—be hard for you to win that one in court." He stepped closer, using his finger to tap Gideon's chest. "A fella your age ought not to get too excited. You might have a heart attack."

Gideon grabbed Reid by his wrist, squeezing, his grip like a steel trap. His voice was now just above a whisper, his eyes burning into the man's languid stare. "If you come back on my land a third time, they'll carry you out of here."

"I take that as a threat. Is it a threat, Mr. Wright?"

"I'll leave that up to your own interpretation."

They packed up the equipment and walked back to their truck. Gideon stood there, watching them drive away. In addition to their stolen water samples, they left him with an ominous warning. His land, which he'd cared for most of his life, could be taken over by government bureaucrats who'd cut a backroom deal with a water bottling company, destroying one of the world's last remaining secrets.

THREE

Max spotted the alligator first. She barked, and danger responded by approaching. We stood on my dock, watching the closest living thing to a dinosaur swim toward us. Max is our ten-pound dachshund, and she has the courage of a lion. We were at the end of our dock on the St. John's River in the heart of Florida. The gator was crossing the river and coming toward us.

I sipped black coffee as the morning sunlight broke through the cypress boughs. A curlew called out across the river like an excited rooster greeting the dawn. The bird waded into the shallows under the cypress trees. The Ocala National Forest, with its thick foliage of cabbage palms and cypress trees, is a primal backdrop that could have been from the Jurassic era. A wood stork with a five-foot wingspan sailed over the river and into the mist.

Max paced the dock, which was elevated on rustic posts high above the river's dark surface. My name is Sean O'Brien, and at a height of six-three, I knew how to determine that the alligator was at least five feet longer than me. I weigh two hundred pounds. The gator would outweigh me by more than five hundred pounds.

The gator was now about fifty feet from the end of the dock. Because of its size, I assumed it was a male. They tend to be longer and heavier than the females. This was one of the old fellas, a senior citizen, so to speak, living in this part of the river. It was easy to estimate the gator's length by looking at the space between its knotty eyes and the space between its nostrils. Each inch from the eyes down to the nostrils is equivalent to a foot in length when measuring the gator from nose to tail. I guessed there were twelve inches from the eyes to the wide nostrils. The gator was about twelve feet long.

The big guy was at least fifty years old, maybe older. That would make him older than me. Max barked again and looked up at me. I chuckled. "That gator would consider you only as an appetizer, kiddo. When you bark, you're ringing the dinner bell."

Max barked again.

I shook my head. "Why do you always want to have the last word?" She looked away, ignoring me. The gator stopped swimming toward us. It moved to the right and swam in the direction of a meandering oxbow. The morning light was golden, like gold coins off the steamy surface. I watched the gator as it headed into the mist, disappearing as if it had swum through a curtain in time, following the slow rhythm of the old river.

Max cut her black eyes back up at me and snorted her version of a victory grunt. I picked her up, setting her next to me on one of the two wooden benches I'd built near the dock's end. One bench faced east for the sunrises. The other was a western seat to some of the most spectacular sunsets on the planet. We watched the sun rise above the cypress tree line, the dank smell of wet moss and decaying leaves in the air.

My property is three acres on the river. The home I shared with my wife and daughter is a seventy-year-old, weathered cabin built to give a wide view of the river. On my land is an Indian mound that dates back centuries to the Timucuan people. It's a small hill, rare in Florida, and is almost entirely made of oyster and clam shells. The mound is overgrown but still makes a statement of antiquity, as if it were a monument to a people and a time long gone but first documented when the Spanish conquistadors landed in Florida.

The Timucuan people numbered an estimated 300,000 at the time. Less than eighty years after the Europeans arrived, the Timucuans disappeared, with thousands dying because their immune systems couldn't fight European diseases.

According to my Seminole friend, Joe Billie, there were some survivors. He told me that the Seminole elders said that a hundred or so members of the Timucuan tribe managed to survive, allegedly, by finding something they could ingest or drink to fight off the diseases. These people hid from the Spaniards and later fled in long dugout canoes to the islands of the Bahamas and Cuba. When the last canoe was paddled over the ocean horizon, the Timucuan were forever gone from a land that they had lived on for thousands of years.

Max and I heard the door to the cabin's screened-in porch slam. My seven-year-old daughter, Angela, came down the stairs, my wife, Wynona, following her. They held hands as they walked the fifty yards from the cabin to the river. Max's tail was like a maestro's baton, moving with the excitement of an orchestral crescendo.

"Daddy!" shouted Angela. "Breakfast is almost ready."

Now Max was even more excited. Food. Bacon. She had a limited vocabulary, but the word *breakfast* was one of her favorites. We watched them walk down the dock, two of the loveliest ladies I'd ever seen. Angela, with her dark brown hair and dimples, wore a blue sundress. Wynona's black hair hung past her shoulders. She had high cheekbones and flawless olive skin. Most importantly, she had a heart that equaled her beauty. Her mesmerizing brown eyes were rich and soft. Wynona's mother is full-blooded Seminole. Her father, who died before she was a teenager, had been an Irish sailor who fell in love with America and Wynona's mother. He chose not to sail away, became a citizen, and worked in a marina until his death.

"I helped Mom make breakfast," said Angela, sitting down next to Max and me.

I smiled. "Did you make pancakes?"

"Nope. Scrambled eggs and turkey bacon. We squeezed juice from some of the oranges we picked off our trees."

"I'm hungry just listening to you."

She nodded and grinned, showing her missing lower front tooth. Wynona sat beside us and took a deep breath. "What a lovely morning down by the river. I heard Max barking. Was she talking back to the blue herons?"

"Not this morning. She was voicing her concern over a large gator that came into Max's personal space, you know, fifty feet out in the river."

Wynona smiled. "Max commands a wide berth. After breakfast, Angela and I wanted to know if you'd come with us to the DeLand farmer's market. It's only on Saturday mornings, and I've missed it the last couple of weekends. Will you join us?"

"How could I turn down that invitation?" Angela looked up at me, beaming.

***

Two hours later, we were among dozens of people strolling through the open-air farmer's market. It was under lofty live oaks in a grassy field near downtown DeLand, a small town about forty minutes west of Daytona Beach. Most of the booths were white, tent-like structures, not unlike something you'd see at art shows. Angela was wide-eyed, taking in the festive atmosphere, which included music and face painting; food truck offerings of barbecue, tacos, and pizza; and vendors selling cotton candy, cookies, and ice cream.

The farmers' stands were filled with vine-ripe tomatoes, ears of sweet corn, lettuce, bell peppers, yellow squash, cucumbers, and more. There were beekeepers selling honey in many varieties, from Tupelo to orange blossom. I could smell ripe strawberries and tangerines from one fruit stand. A large-boned farmer in a white T-shirt and denim overalls boiled peanuts in a kettle filled with steaming water. He used a red rag to mop the sweat from his bald head.

I held Angela's hand as Wynona bought ears of corn, tomatoes, and two jars of honey. For most people, it was a breezy Saturday morning at a farmer's market filled with fresh fruits and vegetables. For me, not so much. Blame it on working as a homicide detective with the Miami-Dade PD for eight years. Maybe some of my wariness had something to do with experiencing overseas combat in the Army. The real driving force, though, came from the little girl's hand I held.

Wynona and I adopted Angela after she survived a child sex trafficking ring. As a private investigator, I was tracking the ring when I found Angela and a dozen children like her locked in a steel container on a cargo ship headed to buyers in the Middle East. Angela was the youngest child. A thirteen-year-old girl was the oldest. After I rescued them, waiting for the Coast Guard, she hugged my leg, crying, not wanting to let me go. When I lifted Angela up and held her, time stood still for a moment, with warm tears soaking into my shirt. Her parents had died in a car accident, and she became a ward of the state, shuffled into foster care. But there was a bad seed with a connection to human trafficking.

Today, Wynona and I did our best to help heal Angela's scars. As the vendor was counting back Wynona's change after a sale, I watched one food stand that stood out more than all the others. At least to me. Maybe it was because there was no one in front of the man's table that was under a large red beach umbrella. His was the last booth among what appeared to be at least fifty.

As we walked in the direction of the red umbrella, I surveyed the crowd. Families mostly. There were a few young couples without children. Everyone seemed to move with the slow cadence and rhythm of a warm Saturday morning in Central Florida.

Everyone except a man in a black T-shirt and black jeans.

He caught my eye because he seemed out of place, not even pretending to buy produce. He moved through the crowd like a panther stalking prey, stopping, watching the guy under the big red umbrella, and moving on, then stopping again, watching. From the distance, and with his back to us, I couldn't get a good look at his face, only his profile, as he turned his head toward the man sitting at the foldout table under the umbrella.

I had no idea what the man at the table was selling. But whatever it was, the guy in black was very interested. So much so, he was using a long lens on a camera to take photos. At that moment, I felt a strong urge to stop by the red umbrella.

FOUR

Sometimes I wondered if Wynona had a sixth sense, almost a form of clairvoyance. Not in terms of looking into the future, but rather from being acutely aware of her surroundings. Wynona's perception made her very good at her former job as a special agent with the FBI. She worked with the Bureau for eight years before coming back to Florida to take a position as a detective for the Seminole Tribe.

After Wynona was wounded, shot by a psychopath, and underwent a career evaluation during her recovery, she decided to put her badge in a drawer and turn the page to a new chapter: becoming the owner of an antique store in DeLand. At the time Wynona was shot in the stomach, she had been carrying our child—a baby girl who didn't survive the horrific injury. I believe that Wynona looked at Angela as a gift from God, one that she embraced with every maternal fiber in her body.

She held Angela's hand as we strolled through the crowd, the red umbrella still about fifty feet away. The man in black had blended into the crowd, drifting out of sight. But he wasn't out of my thoughts. Wynona looked up at me and said, "Earth to Sean. Come in, please." She smiled. "I know you're not working a case, so what's on your mind?"

Sometimes I wish she was a little less perceptive. But I was grateful that Wynona lived in the moment and lived for her family. "I turned down a potential case recently. I didn't think I could help based on what the person told me. It was more of a police matter than …" I paused.

"Than a man with your unique skillset," she said, picking up on my thoughts.

"Maybe. If I don't believe I can help someone, the last thing I want is to take their hard-earned money to chase ghosts."

"Ghosts are in the past, as in past tense. I'm talking about the present. Penny for your thoughts right now."

"They're free. I just happened to see someone who seemed out of place. He appeared to be surveilling whoever is at the table under that big red umbrella, and he was taking photos using a long lens."

"Where was he standing while doing that?"

"Near the parking lot."

Although I worked as a private investigator, trying to help others, I wouldn't discuss much of my work in front of Angela, even if Wynona and I talked in general terms. Not after what Angela had survived. I pointed to a parked ice cream truck. "Anybody up for an ice cream?"

"Me!" Angela raised her hand.

Wynona nodded, picking up on my desire to change the subject. "Sounds good."

The ice cream truck, which was sandwiched between two food trucks, had a giant inflatable, double-decker chocolate ice cream cone floating from a thick string above it. There were wooden picnic tables scattered among the oaks, where people sat and ate. Music played from a speaker on a utility pole, with Charlie Daniels belting out *Simple Man*.

As I walked by the red umbrella, I looked at the man sitting behind the foldout table. Although he had long white hair and a flowing white beard, he was one of those people who probably would fool an age and weight guesser at the county fair. An old man who didn't appear to be an old man. His skin was relatively smooth. Crow's feet at the eyes. Even from twenty feet away, I could detect a light in his eyes, like someone who knew the punch line to a joke but was too well-mannered to interrupt the person telling the joke.

There were at least three dozen small glass bottles on the table in front of him. Next to the table was a white plastic cooler. I assumed there were more bottles in there. A handmade sign hung at the front. The sign read: *A Waterhole for the Soul – Free Water*. Now, I was even more intrigued.

I motioned to Wynona. "Let's take a quick look over there before we head to the ice cream truck."

As we came up to the table, the man stood. "Hi, folks." His beard parted into a wide smile, and his blue eyes shone like a butane flame. "I'm Gideon Wright."

Wynona smiled. "This is my husband, Sean, our daughter Angela, and I'm Wynona."

"You're a fine-looking family. Anybody thirsty? Here you can sip from the well of life."

Angela shook her head, glancing toward the ice cream truck.

Wynona said, "No thanks, but we might be thirsty after we have some ice cream."

He nodded. "How about you, sir? Would you like a cool sip?"

"Will it quench a thirsty soul?" I smiled.

He returned the smile. "It'll do more than that. It'll restore the core of your body and spirit. I can't promise it'll influence the soul like a baptism, but I can say it will make your body feel better. Think about this: the human body retains two-thirds water, and when that water is filled with contaminants, like burnt oil in a car's engine, you'll sputter and have cold starts every day, even in the summertime. Our blue-green marble of a planet is two-thirds water."

"Where does the water in your bottles come from?"

He grinned and picked up one of the bottles, holding it to the sunlight, like he was toasting the universe. "It's the cleanest and purest water in the world. I should know. I worked as a hydrogeologist for decades before I came back to my old home in Florida. I don't know exactly where the water comes from—nobody does. But my theory is that it originates from a deep aquifer that is separate from all the other Florida springs, and there are about a thousand. I do, however, know where it comes out of the ground and where it travels to the sea."

Wynona smiled. "Where's that?"

"From a spring in the center of two hundred acres I own in the Ocala National Forest. My grandfather bought it long before there was a national forest. The old homeplace is really a cabin. It's comfortable, and it's home. The spring doesn't have an official name. We've always called it Sweet Water Spring because it's the best tasting water in the world."

Wynona looked at the bottle in the man's hand. "Why are you giving it away?"

"Because I don't believe in selling something that is essential to human life. It comes free out of the ground. Who am I to put it in a bottle and slap a price tag on it? I'd rather give it to people to help them with their health. I visit nursing homes, offer the water to anyone who wants it. One of my friends there is a woman who just had her one hundredth birthday. She's been sipping this water for a long time."

"What makes this water different from other bottled water?" Wynona asked.

Gideon smiled. "The things that make this water so special don't have a long shelf life. It's only potent for seven days from the time I bring it up at the bottom of the spring. The water is still good to drink, it's just that the special minerals and fragile natural elements will fade in seven days. When consumed within that period, this water has molecules like none other that feed the body on a cellular level, almost like cell replacement. It will recharge your blood and all your internal organs. I had these special glass bottles made with cork tops. There are seven ounces in each bottle. Good for a sip a day while the water is charged with the force of life."

I listened closely to him. The passion that came from his words was as unfiltered as the water he held in his hand. His intense eyes glowed with contentment, intelligence, and compassion. I nodded. "What do you mean by the force of life?"

"Every single organism on earth needs water to survive. Without it, life would cease to exist. But beyond that, this water on the table is like a salve for the soul. And I don't say that in a glib way. Drank often enough, it has the inert power to extend life."

"Does it stop aging?"

He looked at me with a twinkle in his eye. "No. But it will slow down the aging process because it is the best natural medicine in the world for rejuvenating human cells. As cells die, we experience a gradually weakened immune system as we age. People don't die from *old age*. They perish as a result of worn-out upholstery, springs poking through and stuffing falling out."

We laughed. Angela looked toward the ice cream truck and the dancing cone. I glanced at Wynona. "Why don't you two ladies get in line for an ice cream, and I'll be there in a minute."

Angela grinned. "Daddy, what kind to you want?"

"Chocolate chip."

"Me, too. Maybe."

Gideon pointed to Angela's knee. It was skinned from a fall on the dock. "What happened to your knee little lady? Looks like a slight injury."

"I was running after our dog, Max, and I fell on some boards. Mama put medicine on it."

Wynona smiled. "Last month, the other knee was bloodied a little when she fell in a parking lot filled with crushed shells."

Gideon nodded. "Do you mind if I put a few drops of this water on her scrape?"

Wynona glanced at me for a second. I nodded, and she said, "Okay."

He came around the table with a bottle and opened it. "Do you like magic?" he asked Angela.

She nodded. "Yes."

"This is sort of like magic water. I'll put a few drops on your scraped knee, and it'll feel better soon. You want me to try?"

"Will it sting?"

"No. It'll make your knee feel better. Lift your leg just a bit, okay?" Angela raised her leg, knee bent.

He sprinkled a few drops on her scrape. "All right. It ought to make things better soon."

Angela smiled. "Thank you."

"You're welcome, sweetheart. I hope your knee feels better soon."

As Wynona and Angela walked away, I turned back to Gideon. He set the bottle of water back on the table and looked up at me. "You have a nice family. You're a fortunate man."

"Yes, I am." I glanced around, looking for the man in black. "I have a question that might sound a little bit strange, but it's only an observation on my part."

"Okay. What is it?"

FIVE

MANHATTAN – NEW YORK CITY

Clifton Price was looking for an edge. Something that would take Glacier Artesian Springs to the next level. The company was the second largest water bottling company in the world. A lot of that growth had to do with Price's savvy marketing campaigns and his relentless drive to buy drilling rights to springs and aquifers in eleven states.

Florida, though, was ground zero when it came to his interests and acquisitions. "We can't call it artesian water unless it comes from a spring," he often said in speeches and in television news clips. "No filtered municipal water for our customers." As CEO, he hired the best publicity and public relations people to make Glacier Artesian Springs almost legendary among the brands of bottled water.

The PR hype, using attractive actors, touted the water's health benefits as the best of all bottled water—supercharged, excellent alkalinity, and full of essential minerals. Mankind's internal gas. In blind taste tests, Glacier Artesian Springs was purported to top the next five brands of water. It was Price's goal to make the brand a global phenomenon, number one in every country. He spelled GAS using the first letters of each word, Glacier Artesian Springs. *Put gas in your tank for the long haul,* the slogan said. For the mindset of electric vehicle owners, the slogan was changed to *Recharge your battery with lightning in a bottle.*

Price, mid-forties, with astute dark eyes, and neatly groomed hair held in place by hairspray, exited his corner office with a sense of urgency. He walked down the long corridor in a New York City high-rise tower to the corporate boardroom, his heels scraping against the marble floor.

Price was dressed in a black, tailor-made suit, a silk burgundy tie, and a crisp, white shirt with gold monogramed cufflinks on his shirt sleeves. It was 8:30, Monday morning. This would be the first of seven meetings today. As far as Price was concerned, this meeting was the most important. And it was one that could help shape the future of the company.

He entered and took a seat at the head of a long mahogany table. The room smelled of freshly brewed coffee. Around the table sat eight people: five men and three women. All held the titles of vice president and above. Represented were legal, mergers and acquisitions, finance, research and development, and marketing.

Price opened his leather-bound notebook and looked at the agenda. He read for a few seconds before looking across at Mitchel Greene, the VP of research and development. "You're up, Mitchel. I hear good things are coming from the lab. What do you have for us?"

Greene cleared his throat. He looked over his black-framed glasses, the soft overhead lights bouncing off his bald head. "I do have good news. Excellent news, in fact. After an extensive water analysis, we believe that the water from a little-known spring in Florida is the most perfect water in the world." He took eight pages from a stack of papers next to him. "Please take one and pass them down."

When his colleagues had the paper in front of them, he continued. "This quality report is really off the known charts in terms of water quality. Not only that, but it's also how the mix is coming out of the mouth of the springs that gives it such incredible properties."

"How do you mean?" asked one of the women.

"From what our hydrologists tell me, this spring is unique because it is apparently connected to the deepest known aquifer in Florida, and for that matter, the nation. The water in this vast resource may date back to the days of the dinosaurs, and with it come the natural benefits of water that has never been touched by man or any of mankind's activities like agriculture or drilling. From total dissolved solids to minerals and electrolytes, you can see the list. This water has no equal." He glanced across the table at the CEO.

Price read the notes, leaning back in his black leather chair. "Can you imagine the marketing potential of this water? It's as if we stepped back in time and discovered a liquid pool of natural minerals so effervescent that they're like liquid diamonds in the water. This is a game-changer. I know that we're not the only company looking to add more springs in Florida. Let's make sure we are the only ones in the running to acquire water rights to this spring."

"What's the name of the spring?" asked the VP of marketing, a blond woman in her early thirties.

Mitchel Greene nodded. "The locals call it Sweet Water Spring."

"Does the state of Florida own it?"

"No. It's privately owned by a man named Gideon Wright. According to all the records that we could find, Wright lives in a cabin on the two hundred acres that surround the spring. His land and the spring are tucked away in the Ocala National Forest. The property was purchased in 1869 by a man named Jeremiah Wright, unquestionably Gideon's ancestor."

"Is Gideon Wright married?" asked the senior member of the in-house legal team.

Greene shook his head. "No. His wife died in a car accident years ago. He never remarried, and they had no children. As far as we can determine, Wright has no known heirs. When he dies, assuming he doesn't sell it, the land and spring will either be deeded to the state or one of the nature conservancies will make a bid for it."

Price leaned forward. "What we need to do is either buy the land and spring from Mr. Wright or secure water pumping rights in a long and renewable lease." He looked at the senior VP of mergers and acquisitions at the far end of the table. Tall and tanned and wearing a tailored charcoal gray suit, Roger Heller was the company's number one deal closer. "Roger, go to Florida and meet with Gideon Wright. Use whatever's in your toolbox to negotiate a win for us. I don't care how you do it. Just do it. Secure a deal either through a deed transfer or a water rights lease."

"No sweat—shouldn't be that difficult."

"Don't go into the arena without a solid battle plan. If he has an attorney, make the guy an offer he can't refuse."

Mitchel Greene cleared his throat. "Clifton, from what we've gathered, this elderly man, Gideon Wright, a former hydrogeologist, has no intention of selling the property or allowing water to be pumped and bottled. He told one of the consultants we hired that it might be dangerous if the consultant came back to Wright's spring."

"Mitchel, I don't pay you to tell me what this old man has done or said in the past. It's the future that I want to secure. We will make him an offer that he can't turn down. From what these reports tell me, there are hundreds of millions of gallons of water in this unique aquifer. We want to be the one and only straw that sucks from this special water. If properly marketed, this could become the holy grail of water. We'll tell the public that this is the stuff Ponce de Leon gave his life up to find— the Fountain of Youth. Now, we must go out there and get it."

SIX

Gideon looked at me as if he knew what I was going to ask. The music coming from the weather-beaten metal speaker at the top of a tall pole changed to Willie Nelson singing *On the Road Again.* I stepped closer to the table, shade from the umbrella falling across the water bottles. "As I was walking in this direction with my family, I noticed a man who was watching your booth."

Gideon raised his eyebrows. "What do you mean, *watching?* What man?" He glanced around the perimeter.

"He wore a black T-shirt and dark jeans and had a camera with a long lens. He seemed to be very interested in what you were doing here—perhaps to see who was drinking your water."

"Your wife said your name is Sean, right?"

"Yes."

"You must be very observant, Sean. I didn't see the man."

"I only mention this because of my background. I was a homicide detective in Miami. When you work those kinds of cases, you start noticing things that most people don't see."

"Did you develop that skill as a detective, or was it a gift you had before you started police work—this acuity to spot trouble or even evil?"

"Do you think that's what it was? Was the guy I saw evil? If so, Gideon, why?"

"I'll share some information with you because I sense you're a good man. I've lived long enough to know the difference. To answer your question as to why, there is a lot of value in the water you see in these bottles. Unscrupulous people would like to take water from the spring, label it a magic tonic, and sell it, regardless of the fact that the powerful force within has a short shelf life. These are the unprincipled, immoral

24

people in big corporations who don't care about the balance of nature. They would pump the spring dry if they had the chance."

"Could the guy I saw be a competitor?"

"How does someone compete with a product that's free?"

"To build a brand, sometimes companies give a product away. Maybe he thinks that's what you're doing until you establish a loyal customer base and begin charging for the water."

He shook his head. "I'm not a company. I'm retired. I can't charge another human being for what's essential to life itself—water. I've reached an age where my greatest pleasure is giving back, helping others with the number one thing that makes their lives worth living, and that's good health. It gives me joy to see someone's health improved by this unique water."

"That's noble and as special as your water."

"It's not mine. I'm only the caretaker, the guy who takes it from the well, so to speak, and brings it up to the people. Because of the limited shelf life of the water, I do my best to spread it around as far as I can."

"Do you dip your glass bottles in the spring and then cap them for distribution?"

"No. I dive down to where the water is in its purest form. That's near the mouth of the spring boil. During my tests, I discovered that the water contains unique elements from where it pours out twenty feet below the surface. After thirty-three feet across the white sand bottom, the water begins to lose some of its magic. The farther you are from the mysterious source, the less healthy the water will be."

"I wonder if this is the case with some of the other Florida springs?"

"No. None have the mineral and molecular combination that's in the spring on my property. It's a third-magnitude spring, meaning at least fifteen million gallons a day flow from the source and down the run a hundred yards to the St. Johns River."

"I live with my family in an expanded cabin on the river. We have three acres. No spring, but there's an ancient Indian mound next door."

"Is it a Timucuan mound?"

"That's what I've been told. I'm impressed. I rarely meet anyone who is aware of the Timucuan, or at least their faded memory." I glanced at the ice cream truck. Wynona and Angela were next in line to be served.

Gideon cast a glance across the field to the old oaks before returning his eyes back to me. "The Timucuan knew about the spring that produces this water. At the time the Spanish arrived, there were said to be members of the tribe well over a hundred years of age. But even this water couldn't keep the natives alive after they were exposed to European diseases."

I had to smile. "So, is this water the fabled Fountain of Youth?"

"No, at least not in biological terms. Nothing that I know of can maintain youth or turn back the clock, preventing the body from aging. That said, there are things that can dramatically slow the aging process. It's the right combination of foods, the Mediterranean diet is a good example. Exercise, sleep, and learning how to reduce stress. Water is the best thing in the world to maintain life, but even this water won't prevent aging. Would you like to try it?"

"Yes."

He handed a bottle to me. I pulled the rubber stopper out and took a sip. It was unlike any water I'd ever tasted. Silky smooth. Pure. If primordial could be described as a taste, this water embodied it. I took another sip, swirling the water in my mouth, almost like I was tasting an expensive wine. The water felt as if it had been filtered from the ice ages in dark, cold caverns deep under the earth.

Gideon looked at my expression like a proud man watching his child take its first step without falling over. "Well, what do you think? Do you like it?"

"Yes. It's not like any water I've ever tasted. And I mean that in a very good way. It's soft and pure. Maybe fresh is a better word. It tastes like it was filtered through cold glaciers and layers of ancient rocks, giving it a primal silkiness unlike any other water."

"Exactly. Feel free to take bottles for your wife and daughter."

"Thank you."

"You said that you used to work as a police detective. May I ask what you do now? You look too young to be retired. But who knows these days?"

"When I work, I take on cases as a private detective."

"What kind of cases? I've heard that many private investigators are hired to find out if one spouse is cheating on the other or to investigate who and why money is disappearing in a partner-owned business. Is it work along those lines?"

"No. Like you, I try to help people. They usually turn to me when they've exhausted everything else to solve the problem. These can be cold cases that the police no longer work, or deaths made to appear like suicides but aren't. I'm occasionally asked to locate items for people that have been stolen or to find someone who is missing. All in all, it's putting the obscure pieces of a puzzle together before they're lost and never found."

He nodded. "That sounds like a tracker, someone hired to see a trail where others can't find a path. Do you have a business card?"

"Yes." I gave him one. "Sometimes I get lucky for people." I looked back across the area, trying to peer around the people with paper bags of farm produce in their arms. I spotted Wynona and Angela. They were ordering ice cream. Beyond them, near the parking lot, I spotted the man in the black clothes. He was leaning against the side of a parked SUV, a red Ford Expedition. He held his phone to one ear and was looking back toward Gideon's table filled with mystery water.

SEVEN

Gideon lowered his voice, glancing from my card to me. "Sean, you said that sometimes you'll take on cases to help people who've lost something, right?"

"Yes. Have you lost something?"

He grinned. "In my long lifetime, I've lost plenty of things. Haven't lost my mind yet. Do you take on cases *before* they turn into crimes? Maybe prevent it from happening? Keep the wolves away."

"That would depend on the circumstances. What do you mean? Are the wolves circling around you?"

"I have people who are trying to steal something. The big corporate water bottling companies want the source of this water. Rather than hiring you after the fact, after it's gone, maybe I could hire you to help me prevent it from going. They want to stick their pipes, like giant straws, into the heart of my spring and pump it down. If that happens, the spring could go into distress."

"How?"

"By drastically altering the balance, pressure, and flow of the water from the springhead boil to deep within the aquifer. This would affect the rate at which the minerals pour from the spring. And in a worst-case scenario, the spring could run dry after a few years."

He picked up my card and read it again. "Sean O'Brien. Interesting, your card doesn't say private investigator; it just lists your email and phone number."

"I try not to be too wordy."

Gideon smiled. "Maybe, as a PI, you could investigate this for me. I think it's just a matter of time before one of the large bottling companies cuts a deal with the state and tries to take my land and the water rights. I'd like to be proactive and prevent that from happening. I've caught them on my land trespassing and taking water samples."

"It sounds to me like you might want to hire an attorney rather than an investigator. Yes, they're breaking trespassing laws, but an attorney could file restraining orders that put these people on notice, and it establishes a paper trail on your part."

Angela and Wynona were approaching. Angela held a single-dip cherry ice cream cone, her lips red from the cold treat. Wynona carried two cones. One was a single-dip cherry, and the other had two scoops of chocolate chip. She handed the larger cone to me. I took it. "Do you want a chubby hubby?" I asked.

She laughed. "For a man who has no noticeable body fat, I don't think a little ice cream is going to make a difference."

Angela licked her ice cream, and the scoop popped out, falling on the ground at her feet. She looked up at me, fighting back tears. I handed my cone to Wynona and picked up Angela. "Hey, sweetheart. It was just an accident. Too bad Max isn't here."

Wynona said, "Max would be licking it up right now, and it would be all over her face."

Angela nodded, her frown turning into a smile as she glanced down at the melting ice cream. She looked at me. "I was being careful, Daddy. I didn't get any on my dress."

"That's right. You saved the day. What do you say if I walk back to the truck and get another ice cream? How does that sound?"

"Good."

I glanced at Gideon across the table. "Would you like a cone?"

"Thanks for the offer, but no thanks."

I looked across the area to the ice cream truck to see if the customer line had fewer people. A moving glint caught my eye. It was the sun reflecting off the glass of a wide camera lens. The lens was pointed directly at Gideon's booth. The man in black was snapping more pictures. I stared in his direction, knowing that Angela would be in the photo.

A line was crossed.

I set my daughter down and started walking toward him.

"Daddy!" Angela ran after me. "Wait for me. I'll go with you to get the ice cream."

I knelt, wiping a spot of ice cream from her cheek. "You wait with Mom. I'll be right back."

"Okay." I watched her run around an older couple carrying a cardboard tray of ripe strawberries. When she was next to Wynona, I turned. The man in black was getting into his red SUV. I sprinted across the grass, startling a squirrel, who dropped its acorn and scrambled up a bent and gnarled live oak. The red SUV was leaving the parking lot. I got close enough to read the license plate, memorizing the tag number as the driver kicked up dust with the rear tires.

I walked over to the ice cream truck, bought another cone for Angela, and approached the big red umbrella. Wynona looked at me, her eyes knowing yet accepting the fact that I did what I had to do. Maybe I'd overreacted. But considering what Angela had gone through before we adopted her, the presence of an unknown man with a camera pointed at her violated my sense of personal space. I don't care how long the lens is or how far away the man was at the time.

I silently recited the license plate's number once more, filing that data away until I could research the name registered to the vehicle. If Gideon Wright knew the man's name, I wanted to find out before we left the farmer's market. He might not know the driver, but I could tell that he recognized the SUV.

EIGHT

I kneeled and gave the fresh ice cream cone to Angela. She smiled a toothy grin and took it. "Thanks, Daddy."

"You're welcome." Wynona handed the dripping double-dip cone back to me.

Gideon nodded. "I love to see children being raised with manners today. It seems the words *thank you* don't come as often as they used to."

Wynona said, "Angela is an easy child to teach manners to because it comes naturally to her. She's grateful—she's got an older soul."

"I can relate. That was the way I was raised a long time ago."

I shared with Wynona the gist of the conversation I'd had with Gideon and added, "I suggested an attorney. Someone who deals in property rights and privacy might be the best solution."

She nodded. "Where is your land and the spring?"

"North of here, between Alexander Springs and Silver Glen Springs. My little spring is much smaller than those two and most of the others in Florida. But none produce the combination of life-prolonging minerals in the concentration that my spring does. It doesn't have an official state name because it's on private property. My grandfather named it Sweet Water Springs. That's what my wife and I always called it."

"Does your wife help you deliver the water bottles?" Wynona asked.

"No." He averted his gaze, secluding his thoughts. "She died many years ago. Car accident. We married later in life. But together, it was a life far too short. It was a sweet love and marriage, just like our water sweet spring water. Don't be fooled by the calendar. It only lists the days. It's up to you to live them. We weren't fortunate to have children, although we would love to have raised a daughter like Angela."

Angela smiled. He continued. "There's no one left in my family. So, when I'm called home, I'm not sure who the spring's guardian will be. I made a deal with God, but what happens when I'm no longer here to keep my side of the pact?"

Wynona nodded. "Maybe you can leave it to the state with the condition that it remain as it is in perpetuity."

"That's a noble thought and idea. But the reality is that the public springs are controlled by the water districts in Florida. Most of the board members aren't scientists or people with an environmental background. They're farmers and developers, people who too often have commercial interests in water that's wrapped in plastic and shipped from Florida all over the world. The largest food company, Nestlé, pumps water from six springs in Florida."

"Do they want to pump from yours?" I asked.

"Not that I know of, at least not yet. But other companies do. When word gets out that the water from Sweet Water Spring is the best in the world, it'll become an all-out bidding war in which the big companies will wine and dine everyone from the governor down to the board members in the water district.

"Do you think the guy with the camera is working for one of those companies?"

"Probably. I've had to run people off the property recently. These are guys boldly testing the water on gated land that's posted with no trespassing signs."

Angela finished her ice cream and looked at the clear water in the bottles. "Mama, I'm thirsty."

Wynona looked at Gideon, and he said, "By all means. Please, have some water, and take bottles with you." He handed bottles to Wynona and Angela. I helped to remove the stopper for Angela, and she sipped the water. Wynona did the same. Gideon put his hands in his overall pockets, rocking slightly on his feet, waiting for a response.

Wynona said, "This water is excellent. I haven't tasted water like this in a long time. Maybe never. I grew up on the Seminole reservation. It reminds me of some of the water we'd drink directly out of the springs. When we traveled from the Everglades area up to Central and North Florida, my mother used to fill a few gallon containers of water from

Ginnie Springs. She swore that it was miracle water. But that was years ago, before the growth of agriculture in Florida. I heard that fertilizer nitrate levels are increasing in many Florida springs, causing algae."

Gideon released a deep breath. "Unfortunately, that's correct. My little spring, based on the testing I do, is the purest water I've found on earth. And, as a retired hydrogeologist, I've tested water all over the world."

Angela took another sip of the water. "It's yummy. I like it."

Gideon chuckled. "Good! That makes an old man like me happy."

I finished my water. "Gideon, that man in the SUV, the red Ford Expedition, have you seen it before today?"

"Yes. It was on my land, maybe two weeks ago. By the time I walked from my cabin toward that area of the spring run, where the vehicle was parked, it vanished. The driver didn't take the time or effort to close my gate at the end of the drive. I could tell by the tracks he left next to the spring run that he was probably testing the water. There were tripod marks in the sand. And he left behind a test strip and a small vial. Some people have no regard for nature, leaving their trash wherever they go. He left behind something else, too."

"What was that?"

"A trail camera. He'd strapped it to a tree with the lens aimed back toward my cabin and the springhead. When I took the camera down, I felt violated. Like he was trying to photograph and steal something sacred, perhaps the spirit from the water."

"It appears that his prime intent, or that of the people for whom he works, is to monitor you and to see when you leave your home. It makes it easier for them to return and take more samples from the spring, especially closer to the boil."

"Did you call the police?" Wynona asked.

"I'll call the sheriff's department after I find repeat trespassers. However, by the time a deputy would get out to my place, the intruders would be long gone."

I said, "Maybe you should get your own security cameras. Have a video record if these guys come back."

He nodded. "That's a good idea. I don't think it's if they'll come back; it's when they return."

"I know Florida has hundreds of springs. Why are these people just now encroaching on your land and spring?"

"I think it's because some of the others are pumped dry. That's what happened to White Spring. Now it's not much larger than a swimming pool with green water on the surface. There is no flow anymore. For other springs, their daily water volume is dropping. It's just a matter of time before they go dry. My little spring, with its extraordinary water quality and strong flow, is suddenly being discovered and sought after."

"Unfortunately, water and water rights have been the reasons some have gone into battle."

He rose from the metal folding chair behind the table with the water bottles and rubbed his lower back. "For me, I'm just one man up against large corporate interests with deep pockets, bought politicians, and teams of lawyers. It's not unlike a confrontation between David and Goliath. Maybe I'll find a way to keep them from destroying what I believe is a spring connected to the Garden of Eden. The last pure waterhole left on earth."

***

A half hour later, as Wynona and Angela watched two teenage boys fly kites in an open field next to the farmers market, I made a phone call to my close friend. His name is Dave Collins. He lives on a trawler in Ponce Marina. As a former CIA field operative, he is one of the most intelligent and resourceful people I've ever met. My boat, *Jupiter*, is docked near his trawler. Dave, who is retired, enjoys helping me with some of my cases.

"Hey, Sean. Haven't seen you at the marina in almost a month. I hope the battery on your bilge pump is strong." He laughed.

"Me, too. I'll be down there soon. I promised my family a boat ride on the Intracoastal. If you have a few minutes, maybe you can run down a license plate number for me."

"I can do that in my sleep. Do you have a bigger challenge for me, or should I go back to Sudoku?"

I told Dave about Gideon Wright and the mystery man with the camera and red SUV. When I finished, he said, "You know, Sean, legend has it that the elusive Fountain of Youth, sought after by Ponce de Leon and many others, was or is hidden somewhere in Florida. Many historians laugh at the scenario. They say the fountain or spring, if there was ever any validity to the legend, has probably long since dried up. What if this chap, Gideon Wright, found it or some form of it?"

"If that's the case, it's been Florida's best kept secret for more than five hundred years."

"When I get the information on the tag number, I'll call or text you."

NINE

His words echoed in my thoughts. As we drove from DeLand back to our home, I thought about the conversation with Gideon Wright, including the way he spoke about time. *Don't be fooled by the calendar. It only lists the days. It's up to you to live them.* I glanced up at the rearview mirror. Angela was in her seatbelt, watching the countryside through the window, the afternoon light soft on her face.

Wynona was in the Jeep's passenger seat next to me. She used a blue ink pen to work a crossword puzzle in a book of puzzles she often brought on the road. Gideon's words seemed more profound now—my family with me, time moving like the blur of scenery through the windshield. I thought about little Max waiting for us back at our river cabin, and I thought about something else Gideon said that was seeping into my core, stoking the embers of my purpose.

So, when I'm called home, I'm not sure who the spring's guardian will be. I made a deal with God, but what happens when I'm no longer here to keep my side of the pact?

We were back home. I turned the Jeep into the driveway, driving down our long gravel and oyster shell drive, and parked next to Wynona's car under a shady canopy of live oaks, some of the trees more than two hundred years old. I glanced toward the dock, where a white pelican was standing on the handrail.

After we unloaded the Jeep, we walked around the cabin to the backyard and the screened porch. Max greeted us with excited barks. Angela bent down and gave her a hug. "Hi, Max. Mama and Daddy bought you a toy."

Angela stood up and showed Max a soft rubber bone. Angela used her thumbs, pressing to make the toy squeak. Max lifted her ears, tilting her head. Angela tossed the bone across the porch, with Max scampering to retrieve it. In seconds, Max brought the toy back, dropping it next to Angela's pink sneakers.

"We need to start dinner," Wynona said, unlocking the backdoor that opens to our kitchen.

"Mama, Daddy, look." Angela lifted her right leg and knee. "My boo-boo is gone."

Wynona bent down for a closer look, studying the pink area where the knee was skinned a few hours ago. She stood and met my eyes. "It didn't even scab. It simply healed over with new skin. Except for a pinkish area, there is no scar or trace of the scrape. Sean, what's in that water?"

I smiled. "Maybe it's a miracle tonic for scrapes and cuts. Angela is at the age where she can get a scrape in the morning and have it almost healed by bedtime."

Angela grinned, looked at her knee, and then back at Max. Wynona said, "Angela, why don't you take Max outside, okay? She hasn't gone to the bathroom in a few hours."

"Okay. Come on, Max. Let's go to the backyard." She opened the screened door, and Max flew down the steps, trotting out to the center of the yard, Angela following.

Wynona looked at me. "Granted, a child Angela's age heals quickly after a scrape. I did as a little girl on the res. If it took more than a couple of days, my mother would go down to the medicine man's chickee and return with some concoction that looked like dark mud and smelled of old earth—maybe sulfur. She'd put that on the open cut and wash it off in a few hours. The next day, there'd be a scab in place of a cut. Angela has no scab."

"Angela also drank some of the water after Gideon put some on her scrape. Maybe the combination filled her little body with the right mix of minerals and expedited the healing process."

Wynona looked around, inspecting all her plants and hanging baskets on the screened porch. She pointed to one plant in a clay pot in the corner. "Usually, I have a pretty good green thumb. But that one orchid over there has resisted all the tender loving care I could muster as a gardener."

"Which one?"

"Come on, Sean. With your gift of observation, you probably spotted it fading away before I did. It's the one crying in the corner. Remember the gorgeous lavender blooms?"

"Yes."

"They're a distant memory now. The orchid stopped blooming and basically stopped living. It's strange because I have seven more orchids on the porch that are doing just fine. That poor thing is on its last leg. Maybe some of this water will help."

She reached inside her purse and took out one of the bottles that Gideon had given her. She stepped over to the pot and poured water around the orchid, whose stems were more brown than green.

Wynona chuckled. "If that orchid shows a hint of regrowth, I'll call this miracle water, too."

I said nothing, staring at the sickly orchid, the caw of a crow at the top of a cabbage palm in the corner of our yard.

Wynona nodded. "What's on your mind? I could tell on the ride home that you were deep in thought.

"I was thinking about the guy with the camera and telephoto lens. I was holding Angela next to Gideon's stand when the guy snapped some pictures. I don't like that."

"I agree. But there isn't much we can do."

"I memorized his license plate number."

"Why am I not surprised?"

"Obviously, there's something inside of me that can't let its guard down. I mentioned to you the conversation I had with Gideon when you and Angela were getting ice cream."

"Yes. What an interesting man."

"It looks like he, or at least his land and spring, are in the crosshairs of corporate interests. If this water does have the healthful punch that Gideon says, how can one old man fight that? I feel obligated to help him."

"You suggested that he hire an attorney."

"I did. But, too often, when big corporations flash large sums of money, the lawyers like to meet and talk settlement. That is, an attorney representing Gideon would profit far more from a large settlement than being paid by the hour for a case that is frequently routine. In cases, such as these, the government could be looking to seize land for what they contend is a public benefit, all the while, destroying the right to private property ownership. But even more, a remote spring that has flowed freely for thousands of years with life-sustaining minerals could become a corporate casualty. As a Florida native, that would play hard on my conscience." I looked at the empty bottle in Wynona's hand, heard Angela laughing, and Max barking as they played in the twilight. And I heard Gideon's question.

What happens when I'm no longer here to keep my side of the pact?

***

Following dinner and after I read Angela a bedtime story, I entered my small office in a back section of the cabin. I sat in front of my computer and accessed as much information as I could, initially to find out about Gideon Wright. There wasn't a lot, or maybe I simply couldn't find data on the guy under the shade of a red umbrella with small bottles of water on a table.

A few minutes later, I managed to find a reference to a geologist with the name Gideon Wright who worked with another geologist, Charles Richter, in the 1940s. Richter would develop a scale for measuring the magnitude of earthquakes. Richter died in 1985. There was no notation of Wright's death, or for that matter, his birth. Maybe it wasn't the same man.

It couldn't be unless he was much older than what he appeared to be as he sat beneath the umbrella, giving away water. I used a satellite map to locate what I thought was Gideon Wright's land and spring. I could see aerial images of an old cabin and a spring or creek that wound from near the cabin in an eastward direction until it merged with the river.

I checked the property records, finding a two-hundred-acre parcel owned by Gideon Wright. The property history indicated it had been in the family since right after the Civil War. The land and spring were originally purchased by Jeremiah Wright in 1869. He must have been Gideon's relative. The property was inherited by a William Wright shortly thereafter, then passed on to Gideon in 1935. Before Jeremiah, there was no record of the property being owned by anyone else.

It's certainly not a common name, but was it the same Gideon Wright who gave us the water? And how old was he?

TEN

Gideon was about to make his favorite visit of the week. It was a sunny Sunday morning when he pulled into the lot and parked under the shade of loblolly pines not far from the entrance of Bayview Assisted Living, a sprawling single-story senior care building. Gideon shut off his car's engine and lifted a Styrofoam chest from the seat next to him. In his other hand, he carried a paper bag. He locked his car and entered the facility.

Five minutes later, he knocked softly on a closed door. Room number thirty-one. "Come in." The frail voice was that of a woman.

Gideon entered, walking across the room to the side of her bed. He set the ice chest down, reaching for the hand of the woman in the bed. She looked up and smiled, her lined face radiant. Her long silver hair cascaded over the pillow. She had a delicate nose, emerald-green eyes, and a wide smile.

"How are you, Olivia?"

"I can't complain."

"Let me get some more light in here." Gideon moved over to the window and pulled back the drapes, allowing sunlight to flood the room. "Aren't the support staff supposed to open these curtains for you every morning?"

"Yes. Sometimes they're a little slow."

"It's almost 10:30. I'd say they're in no hurry."

"It's all right, Gideon. It's just a comma on today's page of life."

He smiled and glanced around the room. There was a dresser and mirror with a framed photograph of a young woman and man standing in front of a church. Both smiling. Across from the dresser was a small desk for writing. There were two comfortable chairs and a TV screen on one wall. Under the screen, there was a four-tiered bookshelf lined with books.

"I brought something for you."

She sat up in bed, pushing her long hair behind her shoulders. "What is it?"

He handed her the paper bag. "Open it."

"Okay." She peeked into the bag, lifting out a book, her eyes settling on the cover. "Oh, *Twilight in Paris,* by Stephanie Hammond. This is so nice. She's one of my favorite authors. Thank you." Her eyes welled up. She looked through the window to the sunlight shimmering off the surface of a wide bay in the distance.

Gideon smiled. "I hope you enjoy it."

"I'm sure I will. I'll read it on the patio near the garden. Take me out there now, will you, Gideon? It seems like it's been a while since I smelled the gardenias."

"We'll go out there in a moment. First, I want to give you some of the water. It'll help your eyes and sharpen your vision so you can read every word in the book."

"No word shall escape me." She laughed.

He opened the top of the Styrofoam chest, reaching in and taking out one of the six bottles. "Let's sit on the side of your bed."

He held her hand as she pulled herself from the center of the bed to the edge, legs dangling off one side, feet visible from the ends of her blue pajamas. Gideon removed the stopper from the top of the bottle, handing it to her. "Take a sip, Olivia."

She nodded, slowly moving the glass bottle to her lips and sipping the water. She stopped, holding the bottle in both hands, her eyes closed. In less than a minute, there was more color in her face. She opened her eyes, took another sip, and smiled. "It is so good. This quenches more than an old woman's thirst. It's as if I'm drinking from a holy chalice—raindrops from Heaven."

She stood, setting the bottle down on her nightstand. "I'll be right back." She walked across the room, opening the door to her private bathroom. Gideon stepped over to the window and watched a sailboat in the center of the bay, the wind puffing the mainsail.

When Olivia came back into her room, she was wearing a dark blue robe over her pajamas, slippers on her feet. She looked at the Styrofoam chest on the floor next to her bed and eyed Gideon. "Do you want to visit with the others before we go out to the garden? I don't want to keep our friends from the water."

"I will make my rounds after we spend a little time in the fresh air. The morning breeze is blowing across the roses and gardenias. The lovely scent is almost intoxicating."

***

A few minutes later, they were outside. The large terrace was shaded by a wooden overhang, its floor was made from smooth river stones, and over half its length was lined with colorful rose bushes. There were a dozen chairs. A man with snow white hair sat in one of the chairs, a wooden cane propped on the armrest. He stared past the flowers to the bay, his face reflective, as if he pictured himself behind the wheel of a trawler that was cutting through the center of the bay and heading toward Sebastian Inlet.

Olivia hooked her arm in the crook of Gideon's arm as they strolled outside, the lavender throbbing from the dance of bees, the butterflies floating like pieces of rainbow confetti in the breeze. Gideon and Olivia stopped as the stone path curved back toward the facility. They stood in the shade of a tall canary palm, the bay shimmering in the background.

Olivia stared at the water, her hair barely moving in the soft breeze. "Remember those times when Paul and I would go sailing with you and Heather?"

"I remember."

"We had such fun. I miss my Paul so much, just as I know you long for Heather. The boat we had in those days was made from wood. We'd sail from Miami to Bimini and then down to the Keys. Key West was just a tiny town back then. I remembered folks calling it conch town."

"I met Ernest Hemmingway in Key West once. He made the place famous, and then the tourists started coming in droves. Anyway, it was in the early 1930s, and I had just finished reading *A Farewell to Arms*. So I wanted to let him know how much I enjoyed his book."

She moistened her dry lips. "Traveling, sailing … those were the good old days. I'm not sure how old I am anymore. Every time I feel like my batteries can't be charged anymore, you arrive, and I sip that sweet water. It keeps my kidneys replenished and all the parts in between." She eyed him. "Somehow, I managed to live longer than my son. I've felt guilty about that. I know it's not my fault, but a mother isn't supposed to bury her child. Do you know how old I am, Gideon?"

He smiled. "All I know is how young you are. Look at that." A blue and golden butterfly came within a few feet of them. Gideon slowly stretched out his left arm, palm up. In seconds, the butterfly alighted on his hand, its sapphire wings iridescent in the morning light.

***

Later in the afternoon, after Gideon had spent time with five other old friends in the senior care center, he was driving back to his home. As he drove through the forest and came closer to his gate, he could see a SUV parked there, just off the shoulder of the road. Gideon put on his turn signal, pulling off the road. He stopped his car at the closed gate, pulling keys from his pocket and unlocking the entrance.

A man got out of the SUV. As Gideon turned to walk back to his car, he looked at the man, who was in silhouette in the afternoon light. "Mr. Wright, may I have a word with you?"

ELEVEN

I was taking paper sacks of groceries from my Jeep when I heard Wynona make an odd sound. It was a cross between a shout of surprise and delight. She, Angela, and Max had gone into the cabin before me. They got as far as the screened-in back porch and the door to the kitchen. "Sean, you have to see this!"

"Daddy! Come look," Angela yelled.

Max barked. All three of my ladies were calling me. I almost set the groceries down and rushed up the steps to the porch. I carried the two remaining bags in and put them on the wicker couch next to one of the chairs. Everyone was in the far corner, Max with her tail wagging, a hanging basket of ferns above them. They were looking at something.

I walked up to them and saw the source of Wynona's surprise. The orchid plant had come back from the dead. Not only was it green and healthy looking, but a beautiful lavender blossom was emerging from the top of the plant.

Wynona looked up at me. "All I can say is, oh my God. Look at that. I wouldn't have thought it was possible."

"That flower's pretty, Mama."

"Yes, it is, sweetheart. Pretty just like you."

Angela grinned. "Can I have a popsicle?"

"Okay."

Angela walked from the porch into the kitchen, Max at her heels.

Wynona leaned down for a closer look at the orchid. She put her nose next to the blossom, inhaling. "I don't use the word miracle often. But this certainly defines the word. What is in that water Gideon gave us? First, it heals Angela's scrape in a few hours, and then it brings a very sickly orchid back from the brink and turns it into a trophy-winning specimen.'

44

"It's impressive."

"No, Sean, it's mind-blowing. The gardener in me wants to think of the orchid as if it were in some sort of dormant stage, then the water, with all its delicious minerals, gave it a shot of plant adrenaline. But the pragmatic realist in me can only say, wow."

"I wonder what would happen if I poured some on at the base of our orange trees. Would that create super oranges the size of grapefruits, something that might even break the limbs?"

"Who knows? I'm more than happy with our baseball-sized oranges. But it does beg the question, what's in that water?"

"Whatever it is, it packs a punch. Gideon said that supercharging lasts for only seven days and then fades away, leaving simply pure water."

Wynona stood. "If the water can truly bring back nearly dead plants and heal cuts without even a scab, imagine what it would be worth to water bottling companies or even Big Pharma."

"But they'd have to find a way to extend the shelf life of the water to market it as a miracle cure. When I called Dave and told him what Gideon shared with us, Dave brought up the possibility that the spring water could be what explorers like Ponce de Leon were searching for when they rowed ashore from their Spanish galleons and landed on Florida's shore. Through the centuries, Ponce may have been associated with the Fountain of Youth mission or fable, but he was just like most of the conquistadors, searching for gold and precious jewels. The Fountain of Youth would have been a nice addition."

Wynona looked at her right foot. "Pulling weeds in the flower beds yesterday, I got a bite from a vicious fire ant. When we were at the farmers' market, the bite was swollen, about the size of a green pea. Now it's gone. And I only had a few sips from my bottle of Gideon's water."

"Vicious, eh?" I smiled. "I almost wish I had a few scratches on me. I usually have some from working around the house. But I don't. After I drank the water, I didn't feel any different. The thing that stood out to me was how the water tasted. For those people who say water is tasteless, they should try Gideon's water. It was silky smooth, and it had a taste that I can only describe as earthy, as if it came from glaciers during the Ice Age. He said it comes from an old spring in the center of his two hundred acres north of us, in the Ocala National Forest, somewhere between Silver Glen Springs and Alexander Springs."

"Why hasn't anyone found out about this years ago? Look at the hot springs around parts of the South. There is only one in Florida. These hot or warm springs are touted for their high concentration of minerals. People from all over the world go to those places to soak in the waters, which are said to be medicinal. Gideon's spring seems to have missed the radar of the marketing and PR machines."

"That may be because of what Gideon shared with me. He said, from the limestone mouth of the spring, the water only retains the special minerals and molecules for about thirty-three feet. After that length, it begins to dissipate. By the time it makes it down to the St. Johns River, the water is pretty much like most of the other hundreds of springs in the state."

"So, from the womb, these life-changing elements are only there for thirty-three feet. And they expire after seven days in the bottles. Interesting." Wynona looked down our sloping backyard toward the river, her thoughts seemed as far away as the oxbow in the distance. "I remember my grandfather talking about something his grandfather told him. My great-grandfather was a Seminole medicine man. He learned about plant life from the elders. It was a handed down skill until recent times. Anyway, my grandfather said he always heard about a secret spring deep within the forest. No one knew where it was, and the prevailing thought is that it either dried up or became so covered in underbrush that it was out of sight. The spring was believed to have had strong healing powers. Almost magical."

"How so?"

"According to legend, the first Seminoles who arrived in Florida encountered the few remaining Timucuan Tribe members. They were the ones who somehow survived the onslaught of the European disease. They had drunk the water from this hidden spring. It apparently helped them fight off things like smallpox and other diseases. There's something else, too."

"What is that?"

"These people were said to have been very old—many at least a hundred years old." Wynona looked down at the orchid blooming, lifting her warm brown eyes up to me. "What if Dave's right? What if Gideon's water is what Ponce de Leon was looking for, the infamous Fountain of Youth?"

"That might explain the guy at the farmers' market with the telephoto lens camera. Who is he, and who's he working for?" My phone buzzed in my pocket. I looked at the screen. Dave Collins calling. "It's Dave. I'd like to take this."

Wynona nodded, picking up a sack of groceries and carrying it into the kitchen. I answered my phone, and Dave said, "I ran a check on the license plate. It's registered to a guy named Floyd Shaw."

"Did you look into his background?"

"Sean, never doubt a former CIA operative with way too much retirement time on his hands. Of course. It seems that Shaw has no real job. What he does have is a criminal record. Served five years in Raiford for racketeering, money laundering, and strong-armed assault. He bills himself as a PI. However, he appears to be a former mobster looking for freelance work wherever he can find it."

"Where's he from?"

"The Tampa area."

"I doubt Shaw would be doing this on his own. I wonder who retained his services."

"Wish I could help you there. I can only deduce that it is someone with an interest in Gideon's spring. Maybe someone or some company is pushing for eminent domain—a state takeover of the land and spring. That could be a scene in which the nefarious party might cut a deal with the state to pump water from the springs. Or a third-party property management firm. If given control under the guise of public use after condemnation, they could make millions in a lease while the public plays and paddles in the spring run. That's only a guess, though."

"Probably a good guess. Gideon said he's been running trespassers off the land. Not teens looking to swim in the spring, but rather men with water testing equipment."

"So, somehow, the word's out there. The question is how far out there is it, and what's the value of a hidden spring that could be marketed as the true Fountain of Youth? Throw away the Botox needles and plastic surgeons. Just sip this water and cheat time, maybe even death, for a while. That, my friend, would be worth billions of dollars."

TWELVE

Gideon was used to looking for anomalies on Earth. He spent his professional life studying land and water sources and their complexities. He examined the world's pulse, searching for potential earthquakes, landslides, and even floods. He had a keen eye for natural variances in the terrain. He found those skills helpful when meeting people for the first time. Gideon believed that he could detect a real smile from a fake one. He thought the man approaching him had the rehearsed smile of an actor.

He was dressed in a dark sports coat, khaki pants, and a pale blue shirt. His dark hair was turning gray just above the ears, and his haircut was fresh. He had wiry black eyebrows, a wide grin, and a tanned face. To Gideon, the man's smile appeared phony. "I'm Roger Heller. I saw your no-trespassing sign and didn't want to violate it. So, I thought I'd wait here to catch you coming or going."

"Okay. What can I do for you, Mr. Heller?"

"Just give me a few minutes of your time."

"About what?"

"About your spring. I represent a company called Glacier Artesian Springs. I flew in from New York to meet with you."

"If you'd called, I could have saved you a trip." A car whipped by the men, the blast of wind rattling the wild honeysuckle bushes.

"I understand your reluctance to talk with me. However, if I can have just a few minutes of your time, maybe over a cup of coffee, I can give you accurate information and hopefully something to think about considering your spring. Please, I'd hate to go back without at least having a real conversation with you, and not one on the side of the road. Is there someplace close where we can sit down?"

"Astor is close. There's a diner there called the *Wagon Wheel*. Coffee is always fresh. You can follow me."

"Excellent."

***

Twenty minutes later, they were inside a rustic diner, the *Wagon Wheel*. The walls were made from rough-hewn cypress, and a trophy largemouth bass was mounted to one wall. There were a dozen tables, ten stools along a counter near the kitchen, booths next to windows overlooking the St. Johns River. There were less than a dozen customers. Gideon and Heller sat at a booth.

In an adjacent booth, a man was dining alone. He had a fleshy, round face and scraggly, combed-over hair that didn't do much to conceal his balding head. He was eating fried chicken, mashed potatoes, coleslaw, and biscuits with local honey. He sipped sweet tea.

Heller looked around. "This place certainly has atmosphere. Nothing like this in New York."

"If you're hungry, the food is even better than the surroundings." A server came, and they ordered coffee. Heller turned to face the middle-aged woman, her hair black as coal. He asked, "How's the apple pie?"

"Great. Made fresh this morning."

"Sounds good. I'll take a piece with a cup of coffee."

"Comin' up. Anything else for you, Gideon?"

"No, Becky. Coffee's fine, thanks." She picked up the menus and left.

Heller sat back in the booth, glancing out the window at the dark blue river, a pontoon boat gliding over its smooth surface. "What a lovely place. I'm sure there are alligators in that river."

"Lots of gators. I wouldn't suggest swimming across it." Gideon placed his forearms on the table, interlocking his fingers. "Mr. Heller, what is it you want to discuss with me?" The man in the adjacent booth, his back to Heller, sat behind him, sipping sweet tea from a glass dripping with condensation.

Heller smiled. "I like how you get right to the point. No casual small talk."

"I don't know you. There is nothing casual about this. I can and will be courteous, but not casual. It seems to me you're all business, and you're in the water business."

"We are, and we sincerely believe that Glacier Artesian Spring has no equal when it comes to water conservation and the responsible use of spring water. We never use filtered municipal water, always insisting on natural spring water. We work very hard not to have a negative impact on any of the springs where we tap water."

"You don't tap it. You pump it. How's that really working out for the springs?"

"Very well, as a matter of record. Our usual water take per day is less than five percent of a spring's daily output. If we didn't source the water, all of it would flow into various rivers and eventually become part of the world's oceans. By tapping into pure springs, we can bring the healthful benefits of spring water to millions of people around the world. So many countries lack access to clean, safe water. We're trying to make a positive difference."

The coffee was served, and the waitress placed a blue plate in front of Heller with a slice of warm apple pie on it. "Can I get y'all anything else?"

"No thanks, Becky." Gideon nodded.

Heller looked from the warm pie to the server. "I'm fine. Can't wait to try it." She smiled and left. Heller eyed Gideon. "Mr. Wright, I understand you call your spring Sweet Water."

"Been that name for many years."

"It is sweet water. I'm here because I'd like you to consider a partnership with us."

Gideon sipped his coffee.

Heller took a bite of pie and sipped his coffee. "This is excellent. As I was saying, I'm not looking for an answer from you now. Just please think about a partnership in which we would guarantee not to remove more than ten percent of your spring's total daily output. The pumping equipment would be inconspicuous, as to allow the spring to remain like it is in terms of its natural aesthetics."

"Once touched, it can't be untouched. Ever."

"We are very good environmental stewards. The water is never degraded or polluted by what we do. We'd like to enter into an exclusive water rights lease for ten years with an option to renew every ten years. In the event of your passing, whether you leave the property and spring to an heir or another entity, the lease would continue with whomever has the deed."

"Mr. Heller, I appreciate your offer, but ...."

"Please, let me at least make an offer. So far, I've only proposed one scenario."

The man sitting in the booth behind Heller leaned back a notch, tilting his head and listening. He was a local lawyer, and the scent of new money smelled sweeter than the honey on his biscuits.

THIRTEEN

Even upside-down, Gideon could read the incoming number. Heller's phone buzzed softly on the diner's table. Gideon could see that the area code, 212, was a New York number. "Do you need to answer that?"

Heller shook his head, eyes unreadable like a poker player sitting across the table from Gideon. "No, I can return calls in my hotel room. Right now, I want to be present for you as we discuss this potential partnership. Of all the water bottling companies out there, none has our record of environmental stewardship."

Gideon angled his head and ran his tongue along the inside of his cheek. "I'd prefer that you don't use that word, *partnership,* even in hypothetical terms. I can't partner with your company or any other water bottling company. I made a pact with the man upstairs, and my word is really all I have on this earth. I will honor my commitment."

Heller nodded in agreement, leaning in closer, like an old friend listening to every word. "I couldn't agree more. I believe we must be guardians of the good earth. If not, there will be no more good earth for generations to come. Although I'm a little rusty in my church attendance, I was raised Presbyterian, and I remember something my mother quoted from the Bible. I believe it was in the book of Matthew, and it went like this: 'When you give … your Father who sees what is done in secret will reward you.' Imagine offering clean, mineral-filled drinking water to millions of people. That would be one of the greatest gifts on earth—helping your fellow man."

Gideon sat back on his bench seat, pressing against the booth's vinyl covering. "But it's not a gift if you charge people for it."

Heller glanced around the diner, lowering his voice, perhaps now oblivious to the lone man in the booth directly behind him. "If you are interested in selling the land and spring, we're able to write you a twenty million dollar check to transfer ownership." He paused, waiting for a response from Gideon before continuing. Gideon didn't react.

"However, if you'd rather retain ownership and lease in perpetuity, that is fine with us, Mr. Wright. Either way, we'd love to partner with you. You would be compensated at one point four million dollars per year under the lease. Florida has no state income tax, so after federal taxes, you'd clear a million dollars annually. That sum would be passed on to whoever was deeded the land and spring following your death."

Gideon sipped his coffee. He looked out the window toward an anhinga standing on a cypress stump, the bird's wings outstretched, drying in the sun. "Thank you, Mr. Heller. But no thanks. I'm not interested in either of your offers."

"I understand your hesitancy and reluctance. If that proposed compensation amount is insufficient for you, what would it take to sell the land and springs or lease the water withdrawal rights?"

"It's not about the money. I do all right financially. I've saved and invested my money over the years. But for me, when it comes to Sweet Water Spring, it's never been and never will be about the money. It is always about the health of the spring. You say your company caps pumping at ten percent of the total daily volume. But even that amount from the aquifer, which feeds the spring, might cause a change within it. And that could upset the delicate balance of water pressure and the minerals present in the current environment."

"Our consumption wouldn't be a detriment and create irrevocable damage to the spring or cause it to run out of water. It would be counterproductive to change the water quality because that's where our interest lies. Our business model isn't about change. It's about providing water to people all over the world. Creating a balance and making a difference."

"For a vast profit, of course. Bottled water companies rake in more than 400 billion dollars annually on a global basis. More than 60 billion in the US alone. I don't want my water sold. I'd much rather give it away."

"As novel as that sounds, Mr. Wright, even if you allowed people to come in day and night and fill their jugs for free, you'd never have the massive reach and distribution that we have. Since you're interested in helping others, perhaps you will consider the altruistic benefits of partnering with us, allowing your water to reach thirsty people all over the planet."

"Okay, let's make a deal to give it away and not sell it."

"I wish the world moved that way. But the fact of the matter is that it doesn't. There are enormous costs associated with water rights, pumping, piping, bottling, marketing, and shipping water. We believe our price-point is low enough for most people to afford our product while compensating us for delivering it to them."

"Mr. Heller, thank you for your offer. I can't accept. I'm sorry you wasted a trip." Gideon slid out of the booth and stood.

Heller handed him a business card. "Please take this. Maybe you can sleep on the two offers and think about the compensation. Give us a figure, something we can work with."

Gideon took the card, put it in his wallet, and set a five-dollar bill on the table. Heller looked up. "At least let me buy you a cup of coffee."

"I appreciate that. But I always pay my way in a business setting. Have a good trip back to New York."

"Mr. Wright, may I call you Gideon?"

"Yes."

"Thank you. Gideon, please look at the reality of our times. How long can you continue to keep a veil over that spring? A lawsuit seeking possession by eminent domain would probably not be in your favor because it can be proven that the best use of the spring is in the public's interest by having access to it. You can decide how that will play out: with an extremely fair offer or a condemnation suit."

"Are you threatening me?"

"No, of course not. I just hope you can see the full perspective and come back to us with a counteroffer."

"I'm leaving now. I bid you goodbye and safe travels." Gideon left the restaurant. Seconds later, the man in the adjacent booth got up and walked out the front door into the parking lot.

FOURTEEN

I stood at the end of my dock, staring across the river into a lost time. I watched the wading birds and alligators moving along the rim of the Ocala National Forest on the banks of the St. Johns River. Even from where I stood, I could feel the primal environment in the breeze blowing over the river. The old forest was filled with ancient cypress trees, oaks older than the nation, and strands of cabbage palms so thick you couldn't walk between them. The land here was different from anywhere else in Florida.

The humid air felt heavy—nature's green house, an invisible canopy hanging over the tropical land like the Spanish moss in the trees. It was in this national forest that archeologists discovered the skeletal remains of saber-tooth tigers in muck pits. The skeletons of wooly mammoths, camels, and prehistoric sloths were unearthed from deep within the woods.

Who's to say that a spring—some form of the Fountain of Youth filled with Ice Age water—didn't flow from the heart of the forest? But was it still flowing with water dating back to the Ice Age period, from at least 25,000 years ago? I had my doubts. And I didn't think the water in Gideon's little bottles had any medicinal power beyond that of a healing salve. Maybe it was similar to the minerals and antibacterial properties found inside aloe vera plants.

Although I had doubts about the water and its possible connection to the last Ice Age, I did know that Gideon Wright was very much in someone's crosshairs. I replayed conversations and data in my mind. The guy with the camera, Floyd Shaw, who was stalking Gideon, had a criminal history. Who was paying him by the hour and covering his expenses to conduct the surveillance? Dave's comments were concise and maybe deadly accurate.

Throw away the Botox needles and plastic surgeons. Just sip this water and cheat time, maybe even death for a while. That, my friend, would be worth billions of dollars.

Was the Gideon Wright that I met the one I'd read about online, someone who worked with the guy who invented the Richter Scale? That would mean Gideon was much older than he appeared to be. Was Jeremiah Wright, the original owner of the land and spring, Gideon's grandfather or another relative? And who was William Wright—his father, brother or …? Did William have other descendants still living, or is Gideon the end of the line?

Regardless of Gideon's age and lineage, he was trying to do the right thing with the spring water. And there were people closing in on him and his altruistic endeavors. Gideon's imploring words returned like a smooth stone skipping quickly across the river's surface, striking me in the mind's eye. *I made a deal with God, but what happens when I'm no longer here to keep my side of the pact?*

"Daddy!" Angela and Max were running from our home toward the dock. Angela grinned, her hair silky and blowing in the breeze, Max with her pink tongue just visible, tail like a spring. It was as if they came off the canvas of a Norman Rockwell painting, a little girl, her dog, and oranges on trees in the background.

They came onto the dock, Angela changing from a sprint to skipping. Max shifted between a trot and her own form of skipping, one hind leg barely touching the dock boards. "Daddy, can we go fishing?"

"Not at this minute, but we can next weekend."

"When is that?"

"After you finish your schooling this week. Mom has some fun things planned."

"Okay. I can wait. Max can, too. But when we're in the boat, she can't bark, or else it'll scare the fish."

"That's right. We must keep reminding Max to be quiet when she's fishing with us."

"Uh huh. Mama said she's coming to the dock in just a minute."

"Good."

"Look! What kind of bird is that?"

I turned in the direction in which Angela pointed. A large bird was coming out of the national forest. It had white feathers and a six-foot wingspan, and it flew with the hinge-like wing movement of a raptor or maybe like a pterodactyl had flown. Its black head looked like charred leather. "That's a wood stork."

Angela's wide eyes followed the bird. "He's so big! Bigger than Max. What happened to the feathers on his head?"

"I'm not sure. Maybe Mom knows."

Wynona came down the dock. Angela pointed across the river. "Mama, we just saw a giant wood stork flying."

"You did. They are cool looking birds. Something prehistoric from long ago."

I chuckled. "Angela asked me why it didn't have feathers on its head. I wasn't sure. Do you know?"

"From what I learned as a little girl—I was about Angela's age—when the storks are born or hatch, they do have downy feathers on their heads. But as they grow older, they use their beaks and heads to catch minnows and other things in shallow water and mud, so their feathers wear off. And they don't grow back."

Angela made an exaggerated frown. "Maybe the little minnows eat off their feathers."

Wynona laughed and sat on one of the wooden benches. Max barked at a brown lizard on a dock post. She and Angela trotted off to investigate. Wynona looked up at me, her eyes astute. "You often come down here to be closer to nature, to think, to work through something that's on your mind. Do you want to talk about it?"

"How are you so perceptive?"

She smiled. "Perhaps it's an Indian thing. Or maybe it's just me."

"I feel compelled to help Gideon Wright. He's an elderly man, and someone is stalking him. I have no idea whether his water has unique healing elements within it. But I do believe that he's facing imminent danger. Maybe it'll be fought in court, or he could become a victim rather than a defendant."

"How do you mean?"

"Dave ran a check on the license plate and the owner of the red SUV that was in the farmer's market lot. The owner's name is Floyd Shaw, and he has a prison rap sheet that reads like a mafia enforcer. Gideon told me that his wife passed away years ago. He has no children and no heirs. An attorney can help him with that, but who will help him stay alive if I don't?"

"Do you sense it could get that bad?"

"I do. If nothing else, I want to call him. Tell him what we found. Maybe I'll ride up to Gideon's spring to speak with him."

Wynona stood up from the bench and hugged me. She said nothing, her hands on my back, the wide shadow of a soaring wood stork moving across our dock.

FIFTEEN

Gideon was in deep thought when the man approached. As Gideon was unlocking his car in the diner parking lot, the man who'd been sitting in the adjacent booth said, "Excuse me. Aren't you, Mr. Wright?"

"Yes."

"I'm Percy King. I work as a lawyer. We met a couple of years ago at the Suwannee River Water District hearing. You were there as an expert witness, testifying about the potential degradation of the river if five hundred acres along its banks were rezoned. The developer wanted the land changed from agriculture to residential, meaning the construction of a golf course and more than two hundred homes near the river."

"I recall the meeting, and now that you mentioned it, I remember meeting you, too. You were there representing some of the people from a conservancy trying to buy the property."

King grinned, his round face shiny, a strand of dirty blond hair flapping like the wing of a sparrow in the breeze. "Well, we won. No large development and golf course on a river made famous by Stephen Foster. I hummed that tune all the way back to the office after the ruling."

Gideon smiled. "I wonder how many people know that Stephen Foster never even saw the Suwannee River when he composed that song."

"Maybe he didn't have to see it. He could have heard about it, closed his eyes, visualized, and then came up with those iconic lyrics: *Way down upon the Suwannee River.* Excuse my off-key singing voice."

"You can carry a tune. Well, it was good seeing you again."

"Mr. Wright, I couldn't help but overhear some of your conversation with that gentleman from New York City. I would be honored, sir, to represent you in the event his company pushes further to take your land and spring. I know I'm just an ol' country lawyer, and water companies have teams of legal support, but I was born and raised down here. I know the land and a lot of the people making decisions, from the courthouse to the legislature. Here, please take my card." He whipped out a card from the inside pocket of his sportscoat with the speed of a magician.

Gideon took it, nodding. "I appreciate your offer. I hope it doesn't come to that."

"It's best to be ready for a fight before you're ambushed. When a government, such as the state, county, or city wants something, in this case land and a spring, they can use the powerful tool of waging eminent domain. That's basically seizing it from you. Sometimes, big companies work in cahoots with county commissions and water districts to snatch property under the guise of serving the *best interests of the public.* If that's in the works, I can help you fight it."

"That land and spring have been in my family for 160 years. I can't see an arm of government stealing it after all these years."

"Please, don't take this wrong, but to believe that, sir, is being naïve. Mention it to your wife. If y'all need some legal advice, I'm just a phone call away. My office is on Woodland Boulevard in downtown DeLand. We can meet there or in the coffee shop across the street from my office."

"I appreciate that. My wife passed away long ago. We never had children, and I didn't remarry. It's just me and all the critters around my cabin in the woods next to the spring. Good seeing you again, Mr. King."

"You, too, sir."

When Gideon drove away, King walked back inside the restaurant. The man from New York was still in the booth, finishing a phone call. King strolled back to where he had been eating. He picked up his napkin and wiped his hands. When the man finished the call and stood to leave, King cleared his throat. "How are you, sir?"

The man reached for the check the server had left. "I've had better days. Excuse me, I need to pay this over at the register."

King smiled, pursing his lips for a second. "When I was eating in the booth next to y'all, I just happened to overhear a little of your conversation. I wasn't eavesdropping. I only was having an early supper and minding my business. Regardless, I know Gideon Wright."

"You do? How?"

"I'm a local lawyer. I specialize in water-use projects, eminent domain, probate, estate planning, wills, and just about anything that walks in the door. I can't be too picky if I want to remain in business. Gideon was an expert witness in an environmental hearing concerning the Suwannee River a couple of years ago. I was one of the lawyers on the case. Maybe we can chat."

"What do you have in mind?"

"I might be representing Gideon on some legal issues. He's not my client yet, but he could be. In that event, perhaps I can be a little more persuasive with him. Sometimes a homegrown lawyer can reason with local folks better than outside forces. I don't want to sound disingenuous, but right now the playing field is wide open. Maybe I can figure out a way to lubricate any future resistance. To do that, I might need a little more oil."

"What are you suggesting?"

"For starters, the twenty million you offered Gideon is low. Are you able to double that amount? I would need thirty-five percent over his agreed amount, no less than fourteen million."

"Please, have a seat. What'd you say your name is?"

"Percival King. You can call me Percy. Rhymes with mercy. That's what I tell all my juries." He grinned. "You might be surprised when it comes to the subtle power of suggestion."

SIXTEEN

Although I ran for exercise, sometimes I wondered if the best exercise during my early morning run was more about energizing the mind than the body. I laced up my running shoes at first light and jogged four miles along an old trail near the banks of the St. Johns River. The path wound around gray palms, palmettos, and cypress trees dripping in moss. The ashen morning bowed to a golden light punching through clouds blushing pink with the glow of a new day.

There was no breeze. I kept a steady pace in the humid air. A white mist wafted from the dark surface of the river; turtles with olive-green shells crawled up on partially submerged logs, faces pointed to the sun. The air smelled of wet moss and decaying leaves, and red-winged blackbirds fluttered about the cattails and canebrakes.

As I ran, blood pumping through my body and brain, the endorphins seemed to flow like the river near me. I thought about my next step with Gideon Wright. Now that I knew who his stalker was, some of the man's background, I needed to relay that information to Gideon.

Maybe I should leave it at that. Let Gideon report it to police, hire an attorney, and seek a restraining order if he believes it necessary. But something nagged at my conscience like a pebble in my running shoes. Do I leave an old man to fend for himself if wolves are circling, or do I step in and try to prevent it from escalating? I was drawn to the way he gently treated Angela when he saw the scrape on her knee. The tenderness he displayed as he dripped the water onto her open cut. *This is sort of like magic water. I'll put a few drops on your scraped knee, and it'll feel better soon. You want me to try?*

Since my parents were dead and Wynona's father had died many years ago, Angela didn't have a grandfather. I wasn't looking to find one for her. But I was pulled to Gideon's kindness and keen intelligence. And I was growing more concerned about him and the spring he cared for with such passion. Maybe the fact that he labored to give the water away to as many people as he could reach struck a chord with me.

I sprinted over the old trail in a loop back to my cabin. The last hundred yards, I went from a jog to a full-borne, fast run. My heart was racing, and sweat was dripping off my brow and onto my T-shirt. I stopped at my dock, the surface of the river now reflecting the deep blue of a sapphire sky. After a minute, my heart settled back to its slow beat. I walked up the yard, greeted by the scent of orange blossoms.

On the back porch, I could smell blueberry pancakes on the griddle. Wynona was making breakfast before she took Angela into town— DeLand—to begin their day. Wynona used a backroom in her antique store, *Moments in Time*, to homeschool Angela. A part-time employee watched the store, greeting customers, and making sales while school was in session. If I wasn't working a case, I usually watched Max, or she watched me as we made repairs around the cabin or on my boat moored at Ponce Marina.

I'd left a towel on a small hook embedded into the side of a porch timber. I dried the sweat on my face, arms, and legs. Something in the corner caught my eye. It was the orchid. Now there were two lavender blossoms flourishing on the plant.

The kitchen door opened, and Max scampered onto the porch, sniffing the air, her tail curving like a crescent moon over her rump. Angela, wearing a sundress, followed. "Hi Daddy."

"Good morning to you. Did you have good dreams last night?"

She smiled. "Uh huh."

Wynona, casually dressed for work, came out, a small towel in her hands. She smiled. "How was your run?"

"Good. I spotted a new eagle's nest in a cypress tree near Bartram's elbow, that bend in the river a couple miles south."

"I remember that section of the river. It's beautiful there."

I motioned toward the orchid. "Look at that."

Wynona touched her lips with one hand. "Wow! Maybe this is what Jack felt like when his beanstalk grew to the clouds. He had the magic beans. We have the magic water."

"Mama, who is Jack?"

"He's a character from a fairytale."

"Can you read the story to me?"

"I can, or Daddy can, because he'll make the voice of the giant. *Fee-fi-fo-fum.*"

Angela giggled. They both stepped closer to the plant to get a better look at the orchids. Wynona gently touched the petals of the newest blossom. "Sean, what happens when I return to regular water for this beautiful plant? Will it go into shock and die after it was raised from the dead?"

Angela looked from the plant to her mother, curious. "Just give it a tiny bit of water, Mama. That way it won't drown."

"Good idea."

My phone buzzed. I'd left it on the armrest of a wicker chair before I started my morning run. I picked it up, looking at the screen. Although I didn't recognize the number, I felt compelled to answer. After I did, I recognized the man's voice. "Mr. O'Brien, I hope I'm not calling too early. It's Gideon Wright."

"No, not at all. I'm an early riser."

"Me, too. How's your daughter's knee?"

"It's healed."

"Good. Look, I don't want to bother you, but I was thinking about our conversation. You told me that sometimes you're hired to put the pieces of a puzzle together before they're lost and never found. However, I suppose solving crimes is all about lost and found. Finding the criminal, the lost money, and the motive. I think I found the motive—the reason that man was taking pictures of me and my booth at the farmers' market."

"What do you mean?"

"I just turned down an enormous financial offer for the pumping rights to my spring. If somebody is willing to give me twenty million dollars, and if I refuse their offer, what would they do next? Maybe that would be a motive for something bad. Can we meet the day after tomorrow?"

"Yes, I can ride up to your place. I want to hear more about their offer. And I want to tell you about a man named Floyd Shaw."

***

Percy King was entering his office, thinking about what the biggest payday in his career might be. He was always scavenging, seeking the lawsuit that could net him millions of dollars. And now, that illusive jackpot might come from a hidden spring that flowed with liquid gold.

"Mr. King ..." said his secretary, looking at a flashing light on the phone console board.

He walked past his secretary's desk, his thoughts moving like a human calculator, not hearing what she said.

"Mr. King, can you hear me?"

He turned and made an awkward smile. "Sorry, Gladys. What is it?"

"Line two. It's one of your clients, Floyd Shaw. He said you'd take his call."

"All right. I'll take it in my office." King settled into his high-back leather chair and answered the phone. "Floyd Saw, what's going on? You in trouble again, son?"

"Naw, nothing like that. I've been hired to follow an old guy around. You know, to see where he's going and who he's meeting. I saw you at the Wagon Wheel in Astor, walking out to the parkin' lot to talk with the guy I'm tailing, Gideon Wright. From what I understand, there's a lot of big money interested in a spring on his land. I figured you'd be curious since you were talking with the fella and might want me to keep tabs on him for you, too."

"Who hired you to follow him?"

"C'mon, Percy. You know I can't tell. I got no idea why you ran out into the lot to talk with Wright, but I'm guessing he's got your interest. So, are you going to hire me to let you know what he's up to?"

"Along those lines, but I may have a more lucrative job for you."

"I'm all ears."

SEVENTEEN

Darnell Reid had no idea that someone was watching him. As a hydrologist, he was trained to find water sources, not people. Reid was shooting pool on one of two billiard tables in a bar called *The Pocket* in downtown DeLand. It was almost 10:00 p.m., and Reid had been drinking beer since happy hour. He shot pool with his friend, Blake Owen, a skinny man with a long face, sleepy eyes, and dark, gelled hair that was combed back.

Two bartenders, a college-aged woman and a red-faced, heavy man, filled drink orders. Three servers, all young women, worked the room. There were at least thirty-five customers, with most sitting at tables and some on stools next to the bar. A dozen women were in the mix. From a jukebox, the singer Jewel was belting out the song, *Who Will Save Your Soul*. The bar smelled of barbecued chicken wings and beer.

Two men sat at a corner table sipping beer from bottles. They were watching the game of eight-ball, but more specifically, they were keeping an eye on Darnell Reid. One of the men was Floyd Shaw. The other was Jack Rizzo, a man with a hatchet face, oily black hair, and a tattoo of a coiled snake on his forearm. The words *Don't Tread on Me* were below the image.

Rizzo spoke with a Jersey accent. "How long you wanna wait?"

Shaw looked across the bar at Reid, who was lining up a shot. "Shouldn't be much longer. Looks like our man has had a tad too much to drink. That sure makes a fella unstable. Causes his decision-making process to be scattered. He's prone to make some bad mistakes."

"You still want his car on or near the property?"

"It's not what I want. It's what the client wants. That's the plan. After Reid is reported missing, cops will find the car. They'll search for

66

him and bring in the dogs. We just gotta make it easy for the ol' hound dogs. As Elvis used to sing, you ain't nothin' but a hound dog. So, let's throw the dog a bone." He grinned, taking a pull from his beer bottle.

"Looks like he's finished his game."

***

Darnell Reid watched as his friend Blake Owen called the left corner pocket, using the cue ball to sink the eight-ball. Reid grinned. "Blake, I think I've been hustled."

Owen set his cue stick on the edge of the table. "It's only five bucks. If I was trying to hustle you, it'd be a helluva lot more than that. C'mon, you know me. I just got lucky tonight. That's all. Sometimes lady luck puts one on your cheek. Other times it's in the gut."

"One more game."

"I can't. Debbie texted me. One of our kids is runnin' a slight fever. She wants me to pick up some Tylenol on the way home."

"Gotcha. No sweat. We'll catch up next week."

"You better head home, too. You told me you gotta be at work at eight a.m. Speaking of Tylenol, you'll want to pop a couple of 'em when you go to bed. That way you won't wake up with a piledriver pounding in your skull."

"Thanks, Doc. I'll consider that."

"You and Angie doin' all right?"

"Yeah, why?" Reid looked across the pool table at him through red, watery eyes.

"When we were shooting pool, I noticed that you weren't wearing your wedding ring. First time I've seen you without it."

"Sometimes I leave it on my dresser when I'm working out in the field and in the mobile lab we have. Last year, I was water testing in a spring that was so cold, the water caused my skin to shrink. Almost lost the damn ring in ten feet of water and had to jump in and pick it up off the sandy bottom. If the water wasn't gin clear, I'd have lost it."

Owen grinned. "After that, bet more than your hands was shrinking. Sounds like a cold shower, dude. But, in that case, it was more like a cold bath."

"That never stops me." He smiled lopsidedly.

"Where are you working tomorrow?"

"Volusia County. Recently, we were testing this hidden spring in the Ocala National Forest. The old man that owns the land around the spring is weird. We got into an argument. I playfully tapped the old buzzard with one finger on his chest. Lemme show you." He stepped around the table, using his index finger to poke Owen once in the chest. "The old buzzard grabbed me and almost broke my wrist from the pressure he had in his hands and forearm. It was damn unreal. Like he had superhuman strength in his body for an old dude."

"Some of those old guys who work on farms and shit, or oil rigs, are strong well into their seventies. The ones who've lost their strength will just shoot you if you mess with 'em. I gotta go." He shook Reid's hand, took a five-dollar bill from him, and left the bar.

Reid shuffled in a near stupor to the restroom. A few minutes later, he walked out of the bar and was followed.

***

Floyd Shaw looked across the table at Jack Rizzo. "It's showtime. Let's do this."

EIGHTEEN

It would be the last cigarette Darnell Reid ever smoked. As he walked to his car in the parking lot of *The Pocket* bar, Reid shook a cigarette from a pack he carried. He stopped twenty feet from his car and lit it, taking a long draw and exhaling through his nostrils. A block away, the century-old clock in the bell tower of the courthouse started chiming. In the dark, it was hard to see his watch. He stood by his car, fishing for the keys in his pants pocket.

He heard someone walking over the gravel. "Hey, Darnell," came an unfamiliar voice.

Reid turned around as two men approached. "Do I know y'all?"

"No," said the tallest man. "We don't have time for formal introductions either. Just say we're here to introduce you to someone far away."

"Huh?" Reid wasn't sure what he heard. His vision was blurry, and his head was beginning to pound. "What do you fellas want?"

"We're going for a little ride."

"I'm not gonna go anywhere with y'all."

The taller man pulled a gun, pointing it at Reid's chest. "This says otherwise."

"Hey, you fellas got the wrong guy. What's this all about?"

"Reach into your pocket, take out your car keys, and drop them. Then step back a few feet."

Reid did as ordered. The shorter man picked up the keys and unlocked Reid's trunk. The taller man said, "Get in!"

"Wait just a second. You got …."

"Now!" The pistol was aimed at Reid's forehead.

He slowly walked to the trunk, bile rising in his throat. Reid crouched down and got inside. The men slammed the lid.

***

A half hour later, the two cars were pulled off the road in a remote section of the Ocala National Forest. The lead car was driven by Floyd Shaw. Jack Rizzo, wearing latex gloves, drove Darnell Reid's car. The men got out and walked to the trunk of Reid's car. Soft moonlight poured through the mossy limbs of the live oak trees. Shaw held the gun and nodded. Rizzo opened the trunk. "Get out!"

Reid pulled himself from his trunk, unsteady on his feet, nausea rising in his esophagus. "Y'all are makin' a big mistake. I don't owe anybody money. I'm not screwin' some guy's wife. I haven't stolen anything. Cut me loose, okay? I don't know you fellas, so that means somebody had to send you. Can you at least tell me who? Perhaps I can fix …."

"Shut up!" barked Rizzo.

Shaw motioned with the pistol. "Walk 'til we tell you to stop."

"Walk where?"

"There's a gate fifty feet to the right. Walk in that direction. If you make noise or try to run, I'll shoot you in the back and then put a round between your eyes."

"Look, guys, I have a wife and kid."

"Walk!"

Reid did as he was ordered. When he came closer to the closed gate, he stopped. "Wait a second. I know where we are. We're at that old man's place … Gideon Wright. What the hell's going on? Did he send y'all to abduct me at gunpoint? Is he sitting up there with a shotgun waiting for me? All we did was take some water from his damn spring. That's not stealing."

Shaw looked at Rizzo. "You go over first."

Rizzo nodded, climbing over the gate made from rails of galvanized steel, like cattle gates. He pulled a snub-nosed S&W revolver from his belt.

Shaw raised his Beretta, the tip of the barrel pointing at Reid's head. "Your turn."

Reid made a dry swallow and climbed over the gate. He was followed by Shaw, who gestured to the gravel driveway. "Walk." Reid turned and started walking, with the men following. Within fifty yards, they were approaching the spring run, the clear water like that of a slow-moving creek, fog rising from the surface all the way back to the wide, natural pool and the springhead boil.

They could see the lights from Gideon's cabin two hundred feet from the springhead, set back under cabbage palms and old oaks. Reid shook his head. "There are a lot more and much easier ways for me to come to this old man's place than like this."

"Walk toward the cabin."

Within a few minutes, they were much closer to the cabin, where a pale yellow light shone from its windows. A great horned owl hooted from somewhere in the forest. They could see Gideon's car parked near the front door.

Shaw motioned with his Beretta. "You make a sound, and a nine-mil round will scramble your brains as it blows a hole out the other side of your head. Walk to the left of the cabin." He shoved Reid between the shoulder blades. Under the moonlight, they followed a worn path that led from the cabin's proximity to the old barn.

Shaw looked over at Rizzo, gesturing with his head.

Rizzo nodded and started toward the barn. He used the light from his phone to see where to open the door. Thirty seconds later, he came out holding a shovel in one hand and his gun in the other.

Shaw stepped closer to Reid with his gun hand extended. "Move!"

After walking more than a hundred feet, Reid asked, "Where are we going? I thought you wanted to leave me with the old man."

"Walk!" Shaw ordered.

After another hundred yards, the path became narrower, with branches scraping across the legs and faces of the men. Rizzo looked at Shaw and asked, "How much farther? The mosquitoes are chewing my ears."

"Just a little more. There's a clearing up there. In the daylight, it looks like it could have been a place where people camped a long time ago, maybe back in the days of the Civil War or maybe the Indian Wars." After another five hundred feet, the dense woods opened into an area partially overgrown with scrub bush.

The wind stopped blowing, and the cicadas ended their chants. Across the clearing, about fifty yards away, came the haunting cry of a screech owl. It sounded like the whinny of a horse. Rizzo pointed to the far end of the open land surrounded by woods. "Did you see that?"

"What?"

"A light. It looked like it was a flame from a campfire or maybe a torch. It was on for maybe two seconds."

Shaw stared in the direction, the mosquitoes whining in their faces. "I see nothing."

"I'm not seeing things. Trust me. There was a weird damn light."

Shaw swatted a mosquito. "Maybe it was fireflies."

"It was bigger than that. It was like those weird lights people see in the woods, but the closer you get, the farther away they are. Like there's no starting or stopping point."

"You gotta lay off the weed." He looked at Reid. "Turn around!"

"If you're gonna shoot me, you're gonna do it looking in my eyes."

Shaw gestured to Rizzo, who lifted the shovel.

Although drunk, Reid was scared. "Hold on!" Reid said, lifting his hands up in a defensive posture. Shaw brought the shovel down hard on the top of Reid's head. The blow stunned him, cracking his skull and oozing blood. He fell to his knees in the moonlight, lifting his hands up like he was praying. "Please don't. I have a fam—"

"Shut up!" Shaw raised the shovel and brought it down hard again, the edge of the blade splitting Reid's skull. He fell over to one side, staring across the clearing, a soft light like a candle flame trapped in his wide irises, his body shuddering for a few more seconds before his heart stopped. The screech owl shrieked again. This time it sounded more like the long cry of a young child than the whinny of a horse.

Rizzo looked at the body and glanced around the clearing. "Let's get the hell outta here."

"We gotta bury him first. Shallow grave, remember? You start. I'll finish."

"I'm gonna dig fast. You picked a helluva place to bury a body. This land feels like some old graveyard. We've got one more thing to do after we bury this guy. It's the plan."

NINETEEN

When I'd sipped water from one of Gideon's jars at the farmers' market, I felt two things. The first was the difference in taste from any water I'd ever had. The second was trying to envision the source of the water, the springhead he'd talked about. My imagination took me to an Edenic oasis, where the spring's ancient water flowed out of a deep and mysterious source, far from human intrusion.

That lush and remote scene is the image I had as I approached Gideon's property. He'd given me the directions and said, "It'd be a challenge to set your GPS to get here." He gave me specific mile-marker points, landmarks to watch for, and the exact mileage from the last crossroad. I followed it, coming closer to what he'd described. *"You can't miss the old oak across from my gate,"* he'd said with a chuckle.

He was right.

His gate was directly across the road from a large live oak. As I came closer to the old tree, I could see the entrance to his property. There was no mailbox. No sign with the address hand-painted on it. Nothing. And if you drove at the speed limit, it would be hard to see the gate or the driveway covered with leaves.

But the old oak stood out as nature's milepost. It had the large girth of a bull elephant from trunk to tail. And the tree had the dark gray color of an old elephant's hide. It also had the stoop of age. Some of the heavy lower limbs touched the earth, supporting the rest of the tree.

Before the county road was ever paved, when it was only an Indian trail through the woods, the oak was there as a silent witness through the centuries to all that came down the path. And it still served as a silent sentry, watching over Gideon's gate. If it could talk, maybe the tree could tell me why a car was parked on the side of the road a hundred feet past the driveway.

Gideon said the gate would be unlocked. I'd need to get out of my Jeep to swing it open once I arrived. I turned into the driveway, stopping at the gate. As I got out to push it open, I glanced back at the car farther away. It was a Dodge Challenger, dark blue, too far away for me to read the license plate. I looked to see if there was a silhouette of anyone sitting inside. There was no driver or passenger. That didn't mean there wasn't someone napping in the car.

As I started to drive through the open gate, I stopped, looking back at the lone car. Something inside of me piqued more than my curiosity. I got out and walked toward the Dodge. The dirt on the shoulder of the road was wet and muddy. I could see tire tracks—not one type, but rather two.

I looked through the car windows. There was no one inside, and the lock buttons were down, meaning the car was locked. I moved up to the front of the car. The tire tracks continued for about thirty feet. But they were different from the ones left by the tires on the Dodge. I walked back to the trunk area. I saw shoe prints in the wet dirt. It looked to be three sets, and one had a deep tread pattern, like it came from the sole of a boot. I stood there for a moment, watching, and listening. I could see that the shoe prints vanished in the grass and in the direction of Gideon's gate.

I pulled out my camera and took photos of the tracks—human and tire. I shot video as well. Maybe what I spotted in the moist dirt was nothing. I didn't know, but I did know that the weather would soon erase the tracks. As I started back toward Gideon's driveway, a car came down the road. It was a dark blue Lincoln Navigator. As the car passed me on the opposite side of the highway, the driver glanced toward the cars and Gideon's gate.

Although I could only see his face for two seconds, it was enough time to tell that he was surveying the scene, the parked car, me, and Gideon's closed gate. The car vanished over the western horizon. Maybe the guy was just a curious onlooker. I didn't recognize his face, but I made a mental note to remember it.

I walked back to my Jeep, drove twenty feet down the driveway, closed the gate, and then headed further into the interior of Gideon's property. Within a hundred feet, I felt like I was driving back in time to an old and primitive Florida that few people ever experience anymore.

Red and green bromeliads hung from the oaks like knick-knack decorations. Staghorn ferns grew from one of the largest banyan trees I'd seen. The land was thick with palmetto bush, red flowering hibiscus, and purple button sage. I rode with the Jeep's windows down, the breeze had the earthy smell of rotting wood, mushrooms, and wild mint.

As I came around a bend, it was the mottled sunlight off the surface of the water that caught my eye. From where I was, the spring flowed slowly, maybe twenty feet wide at this point. Looking upriver or toward the source, I could see the spring run getting wider as it meandered around cypress trees adorned with hanging moss, the stream of light vanishing beyond the trees. Butterflies darted along the banks, their wings matching the yellow jessamine growing by the border of the spring.

I drove further down the driveway, maybe another two hundred yards, coming around a bend in the gravel road. To the left, I spotted a rustic cabin and an older model Land Rover up a sloping and grassy yard. I knew that Gideon was expecting me. What I saw to my right, though, almost took my breath away. I stopped the Jeep, staring at its beauty, feeling its primal pull.

I've seen a lot of springs in Florida, but never one like this. The springhead was really a pool of shimmering blue light. It formed a circle, as if a meteor had plunged into the earth a million years ago and opened a near perfect hole. It was probably a hundred feet wide, bordered by wildflowers and century-old bald cypress trees, one with an osprey's nest at the top. The nest was the size of a small car.

I walked up to the spring. It was the clearest I've ever seen and almost hypnotic in the way it glistened on the surface, drawing you closer, as if there was some life force just below the water. The white sand bottom, perhaps twenty feet down, looked like I could reach in and touch it. The illusion had a surreal quality to it. There was an aquatic luminosity about the spring that shimmered in shades of aqua. The molecules in the water were like millions of tiny prisms, snatching the light and weaving it through a mysterious mesh, turning the spring into a blue bowl. At night, the mirage would disappear, returning at the break of a new dawn.

I was drawn to the water like I'm drawn to the sea. Something whispering in the spring touched an ancient trigger in me. I could barely see the underwater mouth or the boil that emerged from dark limestone rocks, which looked as if they opened to a dark cave. I was thirsty and wanted to lay down at the spring's edge and drink to restore the water I'd lost during my morning run and to quench a deep thirst that perhaps only this water could quench.

"Beautiful, isn't it?"

I turned around and saw Gideon smiling as he walked up to me. He was wearing a Panama hat, shorts, a faded blue denim shirt, and sandals. He carried a towel on one shoulder, two small glass bottles, and a plastic trash bag. "Yes, it is beautiful. What a great view you have from your cabin."

"Thank you for coming. Before we talk about the reason you're here, I want to show you something. It may be something you've never seen before now."

TWENTY

Like a magician, Gideon reached into the black bag he carried. He lifted what I thought was a bone. Upon a closer look, I could tell it was a large fang or tooth, much larger than one belonging to a lion, maybe seven inches in length, tapered at one end. He nodded. "It's from a saber-tooth tiger. A friend of mine, a professor of anthropology at the University of Florida, ran some tests on it. The tooth is estimated to be at least ten thousand years old. Maybe older. My friend said the tiger would have been larger than a male polar bear."

"Where did you get it?"

"Here, in the spring. I found it about fifty yards downstream from the boil. It was barely sticking up, maybe an inch, out of the sandy bottom. Animals have drunk water from this spring for a long time." He handed the tooth to me.

I held it in my hand, tracing a finger along the curvature of the bone. It was smooth and had a feel of antiquity, as if I were holding an artifact from a time capsule. "This is amazing." Birds in the trees chirped in a chatterbox crossover of melodies. I gave the tooth back to Gideon. "You have a beautiful and unique place here. I can see why it's so exceptional."

"I'm blessed. I know it's not the Garden of Eden, but I believe it has a genetic bridge through time to it. There is no other spring like this left on earth. That's why I spread the water as far and as often as I can. You're welcome to swim in the spring. I want people to enjoy it."

"I might take you up on the invitation and bring my wife and daughter back here."

"Your family is welcome anytime. Do you mind holding the bag, so to speak?"

"Sure." He handed the trash bag to me. I looked at the two glass bottles he held, the same kind he had at the farmer's market, with rubber stoppers on the mouths of the bottles. He removed his hat, dropped the towel, kicked off his sandals, and dove into the spring. Gideon swam to the center, floating on his back, watching the clouds high above him, his face serene. He turned and went straight down, swimming toward the mouth of the spring.

I could see him pull the caps off the bottles, pointing them toward the boil. He recapped the bottles and shot up to the surface. He swam back to the shore and got out. "Please hand me the bag."

I did, and he covered the bottles in black plastic. "I must keep them from direct sunlight. It doesn't take long for the elements inside the water to fade in the heat and UV radiation of the sun. One of the ironies is that the molecules in the water, inside the spring itself, can absorb the sunlight, bend it out, and refract away the white light, turning the water into the illusion of blue. It's not blue, of course, but it's one of nature's tricks that make the water even more lovely."

"I've seen a lot of beautiful springs in Florida, but never one like this."

He pointed at the pool. "The full health benefits of the water are within those first thirty-three feet. That's a little less than halfway from the boil. If you snorkel down there, you will notice that the fish swimming in that first thirty-three feet are more colorful than the ones found further away from the opening. And I'm talking the same species of fish, the lovey bluegill."

"That's remarkable."

"Please, take this water back to Wynona and your adorable daughter, Angela." He grinned. "It'll cure most of what might ail them."

"Thank you. Not that they're sick, but your water is very refreshing. No, it's much more than that. It's rare. The taste is beyond pure. There's something primordial about that water."

Gideon's beard parted in a wide smile. "The ancient water moves through earth's natural filters of limestone, dolomite, and other soluble rock. With pressure, it rises from deep down with a concoction that I can only call God's marinade. Let's walk up to my cabin to talk. I'm worried. Not for me, but for the health of the spring. The representative from that water bottling company appeared to be the type of person who doesn't know how to take no for an answer."

"What do you mean?"

He picked up the towel, drying most of his body. "Maybe it's because of his marching orders from the people he reports to, or maybe it's just him. Regardless, they wouldn't throw around that kind of money if they weren't deadly serious about acquiring my land and this spring."

"Over the phone, you told me a little about your meeting with him. Give me as many details of the meeting that you can remember."

"Okay." As we walked toward the cabin, Gideon shared the conversation he had with the water company representative. "I have a bad feeling in my gut about him and the people he works for. I've lived long enough to heed those intuitive moments. I think they're like personal radar. And if you ignore the warning, something might move into your personal space and not leave until it's extracted."

"What's this man's name?"

"Roger Heller. I have his card in the cabin. I'll give it to you."

"Just give me his number before I go. I'll remember his name."

He looked at me with a twinkle in his eye. "I believe you will, Sean."

On the cabin's front porch, Gideon sat back in his wicker rocking chair, pensive for a moment. "I spoke with another fella, too. He was there in the diner, a man I'd met a couple of years ago. I didn't remember him until he introduced himself when I was walking to my car in the lot."

"What did he say?"

Gideon walked me through that conversation and added, "He seems like a nice fella. He certainly knows the ins and outs of the courthouses in this area. His office is in DeLand. I might go on and hire him. He seems well qualified."

I nodded, watching a great blue heron stalk the spring a hundred feet downstream from the pool. "Hiring that attorney, since you know of his work, might be a good idea."

"That's a thought. But he's not a private investigator like you. He can't tell me more about that man with the camera in the farmers' market. I'm hoping that you can stop a crime before it happens." He eyed me like a man who knew more than he appeared to know. "What if something were to happen to me? Maybe I die and it's made to look like an accident, but it's not. Who would watch after this place? The bottling company would suck so much water from here that it would drastically alter the aquifer for the worse. Maybe Roger Heller will go back to New York, and they'll leave me alone. I'm not a pessimistic person. But when it comes to this place, I'm paternal and protective. I sure need your expertise if you'll help me."

Gideon wasn't the type of man who pleaded with people to do things. I could tell that he wasn't comfortable asking for help. He was a giver, not a taker. "On the phone, I mentioned a man's name, Floyd Shaw. Have you ever heard that name?"

"No. Who is he?"

"He's the guy stalking you with the camera. And he has a criminal record." I told Gideon the information that Dave Collins had found and added, "Is Shaw connected to Glacier Artesian Springs or someone else? If so, who or where's the connection?"

"Maybe he's acting alone."

"Maybe. But based on his rap sheet, he appears to be a guy someone hires when they want to play dirty." Out of the corner of my eye, something caught my attention. I looked down the driveway. I could hear car tires crunching the gravel. Birdsong stopped. The blue heron flew away. Within seconds, a police cruiser was there, heading toward the cabin and us.

Gideon looked up at me, a drip of water at the tip of his nose. He used the back of his wide hand to remove the drop. "Did you close the gate after you came onto the property?"

"Yes, I did."

"I know I told you that you didn't have to lock the padlock, just to close the gate. It won't blow open. It looks like the police didn't have much of a challenge entering the property. Posted no trespassing signs certainly don't mean much if the police want to come on your land."

"Especially if they are here on official business."

"In all my years of owning this place, I've never had a visit from the police."

"I might know why they're here."

"Why?"

TWENTY-ONE

With a sinking feeling in my gut, I watched the police cruiser come closer. It was at that moment that I understood the deep financial stakes and what the old man sitting next to me was about to face. I glanced at Gideon. "How far does your property go east from your driveway?"

"About fifty yards."

"In that case, there is or was a car parked on the shoulder of the road. Unless there's an easement, it may be parked on your land. I did a quick look before I came in here."

Gideon's eyebrows rose. "You did?"

"Yes. You mentioned radar. Mine is never off."

"I guess that's good and bad. Sort of like creativity and insanity living in different parts of the house. They meet in the kitchen for a midnight snack."

The officers in the cruiser came within twenty feet of us. They parked the car, turned off the engine, and got out. I watched their body language. They moved with measured steps, wary, like two men wondering if a copperhead snake was hiding in the grass. They eyed me and looked at the black plastic bag.

The officer who was the driver came closer, while the other one stood near the open car door, his hand resting near the grip of his pistol. I knew that wasn't a good sign, and they weren't here to ask for bottles of spring water.

The lead officer stopped within fifteen feet of us. He nodded. He had olive skin, black hair, and guarded dark eyes. "Good afternoon, gentlemen. Who is Mr. Wright?"

Gideon moved the black bag from one hand to the other. "That would be me. Is there a problem, officer?"

"There's a vehicle parked not too far from your gate and driveway. Do you know who left it there?"

"No. My friend, Sean, mentioned that when he arrived. I don't know why the car is there or who owns it."

"We know who owns it. Are you familiar with Darnell Reid?"

"Is that car his?"

The officer didn't answer. "I'm Sergeant Garcia. This is Officer Potter." The second officer had a military haircut, a thick neck, and his gun belt squeaked when he walked. Garcia glanced down at the black bag. "Whatcha got in there?"

"Just two bottles of water and an old artifact from the spring, a bone, or more precisely, a fossil from a saber-tooth tiger. They roamed around Florida ten thousand years ago."

"Mind if we have a look?"

"I don't mind. The only problem is the glass water bottles. If the water from the spring is penetrated with the sun's ultraviolet light, it destroys many of the minerals in the water. It's still great to drink, it's just not as healthy for you that way."

"Maybe I can come over there and take a look in the bag."

Gideon wasn't sure how to respond. I smiled. "Did you come with a search warrant?"

"No, but we can certainly get one."

"You mind telling us what this is about? Maybe we can save you some time."

"Sir, who are you?"

"Sean O'Brien."

"Is that Jeep yours?"

"Yes." Garcia looked at me like he was trying to decide whether I was a threat to him.

Gideon lifted the black bag. "I don't mind you fellas looking in the bag. Let's just stand under the shade of the oak next to my cabin."

"All right."

They followed us up to one of the largest live oaks I've ever seen. Some of the massive limbs touched the ground, as if they were balancing the rest of the tree. In the shade, Gideon handed Sergeant Garcia the bag. The other officer stood a few feet away. Garcia opened the bag and looked inside. "Looks like water and one really big tooth." He handed the bag back to Gideon. "I wonder if there are any other bones scattered around here. Mr. Wright, did anybody visit you last night?"

"No."

"Did you go out last night, you know, maybe for dinner or to a bar?"

"No."

The officers exchanged glances. "Anybody in the cabin?"

"No."

"You mind if we look around in there?"

I shook my head. "Not without a search warrant. We've been cooperative with you; it's at the point where you should extend the courtesy and tell us why you're here."

"And how are you connected to Mr. Wright?"

"Two ways. One, I'm his friend. The second is that he is my client." Gideon glanced up at me. "I'm a private investigator. Someone has been following Gideon, taking pictures. We'd like to know why. Maybe that car out there on the shoulder of the road is related to Gideon being stalked. Do you know who owns the car?"

"It's registered to Darnell Reid, the name I mentioned earlier. Does it ring a bell for either of you?"

He looked straight at me, and I said, "No."

Gideon angled his head, as if he thought the officer had more to say. "I recognize the name. There was a man who said his name was Darnell Reid, and he came on my property three times. Each time he ignored the no trespassing signs."

"Did you report that to us?"

"No."

"Why was he here?"

"He and another man, I don't recall his name, were here taking water samples from my spring. They came unannounced and uninvited. This is privately owned property. I asked them to leave and not return. They didn't respect me or my request. Darnell Reid showed up a third time with a different person. I recall that man's name was Lamar Dunn."

The second officer jotted the information down on a notepad, stepping closer. "You said they were taking water samples. Why? Who'd they work for?"

"Some company called Enviro Resources. He said the company was in Tallahassee. I haven't seen those two since then. That was about a month ago."

Sergeant Garcia crossed his arms. "Our office received a call early this morning. It was from Darnell Reid's wife. She is worried. Her husband didn't come home last night after shooting pool in a bar with a friend. That friend told us that he left the bar before Reid did. He said that Reid was going home after he left. Never got there. Highway patrol spotted the car not far from your driveway. A check came back that it was registered to Reid. We'd like to know why his car is parked on your land?"

TWENTY-TWO

Thunder rolled in the distance, and the temperature dropped. A mourning dove stopped cooing in the woods. Gideon glanced over at me before he answered the officer. "I have no idea why that man's car is parked on my property. I went to bed last night at ten o'clock. Slept well. Didn't hear or see a thing until first light. That's when I stepped out on my front porch to the call of a curlew hunting for breakfast in the shallows of the spring."

Sergeant Garcia blew out a deep breath, his eyes searching the grounds. "The last time that Darnell Reid was on your property, did your encounter escalate into an argument?"

"We had a disagreement."

"Did he threaten you, or did you threaten him?"

"No. But he did use his index finger to poke me in the chest. I grabbed his wrist and told him that was enough and to leave immediately, or I was calling the sheriff's office."

"Do you have any other buildings on your property?"

"Yes. An old barn. It's about thirty yards behind the cabin. Maybe Mr. Reid will show up and this mystery will make sense."

Officer Potter nodded. "That's our hope and the hope of his family. We just don't want to see him turn up dead. We'd really like to look around."

Gideon cleared his throat. "I don't have anything to hide. You're welcome to have a look, but as Sean suggested, I think it'd be better protocol if you had a warrant, if you don't mind."

Garcia shrugged. "We don't mind. We can have one within a couple of hours."

There was a stronger clap of thunder in the northeast. The wind picked up, and the breeze through the live oak jostled the Spanish moss.

I motioned toward the driveway, in the direction of the gate. "Did you gentlemen walk around Reid's parked car?"

Garcia nodded. "Of course. Why?"

"Did you see the tracks?"

"You mean tire tracks?"

"That's part of it. But there were two different sets of tire tracks, one that extended at least thirty feet beyond Reid's car. Those tracks don't match the tread on Reid's tires. Also, there were three sets of shoe or boot tracks. You can just make the impressions out in the moist black dirt, but they're present." Both officers stared at me like I was speaking Russian.

Garcia cocked his head, his eyes guarded. "Why'd you approach the vehicle?"

"Because Gideon Wright is my client, and since someone has been following him, it made sense to approach a car parked on his property in broad daylight. Of course, no one was there, unless a body was in the trunk. The physical evidence left behind suggests that Reid met two other people last night. If something tragic has happened to him, it'd be good to have plaster casts of the tire and human shoe tracks before it rains."

The officers looked at me with a mix of doubt and annoyance. Garcia sighed. "We'll be back." They hustled to their cruiser, as thunder rolled over the national forest. I glanced at Gideon. He shook his head, grinning. "Thank you, Sean. I'm not sure what would have happened had you not been here. And thank you for being willing to take me on as a client. I'm deeply grateful."

"When I came here, I was going to tell you that I didn't think there was much I could do to help you. That parked car and tracks in the mud changed my mind. I don't know how much I can help, but maybe I'll find a way to keep the wolves at bay for a while."

"I feel a sigh of relief."

"Don't get too comfortable just yet."

"Why?"

"Because of what I just told those officers. I believe someone was either following Reid when he left the bar or he was abducted."

"Maybe he pulled over to the side of the road because he was having a hard time driving if he was drunk. It could be that he didn't want to risk a car accident. He didn't want to hurt or kill someone."

"That sounds noble. But why would he pull off the road close to your gate?"

"Maybe it was on the way to his house, just something coincidental."

"There are no coincidences in a criminal investigation. He didn't pull off the side of the road. He was either forced off or he was abducted by at least two people at the bar as he walked to his car. He might have been forced into his trunk and driven here. The question is why?"

Gideon stared at the dark clouds like he was looking for a white dove caught in the wind. "My mind doesn't work that way. I try to find the good in people. I've always believed that if you looked hard enough, you could find it. And not only find it but help enrich it through kindness."

"Sometimes. But evil operates without illusions except in the way it often approaches good people."

"What do you mean?"

"You mentioned that this spring and land have an ancient, primal bridge going back to the Garden of Eden. Evil disguised itself even in all that sweet innocence and beauty." I looked up at the old oak tree, pulling some moss from a low-hanging branch. "Like this moss, evil hangs around, always looking for a host. I believe Reid's car is here for one specific reason."

"Why?"

"Someone wants you to be the host. Whatever may have happened to Reid, somebody out there wants you to take the fall."

I dropped the moss to the ground just as a bolt of lightning hit the top of a bald cypress tree less than fifty yards from us. Thunder exploded with the force of a concussion bomb, pieces of cypress limbs falling like shrapnel over the spring, the water now dark.

TWENTY-THREE

A half hour later, Gideon's eyebrows arched as he pointed to something down by the spring. "Would you look at that?"

We sat on rocking chairs under the tin roof of his front porch, the storm quickly passing, the air cooling, sunlight squeezing through the limbs on the enormous live oak. I looked in the direction that Gideon pointed. A rainbow rose from the far side of the spring and made a bow in the sky. "That's spectacular. I can never get tired of seeing a rainbow."

He nodded. "They're rare and beautiful at the same time—nature's prisms, bending light through water droplets. They're God's graffiti, an unstructured arc on a canvas of air, fading as mysteriously as they arrive."

"I agree."

"At a rainbow's end, there's no need for a pot of gold when nature is all the treasure we yearn to find."

I motioned toward the spring. "From here, the rainbow looks like it's on the cusp of the spring, maybe coming up from it."

He smiled. "Perhaps it's going *into* the spring. The perfect arc of a rainbow has no beginning or end. It rises from two separate spots on earth and meets in the middle, creating a celestial bridge, possibly one of the stairways to heaven."

"It's beautiful. I wish my wife and daughter were here to see it."

"Yes, it's better shared. I'm glad you are here today, Sean." He stood. "Come with me. There is something I'd like to share with you."

"Okay." I followed him back toward the gnarled and bent oak tree. Gideon gestured to a black wrought-iron bench. He used the palms of his hands to wipe away the water droplets left from the brief rain.

"Please, sit."

We sat. He looked up and into the branches. "I come out here and talk to my old friend, Seth, the tree. Imagine what this big fella has seen over the five hundred years it has been here. Maybe the tree knows where to tap into the real Fountain of Youth. Or maybe the secret to longevity is its calm patience and observation skills."

"It's endured a lot throughout the centuries."

"Yes. Even through storms, it remains calm and learns to endure. The tree may not walk, but it moves and changes with the seasons. Nature, simply put, is beauty. I wish more people would learn to understand and appreciate the harmony, the song of nature, that wants us to join in and sing with our hearts. We're all just passing through, like the brevity of a comet in the night sky, not even a grain of sand in the hourglass of time. But never think you don't matter, because you do."

"That's why I love my home on the river. The old river has stories to tell if you listen."

"I sit here and listen to the wind in the limbs. Hear the birdsong serenade me. In the silence, I learn to really listen. Something the old oak is good at doing."

"You said it's five hundred years old."

"Yes, an arborist friend of mine said it was at least that old, perhaps older. Consider its history—a silent witness all those years."

"I can imagine."

Gideon reached into the front pocket of his denim shirt and pulled out a shelled peanut. "Watch this," he whispered. He rattled the peanut, the sound barely audible. Seconds later, some of the leaves in the tree moved. He shook the peanut again. A squirrel came down the side of the tree next to him. The squirrel hopped across the leaf-strewn ground, standing on its hind legs with its front paws almost in a praying stance. It was less than five feet in front of us.

Gideon leaned over and held the peanut between two fingers. The squirrel took the treat in its mouth, scented it with saliva, and rocked back on its hind legs to eat it. It left one of the two peanuts in the shell, scurrying about thirty feet and using its paws to dig up some loose soil, burying the remaining part of the peanut before turning to scamper back up the tree.

Gideon looked over at me and smiled. "You can see, he's not a glutton. He had his lunch and stored some away for another time. I think most of us can learn from that little guy. Come with me. There's one final thing I'd like to show you."

We stood, and I couldn't help but laugh. "Don't tell me your next trick will be with a bluebird that flies down and sits on your shoulder."

"Now, that would be fabulous. I'd whistle a tune. No, it's something else. Let me show you what I mean."

TWENTY-FOUR

The path to the back of the cabin was like a trail into the primordial. We walked under the boughs of a large banyan tree. Red, yellow, and white bromeliads grew on the tree, propped up like leafy ornaments. Air plants sprouted in the nooks of the limbs of another oak tree. A staghorn fern, twice the size of a microwave oven, hung from a chain on one of the limbs.

When we walked around the cabin to the backyard, Gideon took me near a small cemetery, pointing to the closest headstone. "My wife's body is in that grave. She would sit with me under the big oak tree. We'd have our coffee and enjoy the dawn of a new day. What a blessing."

"How long were you married?"

"About fifty years."

We moved to a small clearing in the deep shade of oaks and willow trees. There were two white beehive structures. I could see bees entering and exiting them. Gideon looked up at me, his eyes twinkling. "I gave you and your family some water. I would like to give you some honey, too. Within ten miles of here, there are some unique wildflowers. These include orchids, swamp lilies, coneflowers, angel trumpets, and many more. For the bees, this area is a potpourri of delights for them to make some of the best honey that I've ever tasted. I filled a dozen jars two weeks ago. Back in my barn, I spin the honey from the hive frames." He pointed to a weathered barn beyond the cemetery.

"I've always been fascinated by bees. I love their honey, but I respect their work ethic even more. They take care of business."

Gideon smiled. "Yes. I only take a small portion of honey from the hives throughout the season. I've had these two beehives for quite a while now. Let me show you that work ethic you mentioned." He walked toward the hives. "Hi, my winged friends. I know you've been busy bees. Did you fellas make it out to the purple heather near the river? I hope so. It's very sweet."

I stopped. "Gideon, don't you need to put on a beekeeper's suit? Won't you get stung?"

"No, at least I don't think so. The bees know me. I know them. Each hive, like an audience on any given theater night, is different. The bees in this first hive are rarely aggressive. The key is that you don't move quickly or with aggressive motions. You move and work in harmony with the bees. They sense aggression and potential threats. Stand next to me. Move like I do, and they shouldn't sting you."

I really didn't want to walk up on active beehives, especially as Gideon was removing the top from one hive. The bees were flying out, buzzing, circling, and returning to the hive. I walked slowly up next to him and peered inside the hive. There were at least a dozen racks or frames hanging, each about an inch apart. He opened his pocketknife, reaching into the center and lifting a frame. Bees came out with it, their bodies glistening in the bright sunlight.

Gideon scraped some of the wax from the cone, the visible honey shining like liquid gold. "Look at that, Sean. Nature's bounty. Dark and rich, packed with nutrients."

"The bees seem to take it in stride. I believe they like you a lot while they tolerate me."

He chuckled while putting the frame back in position and placing the top on the hive. He held out his index finger with a drop of honey on it. One of the bees alighted on his finger, crawling toward the honey and feeding. Gideon grinned. "We have a reciprocal relationship. We share. I give them homes. They give me a little honey."

Something caught my eye. It was at least fifty yards away—just inside the woods. It was a quick flash, like the kind of light reflected when the sun strikes the side mirrors on a moving car—bright and gone in a second. "Gideon, do you have a small building beyond the big oak and at the edge of the woods? Something with a glass window?"

Gideon looked in the direction I gestured. "No. The only buildings on the property are the cabin and the barn."

"I saw a flash. Let's move closer to the cabin and away from a direct line of sight."

"Okay, but why?"

"Because what I saw could have been the sun reflecting off a rifle scope."

We walked behind the cabin, keeping a view of the cemetery and barn in front of us. Gideon looked toward the barn. "I can't imagine someone standing just inside the woods looking through a rifle scope."

"I can."

He let out a deep breath. "There are some things that happen around here that are, on the surface, unexplainable."

"What do you mean?"

Gideon looked beyond the barn into the deep woods. "There's a clearing back at the far end of my land. Maybe it's two acres, tops. It was said to be the site of a Civil War battle. I found things like rifle minié balls. Buttons from uniforms. An historian friend of mine from the university came down here and used a metal detector. He found more than a dozen old bullets, a belt buckle, and even a rusted bayonet under two inches of dirt. He put the artifacts on display at the history center. He only came here once."

"Why was that?"

"He started hunting for relics after lunch. He was still at it as the sun was setting. He told me he saw a light—not a lightning bug—moving near the bushes, like something was carrying an oil lamp. In a few seconds, it was gone. This professor, whose name is John Hartwell, said it was akin to something guarding the battlefield. It spooked him. He said that had never happened to him at any other Civil War battlefield site, only here."

"Have you ever seen this light?"

"No, but I will say that this land, with its vast limestone topography, not only creates artesian springs but also produces what some geologists call energy vortexing. These are places throughout the world where the electromagnetic fields are more pronounced. This can have subtle effects on electronic devices. Cell phones are a good example. Also, these energy vortexes can give some people a greater sense of place or comfort."

"Interesting."

"Sean, have you ever been to a place—perhaps a remote land—in which, when you stepped off the plane and ventured into it, you felt a greater sense of peace than you would have expected?"

"Yes, once in South Africa. It was in northern Botswana. I felt like I was walking in a very primal land, as if it were one of the oldest places of human habitation on earth."

"That's what my grandfather felt about this land when he first found it."

"What I saw wasn't from the Civil War. It's right here and now. I'm going to walk beyond the barn, staying out of sight, and move through the edge of the woods to circle toward whatever it was that caused that light."

"Rather than a rifle scope, maybe it was a camera lens, like that day at the farmers' market."

"There's only one way to know. I must move toward it. You'd better stay here, out of a direct line of fire."

TWENTY-FIVE

The moment I entered the forest, I pulled the Beretta from my ankle holster. I moved stealthily within the perimeter of the woods, coming up on a banana spider larger than the back of my hand. The yellow and black spider was suspended in the center of a web that was five feet across and attached to tree trunks. I looked at the white zigzag stripe down the middle of a web so thick it might have caught small birds.

I walked around it, quietly as possible, stopping to listen every fifty feet or so. I was listening for the sounds of footsteps or maybe a car engine starting down by the gate. I was now less than a hundred feet away from where I saw the light at the edge of the woods. I looked through the branches and saw Gideon standing where I'd left him, at the back of his cabin. There was a rustle of leaves to my right. I lifted my Beretta. Two squirrels were darting in a circle at the base of a pine tree.

I moved on, coming very close to where I believed the light originated. The air was hot and humid, like a sauna. No breeze. I felt a drop of sweat rolling down the center of my back. I weaved through what looked like a path used by deer and other animals, barely visible, just a rough depression in the leaves and weeds. I raised my Beretta, coming within twenty-five feet of where I thought I'd seen the reflection of light, using my left hand to push down limbs and leaves. There was nothing, at least not visible from that perspective.

I looked back across the lawn toward the cabin. I knew that I was almost at the exact spot where I'd seen the light. I listened for more than twenty seconds. The only sound was a deerfly buzzing near my head. I entered a very small clearing, probably ten feet wide in a semicircle. No one was there.

But someone had been there.

The weeds, a foot high, were flat in a few places, the result of someone standing in those spots. I stared at the grass and the area of bare ground. Whoever had stood here, was a smoker. I saw the remains of a partially smoked cigarette. I picked it up and smelled the burned tobacco. It was new and the ash still warm. I slowly stood, looking at the grass, weeds, and exposed ground. I could see where the intruder exited. I followed the trail as closely as possible.

There are times like this when I wish I had the tracking skills of my friend Joe Billie. As a Seminole, he grew up on the res with Wynona and was like a big brother to her. Joe could spot anomalies on or off a trail that few people could see. He taught me to be a better tracker by sharing his powers of observation. On days like this, I was grateful for his expertise and willingness to teach.

I could see where the intruder had taken the path of least resistance, weaving around taller weeds and bushes. The trail he'd left was a zigzag path, like the crisscross stripes of the banana spider's lettering on its web. The trail was pointing toward the highway. I moved as quickly as I could, trying to trace the footsteps. I walked faster, no longer following the hard-to-see imprints and simply getting closer to the highway.

I heard a vehicle's engine crank. I was getting close to the county road. I sprinted, tearing through vines, spider webs, branches, and small trees. I could hear the vehicle leaving, tires spinning on dirt and connecting with asphalt, the screech of rubber on the pavement. I burst out of the foliage with my Beretta gripped in both hands.

In the distance, just as the highway faded into a curve, I could barely make out the vehicle. It wasn't a car or truck. It was an SUV. I holstered my pistol and walked the distance back across the wide yard up to Gideon's cabin. As I came closer, I could see that he was no longer standing behind his home. He was sitting on the wrought-iron bench under the tree.

I looked at him and shook my head. "I thought you were going to stay in the back until I could find out whether that flash of light came from a rifle scope."

"I was, but then, after you'd been gone about ten minutes and I didn't hear a gunshot, I came around the opposite side of my home, keeping this old tree between me and the spot where you'd seen the light flash. I figured that person, if there was one, couldn't shoot through an oak tree this large. So, I took a seat under the strong arms of my old friend." He chuckled.

"Someone was back there. I could see the imprints he or she left in the grass and weeds. And I found a cigarette butt. The remaining ash was still warm. I followed the tracks to the highway, where a vehicle spun its tires and sped away."

"Do you think the person was carrying a rifle?"

"I don't know. It's possible he had a camera because the vehicle I saw leaving in the distance was an SUV. And I think it was the same one I saw that day at the farmer's market."

Gideon said nothing. He looked down toward the spring, where a white heron stood at the edge of the water. "Sean, I'm not fearful for my safety. I've lived a blessed life. But I am fearful for the land and the spring. With this kind of clandestine activity going on around me, perhaps someone is trying to build a case, documenting my activity, to serve them in a bogus and nefarious way."

"What do you mean?"

"When I met that lawyer, Percy King, the day I'd finished speaking with Roger Heller from Glacier Artesian Springs, Percy mentioned the possibility of eminent domain being served on my land. He even suggested that some local county commissioners or water district board members could be, to use his words, working in cahoots, conspiring to leverage the power of eminent domain to seize the land. He said he could help me fight that battle."

"You think someone following you around and snapping photos of your life can contribute to an eminent domain seizure case?"

"Perhaps. Why else would they be doing it. Pictures and politicians can both be manipulated to tell the story someone wants told. Maybe they want it to look like I am old, feeble, and cognitively challenged. With no heir, the government might try to pay a fair market price for this land and move me out and into some senior care facility. I hate to think that way."

"I'll do what I can to protect you and your land."

"Now that I have your PI expertise, maybe it's time to get legal support, too. I might visit Percy King."

TWENTY-SIX

It took Gideon two days to reach a decision that he hoped he wouldn't regret. If Darnell Reid didn't show up alive somewhere, Gideon assumed the police would return to his home with a search warrant. Because he was innocent of any crime, that prospect didn't worry him. What did bother him was something the man from Glacier Artesian Springs said that day at the diner. His snide remark, combined with the fact that Gideon was being stalked by a man named Floyd Shaw, prompted him to take Percy King up on his invitation to meet.

As he parked on Woodland Boulevard in downtown DeLand and walked toward attorney Percy King's office, Gideon thought about the conversation he had with Roger Heller in the Wagon Wheel. *Mr. Wright, how long can you continue to keep a veil over that spring? A lawsuit seeking possession by eminent domain would probably not be in your favor because it can be proven that the best use of the spring is in the public's interest by having access to it. You can decide how that will play out: with an extremely fair offer or a condemnation suit.*

The receptionist in the law office, a middle-aged woman with blond hair like a beehive, escorted Gideon from the small lobby down a short hallway to Percy King's office. He was seated behind a desk piled with file folders. Partially hidden behind the stacked paperwork, King looked like he was sitting opposite a flatbed truck. He was not a tall man, but he had a big smile.

The toughest decision that King had to make in college was whether to study law or drama with hopes of becoming an actor. At five-foot-six, he chose law school and kept his performances exclusive to the captive eyes and ears of juries and judges.

"Good to see you, Gideon." King shot out from behind his desk, right arm extended for a handshake, belly protruding over his belt buckle. He pumped Gideon's hand and motioned toward one of the four chairs in his office. Gideon sat, and King grabbed a yellow legal pad from his desk, sitting in a chair across from him. "Can I get you something to drink? Coffee? Water?" His drawl, which was mostly part of his repertoire as a lawyer with southern roots, was syrupy.

"No thanks." Gideon looked around the office at the framed certificates, degrees, and pictures on the walls. Most of the photos were of King standing next to politicians at some social event. "I appreciate you seeing me without having to wait a couple of weeks to get in here. I know you're a busy lawyer."

"But I'm not a doctor, so my appointment book is more flexible to meet the needs of my clients." He leaned back, his leather chair squeaking. "Okay, let's start from the beginning. On the phone, you mentioned that the police came onto your property. Have they come back?"

"No."

"Good. If they do return, don't do anything until you call me. Unless I'm in a courtroom or on my deathbed, I'll answer my phone, or I'll return your call within a few minutes."

"That's good to know. Service like that is rare today."

"It's what country lawyers do, or they should. If not, they ought to take a position as a corporate lawyer, and it'll be a job most of 'em will hate and later regret. I like helping people, especially local folks. It's repeat business."

"Wasn't this building a Kresge department store in the 1920s?"

King's thin eyebrows arched. "Matter of fact, it was. Not too many people today know that. You must be a historian."

"The exterior bricks were painted dark red in those days. I remember one time—never mind, I don't want to digress."

King nodded, not sure how to respond. "Yes, the good old days. Let's talk about the present and your future."

"All right. You told me what type of law you practice. I know criminal law isn't your specialty. Maybe I can work with you on civil law, and there's someone you might recommend when it comes to criminal law."

"Well, first, as far as I'm concerned, most lawsuits that deal with man versus man have varying shades of dishonesty or criminal components to them, like someone attempting to cause harm to another fella or filing frivolous lawsuits to obtain unjustified money. It's not a perfect system. But I do know how to work the system, because I know how it works. In terms of the criminal prospect, right now, there has been no crime committed. At least none that we're aware of, right?"

"Yes. Although, as I mentioned on the phone, I'm a little anxious about the car that was found on my property. The authorities are still searching for the owner, Darnell Reid."

"If they find him, and if, God forbid, he's dead, you have nothing to worry about because you're innocent. The truth is the sharpest knife in a courtroom. It has a profound way to cut out the fat. I can represent you in anything from a civil to a criminal case. Let's focus here for a moment. You told me that the protection of the spring is your life's motivation."

"It is."

"Unfortunately, urban spread is inevitable, especially here in Florida. You have a large piece of property buffering the spring. The state park service has been trying to buy land in that general area to protect the aquifers from agricultural runoff and housing development. Your spring is one of dozens that are of high magnitude, meaning they flow with a lot of water. I believe in preventive medicine. In other words, taking care of something before it becomes sick."

"I agree—it's been my mindset all my life."

"I can see you are in excellent shape for someone who probably could be my grandpa. My hat is off to you, sir. Isn't a Civil War battlefield on your land?"

"Yes. The back part. Lots of minié balls, brass buttons, and even an old sword have been found scattered under the pine straw, leaves, and sand. Before that, I heard the Spanish fought a band of a hundred Timucuan warriors in the same area. It's almost as if history is repeating itself three hundred years later."

"I can petition to have the area designated as a federally recognized historic site. That will help reinforce the unique historical value of the land. Not unlike an old shipwreck lying off the coast of Florida, protected by law and the significance of antiquity. That would be a good start. We can generate favorable publicity and public relations through that."

"Okay. What else can we do?"

"We can be ready to fight any attempt from a local or state government that tries to seize the property by eminent domain. That would be a long and drawn-out fight. Hopefully, if we play our cards right, it will not come to that. You might consider opening the spring on a limited basis to the public—not as a commercial enterprise, but as one in which you are shown to be philanthropic. That way, a government can't seize the land with the pretense of turning it into a state park if you are, in essence, doing the same thing by allowing the public in there on a controlled and measured basis."

"I enjoy sharing. All I ask is that people respect the water and land."

"You'll need some sort of life insurance policy to make that happen."

"What do you mean?"

"You told me that you have no family left, no heirs. In the event of your death, you'll need someone—an executor of your will and your wishes—to maintain the land in perpetuity, just as you would. If you can leave enough money in the bank to allow for expenses, such as property taxes and any legal fights, you will ensure the spring remains like it is for generations to come."

"Are you suggesting that you would be the executor?"

"I'd be honored. We could do that for a minimum fee, mostly to draw up the papers. Once everything is in order and the agreement is signed, we carry on with our lives as we always have. You will then have peace of mind knowing that your land and spring will always be protected in the event of your death. There will be no homes or fancy country clubs built there. How does that sound to you?"

"Would you become the owner after my death?"

"Steward of the land is more accurate, fulfilling your will and wishes precisely to a tee, to your specifications. The deed may transfer to my name, but the most important thing is that your wishes and goals that you hold in your heart would become mine in a shared mission to protect the spring and land." King had the appearance of a man who thought he was about to win a card game: poker-faced, with lively eyes and wet lips, eager for the turn of the cards.

"Let me think about your offer."

"Certainly. Please don't overthink it or ponder it too long. From what I could hear in the diner, it sounds to me like that fella from the big water bottling company won't take no for an answer."

Gideon looked out the second-floor office window at two college kids walking toward a coffee shop. He cut his eyes back to King. "Maybe that man, Roger Heller, is behind someone stalking me."

"What do you mean?"

Gideon shared the information and added, "I never would have learned of Floyd Shaw's name if it hadn't been for a man that I met at the farmer's market here in DeLand."

"What man?"

"He was there with his family. They live in a remodeled cabin across the river from the national forest. He's a private investigator. His name is Sean O'Brien."

King jotted the name down on his legal pad, double underlining it. "As your lawyer, if I do represent you, Gideon, I'll need to meet Mr. O'Brien. All in your best interest, of course. In the meantime, I'll draw up the paperwork for you to review."

TWENTY-SEVEN

Puzzle pieces. I thought about those two words as I sat in front of my computer in the small room I used for an office inside the cabin. I'd been spending time doing what I normally do after a crime has been committed. But in Gideon Wright's case, there was no crime, at least none that we were aware of. Typically, I was hired after a crime had gone cold, with the police moving on to other pressing work.

In my work, the puzzle I was referring to was part visual and part intuitive. A jigsaw puzzle is the best example of a visual representation of an event—a crime with all the players on stage. What you must do is find the tiny pieces and match colors and shapes in order to build a complete picture. The intuitive part is without form, like an architect's design in his or her head before the idea is ever drafted on paper or on a screen. It's an instinctual way of looking at what is and imagining what can be. This is true whether it's designing a building from the ground up or adding onto an existing structure.

Both skills are needed in a criminal investigation. This is especially true when a crime is brewing, like a carrion bird circling high in the sky, with the prey or victim wounded but not yet dead. I looked at the whiteboard on the wall above my computer screen. I'd used the internet to find photos of the players—at least the ones I knew about thus far in what could become a deadly game.

Gideon's picture was right in the center. A photo of Floyd Shaw was in the upper left corner, with dates and two informational bullet points under it. In the top right corner was an image of Darnell Reid. I'd printed my digital pictures of tire and shoe tracks. In the bottom left corner was a photo of Roger Heller. It wasn't hard to find Heller's picture online.

The murky path didn't stop there. Although I had no idea to whom Heller reported at Artesian Springs, I knew the buck stopped with the

CEO. His name was Clifton Price. I stared at his smiling photo and reread his biography on my computer screen. If I found more puzzle pieces connected to him, I would dig further into his background. If not, I'd move on.

The last person—someone who was a potential player in either a good or bad way—was the lawyer, Percy King. After Gideon shared the conversation that he'd had with King that day in the Wagon Wheel parking lot, I thought it might be a good thing—serendipity. Gideon being at the right place at the right time. Or the chance meeting could have been planned and executed but just wasn't played out yet. King's smiling picture rounded out my known and potential players.

"Daddy, Mama says dinner will be ready in five minutes."

I turned in my chair to see Angela standing in the open doorway to my office. Next to her stood Max, with a green squeaky toy in her mouth. "That sounds good. I can smell it from back here. Smells like pizza."

She grinned. "It is pizza. I helped Mama stick the pepperoni on before she put the pizza in the oven."

"I'll be there in just a minute."

"Okay. I'll go tell Mama." They vanished in a blink, Max's squeaky bone sounding like a fledgling bird that had fallen from its nest. I thought about the bone or saber tooth that Gideon had shown me, and I remembered what one of the deputies had to say. *I wonder if there are any other bones scattered around here.*

On the white board, I stared at the images of the tire and shoe tracks. My mind went to places I didn't want it to go. I could see the macabre puzzle pieces, and they would never be snapped together to form a pretty picture, just the opposite. They would paint a picture of evil, maybe in a place where it too often was found. I shut down my computer and walked into the kitchen.

Wynona was just taking the pizza out of the oven. She looked over her shoulder at me and smiled. "You're just in time to cut the pizza. I know a Thanksgiving turkey is a bit more challenging, but the pizza, with its round shape, can be a test to get the perfect triangle."

I used the roller blade to cut the slices. "That reminds me of something Nick Cronus said when we had a pizza delivered to Dave's boat."

"What was that?"

"Nick, chewing thoughtfully, looked at the slices in the open box and said he wondered why a round pizza was delivered in a square box and served in triangles."

Wynona laughed. "That sounds like something Nick would think about and say right in mid-bite. Okay, the salad is done, and the pizza is cut. Who wants to eat on the back porch table?"

Angela's hand shot up. "I do! Max does, too. Right, Max?" She made one of her doxie nods, and we all walked from the kitchen to the screened porch and sat around our round wooden table. Although the tabletop is smooth, it is as wide as a wheel off an 1890s stagecoach. As we ate, I got to hear more about their day, especially the homeschooling.

Angela finished a bite of pizza. "I still like art the best. My second best is reading."

Wynona nodded. "Her reading comprehension is a grade level higher than the grade she's in right now. Her writing skills are up there, too."

I smiled. "That's my girl. The more you read and write, the more you'll learn. How are you coming in math?"

"Are those numbers?"

"Yes. Most people say math, but addition, subtraction, multiplication, and division are really called arithmetic. Numbers help you figure out things like how much money you have in your piggy bank, what to pay for a toy or groceries, and how much change you should get back."

She used a paper napkin to wipe her mouth. Max sat next to Angela's chair, watching her every move like a meerkat looking across the savannah. "When Mama shows me how to do a problem, I can do it. But when I get different problems, I have to ask for help."

"I still ask for help. Nothing wrong with that, right?"

"Right." She bit off a piece of pizza.

Wynona smiled. "Her math skills—I mean arithmetic—are getting better. She'll do fine as she advances."

***

An hour later, we'd finished dinner, Angela had bathed, and she was ready for bed. After I read her a story and tucked her in, I joined Wynona in the kitchen. The small TV screen in the corner of the counter was on, the sound muted. Wynona poured two glasses of cabernet. She handed me a glass and made a toast. "Cheers. To a peaceful resolution with your latest case."

I smiled. "I'll drink to that." We sipped the wine. I'd filled Wynona in on all the details I had thus far and listened to her thoughts. She was the one who suggested that I put up a whiteboard—a crime wall—for keeping tabs on the innocuous pieces that were drifting around my periphery like flotsam scattered in the surf.

Wynona gestured toward the rear door. "Let's go back on the porch. It's a balmy night in Florida, and the crickets and frogs are competing for our attention like it was a singing contest."

As we started to leave, something flashed on the TV screen. I reached for the remote. "Let's wait a minute. There's a graphic on the screen and a photo." I turned up the sound.

A TV news anchorwoman said, "Coming up next on Channel Seven Eyewitness News, the investigation expands in the hunt for a missing man whose car was found on the edge of the Ocala National Forest."

TWENTY-EIGHT

We sat through two mind-numbing commercials. One was an attorney in boxing gloves selling his services as a personal injury lawyer. The other was the owner of a used car lot, standing in the bed of a pickup truck and shouting. The newscast finally appeared on screen. A graying anchorman with a deep voice said, "Tonight, the investigation is widening in the mysterious disappearance of a Lake County man who was reported missing three days ago. Channel Seven's Patti Fleming has the latest."

The image cut to the abandoned Dodge Challenger, the one I'd seen. But the car was not on the side of the road. It was inside a garage at a police compound. The reporter's narration began. "Police would like to know where to locate the owner of this car. The Dodge Challenger was found on the side of Highway 19, near the Ocala National Forest. Its owner, Darnell Reid, was not in the locked car."

A photo of Reid appeared on the screen, and then it switched to the exterior of a one-story bar with neon lights. The reporter continued. "The last time anyone saw Reid was here at The Pocket bar, where he'd spent part of the evening shooting pool with his friend Blake Owen."

The video cut to an interview with a man. "After shooting a few games with Darnell, I left. He said he was going home, too. Because he had been drinking, I tried his cell phone about an hour later to make sure he got home okay. There was no answer. I wanted to leave a message for him, but I never heard the voice prompt. So, I hung up."

The images cut to a daytime aerial perspective of a massive, forested area. The reporter continued. "Down there is the Ocala National Forest. At more than 620 square miles, it is the oldest national forest east of the Mississippi River. The forest is laced with many lakes, rivers, springs, swamps, snakes, and alligators. In addition to the natural dangers, the area has been the scene of many deaths and murders during the last three decades. It was here where serial killer Aileen Wuornos left some of her victims."

The video cut to a ground shot of the forest, with egrets rising from wetlands by the dozens and flying over the bald cypress trees in a flapping cloud of white. The reporter's narrative continued. "Law enforcement and volunteer search crews have been walking through parts of the forest looking for clues. So far, nothing."

The video cut to an interview with the sheriff, a man in his fifties with a rugged, tanned face. "Unfortunately, the exterior security camera at the bar wasn't working the night Darnell Reid left. What began as a missing person's report is now a criminal investigation. We hope to find Mr. Reid alive, but each day those hopes diminish."

"Do you think Darnell Reid was kidnapped?"

"There has not been a ransom attempt. Our detectives are pursuing all leads."

The shot cut to the reporter standing on the side of the road, thick trees, and vines in the background. "Darnell Reid's car was found a few feet from where I'm standing. Investigators say there were no signs of him or a struggle. It's as if Reid parked his car and vanished. I'm told that the ground search will continue tomorrow. This time, deputies are bringing canine tracking dogs, and they'll be using cadaver dogs, too. From the edge of the Ocala National Forest, this is Patti Fleming. Now back to the studio."

Wynona raised her eyebrows. "Let's go on the porch. Sounds like the police are in body recovery now." We sat in the wicker chairs, Max between us. Down by the river, a chorus of frogs sang competing tunes. The air was cool, and the stars were smoldering but cold and distant, like ice crystals in the inky sky. A whip-poor-will called out from the live oaks.

Wynona sipped her wine and looked at the lavender orchids in the corner. "They seem to bloom at night. When I come out in the morning and discover a new orchid bloom greeting me, I smile the same way the squirrels and birds do. The tribe's elders believed that some plants have a distinct spirit. Maybe, in a strange botanical way, that might be the case with those orchids. If they die, I will feel so guilty, like I've committed a crime. Speaking of crime, do you think Darnell Reid was killed?"

"I'd bet on it."

"Do you think someone would set up that kindly old man, Gideon Wright, to take the fall if a body is found?"

"Maybe. And that is because of the correlations I'm seeing. Gideon knew Reid from the times he trespassed on his property to test the spring's water, take pictures, and scout the area. Another man, ostensibly a second water tech who was last there with Reid, might testify that he saw Reid push Gideon's buttons, causing an argument. It's not by chance that Reid's car was on Gideon's property. I don't know if those two deputies that drove up to his cabin took pictures of the tire and shoe prints before the storm arrived. At this point, I can offer the photos I took, giving them to the sheriff's detectives. One vehicle had wider tires than those on the Dodge."

"The images usually aren't as good as plaster casts, but they'll do if they can find the vehicle with the wider tires and the people who were wearing those shoes the night Reid had gone missing."

"Or, if they find Reid, maybe one pair will be accounted for. That means tracking down two more. I don't think they'll have to go far from where that car was found to find Reid."

"The news report indicated deputies and volunteers have been searching through parts of the national forest."

"Their next move will probably be to search Gideon's land."

"They may not find a thing."

I said nothing, listening to the whip-poor-will in the trees.

Max uttered a slight whine, the kind she makes when she needs to answer a call of nature. Wynona glanced over at me and smiled. "It looks like your gal pal wants to go outside."

"Is it my turn?"

"Max is staring at you with her big brown eyes."

"You have big brown eyes, too."

"But I don't need you to escort me to the bathroom." Wynona smiled and finished her wine. "As you two make the rounds outside, I'm going to shower and get ready for bed. You're welcome to join me."

"In bed or the shower?"

"Both." Wynona smiled, touching my hand as she got up and went inside.

Max led the way to the backyard. As she went through her nightly routine of sniffing and turning in half circles while looking for the perfect spot to pee, I watched dark clouds build over the national forest, covering the stars in the northern sky. A full moon was in the east, and clouds were moving like gray smoke in front of it. As the moonlight dimmed, I saw another light.

This one was manmade.

It was coming from the road in front of our cabin. "Max, let's take a look down the driveway." We walked around the cabin.

My crushed shell driveway is two hundred feet from the cabin to the county road. We don't get much traffic, just the occasional car or pickup truck. Rarely anything after midnight. I watched a car's headlights approach the area where my driveway connects to the road.

The person in the car slowed down. The driver went from going at least forty miles per hour to maybe ten or less. The car slowly cruised by our driveway, stopping. I stood near a massive live oak. I didn't move, standing still in the dark, with crickets chirping and Max watching the headlights.

As the car passed our driveway, I could see the brake lights flashing and the driver tapping the brakes twice. The brake lights became brighter, and the car almost stopped again. In the dark, I couldn't determine the color of the car. And, from that distance, it wasn't easy to be sure of the exact model. I knew it was an SUV. Maybe a Ford Expedition. Was the SUV red?

And if so, was Floyd Shaw the driver?

TWENTY-NINE

The next day, Gideon Wright was standing in the stillness of the small graveyard when he saw motion from the corner of his eye. He just finished a prayer and stood straight after he'd placed fresh flowers next to his wife's headstone. To his left, past the cabin and barn, was the gravel and dirt driveway that led to the main gate. Someone was walking up the drive, heading in the direction of the cabin. Gideon watched the woman from about fifty yards away.

He took a deep breath, shaking his head. Gideon looked down at the grave. "We have company, Heather, a young woman. Maybe she's lost." He turned and walked around the few headstones, moving toward the woman coming up the driveway. She stopped, staring in his direction for a few seconds.

"Can I help you?" Gideon asked.

The woman didn't say anything. She just stared and then started walking toward him. When she came within twenty feet, she stopped and moistened her lips. "Hi, I apologize for the intrusion. I saw the signs at the gate. I didn't have a phone number or a way to reach you online."

"I've never been online. Been to lots of other places, though." He smiled. Something about the young woman looked familiar. She appeared to be in her early thirties—anxious, maybe a little afraid. Her dark auburn hair caught the soft breeze. She had a refined nose, high cheekbones, and full lips. Her eyes reminded Gideon of the color reflected from the spring when there were no clouds in the sky, when the water was like a ceramic blue bowl.

"I felt odd climbing over your gate. That spring is the most beautiful I've ever seen. In the sunlight, it looks like liquid diamonds flowing over the stones."

111

"Are you connected to Glacier Artesian Springs or any water bottling company? If so, you can leave the way you came."

She shook her head. "No, and I'm sorry for climbing your gate. It's something I wouldn't ordinarily do. But this isn't an ordinary visit. At least I don't think of it that way. The last distance from the road up to here is the end of a three-thousand-mile journey, I hope."

"Who are you?"

"My name is Margaux Brennon. Are you Gideon Wright?"

"Yes. Why do you ask?"

"With your permission, I'd like to tell you that by sharing with you how and why I came here."

"Okay. You said you had traveled three thousand miles. Where is your home?"

"That's a good question. I left where I was living in Seattle for a change of pace, maybe even a change of place. I ended a bad marriage. To be frank, it was a shitty marriage. I sold or gave away those things that I used to think were so damn important, and I've turned the page."

"Why are you here, Ms. Brennon? And why are you staring at me like I have soup dripping from my beard?"

"I'm sorry. I don't mean to stare. It's just that your eyes resemble someone who used to be in my life."

"Used to be?"

"My grandmother. She's gone. I mean, she's not alive anymore, and I'd like to think she's gone to a better place. If she didn't, I don't have a chance."

Gideon chuckled. "Sounds as if you've had a rough patch or two."

Margaux nodded. "A lot more than two, but I stopped counting. I'm not here to lament my life. I'm here because of this." She opened her purse and lifted out what appeared to be a small, leather-bound book.

Gideon eyed it. "Is that a Bible?"

"No. It's a diary. I found it in my grandmother's attic when she passed away. She raised me after my parents were killed in a car crash. They were hit by a drunk driver. I never called it a car accident. Something like that is intentional. When someone drinks themselves into oblivion and becomes too shitfaced to drive, somewhere after that first drink, that person decides that the next few hours are all about them. This was my great-grandmother's diary."

"Did that really bring you all the way here?"

"It's what's inside the diary, maybe what was inside her, that brought me here."

Gideon was quiet for a moment. The mockingbird flew to the gable of the barn and chattered. Gideon motioned toward the small cemetery. "If you would, Margaux, please follow me." He led her across the grounds to the graveyard. The headstones were clean and easy to read, except for the one in the shade of a large live oak.

He pointed to the headstone with the fresh-cut roses. "My wife is buried there. This is the Wright family cemetery. Not many folks here because we never had a large family. Lots of love, though."

Margaux looked at the headstones, her eyes settling on the one with the roses. "*Heather Wright - Beloved Wife and Friend to All.*" She looked over at Gideon. "That's a sweet and loving inscription. I'm sure you miss her dearly."

"I do. But I have no idea why you're here. If you have something to tell me, we can go onto the cabin's front porch and talk in the shade. But you're probably wasting your time."

***

Twenty-five miles from Gideon's home, a new search team was going to hit the road and head in his direction. In the back parking lot of the sheriff's department and criminal justice complex, twenty deputies, two bloodhounds, and a black Lab—a cadaver dog—were about to get into vans, cars, and pickup trucks to take the search for Darnell Reid to the next level.

The lead tracker, Captain Ron Morris, was a rawboned senior deputy who was a big game hunter and a former tracker in the Army. He stood in the parking lot as his men gathered around in a half circle. "Okay, we have a warrant to search all buildings on the property. This includes the home and the barn. We'll cover his entire two hundred acres."

One of the deputies who was holding a bloodhound's leash asked, "What if we don't find anything there? Do we keep going?"

"If we come up empty-handed, we'll fan out and search the adjacent terrain. Slap on the sunscreen and lace up your snake-proof boots.

113

Rattlers are in the scrub bush. Moccasins in the swamps. We're going out there in God's country. No tellin' what we might find—it could be a place where bodies are dumped way back up there. Any questions?"

The stocky deputy with the black Lab raised his hand and said, "Captain Morris, I'd suggest that Buck and I work the center area in a zigzag fashion between the two bloodhounds. Because Buck is smelling for a cadaver, it's a different kind of trail or approach. We'll look for anything that appears slightly out of place. Stuff like leaves or sticks higher than the surrounding ground. Maybe there will be a fresh grave under some of that."

"Understood. I have the search warrant. Jason, Rob, and I will serve it. As I understand it, Gideon Wright is an older gentleman. We need to be as respectful as possible, not wanting to give him a heart attack. After we search his house and any other structures, we'll fan out across the property and head deep into the national forest if need be. I've been with the department for almost twenty years now. We've recovered more than forty bodies from the Ocala National Forest in my time. The old forest seems to attract people who commit suicide and people who commit murder. Get ready. We leave soon."

As the deputies loaded equipment into the vans, one deputy stood with a carrying case opened on an outdoor table near the rear of the building. He was prepping his drone for aerial surveillance. The dogs barked, already sensing the excitement of following a trail of death.

THIRTY

I thought an in-person appearance would be better than a phone call. I walked into the county sheriff's office lobby and smiled at the receptionist hunched behind the plexiglass partition. A small, round hole was in the glass to allow for conversations to be heard, somewhat. She was in her early thirties, with shoulder-length mousy brown hair. Her eyes were puffy, maybe from allergies.

"Can I help you, sir?"

"Hope so. I'm here to see Sheriff Warren."

"Your name?"

"Sean O'Brien."

"Is the sheriff expecting you?"

"I have some evidence in the case of the missing man, Darnell Reid." I motioned to the file folder I was carrying.

"Lemme see if he's in his office." She punched three buttons on her phone console. "Hey, Sylvia, is the sheriff available? I have a gentleman here in the lobby, and he says he has some evidence he wants to give him. It's in reference to the Darnell Reid missing persons' case." She was silent for about fifteen seconds, nodding. "Okay. I'll tell him." She set the phone back on the cradle and looked up at me. "The sheriff's busy right now. Detective Richard Lofton will meet you here in the lobby. You can have a seat if you'd like."

"Thank you."

I sat in one of six hard plastic chairs against one wall, with a green plant in the corner. The opposite wall had framed photos of the sheriff and the senior members of his department. After a minute, a door to the far left opened, and a man in pressed dark jeans, a tan sports coat, and an open shirt came up to me. He wore pointed-toe boots, walking like he'd been in a saddle all day. His square face was sun-kissed, with a downturned wide mouth and wary eyes. "I'm Detective Lofton. Can I help you?"

I stood. I was probably three inches taller than him. "Maybe I can be of help to you, Detective. I'm Sean O'Brien."

"What information do you have?"

"It's more than just information. It's tire and shoe tracks I found in the dirt around and near the car owned by the missing man, Darnell Reid."

"How'd you come across them?"

"I was visiting my client, Gideon Wright." I paused to see if there was name recognition. I could tell that he knew of Gideon. "Not far from his gate off Highway 19, there was a car parked. It was Monday, the twelfth. I walked over to see if the driver or anyone else might need assistance. But there was no one in the vehicle, and it appeared to be locked. I couldn't help but notice the tracks, so I thought I'd take a few photos just in case they might be needed."

"Are you always so visionary?"

There was a slight edge to his voice, and his eyes were impassive. "Not long after I took the pictures, two of your deputies came onto Gideon's property. They were curious as to why Reid's car was parked off the side of the road and on Gideon's land. After they questioned him, I told them about the tire and shoe prints. But it was right before a storm threatened to blow through and dump rain. I don't know if the deputies had time to take their own photos, so I thought I'd give these to your office."

I opened the folder, handing him five 8-by-10 photos of the tire and shoe tracks. He nodded. "Thank you. You're right. I don't think the deputies had a chance to take their own photos. No time, of course, to order plaster casts, considering the weather."

I took a pen that was clipped on the side of the folder, pointing to the tire tread marks. "The smaller tread prints came from the car driven by Darnell Reid, or rather the car he owns. The wider tracks were from the tires on another vehicle, which must have been about forty feet in front of Reid's car and off the road. Here are the close-ups of the shoe or boot prints. As you can see, there are three separate and distinct impressions in the mud."

He put on wire-framed glasses and studied the images. "I see the differences. One of the prints looks to have come from a work boot."

"Probably, and one of them might have come from Darnell Reid."

He grunted. "Mr. O'Brien, you said from the car driven by Darnell Reid … or rather the car he owns. What do you mean by that?"

"Reid might not have been driving that night. If he was abducted in the bar's parking lot, maybe one perp drove the lead vehicle and one drove Reid's car."

"Then where was Reid?"

"In the trunk."

He looked back down at the photos, his face pinched. He eyed me. "You said that Gideon Wright is your client. Are you a PI?"

"More of a consultant."

"Did he hire you because we found Darnell Reid's abandoned car not far from Wright's driveway?"

"No. He hired me before that, for another reason."

"Is it related to Darnell Reid?"

"I don't know. I do know that Reid and another man, both claiming to be water quality techs, ignored the no-trespassing signs, and went onto Gideon's land to test the water in the spring he privately owns."

"Why would they do that?"

"That's a question I'd like to have answered. If you find Reid, you might want to ask him that."

"At this point, Mr. O'Brien, Reid is a missing person. However, if we find his body, that becomes a drastic change of events. It'll create an investigation wave that will wash over Gideon Wright's property. Is he involved in Reid's disappearance? We don't know that. If we do find Reid's body out there in the national forest, we'll come knockin' on Gideon's door."

I gave him the file folder. He put the photos inside the folder. "Detective, you have three sets of shoe or boot prints. One is most likely Darnell Reid's. The other two are probably his kidnappers. If you find a body, you won't find a shoe in Gideon Wright's home that will match those."

"In these photos, there is one image of the Dodge. The rest are close-ups of the shoe and tire prints. How would I know for certain that these prints came from the ground around Reid's car?"

"Let me show you how. I took more than just pictures. I also shot video." I found the file on my phone, hit the play button, and held the phone screen to where Lofton could see it. "Okay, here's a wide shot of the car. As you can see, I'm walking toward it, and as I come to the rear section, I point the lens to the ground. You can see the same prints on the photos in your hands. I shot video of the wider vehicle tracks in front of the Dodge. I'll email the files to you."

"You call yourself a consultant for Gideon Wright. I got a feeling you're a helluva lot more than that." He turned and walked away, his hard soles and heels echoing off the tile floor.

I thought about how often I tried to work with detectives on cases, particularly homicides, where I came up against hesitancy on their part. I worked mostly cold cases, which you'd expect they would welcome another set of eyes. But that was not always so. Maybe it was a territorial issue, or it was because they didn't believe a particular cold case could be solved and might be thought incompetent if it was. Or, if their caseloads were too full, they harbored guilt for neglecting them. Egos also played into the reluctance, as if taking information from a PI would jeopardize a case that they'd already put behind them.

At the door, he looked back toward me. "FYI, Mr. O'Brien, we have some of our trackers and canines canvassing that area. They have a warrant to search Mr. Wright's home, too. Thanks for the photos." He exited through the door.

THIRTY-ONE

Margaux sat in a rocking chair on the cabin's front porch, watching a blue heron stalking at the edge of the spring pool. "There's nothing like this in the state of Washington. Granted, there are beautiful places: the Pacific Coast, the lakes, rivers, and waterfalls. But nothing even close to this. It has a primeval feel to it, like it's stuck in a time warp."

Gideon sat in a rocking chair a few feet away from her, his legs crossed at the knees, broad hands on the armrests. "The Pacific Northwest is a beautiful place. I did some geological surveys up there in nineteen ... well, it was many years ago. Ms. Brennon, you'll find that I'm a patient and careful listener. What is it that you came here to say?"

"Please, call me Margaux."

"Okay."

"It's not what I came here to say, it's what I came here to find." She rested the diary on her lap, the breeze fanning the hanging moss. "Before my great-grandmother married my great-grandfather, she had been deeply in love with another man. She became pregnant with that man's child. When she told her parents, they were furious, and her father threatened to disown her. She was only nineteen. The family already was moving from Florida to San Francisco. My great-grandmother was forbidden to tell her boyfriend that she was carrying his child. That baby, my grandmother, was born in San Francisco. Five years later, my great-grandmother met another man; they married and had a son. When he was a teenager, he took his own life by jumping off the Golden Gate Bridge."

"That's a sad story."

"Unfortunately, it becomes sadder. I'm sorry. I didn't come here to burden you with ghosts from the past."

He smiled. "I'm not afraid of ghosts."

"I hope you aren't afraid of the truth. Some passages in my great-grandmother's diary are painful and yet so beautiful. Most were written while she was pregnant, thousands of miles away from the man she loved, and some were written in the three years after she had her baby."

She opened the diary to a page marked with a yellow ribbon and read. "Although just a toddler, our daughter has your expressions: the way you look at something new and how you narrow your eyes, finding the grit deep inside you to tackle a problem. Lily does those same things. There is no denying that she has your eyes, your smile, and your dimples. It is my hope and prayer that one day we will be united as a family." Margaux paused, looking away.

"What happened to them?" Gideon's voice was low and soft.

"My great-grandmother died from leukemia at age fifty-three. Her husband had died years earlier, overseas in the war. My mother, Victoria, was my grandmother Lily's only child, and she died along with my father, as I mentioned, in the horrific car wreck. I have no siblings and no living family unless you are my great-grandfather. I believe you are. My great-grandmother wrote about this land and this beautiful spring in her diary. She also wrote about you, Gideon Wright, the young man whom she loved so much. When she was taken away, he never knew she was carrying his child. I'm sorry that you're getting this news decades later."

Gideon looked at the diary and then down at the spring, the breeze jingling windchimes hanging from an eave on his porch.

Margaux chose her words carefully. "If this is too painful, I can get up and leave. I'll never come here again. But after I found and read her diary, and after I did some ancestral research, I was surprised to find no record of your death in any Florida counties or anywhere else for that matter. After I read and closed the cover on her diary, I couldn't stop thinking about her words, what she went through, and how she lived in this tropical paradise before being moved across the country. She was forced to turn her back on the man she truly loved with every fiber of her being. God, I ache for a true love like that. Her diary is better than any romance novel because it's a real love story. And you're real."

Gideon looked at her, searching Margaux's face. "As much as I want to believe you, what if this is some kind of elaborate ruse?"

"It's not."

"But I don't know that."

"You have my grandmother's eyes and smile. If you shaved off that beard, would I see dimples, too? I had a law practice back in Seattle. I graduated from law school at Stanford. After working with a firm for six years, I went solo. Many of my cases were family law. More and more, the term *family tree* has become convoluted as people have done ancestry DNA tests and uncovered genetic roots. The offshoot is that they began to discover family members they never knew existed. Imagine living all your life believing you are an only child—you have no siblings—and years later, someone calls you and that person says she believes you are her sister or brother, mother or father. It's happening all the time. For the first time, unknown siblings are meeting. For some, it's a great thing. For others, not so much." Margaux leaned closer to Gideon.

He stared closely at her. "Your great-grandmother, what was her name?"

"Tiffany Ann Harper."

Gideon made a dry swallow. The breeze stopped, and a cardinal called out from a tall cabbage palm tree. "Tiffany," he said in a whisper. Gideon cleared his throat, his thoughts going back far in time. After a moment, he looked at Margaux. "You said that you have no living family members."

"Unfortunately, that's correct. My ex-husband and I didn't have children. The marriage lasted seven years. He's back in Seattle."

"My wife, Heather, is here, of course. We were blessed in many ways, but having children wasn't one of them. Tiffany Harper was my girlfriend for three beautiful years. I was heartbroken when she moved away. I eventually met Heather, and we lived a blessed life. After my wife passed away, I never remarried. My brother died years before her, and I was his only family. So, naturally, I assumed that I had no living family members. And then you show up."

Margaux made a self-conscious smile. "Why do I feel like a cat that just brought a dead mouse to your door?"

"I'm sorry. I didn't mean it like that. I have no issue with or ill will toward you, Margaux. It's just that this is quite a surprise, and it comes at a rather trying time in my advanced years."

"I didn't come here to interfere with your life or even to be part of it. We can be like ships cut from the same timber and passing by in the straits of life. I didn't travel here like some crazy, distant relative showing up to lay claim to your property or possessions after your death. I've decluttered, done well in my career, and I've invested wisely, too. I passed the Florida bar exam recently. I can work here if I choose. Key West sounds like a good place. I need nothing materially from you. Something spiritual, well, that would be a breath of fresh air."

"What do you mean by spiritual?"

She opened the diary and made a dry swallow. "This is how my great-grandmother, your Tiffany, described it." She looked down and read. *"Gideon, I feel so lost without you, like a tiny bird flying against the winds of change. After falling in love with you, I don't have to keep the hope of finding real love alive because I found it. The depths of those feelings are forever fused in my soul. Giving birth to our child will never allow that spark of love to die, because every time I look into our child's eyes, I will see a part of you. It's the part I long for late at night when I'm all alone. I remember the scent of your skin after we swam in the spring, and the look of morning sunlight in your blue eyes. Your love fanned a fire in my soul that will never die. Maybe it will dim with time, but it will never die. I know you loved me—you said so. But I hope it was as deep as what I felt for you. When you look at that beautiful harvest moon over the spring, I want you to think of me as something of beauty, as I shall always think of you."* With all my love, Tiffany.

Margaux closed the diary and looked over at Gideon, tears flowing down his cheeks and into his snowy beard. Margaux felt her own eyes tearing. She sniffled. "I'm sorry to read something to you that's so painful all these years later."

"It's not that what you read is painful, it's poignant. Through your voice, the way you spoke, I could hear Tiffney's voice from so long ago." He smiled, using both hands to part his beard on his right cheek. "If you look closely, Margaux, you might see one of my dimples."

She leaned forward. "Yes! I can see it. And I can see it through my tears, Grandpa."

THIRTY-TWO

The car caught my eye, and the license plate piqued my curiosity. The car was parked in Gideon's driveway a few feet short of his gate. I started to pull my Jeep up behind it but decided that wouldn't be a good idea considering the last car I saw on Gideon's property was abandoned not too far from his gate. Déjà vu is a feeling. Serendipity is usually a good thing. I didn't think the car represented either, at least not upon my first observation.

This one was a Subaru Outback with plates from Washington state. I got out of my Jeep, snapped a picture of the rear license plate, and used the key Gideon had given me to unlock and open the gate. I drove around the car and through the gate, relocking the chain around the posts and driving toward Gideon's cabin.

As I rounded the last bend in the gravel driveway, I spotted two people standing near the spring. One was Gideon. The other was a woman. I assumed that she was the driver of the Subaru. I'd soon find out.

I parked and walked over to them. Gideon grinned. "Sean, it's good to see you. Thanks for calling me from the sheriff's department. Maybe those pictures you took will help them with their case."

"Let's hope so."

"This is Margaux Brennon. Margaux, meet Sean O'Brien. I first met Sean and his family at one of the farmers' markets I attend to hand out water from my booth. Sean is a private investigator."

I looked at the woman. She appeared to be in her mid-thirties and had a naturally pretty face with no traces of makeup. Her smile was wide, like Gideon's, with a slight trace of dimples when she smiled. "It's nice to meet you, Margaux."

"Same here, Sean. Gideon told me a little about you—more about why he sought your services. I hope you can find the man with the camera and discover why he has a habit of stalking an elderly gentleman."

123

"He won't be too hard to find. If possible, I like to share some of that investigative work with law enforcement agencies. That's one of the reasons I gave the pictures I took of the tire and shoe prints found near the abandoned car on Gideon's property, just south of his gate. Sharing data with the police usually results in a better outcome."

"Better? Would that be for the perpetrator or the police?"

I smiled. "The police. If there's too much resistance from them, I'll circumvent and find some form of restoration or reconciliation for the victim or a member of the victim's family."

She nodded. "I like your choice of words. If I'm translating accurately, I believe the word *justice* for the victims would fit well."

I said nothing. A limpkin broke the silence by shrieking from the thick cypress trees west of the spring.

Gideon cleared his throat. "Margaux lived in Seattle. She's an attorney."

I nodded. "Criminal law or civil?"

"A little of both. I was a prosecutor for three years before joining a firm and then starting my own practice. I'm particular about the cases I take, choosing them for what I consider to be the right reasons."

"The best reason is that someone is a true victim. Is that your Subaru at the gate?"

"Yes. I love that old car. I bought it ten years ago, and it has never given me a bit of trouble."

"You lived in Seattle; does that mean you've left the city?"

"Yes. Me and my little dog, Lily. I decided to turn the page on a few trying chapters and head to the Sunshine State. I took a six-month lease on a condo over at New Smyrna Beach. I love it there. I might practice law in Florida, but only with select cases and clients. Cases of true injustice—clients who've been harmed and have few places to turn for help. Like you said, true victims."

I hadn't known Gideon for long, but I knew him well enough to detect that he was already harboring a fondness for or at least a personal connection with Margaux. I waited for him or her to tell me what that was, although I could guess. It was apparent in their physical traits and subtle body language.

Gideon smiled. "Sean, I was telling Margaux about the history of the spring and this land. I gave her a brief explanation of the mineral elements in the spring water, at least from the boil to the first thirty-three feet."

Margaux gestured toward the spring. "I have some food allergies. I'm hoping I can sip this water before a meal and not break out in a rash from eating cheese or dairy. I so miss pizza."

Gideon chuckled. "I don't know if it'll prevent your allergies, but I'd bet it'll quickly heal any rash you get, for any reason." He motioned toward the cabin. "Let's go sit on the porch and have some iced sweet tea. I used the spring water to make it. Sean, when I met you and through our subsequent talks, I told you some of my history. You saw the grave of my beloved wife, Heather. What I didn't mention, because there was no reason to do so, was that, before Heather, I fell in love with a woman whom I wanted to marry."

I said nothing, listening as we walked up to the porch.

"We talked about marriage and had planned to do so after I earned my university degree. But that was not to happen. Tiffany was her name. And if what Margaux shared with me is accurate, as I believe it to be, then this young woman standing beside me is my great-granddaughter."

THIRTY-THREE

When I'd earlier seen the Subaru at Gideon's gate, I thought about the difference between déjà vu and serendipity. The latter usually indicates the occurrence of something positive, but unexpected. Déjà vu, though, is often the feeling that you get when you're experiencing something you've faced before. There's also premonition, which is a type of psychic radar—getting a tiny glimpse of a future event.

At that moment in time, sitting in rocking chairs on Gideon's front porch, talking with him and Margaux, I had no feeling of déjà vu or a foreboding hunch. But I've often had to rely on a sense that is beyond sight and sound. It has to do with motive and the law of probabilities—cause and effect. I listened to Gideon and Margaux with a mixture of happiness for them and a dash of suspicion to flavor this new family soup.

An hour later, after each of us had finished our first glasses of iced sweet tea, I wanted to run a background check on Margaux Brennon. Not because I disbelieved her or thought that she was lying, but rather because I wanted to prove that she and what she represented were real. Also, it was because of my experience in criminal cases.

As a detective investigating homicides, I rarely found evidence that could be considered a coincidence. It was seldom accidental and usually connected to greed, lust, or jealousy. But I knew that Margaux's coming to Florida and seeking out Gideon had nothing to do with homicide. This was a lost relative reaching out to another. You put a saliva sample in a container, mail the little kit off to the land of Oz, and find that your gene pool comes from fifty-seven countries, and the wicked witch of the west was your aunt, and you're related to a serial killer.

It happens.

But for them, there was no DNA test yet. Only a diary and a family connection are illustrated in it. If the diary was real, and I didn't believe that it wasn't, I was happy for Gideon. Here was a kindhearted man who had done so much for others, and now he had a sweet interlude in his life. A life ring was tossed his way, which could go a long way toward protecting his spring and property. It's a nice fantasy transition for this primeval land that managed to hide in a crack of time, snuggled in the protective womb of the cosmos, resistant to the yin and yang of a growing Florida.

Margaux set her tall glass of tea down on a coaster atop a small table on the porch. She looked over at me. "Sean, I can't read minds, of course, but like you, I've been around the block in the criminal justice system. I know that to you, and probably to Gideon as well, this juncture may seem somewhat poorly planned, gratuitous, and presumptuous. But it's not."

"I'm not here to judge, only to consider the facts and what some might call coincidences."

"I understand. In terms of planning, I didn't plan it. I discovered it. I found that old diary inside a chest in my grandmother's attic after her death. When I read it, I sat on the floor and cried. Not for me, but for my great-grandmother and her daughter, who was my grandmother."

Gideon leaned forward in his rocking chair. "We're not doubting you or suspicious of why you came here. It is what it is, that's all."

"You have every right to be skeptical. After you shared the stories of the trespassing and the water company's aggressive posture and veiled intimidation, I would be suspicious of any long-lost relative showing up out of the blue. It's like winning the lottery and hearing from Uncle Harry's estranged second cousin."

Gideon's eyes were mixed with sadness and empathy. "You only could be long lost if I knew you existed. I didn't, so you weren't found at my doorstep. You simply came across an old bridge connected to my past, and here you are." He looked at me. "Sean, I think Margaux's arrival here is a good thing. Perhaps a blessing in disguise or a happy turn of events."

I eyed Margaux. "May I see the diary?"

"Of course." She handed it to me.

127

I opened the leatherbound cover. The pages had the smell of yesterday—the musky scent of the past with the hint of vanilla. Although the black ink had faded somewhat, the penmanship was lovely. I gave it to Gideon. "Does this look like Tiffany's handwriting?"

He put his glasses on and read a page from the center of the diary. Gideon didn't have to answer. His eyes were wet. "Yes. Even after all these years, I still remember how lovely and distinctive it was."

"I'm sure, as my Greek friend Nick Cronus says, this is not a Trojan horse of deception. You're right, Margaux. Your arrival, in view of what's been happening on Gideon's property, is curious in terms of your timing. That doesn't mean it's suspect or there are ulterior motives. The idea that you two are the only family left is a powerful potential bond for you both. But I think, in view of the circumstances, that the proof of concept—the test of time, if you will—comes from your future actions."

She smiled, nodding. "I couldn't agree more. All I would like to do is spend some time with Gideon. If he doesn't want that, I will get in my car and drive away, never to return. But it is my heartfelt hope to get to know him better and give him the chance to know me. We can take it from there." She looked at Gideon. "Maybe I could drive over here a couple of times a month from my condo and take you to lunch or dinner. I can even make dinner for us. I'm a pretty good cook, especially with Mexican food. Sean, I would hope that you can join us occasionally for dinner. Please bring your wife and daughter, too."

"I would like that, thanks."

"Great. On that note, I need to find a bathroom. The tea is testing my bladder."

Gideon motioned toward the cabin's screened front door. "When you go inside, walk past the kitchen to the right. The bathroom is down at the end of the hall, on the right."

"Thanks." She stood with her purse, left the diary, and went inside.

After a moment, Gideon looked over at me. He stopped rocking in his chair. "Well, what do you think? I need your honest opinion. How do you read this."

"I only can give you an honest opinion. That's the way I work. However, my opinion means nothing. It's a judgment call, and I don't know enough about Margaux to make that for you or her. My gut feeling is that she's the real deal. I'm not completely sure, but based on her story, body language, the way she speaks, and the obvious warmth and humility in her heart, she's either a great actress or the real thing. I would like to believe the latter."

"Me, too. In my case, it's a little different. When I look at her and listen to her talk, I hear a voice from my past. I hear a touch of Tiffany coming from Margaux's lips. The way she read that passage from the diary was like Tiffany sitting right here on the front porch and speaking directly to me. It hit me to the core. I can look at the physical traits and the subtle mannerisms in Margaux and see glimpses of Tiffany. I don't have DNA proof that she's my great-granddaughter, but the compass in my heart, the one that I lost so long ago, is now pointing to her. Maybe that's the true north direction of the heart. It sure feels that way."

"For you and for her, I hope that's the case. I can get DNA proof quickly if you two agree to a cheek swab. I have cotton tips and plastic baggies in my Jeep."

"Of course. Let's ask Margaux when she comes back out here."

"I will run a background check on her. I have no doubt it'll reflect much of what she told us. I'll look for any inconsistencies. But the big thing won't be some event in a past that's probably clean. What Margaux does or does not do with you will depend on her actions now and in the future. She needs to earn your trust. For what it's worth, that last sentence is my honest opinion." I smiled, and he laughed.

Margaux came out the screened door, stepping past me to take her seat in the rocking chair. I could smell the scent of lavender soap on her hands. She looked over at Gideon, a concerned expression on her face. He picked up on it and said, "Margaux, Sean has access to DNA testing. He's offered to do it here and now. I have no problem doing it. Will you? And that question doesn't mean that I don't believe you because I do."

"Yes, I'm happy to do that." She looked over at me.

"Okay. Wait here." I retrieved the cotton Q-Tips and two plastic baggies from my glovebox, returned to the porch, and swabbed the inside of their cheeks, placing the swabs in the air-tight bags. "I can get the results back quickly."

Gideon smiled. "Excellent. Thank you."

Margaux nodded and looked over at Gideon. "I'd like to ask you something, and please don't think that I'm prying or being nosey in any respect. Walking by the kitchen, I couldn't help but notice a legal contract on the counter. I only saw the top page, and I would never read it without your permission. But if you're considering entering into a legal and binding agreement, or if you've already signed one, I'd be happy to look at the contract. I just would be another pair of eyes working on your behalf. If you'd rather not, that's fine, too."

He shook his head. "No, I haven't signed it. The lawyer's name is Percy King. Sean, I told you about him. Anyway, he put together the terms of the agreement. It's a contract that will protect the land and spring after I'm no longer here to care for it."

"When did you receive it?" I asked.

"A couple of days ago. Percy had a courier bring it out here from his office in DeLand."

"I wonder why he didn't send it registered mail."

"He didn't say. He's supposed to come pick it up this afternoon, unless, for some reason, I decide not to sign it."

I looked over at Margaux. Her eyes said it all. She was afraid for him, and I could tell. I glanced at Gideon and said, "I think it'd be a good idea to have Margaux read it."

He nodded. "That's fine. Would you like to read it out here on the porch or inside the cabin?"

"On the porch is fine. I'll go get it." She left.

I looked over at Gideon. He winked and said, "It looks to me like she's starting to earn that trust right now. I wonder if she'll find something in the contract that's a red flag."

THIRTY-FOUR

The dogs wanted to hunt. They knew the drill. The K9 sheriff's deputies loaded the bloodhounds and the lone black Lab into cruisers. The other members of the search team were all locked and loaded with gear as they walked from the criminal justice building to the awaiting vehicles.

Captain Ron Morris, now wearing wrap-around dark sunglasses, said, "The news media might be there when we arrive. If they try to interview any of you, refer them to me. Otherwise, it's strictly no comment. Understood?"

The men nodded, and the black Lab made an anxious whine, angling his big head as if he could understand Captain Morris. They pulled out of the compound, five police cruisers and two tactical vans, the drivers following in a convoy as they set a course to a remote section of land off Highway 19, the property and home owned by Gideon Wright.

***

She didn't rock in the chair. Margaux barely moved as she read the five-page legal agreement. She'd taken a small pad from her purse, jotting notes as she read. When she finished, she went back and reread one of the pages. Margaux looked up at Gideon. I could tell she was searching for the words, or the best way to string the right words together. "Thank you for giving me a chance to read this."

He nodded. "Well, what do you think? Does it seem fair to you?"

"No. Not by a long shot. It's window dressing, or what I'd refer to as a legal shell game."

"What do you mean?"

"There is nothing on this contract that offers third-party checks and balances. There is nothing to ensure that, upon your death, your final wishes are carried out exactly as you've instructed. First, you're strapped with depositing thousands of dollars into a joint bank account, one to which Mr. King has access. The money would ostensibly be used to buy insurance, pay property taxes on the home and land, and for what he terms as annual upkeep and maintenance. But at what cost? There are no itemized expenses. It's capricious, giving King the arbitrary authority to withdraw the funds whenever he wants."

Gideon grunted. "I suppose there must be some element of trust given to the executor. I would hope an attorney like him, with a long history and career in the county, would abide by the terms of the agreement and not withdraw funds when it isn't needed or justified."

"But there is no way you can be sure, especially with no other oversight. There is no board—no one to keep tabs on it. But that doesn't bother me as much as paragraphs seven through ten on page four. If the deed to the home and land is transferred to King, he can do whatever he wants. He can sell the land and lease the water rights to bottle companies."

"I can add addendums to the agreement."

"The agreement states that the executor will strive in good faith to keep and maintain the home, spring, and property in their current status quo. However, should an act of God or an unforeseen event arise, requiring more funds than what is in the bank, King would be at liberty to liquidate the property and then divvy up a portion of the net sales to the two charities you included—the Salvation Army and the Nature Conservancy. He could sell to a housing developer or cut a deal with the state to buy the land and spring for a park."

She looked at her notes. "This contract is far too vague and ambiguous for my tastes. It gives Percy King the legal right to do whatever he wants with this marvelous land after you're gone. And there is no one in the courthouse, not the county clerk, property appraiser, sheriff—nobody with the authority to stop him." She looked over at me.

"I agree with Margaux. I'm not suggesting that Percy King is a shady or crooked lawyer, someone with ulterior motives to sell all of this when you're not here. But that contract gives him the legal teeth to do just that."

Gideon sat back in his rocking chair, his eyes filled with private thoughts, bees humming in the purple lavender growing in the yard along the porch. "I've seen Percy take on housing developers and not back down when it came to rezoning riverfront property. I don't have complete faith in him, but based on his track record, I have no reason to doubt him."

Margaux nodded. "Someone was paying him to fight waterfront development. I seriously doubt that an attorney not affiliated with a large firm would spend his time and resources on a case like that unless he was paid handsomely to do so. I advise you not to sign this agreement in its current form. I can rewrite it to be equitable, adding legal clauses that'll ensure methods to prevent a sale or division of the land for any reason and to safeguard it to remain as is for perpetuity."

Gideon shook his head. "No, don't go to the trouble."

"It's no trouble at all. Basically, it will give you a counter-agreement that will do what it's intended to do. There will be nothing vague, subjective, or containing loopholes that King or anyone can use to change your wishes."

Gideon didn't respond immediately. I could tell he was deep in thought. A black and yellow bumblebee flew up from the lavender blooms, its wings creating enough circulation to sway the wind chimes before the insect flew away. "Rather than rewrite what you consider a lopsided contract to make if fair, let's do away with it and start from scratch. At this point, I don't see a reason for Percy King to become the executor of this land after I am no longer here. I think you'd be a better attorney."

***

The sheriff's entourage converged near the gate to Gideon's home. The cruisers and vans were parked off the shoulder of the road. When they walked up to the gate, Captain Morris turned to one of his deputies. "Let's run a check on those plates. I'd like to know who's in there."

The deputy, his chest like a rain barrel, snorted. "Will do, Captain."

"It looks like there's a padlock locking a solid chain around the gate posts. Scott, get the bolt cutters and cut off the lock. When we open it up, my vehicle with Don and Wayne will be in the lead. We'll serve the warrant at the house. The rest of y'all follow us."

When they cut off the lock and swung the gate open, the dogs barked, knowing the hunt was about to begin.

***

Margaux was answering one of Gideon's questions when we heard dogs baying. I'd been around dogs long enough to recognize the barks. They sounded like they were coming from bloodhound tracking dogs. That meant the cops were either at the gate or already had passed through it. If they were through, I knew they had a search warrant. At that moment, I was glad that Margaux Brennon was here.

I had a feeling that she was about to earn her keep.

THIRTY-FIVE

The bees left the flowers alongside Gideon's porch. Although the weather was good, I felt something bad was around the corner. It was like a sandstorm that can change directions, as if it had an intent to come for you with a heavy cloud of confusion. Through the low-hanging branches of the oaks, I could see the reflection of sunlight off chrome bumpers as the caravan of sheriff's cruisers arrived on Gideon's property.

We kept sitting, Margaux, Gideon, and me, waiting for the vehicles to stop. I spotted two K9 units, the back windows partially down, with two bloodhounds in one cruiser and a black Lab in the other. The driver of the lead car came up and parked behind Gideon's Land Rover, and the second vehicle parked behind my Jeep. All the men got out. The K9 units, dogs, and their handlers, stayed about a hundred feet away from us, closer to the spring than the cabin.

A tall deputy with graying hair at the temples and two other funeral-faced deputies approached the porch. The tallest man nodded. "Hello, folks. Who here is Gideon Wright?"

"That would be me?" Gideon braced both hands on the armrest of the rocker.

Margaux stood.

"Mr. Wright, I'm Captain Morris with the Volusia County sheriff's office. Sir, we have a warrant to search your home and any outbuildings that you have."

"Why? What's this about?"

"We're looking for any evidence that can help us find the whereabouts of a missing person—Darnell Reid. I understand that you know him?"

"I met him. Don't *know* him."

Margaux cleared her throat. "Captain Morris, may I see the warrant?"

"And who are you, ma'am?"

"I'm Margaux Brennon, Mr. Wright's attorney." She moved to the first step, extending her hand. He gave her the search warrant, his eyes guarded. Margaux took time to read the warrant. After a minute, she looked straight at him. "This is a very vague and general warrant. Can you tell me why the judge would sign something that wasn't specific in terms of what you are looking for and where? With something like this, which is not standard protocol, you could go into my client's home and search through every nook and cranny, down to his underwear drawer."

He managed to fake a smile. "With all due respect, Ms. Brennon, sometimes law enforcement doesn't know what it's looking for until we see it and have reason to believe it could be linked to a crime."

"With mutual respect, Captain, based on what you told us, you have a missing person, and that's not a crime until proven so."

The breeze tinkled the windchimes as he remained silent. After a noticeable number of seconds, he retorted, "We have a warrant to search the premises. If you have a problem with that, you can take it up with the judge."

"Obviously, I can't file a motion right now, but what I can and will do is be in the home with your men. As Mr. Wight's legal counsel, I not only have that right, but I have the obligation." She turned around and opened the screened door, using her hand to motion them inside. Captain Morris and three other deputies entered, followed by Margaux. The rest of the officers stayed in the yard under the shade of the old oaks.

Gideon leaned toward me, lowering his voice. "Margaux sure knows her stuff. She's not very big or tall, maybe five-four, but she has the confidence of David taking on Goliath."

"I've been part of police units serving search warrants. Most of the time, we were concerned about the unknowns when knocking on a suspect's door. You never knew what the answer would be. Most of the time, it was routine. Sometimes, though, we were met with gunfire. I'm sure the captain has seen that kind of resistance. But I doubt he's ever encountered an attorney already on the scene of his search, someone to accompany them inside."

After about ten minutes, the men came back onto the porch, with Margaux following. Captain Morris looked at Gideon. "Sir, where is your shed?"

THIRTY-SIX

The birdsong was replaced with the clipped and hollow sound of police radios in the yard, a silent spring flowing in the background. Gideon stood up from his rocker. He glanced at Captain Morris. "I don't have a shed. I do have an old barn, built out of cypress and heart of pine by my grandfather and his brother."

"Where is it?"

"Back of the cabin. A pine straw trail leads to it. You'll pass by my family cemetery."

The captain cleared his throat. "Thanks."

"From this old home place—the cabin, to the barn, cemetery and spring—this land has been in my family since the Civil War. As you roam about, please remember that and respect this special place; it's a sacred land molded from God's hands and much the same as when we first found it."

"We understand." He signaled to his men. "Chuck, you and Harold search the barn. We'll all meet to the east of it. I have a property plat of the land. It makes a very large rectangle and goes deep within the national forest. We'll keep it between the fences." Two of the men headed toward the barn; the rest moved fifty yards to the southeast. The bloodhounds and Lab were now part of the search team as the men and dogs fanned out and started walking in a parallel line, each team member about fifty feet away from the next man.

A lone deputy stood next to one of the cruisers parked farthest away from the cabin. I watched him remove from the back of the vehicle what looked like a dull gray suitcase. He set the suitcase on the trunk, unlatching and opening it. I thought he was going to assemble a special weapon. He removed a drone and began assembling it.

Margaux turned to Gideon. "I'm going to follow those two men to the barn. Do you keep any horses or cows in there?"

"No. We had horses when I was a boy. After they passed, there were no more. I use the barn mostly for storage and to bottle honey."

"Okay." She walked down the porch steps, following the two deputies who were heading along a path toward the barn.

Gideon looked at me. "She sure wants to be there when they search it. They won't find anything but old tools. The barn has a fine hayloft under its tin roof. Those times when I couldn't sleep after Heather's death, I used to go out there. I had an old wool horse blanket up in the loft, under the straw. I would lie down and watch the world through the loft's open window. I used to love the view in the moonlight over the cypress strands. Sometimes, I'd even see a shooting star, make a wish, and drift off to sleep."

***

Margaux kept her distance as the two deputies searched through the barn. One man was tall and wide-shouldered; the other was shorter, with a fleshy face and a shiny forehead. They opened the doors to the four horse stalls, inspecting them. Then they used a rake to sweep back dried hay on the hardpacked dirt floor, looking for a trapdoor. They looked at an axe, a double-edged sickle, pruning shears, and other tools. "No visible sign of dried blood," the shorter deputy said.

"I'll check up in the loft." He climbed a ladder that looked more like a flight of wooden stairs, each step creaking under his weight. After a minute in the hayloft, the deputy came back down, shaking his head. "Nothing but a framed black and white picture of a woman. Looks old. There's hay all over the place, and a blanket that was neatly folded. I shook it out and couldn't find anything. No blood. Nothing. The window is open."

He picked a piece of straw from one of his boot laces, glancing back up toward the hayloft's open window. The sunlight was streaming inside and striking the floor of the barn. A sparrow flew in through the opening, alighting on the timber near where Margaux was standing. The little bird turned its head, eyeing her. Margaux smiled.

The men made a final cursory check, glancing at a rusted *Purina Chow* sign nailed to one beam. Above the rusted sign, a carved wooden cross hung from the timber. The taller deputy pointed to a burlap sack covering something in a darker corner. He reached out, lifting the bag. "It's a headstone. Gideon Wright's name is on it and nothing else—no date of birth is inscribed into it."

"Maybe the old fella's keeping it out here until his time comes. Speaking of time, what time is it? Feels like we've been back in here for longer than necessary."

The taller deputy checked his phone screen. "The clock on my phone's kind of weird. The time's flashing and then fading out and coming back with a different time."

The other deputy checked his phone. "Mine is doing the same thing. Maybe there's a big magnet somewhere among all these tools."

"Let's join the rest of the team. This place looks like an old stable where the four horses of the apocalypse might be boarded until they're needed." The men laughed as they walked past Margaux to join the search party.

When the staccato noise of police radios faded, Margaux could hear the soft chirp of the sparrow. It flew from the rafter to the headstone, landing on a board near it. Margaux smiled. "You're right. They should've covered it up before leaving the barn." She walked over to the headstone and picked up the burlap sack.

The sparrow flew up to a rustic beam that supported the timber holding the cross and animal feed sign. Margaux stared at the name on the headstone: *Gideon Wright*. She had an idea when he was born but didn't know for certain. She covered the headstone and walked back toward the entrance of the barn.

Margaux looked at her watch. It had stopped, the second hand not moving. The sparrow flew from the timber through the hayloft's window, the sunlight absorbing the bird in a vacuum of bright white. Margaux stared at the light. A breeze blew through the barn's open doors, stirring the hay on the floor. Her eyes followed the light from the loft to the floor. Margaux looked at the dust dancing inside the light beam, the sun warming her hand and arm. Along with the warmth, she felt a sudden sense of peace.

She hadn't been sure that seeking out Gideon would be a good thing. Now, she was convinced it was. A cloud moved over the sun, the fading light making the barn grow darker. Margaux had faced her share of dark times in the past. Those times made her better for having walked through them. It made her the woman she is today. Now that she found Gideon, the last living member of her family, she wanted to squeeze out more time from whatever was left and help him if she could.

She looked across the barn at the burlap sack on the headstone. In the dim light, she thought is resembled a winter shawl draped over stone shoulders.

Margaux turned and left the barn as the hounds howled in the woods.

THIRTY-SEVEN

I stood on Gideon's porch, listening to the dogs' baying. There is a certain cadence to a hunt. When a dog detects a scent, it will sound an alarm, and the baying will become more excited. Everyone follows that hound's lead. The dogs and men, all eager, share the anticipation of finding the prey. Whether it is hunting for bears, boars, deer, rabbits, or criminals, as the circle closes, the fervor becomes more intense.

That was what I was listening for as the search party moved deeper into the forest—the bellowing of the hounds and the shouting of men. The mutual communication between man and dog is a partnership that goes back centuries.

I heard a small motor—the noise of a drone. The deputy, who had assembled the drone on the trunk of the sheriff's cruiser, was now flying the aerial eye in the direction of the search party. He watched the drone on a monitor screen as it soared about a hundred feet above the tree line. In seconds, it was gone.

"What'd they do in the barn?" Gideon asked Margaux.

"They looked in the stalls, the hayloft, and around the tools and storage areas. They found nothing but a few spiders."

"The police shouldn't even be here. It's a waste of time and taxpayers' money. The fella they're searching for, Darnell Reid, isn't here. When he did come on my land, it was to take water samples from the spring. I can't imagine he'd have any reason to return. Sean, earlier you said that if he came back, he wasn't doing it of his own volition. Why would someone force him here? And if they did, where is he?"

"Those are two good questions. And I think they could be answered by the tire tread prints in the mud and the three sets of shoe or boot prints. Unfortunately, the shoe prints vanished in the thick grass along the road.

The people wearing those shoes could have marched Reid into the woods. Or they might have put him in the trunk of their car and driven away to who knows where. It's the question of *why* that intrigues me."

Margaux nodded. "The mysterious motive. Care to guess the reason?"

"I believe it's not connected as much to the land as it is to the spring."

"Gideon told me about the unique mineral content of the water. Unfortunately, the shelf life isn't very long. But even after that expiration, he says the water is still some of the best in the world."

Gideon nodded. "The best."

"Look at the value of spring water of that quality. In many places, even in this country, real spring water is getting harder to find and much more expensive. California is suffering such a severe drought that they're rationing water use. In that state, don't think about taking a long shower or you may see the water police at your door." She smiled and sipped the last ounce of diluted iced tea from the bottom of her tall glass.

Far in the distance, almost drowned out by the hum of bees, I could hear the barking of the tracking dogs becoming more anxious. I didn't know if Margaux or Gideon could hear what I heard—the change in the dogs' tempo or the faint barking. I could see that something had caught Gideon's attention. He closed his eyes and tilted his head in the direction of the muffled but excited barking. I was amazed that a man at his age still had an acute sense of hearing.

***

Captain Morris and two of his men stood near the clearing in the woods, with the bloodhounds to their left and right in the trees and the black Lab and his handler approaching. The Lab raised his big head, nostrils testing the wind. The dog barked, pulling at the deputy's leash. Morris lifted his radio microphone. "Ed, fly the drone southwest from where it is. Some of us are at the edge of a large clearing. Mostly barren except for high grass, weeds, and some scrub oak. See if your camera can pick up any anomalies. Anything that looks out of place."

The drone operator keyed his radio. "Ten-four. On it. Should be above the area within thirty seconds."

"We're going in. Keep me posted." Morris gestured toward the clearing, which was longer than a football field. As the men approached, the Lab sniffed the ground and grass, raised its head, and looked to the far left.

The drone was flying above the clearing, and the baying of the bloodhounds coming closer. As the rest of the searchers arrived from different points of entry, the dogs were bellowing. Two vultures circled high above the clearing, their black bodies like ink silhouettes floating against the pale blue sky.

The drone pilot saw something on his screen. He flew lower and closer. At a hundred feet above the clearing, the drone was now flying in one spot like a hummingbird. He picked up his radio. "Captain, directly below the drone is something that looks like sticks and branches sort of piled together in one spot."

Morris looked from the hovering drone toward the ground. "Ten-four. You can pull it back some, Ed. We'll let the dogs take it from here." Morris motioned to the deputy with the Lab. "Let's go."

The Lab, followed by the bloodhounds, worked the clearing in a zig-zag fashion, sniffing, stopping for a second, and continuing. In less than a minute, the Lab was approaching the area first spotted by the drone's camera. The cadaver dog barked at the site, walking around it, sniffing, and looking back as the men and other dogs approached.

Morris turned to two deputies. "Let's get these branches off that spot. We could be looking at a grave that isn't supposed to look like a grave." The men began removing the branches. All the limbs had brown, dead leaves. A long black snake slithered out from the pile, vanishing in the grass and weeds. Morris looked around at his men. "Who brought the shovels?"

"I got one, Captain." A stocky deputy motioned with a wave.

"I brought one, too," a red-faced deputy said. The men removed two small metal shovels from their backpacks and unfolded the hinged handles. "I can start in the center. Jimmy, maybe you can begin at one of the ends."

Morris nodded. The deputies used their shovels to dig, quickly uncovering the sandy dirt. The Lab and bloodhounds paced anxiously. As the stocky deputy thrust the blade into the earth, he struck something, and the odor hit him. "Whoa." He stopped digging. The sickly-sweet smell of death mixed with the pungent odor of rotten eggs rose from the ground. They used the edges of the shovel blades to carefully scrape away the sandy soil. "Got something."

"So do I," said the other deputy. He used the side portion of the shovel to remove more of the soil. "I'm seeing clothes. Pants, belt buckle, shirt."

The other deputy said, "I see a man's chest." He scraped back dirt. "Damn! I can see his face. At least what's left of it. The smell is coming right up. Captain, this may be our missing person, Darnell Reid."

Morris motioned to another deputy, who put on latex gloves and used a small hand brush to sweep dirt from the opaque face of the dead man. The deputy held his breath, blowflies circling his head. Morris turned to another deputy. "Radio back to dispatch and tell them to get homicide headed this way. Same thing for the coroner. Have them call his office. We have a murder victim."

He keyed his radio mic to speak with the drone operator. "Ed, is Gideon Wright still at his house?"

"Ten-four."

"If he starts to leave, tell him not to go anywhere. Homicide detectives will want to speak with him real soon. Watch the gate. I'm sending two more deputies to help you."

THIRTY-EIGHT

Within the next hour, Gideon Wight's life would dramatically change. From the porch of his cabin, when I saw the dark blue Ford van arrive, I knew what the searchers and dogs had found. A body had been discovered in the woods. The coroner's van was followed by two more sheriff's cruisers, and two unmarked cars driven by detectives.

As the drone operator was packing his machine back in the case, a TV news truck arrived. Two additional deputies were near the drone operator, watching the cabin and driveway. They flagged down the driver of the news truck, motioning for the man to stop and go no further onto the property. The driver and a woman dressed in a business suit—a reporter—got out and spoke with a deputy.

Gideon and Margaux watched the parade of emergency vehicles and the arrival of the news media. Margaux touched her hand to one of the cypress posts that supported the roof gable over the porch. She smiled at Gideon. "We'll get through this."

Gideon took a deep breath. "I hope so." He looked from the scene back to me, his face troubled. At that moment, I didn't believe he was concerned for his future. Gideon knew that he didn't commit a crime, but I could tell that he was uneasy about what this might mean for his cherished spring. "Sean, I wish you knew who left those tire and shoe tracks on my land. Because, right now, seeing what I'm seeing, it looks like those tracks are leading to me."

"I have no doubt that they found a body back there in the forest. It's probably Darnell Reid. When I worked as a homicide detective, my colleagues often talked about how murder usually was caused by one of the four Ls: love, loot, lust, or loathing. I always thought that narrowed the playing field a little too much, but those four do sum up the top

145

reasons. However, none of them lead to murder by themselves, it's the intensity of the triggers that do."

Margaux looked from the TV truck in the distance to me. "What do you mean?"

"The thread of evil weaves itself like a spider's web. In Gideon's case, I think it's about entrapment and deception, where someone is trying to remove him from this special place so the spiders can crawl in and take the land and spring. Lusting after his spring and the loot that can be derived are very powerful triggers."

Margaux folded her arms across her breasts, watching the deputies keep the arriving news media from driving through the property toward the crime scene. "Do you really believe someone would murder and blame Gideon in order to gain access to his spring? Why not just kill him?"

"That might be too convoluted and drawn out. It would take way too much time to go through probate to try to gain rights to pump water from here." I looked over at Gideon. "Please don't take what I'm about to say the wrong way."

"I won't, and I have an idea what you're going to say."

"In the ruthless world of corporate greed, white-collar crime is some of the most nefarious and often the most difficult to track. It hides behind layers of pretentious people and deceptive balance sheets. Because of your age, a perp or a group of like-minded perpetrators might agree that, if you're arrested and convicted, you wouldn't live long in prison. In the meantime, if you've signed the deed over to a third party, the property and water rights could be adjudicated quicker and with greater public relations value."

"PR value? How?" Gideon asked.

"Because you'd be labeled as a convicted killer, and the transfer of property rights would be easier to justify in court."

Gideon rubbed his temples. His eyes showed no indication of fear, only a quiet insight into what was happening around him. The more I was around Gideon, the greater admiration I had for him. His land, no doubt, was a crime scene—capital murder. And out of the blue, he now has a great-granddaughter he never knew existed. If she wasn't who she appeared to be, my heart would hurt for the old man. I knew that most people have a breaking point. It usually happens as layers of bad events and distress fall around them like acrid ash. Their circumstances become suffocating, and they become helpless, forgetting how to fight for survival.

***

It didn't take long for the detectives to emerge from the woods and make their way to Gideon's cabin. They parked their unmarked car behind one of the sheriff's cruisers near the cabin, got out, and walked toward us. They both wore sunglasses. One detective was a woman, olive skin, dark brown hair to her shoulders, and an impassive face. I recognized the man. He was Detective Richard Lofton. They came near the bottom step. Lofton removed his dark glasses and looked up at me. "Mr. O'Brien, why am I not surprised to see you here?"

"Probably because you know Gideon Wright is my client."

He shifted his eyes to Gideon, nodding. "I'm Detective Richard Lofton. This is my partner, Detective Sylvia Ortega. Are you Mr. Wright?"

"Yes."

Lofton studied Gideon's face for a few seconds. "Margaux didn't wait for him to ask her something. "I'm Margaux Brennon, Gideon's attorney."

THIRTY-NINE

They were beginning to look like a posse from the Old West. Members of the news media were being corralled behind yellow police tape at a bend in Gideon's driveway, held at bay by anxious deputies. Sheriff's cruisers drove around the trees and tape as they went back and forth, heading back into the woods.

The TV van driver parked and began unloading his camera and gear as a reporter, a woman with golden hair reflecting in the sunlight, approached two of the deputies. She smiled a model's runway smile. "We've been following the calls on the police radio. It looks like you guys found a body back in the forest. Is the deceased a man, woman, or a child?"

"You'll have to speak with the detectives or Captain Morris. He's leading the recovery efforts. The detectives will take it from here."

She gestured toward the cabin, which was about eighty yards away. "Are those detectives talking to people in that house?"

"That's a good bet."

"Can we drive up there and wait for them to finish?"

"No. This is private property."

"Is someone in that cabin considered a suspect?"

"Ma'am, why don't you stand over there with the rest of the news folks. If the detectives or the sheriff decide to have a news conference, y'all will be the first to know."

***

Detective Lofton feigned a surprised reaction. "Well, Ms. Brennon, your presence seems timely because our search team recovered a man's body on your client's property." Lofton and Detective Ortega watched Gideon for a reaction.

Gideon looked from the growing band of news media in the distance to the detectives. "I'm very sorry to hear that. I had nothing to do with the man's death."

Detective Ortega said, "Good to hear. In that case, I'm sure you will have no problem speaking with us."

Gideon lifted his hands, palms out. "Of course not. I'm happy to help if I can."

"From the description, we believe the body is that of Darnell Reid. An autopsy will confirm that. The victim's body was found in a shallow grave. It is my understanding that you and Reid met."

Gideon glanced at Margaux. She nodded. He turned to Lofton. "The only reason we met is because Darnell Reid was trespassing on my property. Not once, but three times, maybe more. I'd asked him to stay away and respect private property and the posted no-trespassing signs, but he kept coming back."

Detective Ortega took notes. "Why is that, Mr. Wright?"

"Reid said he was conducting water tests on the spring. I told him that he didn't have the authority to do that and to leave. He returned."

"What'd you do then?" asked Lofton.

"Told him again to take his equipment and leave the property."

"Did he refuse?"

"He was reluctant. But he and his colleague eventually left."

"Do you know the name of his colleague?" Ortega asked.

"He was introduced as Lamar Dunn."

As the detectives jotted notes, I said, "You had two deputies here the day Darnell Reid's car was discovered near the road on Gideon's property. They were Sergeant Garcia and Deputy Potter. Gideon told them everything he's telling you. I assume you've seen that report since you knew that Gideon met Darnell Reid."

Detective Lofton stared up at me as if I spoke Chinese. "We appreciate your input, Mr. O'Brien. We can do our own investigation."

"I mentioned the previous police report to you when I delivered the photos of the tire and shoe prints left in the mud near the entrance to Gideon's driveway." Lofton exchanged a quick glance with Detective Ortega. She seemed slightly confused by the information.

Lofton eyed Gideon. "After you ran those guys off the last time, did you ever see Darnell Reid on your property again?"

"No."

"If you had, how would you have handled that encounter?"

"Hold on," Margaux said, stepping forward. "My client is more than willing to tell you the facts as he knows them. He will not answer any hypothetical questions."

Lofton nodded. "All right. I'll rephrase the question. Mr. Wright, obviously Reid didn't dig his own grave on your land. Did you see or hear anything or anyone last Tuesday night, the evening after Darnell Reid was seen leaving a bar called The Pocket in DeLand? Any movement, or maybe even flashlights in the night here on your land?"

"No, I didn't see or hear anything."

"Having walked around the crime scene on your property—"

"With all due respect," interjected Margaux, "what if the victim was killed elsewhere and taken back in the woods for a burial? The location is certainly part of the crime, but not necessarily where he was killed."

"Forensics will help us determine that."

I said, "Something else that might help you determine that are the photos of the shoe or boot tracks. Maybe the shoes on the body will match one pair. The other two shoe prints are most likely that of those perps."

The detectives didn't react to what I said. Lofton looked over at Gideon. "Mr. Wright, last Tuesday night, was the gate at your driveway entrance locked?"

"Yes. It's always locked at night. Often during the day as well."

"Did Reid or his partner, Lamar Dunn, tell you who they worked for … who was asking them to take water samples?" Detective Ortega inquired.

"Reid was hesitant. He said they were consultants. Dunn said they were hired by a company called Enviro Resources out of Tallahassee."

Ortega glanced at Lofton, and he said, "Thank you for your time, Mr. Wright. We may have additional questions. If so, would you come to the sheriff's department to be interviewed?"

"I have no problem with that."

They put their notepads away, walked to their unmarked car, and left, stopping near the yellow tape down the driveway. Deputies allowed another car, this one a black Cadillac, to drive around the tape and head toward the cabin.

The driver parked near my Jeep, got out, and walked up to the porch. His belly hung over his belt buckle, blue sports coat, open shirt, and khaki pants, the breeze blowing strands of oily hair from his bald spot. His round face was shiny, which looked as if he had been rubbing baby oil on his fleshy pink cheeks. He flashed the mock grin of a used car salesman. He took us all in with the sweep of his deep-set eyes. "Hi, Gideon. It looks like you've got a lot goin' on here today."

Gideon nodded. "It happened very fast. It's still happening."

"I don't think the deputies were gonna let me through to come see you. When I told them I was your lawyer, they yielded."

The man looked at me and then at Margaux. "I'm Percy King at y'all's service. Looks like my client, Gideon, is gonna need a big dose of legal help."

Just above the tree line, the sound of a news helicopter was coming closer.

FORTY

I looked from Percy King's expectant face to the sky and watched a TV news helicopter fly over the property. The pilot made a circle above the clearing deep in the forest. I could see a news cameraman strapped in the open door of the helicopter, videotaping the police proceedings on the ground. King made an awkward grin and said, "Looks like this is a big story. It might wind up on cable news and become a nationwide story by tonight."

He came up the steps to the porch. I stood to the left of Gideon, who was seated in his rocking chair. Margaux sat back in her chair. King cleared his throat. He stuck out his hand to me. "Hello, sir. What's your name?"

"Sean O'Brien." I wanted to let Margaux introduce herself to see whether she'd tell him that she was Gideon's attorney, his great-granddaughter, or both. And, more importantly, I wanted to gauge Percy King's reaction, especially after Margaux had given us her assessment of the proposed legal contract.

King turned to Margaux. "And who is this lovely lady? I doubt that you're with law enforcement, sitting up here on the porch sippin' iced tea."

She smiled. "You'd be right, Mr. King—"

"Please, Percy will do just fine, ma'am. I'm a simple country lawyer. I never use that mister stuff when I engage in adult conversation." He cut his impassive eyes over to Gideon. "That iced tea sure looks delicious. Did you sweeten it with your own honey, Gideon?"

"Yes. Would you like a glass?"

"That would be nice on a day with humidity, like an Army blanket."

Gideon got up and walked into his cabin. King looked around the property, his eyes taking in the spring and the presence of police and

152

news media activity. "The last time this land saw so much commotion was during the Civil War."

Gideon returned, handing King a tall glass of iced tea. "Thank you, sir." He set his phone down on the oak table in front of the chairs, sipping the tea. His phone buzzed. Although the caller's number appeared upside down from where I stood, I could see the area code. I memorized the number. He set his glass down, picking up his phone and slipping it into his pocket. He fixed his cat eyes on Margaux. "Ma'am, are you a friend of Mr. O'Brien's?"

"I just met Sean. I'm Margaux Brennon. Gideon Wright's attorney. As I understand it, he never officially hired you."

King's face melted. The grin turned into an upside-down frown. "With all due respect, ma'am, Gideon and I have a legal agreement in the works. Just dotting the i's and crossing the t's. I'm here today to pick up his signed copy." He looked over at Gideon.

"I haven't signed it."

"Well, let's hash it out and make it amenable to your wishes."

Gideon released a deep breath. "I appreciate your offer to help me, Percy. However, since Margaux arrived, I see the need for a new legal strategy. Also, I like to keep this kind of business in the family whenever possible."

Percy's deep-set eyes went dark. Something was smoldering down in the twin pits that looked as hard as lasers through green marbles. "Gideon, you have no living family. I'm the closest thing to that because I'm local, and I share many of your values, including the same environmental and ethical principles. Although we might not have the same bloodline, we both have those southern-bred, old Florida-style character traits, and we sure as certain share an ideology when it comes to protecting this land and spring."

Gideon stood. "All things considered, I think it's in the best interest of the land and spring to be handled by my great-granddaughter. I'm sorry it didn't work out for you, Percy. But there's plenty of other business in the county. Gideon glanced at Margaux, then back at King. "I won't sign the agreement, Percy. Just send me a bill for your time."

The sound of the TV news helicopter continued in the distance, over the forest. King fought to keep his anger in check. I had an idea that he would take a parting shot. He looked at Gideon and made an impish, insincere grin and said, "This woman may turn out to be an imposter. She might have been sent here to con you. Be very careful what you agree to do with her. You never know the kind of ulterior motives some people carry."

Margaux smiled. "Mr. King, that so called agreement you gave Gideon to sign carried the ultimate ulterior motive. In the event of his death, you would have received the key to the city, so to speak. All of this—the home, land, and spring—would have fallen into your hands through something disguised as an estate trust. It's an egregious and deceitful contract because you would have assumed the property deed and complete control and been free to do with it what you will."

He shook his head, holding both hands up, palms out. "Ms. Brennon, you have no idea what you're talking about. You are slanderous in your negative assertions as to my impeccable integrity as a lawyer. I take exception to that. You assert that my honesty and legal skills would not be in the best interest of Gideon's wishes. Should, for any reason, the land and home ever need to be sold, Gideon's favorite charities, the Salvation Army and the Nature Conservancy, would have stood to gain substantial contributions."

Margaux's smile was disarming, cutting through the façade like a legal razor. "If what you're attempting to do in this so-called estate planning and disbursement agreement were taught in law school, either the school would be shut down as fraudulent or the course would be taught as an example of how to recognize probate estate fraud. Have a good day, Mr. King."

He started to rebut her but looked over at Gideon. "Mark my word, Sweet Water Spring will turn sour faster than you'll realize." He walked down the steps, marching back to his car with a fast waddle, his thighs thick in his pants like fire plugs. The helicopter flew so close over the cabin, the prop blast caused the Spanish moss to flap from the tree branches, like a storm blowing across the hand.

Before I left Gideon's home and property, there was a question I had to ask. And it was one that I wanted to gauge Margaux's response to as well. I stood in front of them, my back to the deputies and news media in the distance. "Gideon, you hired me to find the identity of the guy stalking you with the camera at the farmers market."

He sat in his chair, looking up at me through clear, thoughtful eyes. "Yes, I did. And you did that."

"I gave you his name and what I believe is his home address. My question now is, do you want me to continue? Do you want me to walk through this web and see who hired Floyd Shaw and the person Shaw works for? I can try to see how far up the corporate ladder this might go."

Gideon didn't hesitate. "Yes. Please stay on the case until it's resolved."

I said nothing.

Margaux nodded. "I agree with Gideon. Please remain on the case, Sean. My lawyer's intuitive sense is that you are a man who delivers results. The results in this case could have repercussions for many years to come."

***

As King pulled out onto the highway from Gideon's driveway, he drove less than a mile before making a call. When the call was answered, he said, "There's a new problem with Gideon Wright."

"We pay you to fix problems."

"Most of them, I can. But this one is a little out of my control."

"Spit it out."

"We did our due diligence. There was no indication whatsoever that Wright had any living family. His great-granddaughter is here, sitting on Gideon's front porch with him and a PI named Sean O'Brien, sippin' sweet tea like one cozy family."

"Solve the problem, or we'll find someone else to do it. We will have those water rights, with or without you."

FORTY-ONE

Later that night, I looked up at the white board in my home office and added a new photo, one of Margaux Brennon. Not that I was distrusting her, but rather the fact that she now was a shard in a jigsaw puzzle with a growing number of pieces. Regardless of the diary or the family history connections to Gideon, I knew that the DNA testing was the right move to prove the bloodline. As I started to go to the internet to continue my research, Wynona stood at the open door. "It looks like the playing field on your board is expanding." She smiled.

"I've told you as much about Margaux Brennon as I know. I'm not adding her up here in terms of being suspect or dubious, but rather as one of the puzzle pieces."

"You said that you have no reason to doubt that she isn't who she says she is … it's just that her timing is questionable, right?"

"Yes, the timing is, at best, coincidental. But she appears credible. Apparently, she left a bad, childless marriage back in Seattle and moved across the country to start a new chapter in her life. Margaux thought she has no other blood relatives left on earth. Gideon Wright thought the same thing—that was until Margaux read that old diary a few months ago and decided to do some genetic and historical family research."

"You said that Margaux had no hesitations about doing the DNA swabs. If she'd had reservations, it would speak volumes."

"Dave Collins can push the results through quickly for me. I believe he only pretends to be retired from the CIA."

"You're lucky to have Dave as a friend and as a backup."

"I agree."

"Maybe I can meet Margaux Brennon at some point."

"That'd be good. I'd like your assessment. Those years as an FBI agent have given you a different perspective than most people."

Wynona smiled. "But that can be a double-edged sword. I find myself looking for motive if the fish market is selling fresh fish and doesn't mention that it was previously frozen." She laughed.

"That's why we try to get our fish from Nick Cronus as often as we can. Speaking of Nick, I'm heading to the marina tomorrow to meet with Dave. If Nick's boat is in, I'll buy some of whatever he has caught."

"Let's have a glass of wine on the back porch. I'd like to hear more about all the activity on the property of a genteel old man who restored life to my most challenged orchid. The benevolent rescue is coming from the water he gave us. Angela's about ready for bed if you'd like to read her a story."

"I would."

***

An hour later, I was uncorking a bottle of cabernet in the kitchen when the local news came on the TV tucked in a corner of the kitchen counter. Wynona motioned toward the screen. "It looks like the murder in the national forest is their lead story."

I turned up the sound as a square-jawed anchorman said, "Off the top tonight on Channel Seven Eyewitness News is the story of a body found in a remote section of the Ocala National Forest. And it was found on land owned by one family for many years. Anna Hart has more on the story."

The video opened with dozens of emergency lights flashing as police cruisers streamed in and out of the national forest. The reporter's narration began. "Sheriff's deputies were using canine tracking dogs and a cadaver dog to search parts of the Ocala National Forest before finding a man's body in a shallow grave. They'd been searching for a missing man, Darnell Reid, who vanished from the parking lot of The Pocket bar in DeLand. Authorities aren't saying whether the body is that of Reid, nor are they sure of the cause of death."

The video cut to an interview with detective Richard Lofton. "Until we get the results from the autopsy, we don't know exactly how this man died. We do know it is a homicide, and due to the condition of the body, we believe it could be that of the missing man, Darnell Reid. If so, the family will be the first to know."

"Do you have any suspects?"

"Not at this time."

The video cut to a shot of Gideon's cabin in the distance. The reporter continued. "The land where the body was found, which abuts the national forest, is owned by Gideon Wright, an elderly man whose family was said to have settled here before it was designated as a national forest. Investigators say that Wright told them he didn't see or hear anything on his property the night Reid disappeared. Why was the body buried in a remote part of his land? Currently, detectives don't know."

The image cut to a live shot of the reporter standing just off the shoulder of the road. "They do know that Reid's car, a Dodge Challenger, was found here, not too far from the entrance to Wright's driveway. Detective Lofton told us that he has reason to believe there was a second car here that night, too. They managed to take photos of a second set of tire tread prints as well as shoe prints in the mud. They're hoping to match the tire prints to a car and the shoe prints to suspects. Reporting live from the scene, Anna Hart. Now back to you in the studio."

I muted the sound, and we walked from the kitchen to the back porch, Max trotting behind us. We took seats in our wicker chairs, watching a crescent moon rise over the bald cypress trees along the riverbank. Wynona sipped her wine, her eyes thoughtful. She looked over at me, with Max curled on my lap. "Not that you wanted credit for those photos, but the investigators would not have them had you not used your phone's camera, printed the photos, and given them to detectives along with the digital versions and the video."

"Makes no difference to me as long as they can find the perps. Remaining anonymous allows me to stay in the background."

"Unless it's a fluke, the number one reason to bury that man in the back of Gideon's property is to frame him for murder. Get the stubborn old man out of the way, lock him up in prison, quicken his death, and buy the property or water rights from whomever assumes them. Do you think that lawyer, Percy King, is compromised and playing both sides of the fence, trying to act like he's representing Gideon while working for someone who wants access to his spring?"

"I do. Is that someone with Enviro Resources, the company attached to Reid, or someone with Glacier Artesian Springs who made the offer to Gideon, or someone else?"

"Those are excellent questions."

"I think some of the answers will come from this guy, Floyd Shaw, if I can find him." I sipped my wine and rubbed Max's head, her eyes closing, and heard the shriek of an owl coming across the river.

"If these people are so desperate for this special water, ready to market some imaginary form of the Fountain of Youth to the world, just how far are they willing to go to secure water pumping rights? What would they do to his only relative, who now may inherit the cabin, land, and spring, if they were willing to kill someone remotely linked to her great-grandfather to frame him? Is Margaux's life in danger?"

I didn't know the answer to her question. I looked over at Wynona, beads of yellow moonlight catching in her brown eyes. "Maybe. I do know this. Based on what I've seen thus far, I believe Margaux Brennon has moved from a bad place in her life, traveling across the country, only to get herself into a worse position. She could be stepping into the crosshairs of ruthless people who see the spring not only as a source of perhaps the world's best natural water, but as the source of hundreds of millions of dollars in profits."

"The price of youth. It may be as illusory as the water, but it's an eternal quest."

Wynona reached for my hand. "Your visit with Gideon offers a great perspective that too few people take the time to see. The old tree he sits under and talks to, the critters he befriends, the bees he keeps—what a unique man. I'd love to take Angela there the next time you go."

"Gideon invited us to the spring. But I want to get to the bottom of this case for him first."

"What you shared with me about him reminds me of time I spent with Seminole elders on the res, especially our shaman or medicine man, Josie Tiger. He was never a beekeeper like Gideon, but he knew more about plants, animals, and the interconnection of nature than anyone I've ever known. I miss his wisdom, and I often think of him. He used to travel all over Florida, searching for various plants he'd bring back to the res and use for medicines. He may have picked a few plants from the forest around Gideon's place, and he might have sipped water from that spring. When Josie died, he was 106 years old. Age, though, wasn't important to him." She smiled. "Today, our culture is obsessed with looking younger."

"More than five hundred years ago, that attraction drew Ponce de Leon across the ocean to the Caribbean islands and up to Florida, where the Indians talked about a fabled spring with the magic to maintain or restore youth. Today is no different. The pirates from then and now are only five centuries apart. Tomorrow I'll see if I can bridge the gap in time."

FORTY-TWO

Gideon and Margaux moved from the cabin's front porch to the kitchen. As they cooked together—chicken sautéed in olive oil, green beans, and rice—they talked at length, mostly about family. Gideon answered as many questions as possible about his side of the family. They sat at a round, wooden table and ate, the conversation continuing.

She looked across the table at him. "Having read Tiffany's diary, I think that I have a good insight into her personality, who she was as a person. But, as the woman you fell in love with, what was it about her that attracted you."

"It's hard to put my finger on one specific thing. However, looking back, I believe it was her heart that first mesmerized me. Yes, she was beautiful, smart, and filled with a zest for life, but it was her heart—her compassion for others and her desire to do right by them—that I found so compelling. I was smitten by it. She was like loving fresh air—you take it all in."

"How so? And I ask this from the position of her great-granddaughter, someone who hasn't succeeded thus far in the love department. My ex blames the demise of our marriage on me. He said I was too focused on my career and not on him, not on building a family life together."

"What do you think?"

"In retrospect, I believe some of what he said was true, but he was wrong about me not wanting a family. I would love to be in love. Just the idea seems so damn lovely. But before our marriage, I had a spattering of boyfriends and, for various reasons, none ever seemed to be what I was looking for in a man. They all fizzled. Or maybe I fizzled. And now here I am, alone, in a new state, trying to start the next chapter in my life. No,

I'm done with new chapters. I want to start a new book. I just don't know if that's possible anymore."

He looked at her, the soft light from a lamp in his eyes. "First, you're not alone. I'm here. Secondly, you simply haven't met the right man, someone who appreciates you for who you are, not who they want you to become. You asked me how Tiffany was like loving fresh air. Well, she was comfortable with who she was, which allowed her to give life real meaning and a sense of purpose. She touched my soul with her love and asked for nothing more than for me to do the same. When you can find a man who offers that, gives unconditional love, and touches your soul, you will know what to do. Tiffany did that for me. And later, after she was long gone from my life, and after the pain faded, I met Heather. I was blessed with real love twice."

"You're making me cry." Margaux reached for a napkin, dabbing her eyes.

"Margaux, to find a healthy kind of love, though, you must be healthy yourself, meaning comfortable in your own skin. When you are, it's easier to recognize the positive qualities in others and identify the flaws that are deal breakers."

"Thank you for sharing some of your wisdom."

"You're welcome."

After dinner, Margaux cleared the table. "Let me wash the dishes. You did most of the cooking. And it was delicious."

"I usually eat alone. It's nice to have you here."

"I'm loving every minute of it. But when I'm done with the dishes, I need to get on the road and head back to my condo."

"Why don't you stay the night? It's getting late, and I saw fog drifting outside. There are mostly two-lane county roads from here to New Smyrna Beach. I don't want any drunk drivers crossing the centerline and crashing into your car. Now that I've found you, or since you've found me, I don't want to lose you."

She smiled. "That's mutual. My little dog, Lily, named after Grandma, is home alone. I called earlier and asked my neighbor, Kim, to walk and feed her. I can call again and see if Kim will walk Lily in the morning."

"Good. Please call your friend Kim. You can give her some of my honey tomorrow. We have a lot of catching up to do. In your case, at least thirty-five years' worth."

She smiled. "I don't want to intrude at all."

"No intrusion. This old place has three bedrooms and two bathrooms. You can stay in the bedroom on the left side. My room is on the opposite side of the cabin. We can have coffee and breakfast in the morning. Then, if it's not storming, you can safely travel, and I won't worry about you."

"Thank you." Margaux stood at the kitchen sink, washing and drying the dishes. She looked through the window above the sink, fog like smoke on the ground, the yard, and trees illuminated by moonlight. Something caught her eye. She stared into the night, stopping the running water. There was movement. "Grandpa!"

"Yes, what is it?" Gideon rose from his chair at the kitchen table.

"Outside! I saw something."

"What?"

"A man. At least I think it was a man. The window is a little steamy from the hot water. And there is some fog out there. But through the window, I believe I saw someone standing near the big oak tree. It looked like he was starting to walk toward the barn or the back of the cabin.

Gideon stood from the table, stepping to a window, and parting the drapes to peer outside. "Are you sure what you saw wasn't a deer? We have a lot of deer on the land, some black bears as well."

"Unless the bear was standing on its hind legs, it was a man."

"Was he carrying a gun?"

"I couldn't tell."

She dried her hands with a towel and walked from behind the sink to Gideon. "What can we do? Maybe we should call the sheriff's department."

Gideon walked into another room and returned with a long flashlight. He headed toward the front door. "I'll be right back."

"Wait! Where are you going?"

"Outside to have a look around. I'm turning on the floodlights. That ought to scare him away."

"Not if he has a gun. Please stay inside. We'll call the sheriff's office."

"It'll take them forever to get way out here. Don't worry. I'm just going to stay on the porch."

As he left, Margaux opened a kitchen drawer, found a butcher knife, and headed out the door.

FORTY-THREE

It was Max's final walk of the night when I saw something that made me think of Gideon. Max and I were walking down the backyard toward our dock when I looked at the night sky, spotting a fiery meteor streaking across the heavens. I remembered what Gideon said about meteors. *We're all just passing through, like the brevity of a comet in the night sky, not even a grain of sand in the hourglass of time. But never think you don't matter, because you do.*

I thought about our conversations during the period that I was alone with him, and I remembered the conversations when Margaux was with us. For the good of both, I hoped they were family, had a similar ideological makeup, and could find a sense of harmony. Was she still there, continuing to spend time with Gideon, or had she returned to her condo?

I had a sudden urge to call Gideon, and I didn't know why. It was just an impulse and not a reaction to something known. It was the unknown that occasionally touched my tripwire and moved some internal needles. I had a gut feeling that something wasn't as it should be. But that was an understatement, considering what was happening to Gideon. I didn't want to check up on him, but as my client and friend, I wanted to check in with him.

Max and I walked onto the dock, watching the mist floating up from the river and swaying in the glow of the moonlight. Frogs were bellowing on both sides of the river. There was a splash near a cypress tree in the shallows. I glanced at my watch. It was getting late—maybe too late to call him. I didn't know whether he read or sent text messages, so I copied Margaux.

I reached for my phone and sent a quick text. *Hi, Gideon and Margaux, it's Sean. I hope you two are having some quality time together, regardless of recent events. Gideon, if you're awake, give me a call. If not, we'll talk tomorrow.* I picked up Max, and we watched the moon come out from behind a cloud.

***

Gideon turned on the floodlights that he had attached to every outside corner of the cabin. He stepped out into the night on his front porch. Beyond the reach of the lights, he used the moonlight to survey his property from the porch. He listened to the sounds of the night, holding a flashlight. Margaux, knife in her hand, came up behind him. A plank on the porch groaned. He turned toward her, whispering. "You're supposed to stay inside."

"Have you seen anything?" Her voice was low, anxious.

"No. I've been using the moonlight to see, listening to the night sounds. The owls and nighthawks are silent."

Margaux nodded, took a deep breath, and held up the knife, its blade shiny under the moonlight. "I brought this for our protection."

Gideon looked at the knife. "Let's hope we don't need it. Come on."

"Where are you going?"

"Toward Seth."

"Who's Seth?"

"The big oak. That's where you first saw the trespasser." Gideon turned on his flashlight; the beam was as intense as a train light. Fog floated like clouds over the damp ground, making it look as if the land was tucked into a dreamy blanket of white. It was quiet, like walking through deep snow in the woods. He pointed the flashlight toward the spring, where a mist was rising from the water. Margaux followed him, gripping the knife handle. The only sound they could hear was their own breathing.

Gideon aimed the light toward the trees and the area around them. He came closer, searching for signs of shoe prints. "Can't see any indication that a man was standing or walking around here. But it's harder to tell in the fog."

"I saw someone. It wasn't a bear or a deer."

"Let's walk around the back of the cabin."

"Maybe that's not such a good idea."

165

"With all the floodlights, it's like a rocket launch out here tonight. Plus, this flashlight is one of the brightest on the market. It'll almost blind anyone who looks toward it in the night. Maybe our presence will scare the intruder away."

"And maybe he's standing on the back side of the cabin with a gun in his hands." Margaux felt her phone vibrate. She pulled it from her back pocket, looking at the screen. "It's Sean O'Brien. He just sent us a text. He wants to call you if you haven't gone to bed yet. I think we should call him while we're standing out here."

"Okay."

***

I was walking back to our cabin when my phone buzzed. Margaux calling. "Sean, I'm with Gideon. We made dinner and had a long talk. He invited me to stay the night. There is a lot of fog around here. I was doing the dishes when I saw a man walking in the yard through the kitchen window."

"Where are you two right now?"

"In the yard, near the big oak tree. That's where I first saw the person."

"Could you tell if he was carrying a gun?"

"No, not from where I stood in the kitchen. And the fog was swirling around him."

"Are you or Gideon armed with a gun?"

"No, he doesn't own one. But I'm carrying a large knife. Gideon turned on the floodlights, and the place is well lit up. He wants to walk toward the back of the cabin. He's carrying a flashlight with a very bright beam."

"I wouldn't advise going too far on the property. Don't go into the woods. If you do go toward the back, keep me on the phone. Put the speaker on so the person can hear that you are in immediate touch with me. Did you or Gideon call the sheriff's office?"

"No. Not yet. I advised him to call them. I'd like it on a police record that there was a trespasser on the property. And I hope the word *was* now is the accurate term. Hold on a second, Sean. I'm putting you on speakerphone. Okay, we're here."

"Gideon, my advice is to just go back inside the cabin and call the sheriff's office."

"How far away do you live, Sean?"

"About fifteen minutes if I hurry."

"You'd probably get here before the deputies. Trust me on that. We are walking to the left of the cabin. My floodlights have the grounds lit up like an airport."

"I'm heading your way. In the meantime, I'll stay on the phone with you."

"All right. Everything looks fine in the backyard. The beehives are like you saw them. The graveyard is misty, but there is no sign of anyone."

"How about your barn? Will your flashlight beam go that far?"

"Absolutely."

There was a twenty second pause. I could hear them walking. They stopped. Only the sound of screeching cicadas came through the phone. I heard them mumble something before I asked, "Are you okay?"

Margaux responded. "Yes. Let's stay away from the barn."

Gideon's voice sounded anxious. "I don't remember leaving the barn door open. When I had livestock, I always closed it. And I continued that practice today. Sean, the main door to the barn is open."

"Don't go any farther. I'm on my way. Go back inside the cabin. Make sure the deputies are on their way, too."

FORTY-FOUR

I swapped Max for my Glock and put the gun under my belt and the Beretta in my ankle holster. Standing in our kitchen, I told Wynona what happened and added, "Maybe the sheriff's deputies have a cruiser somewhere in the vicinity and will be there before I arrive."

"Why didn't Gideon and Margaux call them first?"

"It could be because of all the upheaval that Gideon has been experiencing lately. He's a solitary man, someone who's a problem solver. But, under these circumstances, the more he goes the do-it-yourself route, the greater the odds are for something bad to happen."

Wynona held Max in her arms. "Maybe they frightened off the man that Margaux saw."

"That's a possibility, or he might be hiding out in the barn. Margaux said she'd call the sheriff's office. If the police are responding from DeLand, I'll get there faster."

"But should you be the first responder? And I ask that only because of the ongoing investigation that the sheriff's detectives are conducting. Perhaps they should arrive first, and you come later?"

"I need to make sure that Gideon and Margaux are safe. I don't care who gets there first."

"I understand. You said they went back inside the cabin and locked the doors. Unless there is some homicidal psychopath hiding on Gideon's property, they should be safe until deputies arrive."

"I won't be gone long. Too bad this is happening when Gideon and Margaux are getting to know each other." I leaned in and kissed Wynona. "I'll call when I'm heading back home." I patted Max on her head, turned, and left. Seconds later, I was driving north toward Gideon's cabin.

***

The fog on the road slowed down my approach to Gideon's house. At his gate, I assumed I'd arrived there before the sheriff's deputies. The new chain was locked, and there was no sign of any vehicles parked off the road. I got out, using my tactical flashlight to search the immediate area for tracks. I couldn't find any in the foggy night.

I opened the gate, left it unlocked for arriving officers, and drove down the gravel driveway to Gideon's cabin. I shut off the Jeep's headlights. I knew the way well enough to drive by the light of the moon. I called Gideon and said, "I'm here, and I'm parking near Margaux's car. From there, I'm walking down to your barn."

"Sheriff's deputies are on their way. Do you think you ought to wait for them?"

"No. They'll use flashlights and check around your place. I'm doing the same thing, but I'll look for a *reason* the perp may have been on your property."

"What reason?"

"If he didn't come here to hurt you, then why be outside your home? It might be because he wanted to leave something."

"What?"

"I don't know. It could be something that might be used against you. In other words, when they killed Darnell Reid and dug his grave on the back of your property, they didn't end it there. Maybe one or more returned to leave bogus evidence that will put you in more jeopardy."

"I hope that you're wrong. Perhaps the trespasser was like some folks I get, people sneaking onto the property to swim in the spring."

"I doubt they'd do that at night in Florida. I'm heading back toward your barn."

"Hold up a quick second. Margaux is standing next to a window, peeking through a crack in the shades. Margaux, can you see Sean?"

I heard her say, "No. Only dark and fog."

Gideon said, "She can't see you or your flashlight."

"That's good. It means the perp or perps might not see me either. I'll be knocking on your front door soon." I clicked off, holding my Glock in one hand, the dark flashlight in the other, walking beyond the floodlights toward the barn. I could see bats flying in and out of the perimeter lights.

I approached from the rear of the barn, the air moist and the fog crawling up the bottom of the weathered boards like smoke from a ground fire. I stood still at the back of the barn, listening. I placed my right ear against the outside wall. There were no sounds coming from inside.

I kept my flashlight off, walking around the entire perimeter until I came to the front side of the barn. The large entrance door was open. I stooped down and picked up a rock the size of a walnut. I put the rock in my jeans pocket.

I knew there was only one way out. If the perp was in there, he'd have to run right by me to exit. I lifted my flashlight, stepping into the darkness of the barn, and turned on the light. I held my Glock with my arm extended, the muzzle following the sweeping beam of the flashlight. I spotted a mouse scurrying toward the rear of the barn. The dank air smelled of hay, leather, and a trace of horse manure in the stalls.

I aimed the flashlight up toward the second story, the hayloft. A block-and-tackle pulley hung from one timber. I stood behind a post, looking into the light beam for signs of dust or bits of hay falling from the cracks in the weathered boards above me.

I glanced down at the hard-packed ground strewn with straw and cypress mulch, aiming the light into the stalls, walking by each one. There was a tuff of horsehair pinched in a cracked board. A bridle, its leather splintered from age, hung from a rusted nail in a post.

Spiderwebs were in most corners. A few corn kernels were still in one of the feed troughs. I walked quietly by a wall of tools—a rusted pitchfork, pickaxes, post-hole diggers, rakes, hoes, a scythe, and a shovel. All the tools, except for one, were hanging on hooks in the wall.

The shovel blade was on the floor, the handle propped up against the wall. It was the lone outlier. Maybe it meant nothing more than the fact that the last time Gideon used the shovel, he simply set it back in a corner next to the wall of tools. I didn't pick up the shovel, but rather used the light from the flashlight to look at it.

Something moved.

I heard a noise in the hayloft. I started up the ladder rungs that led to the loft. Halfway up, one of the steps groaned under my left leg. I stopped, held my breath.

The noise returned. Something moving. The sound was coming from a far corner of the loft. I didn't know whether it was a rodent or a human. I did know that, as I got closer to the second floor, and when my head popped through the entranceway at the end of the ladder, a perp could shoot me because he'd most likely see my head before I could take in the entire loft and spot him hiding.

I reached inside my pocket, took out the rock, tossed it into the loft in the opposite area from where I heard the noise. The rock made a thud on some of the boards, rattling to a quiet stop. There was no other sound. I popped through the opening in the loft floor, aiming the flashlight toward the area where I'd heard the sound. I saw three mice in one corner, all staring back at the light. "Three blind mice," I whispered.

I came down, stood in the center of the barn, and shined the flashlight on the walls and over the tools, looking for any indication that anything other than the shovel seemed out of place or that something wasn't supposed to be in the barn. But without knowledge of the inventory of tools and assorted farm equipment, I couldn't be certain what belonged and what didn't.

I headed toward the exit, turned off the flashlight, and bolted through the open doorway. I wasn't met with a barrage of gunfire. *Who had Margaux seen standing in Gideon's yard? And where was that person at this moment?* I stayed in the dark shadows beyond the cabin's floodlights as I walked back to where Gideon and Margaux were. When I got to the front porch, I could see headlights raking along the boughs of the oaks.

Someone was coming.

FORTY-FIVE

I stood on Gideon's porch, watching a sheriff's cruiser arrive. Gideon and Margaux came out of the cabin, standing beside me as the deputies parked. "Did you see anyone back there?" Margaux asked.

"No. That doesn't mean that a perp didn't enter the barn. I just didn't see anything abnormal for a barn, such as blood spatter, fresh mud, or shoe tracks on the floor. Gideon, since you know the interior of your barn well, you might want to look around in there tomorrow to see if anything is out of place or if something new was added. Just don't touch anything if you notice something different."

"I'll do it at first light in the morning. Sunlight coming through the open doors and the hayloft will help."

"When was the last time you used your shovel?"

"A few weeks ago."

"Did you hang it on a hook on the wall?"

"Most likely, although I can't be sure."

Two male deputies got out of the crusader and approached the porch. The shorter one was in his mid-thirties, and the other was in his early twenties; both looked leery—not sure why three people stood on the porch if a prowler was stalking the house. They carried black tactical flashlights. The older deputy said, "We're responding to a call about an unknown suspect seen around your home."

Gideon nodded. "Yes, officer. This property is posted with no-trespassing signs. My granddaughter made the call because she saw a man."

"What'd you see, ma'am?"

"There was a man standing near that large oak. I was doing dishes and saw him through the kitchen window."

"Can you describe him?"

"Not very well from that distance. It was foggier than it is now. But I could see that he was wearing dark pants and a black hoodie, and that the hood wasn't covering his head. I think he walked toward the back of the cabin, in the direction of the barn."

"Where is that?" asked the younger deputy.

"About a hundred feet behind the cabin, on the other side of a small cemetery."

"Who are you, sir?"

"Sean O'Brien. I'm a friend of the family. I was on a phone call with Gideon and Margaux just after the perp was spotted in the yard. I live rather close to here, so I came over to see if I could help. I didn't get to Gideon's home long before you fellas arrived."

The deputies didn't respond. After a few seconds, the older one nodded. "We'll have a look." He paused, eyeing Gideon. "I know y'all had a body found on the back section of your land. Maybe the prowler is connected to that."

He looked up at me. I nodded. "I'd bet the farm on that."

"You folks ought to stay on the porch or in the house." They turned and left, walking down the left side of the cabin, their police radios crackling and flashlights ablaze. Because of that potential approach, I came earlier and was stealthy in my search.

Gideon cleared his throat. "Sean, thank you for having the first go to look around the place. I suspect that the prowler was gone by the time you went back there."

"There was no sign of a vehicle anywhere near your gate when I arrived."

"There is an old logging trail that runs adjacent to my land. It would take an off-road vehicle to go down it, but it can be done."

"Where is this old trail?"

"When you leave my gate, turn left. Go about fifty yards. It's very close to a utility pole, and it sort of makes an alcove at the entrance between the trees. Maybe he parked back in there."

Margaux folded her arms. "Will he come back? Why was he here?"

I said nothing, staring out into the night at the massive oak tree.

"What are you thinking, Sean?" Gideon asked.

"That your old friend, Seth, might once again have witnessed something near it. Margaux, when you spotted the perp, exactly where was he standing?"

"I'd say it was about thirty or forty feet to the right of the tree."

I stepped off the porch and went to the area she pointed toward. I used my flashlight beam to examine the wet ground, which was mostly grass and leaves. The fog swirled around my ankles. A breeze came from the west. The fog had lifted enough for me to notice a cigarette butt ground into the grass. I kneeled and looked closely at it. I used a twig, pushing one end into the dirt, to mark the spot before retiring to the porch."

"Did you find something?" Margaux asked.

"Yes. A cigarette butt." I looked over at Gideon. "And from what I can tell, that cigarette butt matches the one I found in the woods when you were showing me the beehives, and I had spotted a reflection on glass from the edge of the forest and went to investigate."

Gideon took a deep breath. "Then this could be the same stalker."

Margaux's eyebrows rose. "Glass? What kind of glass?"

"Either from the telephoto lens of a camera or the scope on a rifle."

FORTY-SIX

Some physical tells can't be faked. Good poker players can come close, but even they can't hide the dilation of the pupils in their eyes or the beat of their heart visible in the carotid artery. Just the thought of Gideon dying from a killer's bullet caused physical reactions in Margaux. She leaned against one of the porch timbers and touched her throat, eyes wide in the night, a moth orbiting the porch lamp.

"Sean, someone has a massive interest in Gideon's fate, and that person or persons must be stopped. My great-grandfather must be protected."

"That's why I'm here." I could hear the static of police radios as the deputies made their way back around to the cabin. The twin beams from the flashlights were bouncing along the trees as the men walked toward the front of the house.

They came to the bottom step, with the older deputy speaking first. "All looks clear in and around the old barn. Saw a mouse and a black widow spider, but that was about it."

The other deputy nodded. "You've got plenty of floodlights around here. I'd suggest you keep them on at night. The prowler is probably gone. Let's hope he doesn't come back. But call us if you see or hear anything suspicious."

"Thanks for coming out here tonight, officers," Gideon said.

As they started to leave, Margaux raised one hand. "Wait please. Sean found a cigarette butt not far from that old oak. Maybe you can take it as evidence."

I pointed. "It's over there. I used a twig and stuck it in the ground near the butt to mark the location."

A call came over their radios. The older deputy pressed the microphone on his shoulder and said, "We're finishing up a 10-66 at the Wright home off County Road 19. We'll be en route in a couple of minutes."

175

"Ten-four," said the female voice on the radio.

The deputy eyed me. "We appreciate you marking the spot where someone left a cigarette butt. Except for trespassing, no crime appears to have been committed. We don't need DNA evidence on trespassing calls. Y'all have a good rest of your night."

"Wait a second," Margaux said as she took a step forward. "This is greater than trespassing. As you mentioned earlier, a dead body was found on the back of this property. It was placed there because someone is trying to frame my grandfather. The DNA on that cigarette butt could match that of the killer if you catch him."

I said, "Detectives Lofton and Ortega are investigating that murder. They could have an interest in the evidence that might be found on the cigarette butt."

The deputies exchanged glances. The senior officer said, "All right, we'll take it with us." He looked at the other deputy. "Chuck, you wanna get on a latex glove and put the cigarette butt in an evidence bag?"

"Sure." He walked to the cruiser.

The other deputy eyed me. "To save time, why don't you show us exactly where you stuck that twig in the ground?"

"Okay." I led the way, pointing to the stem. The younger deputy came up, knelt, and placed the cigarette into a small plastic bag. He sealed it, and they left without saying another word.

I walked back to the porch. "One thing the deputy mentioned was wise—keeping the outdoor lights on at night—at least until this thing is over."

Gideon nodded. "Good suggestion. Margaux has decided to spend the night. I'd feel better for her and for me if she stayed. I don't want any creeps following her back to her condo. Not that it would occur, but who knows what they'd do?"

"Goodnight. Don't hesitate to call me if you need something."

They thanked me, and I left. I put the padlock back through the links in the chain, locking it. I took a left out of the driveway and drove fifty yards toward the utility pole. I pulled off the road, stopped the Jeep, and got out. I took my Glock, walking through weeds to the spot that Gideon mentioned. It was an egress into the scrub brush. It would be hard to see in the daylight and harder to spot in the dead of night.

I used the flashlight beam to follow the rough trail. I went another thirty feet and saw flattened weeds where tires had rolled across. I walked farther along the trail, using the bright beam to track, watching for a bare spot or area of dirt where the tires could have left tread marks. I moved up a hundred feet and saw where the vehicle had stopped and later exited.

I smelled human urine in the still air. There was less than three feet of open dirt in one area. I hit the spot with the light. Tread marks were on the moist earth. I knelt, studying the pattern, and used my camera to take pictures. I would compare them to the others I'd taken of the tire tread patterns. The new photos would corroborate what I could see.

The tread came from the same vehicle that left them near Gideon's gate.

FORTY-SEVEN

I like to think of Ponce Marina as my extended office. I felt that I did some of my best work up in the flybridge of my boat, *Jupiter,* overlooking the Ponce Lighthouse and the Halifax River, the latter leading two miles away to Ponce Inlet and the Atlantic. I could conduct criminal research from the flybridge while enjoying the wash of sea breeze over the marina, which harbored more than 150 boats.

A couple of my best friends live on two of the boats. One was Nick Cronus, a commercial fisherman. The other, Dave Collins, helped me with some of my cases, usually working from his computer. But, as a former CIA operative, he is field-savvy and can read people and situations well.

I thought of that as I pulled my Jeep into the marina parking lot. Max was with me, as she often was, because Wynona was homeschooling Angela from the antique store Wynona owned in downtown DeLand. Max rode shotgun, sticking her head out the open window. I parked, picked up a brown paper bag with a bottle of Gideon's spring water in it, and we walked toward the Tiki Bar seafood restaurant. Well, I did the walking; Max did the trotting—the smells from the restaurant's kitchen almost caused her to saunter on her short hind feet.

The Tiki Bar was a single story structure made of weathered wood that resembled faded driftwood. The exterior of the roof was thatched and made from layers of dried palm fronds. The rustic restaurant was built on sturdy pilings above the marina's waterline, with a view of the docks and the river.

We walked through the open, screened door, Max beelining toward the bar. Not because she wanted a drink, but because the owner, Flo Spencer, gave her foodie handouts. From the vintage Wurlitzer jukebox in the corner, Lyle Lovett sang *If I Had a Boat.*

I quickly surveyed the room. About a dozen people were sitting at the tables. There were five customers at the bar. The walls were adorned with all things nautical. Fish netting. Starfish. Shells. A brass dive helmet from the days when divers walked the ocean floor harvesting natural sponges. A ten-foot trophy marlin was mounted and displayed, hanging on the wall behind the bar.

"Miz Max!" shouted a woman setting two plates of grilled shrimp and scallops on a server's tray at the bar. The woman was Flo, the owner. She was in her mid-sixties, with silver-colored hair pulled back. She had a lovely profile. But mostly, she had a wide smile that would light up a room or disarm a potential bar fight. She came out from behind the bar, wiping her hands on a white towel.

"Hey, Sean," she said, picking up Max and cradling her in one arm. "How's my favorite doxie?" At that moment, eyes bright and tail a blur, I thought Max might speak. She made a slight bark, glancing back at the bar like someone who wanted a bartender to refill an empty glass. Flo laughed. "I know what you want. I have some hushpuppies back there that I know this little puppy loves." She looked up at me. "How's the family—Wynona and Angela?"

"Fine. They're at the antique store."

"Isn't Angela a little young for you two to put that child to work?" Her loud laugh was a cackle.

"Angela only works part-time." I smiled. "The real story is that Wynona homeschools Angela in one of the backrooms. An employee handles the customers while school is in session."

"I wish my daughter, Shannon, could homeschool my grandson. He's in the third grade and attends a public school that needs to do a better job educating kids. But don't get me started. You here to take out the boat?"

"Not today. Is Nick's boat in the marina?"

"Yes. I bought fifty pounds of fresh grouper from him this morning. He had breakfast at the bar. I haven't seen Dave yet. He usually has breakfast at one of the tables in the corner, always carrying at least one newspaper. That man is so darn smart." She used her head to gesture toward the bar. "Let me get my gal pal, Maxine, a tiny treat." She carried Max behind the bar. The customers, three commercial fishermen that I

179

recognized, grinned as Flo reached inside a plastic serving basket with wax paper and took out a sliver of food. Max inhaled it.

"Come on, kiddo. We must go." I stood at the server's entrance to the bar as Flo set Max down. She trotted, following me to the screened door leading to the docks, Flo already was engaged in conversation with one of the customers sitting on a barstool.

Max and I walked down to L dock, heading west toward my boat, *Jupiter*. Max knew the way, taking the lead. We passed by dozens of sailboats, sport fishing boats, and gleaming white yachts, some more than a hundred feet long. There were a few houseboats, and the song *Windows Rolled Down* by Amos Lee came from one of them. The breeze smelled of barnacles baking on the dock posts in the sun, creosote, and suntan lotion.

My boat was at the very end of the dock. *Jupiter* is a 38-foot Bayliner, one that I bought years ago when I left my job as a detective in Miami after the death of my wife, Sherri. I piloted it north, up the Intracoastal, stopping at marinas along the way. When I arrived in Ponce Marina, I dropped anchor. One month turned into two, and so on. I lived on the old boat before buying the cabin on the St. Johns River, about an hour's drive away. It was when I lived on *Jupiter* that I became friends with many people in a transient place. Dave Collins and Nick Cronus are two of the full-time liveaboards here.

We walked by Nick's boat, *St. Michael.* It had the classic lines of fishing boats that sailed the Mediterranean a thousand years ago, with a high bow that could withstand towering blue-water waves. There were a half dozen fishing rods and reels stored neatly in the cockpit. The door to the salon was closed. If Nick was home, most often, it would be open. Max stared at *St. Michael* and barked. She glanced up to me. "Looks like Uncle Nick isn't home, Max. I know Dave is there because I called him. Let's go see."

Across the dock from Nick's boat was *Gibraltar*, a 42-foot Grand Banks trawler. It was spotless, the bow moored toward the dock, the cockpit in the opposite direction. We walked down a short auxiliary dock to the stern. I could hear soft jazz coming from the salon. Dave was humming to the tune *The Stars Fell on Alabama.*

"Permission to come aboard?" He came out of the opened doors to the salon, looking up at Max and me.

"Well, it's about time you two got here. Was Max driving?"

"No, she was watching the GPS."

"Speaking of GPS, I have a better idea how parts of Gideon Wright's case might be aligning. But one part seems out of sync." Dave was in his late sixties, with a full head of snow-white hair and a trimmed beard to match. Although a connoisseur of fine foods, wine, beer, and gin, he had a flat stomach, a wide chest, and thick shoulders. His pale blue eyes often were unreadable. Always unflappable.

"What do you mean, out of sync?"

Dave looked from *Gibraltar's* cockpit to a Tartan sailboat easing from its slip across at M dock. "Let's discuss it in the salon." He looked at the brown paper bag in my hand. "What's in there, a fine spirit from Ireland?"

"No, it's water. And no one on earth knows where it's from."

FORTY-EIGHT

I heard the unmistakable sound of flip-flops coming across the dock. Max did a double take when she saw her pal, Nick Cronus, strolling up to us. "Hey, Hot Dawg! Where you been, my lil' furry friend?" Max barked once, turning in a half circle. Nick reached down with one of his large hands, scooping her up. Born in Greece, Nick still spoke with a Greek accent. He was in his mid-forties, with dark olive skin, a mop of wavy black hair on his head, and a walrus moustache. His black eyes flashed with a wry sense of humor, and his heart of gold was noble and boundless.

Nick looked at me. "If Wynona and Angela aren't with you, I know your visit to the marina has something to do with business."

"That's why Dave's on speed dial. He's better at research than I am."

Dave shook his head. "I doubt that. I'm just better suited to track criminals online than on foot. Though that wasn't the case thirty years ago."

We sat at a round table in *Gibraltar's* salon, a bar with three stools to our right, Dave's laptop computer and papers on a cypress coffee table in front of the couch, and a stack of National Geographic magazines near the laptop. Dave looked across the round table to me, with Max at my feet. "After you emailed the names of the known players with their brief bios to me, I spent time online. One of the ancillary benefits of working as an occasional consultant with the CIA is that I can access some of the agency's databases through the dark web."

"What'd you find?"

"I will begin with the man in the middle, Gideon Wright. But before that, let's examine what we know thus far. Police are investigating the death of a man found in a shallow grave on the back side of Gideon's property. This land is where a unique spring flows, with perhaps the best water in the world. Water that may be marketed with a discovery that has piqued man's interest since Ponce de Leon and his conquistadors scoured Florida for the magical drink that could slow aging."

Nick leaned forward in his chair. "You got my attention now. I'm starting to see some gray in my hair, and all this time I thought I'd age like the Greek god Adonis." He chuckled, his dark eyes roguish.

I reached in the paper bag, took out the bottle of water, and put it on the table. "Dave, can we have three glasses?"

"Of course." He got up and came back from the bar with three cocktail glasses.

I poured some water into each glass and put one in front of Nick and Dave. "This water came from Gideon's spring. It was bottled a few days ago. You guys can sip it in its purest form." I lifted my glass in a toast. "To life."

"Cheers," Nick said. They lifted their glasses and sipped the water. "This is good stuff. Smooth and crisp, as if squeezed from some big ol' iceberg."

Dave nodded. "I've consumed water around the world, from the Scandinavian countries, all through Europe, and Japan as well. I've never tasted water quite like this. Perhaps it's because this has such a pure flavor." He took another sip. "I concur with Nick's analysis. It's smooth, but more than that, it's silky. Maybe it did come from an iceberg or at least the last ice age, somehow flowing down through an underground river to a hidden aquifer in Florida where it rises through the limestone to see the sunlight, streaming from the spring to the St. Johns River and out to the Atlantic."

Nick held up his glass to the light, studying the water. "What a trip, maybe one that started thousands of years ago." He knocked back his water, finishing it. He set the glass down. "Why are you carrying it around in a paper bag?"

I pushed the cap back into the bottle. "Because the properties in the water fade in sunlight. It's still excellent to drink, but the natural elements start to decline."

Dave put on his bifocals and read from a legal pad. "So, we have a unique spring and a murder. That definitely hints at what the value of the water pumping rights could be and why someone would drop a body on Gideon's land, ostensibly to frame him."

Nick looked at me. "Do cops think the dead guy was killed someplace else and dropped on Gideon's land?"

I gave Nick a summary and added, "Based on the three shoe or boot tracks I found, I believe Darnell Reid was alive when the other two brought him to Gideon's property. I think, probably at gunpoint, they marched him into the woods, killed him, and put the body in a shallow grave that would be easy for cadaver dogs to find. Since Gideon knew Reid and ran him away from the spring, it established a connection and a possible motive."

Dave looked up from his water at me. "It'll be up to you to connect the dots. You said Reid and a tech named Lamar Dunn were working for Enviro Resources. It's a lab that is retained by every group, from the EPS to water bottling companies. I discovered that Glacier Artesian Springs hires Enviro Resources to test springs in Florida. Unless I have the wrong man, and I don't think that's the case, Gideon Wright is getting up there in age. You said he appears stout and physically fit for a man his age. Perhaps it is because of this water." He gestured to the bottle.

I said nothing, thinking about Gideon swimming in the spring.

Dave glanced down at his notes, setting his laptop on the table. He tapped the keyboard. "We'll look at the rest of the known players after Gideon Wright. He has an impressive background in hydrogeology. Wright was and possibly still is an expert in the theory of earth's hot spots and tectonic plate movement, as well as how this affects water tables. He is a specialist in ground water and how to safely tap it for human consumption. From what I gather, he retired about thirty years ago."

I leaned forward, glancing at Dave's notes. "You mentioned that he's getting up there in age. What does up there mean?"

"Try ninety-nine. I've checked birth and death records, university records, and employment histories. He was born in Jacksonville."

"He doesn't look ninety-nine. He can swim like a fish in a spring with what appears to be a robust current as the water flows out of the boil underwater."

Nick grunted. "Back in Greece, on the isle of Mykonos, some of the old men swam in the ocean up 'til they died. And I'm talkin' about fellas in their nineties."

Dave looked at me. "You said Gideon's very fit, but how about his mind, his cognitive abilities? Does he have difficulty with thought or speech?"

"No, not at all. Maybe the water helps prevent mental decline."

Nick grinned. "I want a jug full. So, this gent's been sippin' real tonic water for years. How'd Gideon find this stuff?"

I gave Nick a briefing. He leaned back in his chair and said, "Some old sailors I've known believe the Fountain of Youth was on Bimini, but it was lost after an earthquake."

Dave grunted. "No one in history is tied more closely to the legend of the Fountain of Youth than Ponce de Leon. The city of St. Augustine has marketed that alleged connection for years. There are some other places in Florida that claim to have the original Fountain of Youth that Ponce sought."

Nick chuckled. "In Florida, there are shopping centers, highways, and even towns named after ol' Ponce."

Dave nodded. "He wanted eternal youth so much that he was willing to face the fierce Calusa warriors to find it. One of those warriors shot a poison arrow into Ponce's thigh. He and his men managed to get back on their ship and flee to Cuba, where he died at age forty-five. That's a sad twist of fate in Ponce's demise—to die young while searching for eternal youth. This inlet and that lighthouse in the distance bear his name."

Nick looked up from the bottle of water at me. "Maybe Gideon Wright did find the water that Ponce searched for."

"Ponce may have searched for a legendary youth-giving spring, and who knows—is Gideon's spring what he was looking for? Now, more than five hundred years later, we know that Gideon's spring can't provide eternal youth, but it does have a perfect concentration of minerals to help heal the body and might even slow aging a bit."

Nick leaned forward, resting his beefy forearms on the table. "I'm thirsty."

Dave nodded. "Perhaps this unique water from an unknown source deep within the earth is so pure that it can actually slow down the aging process, possibly by replenishing the human cells and lowering acidity in the body. Sean, you said the water is only potent for thirty-three feet from the underground opening and that the water, when bottled, has a shelf life of seven days in that powerful form."

"That's what Gideon says. The day we met him at the farmers' market, he sprinkled some of the water on Angela's skinned knee. It was a fresh scrape. By the time Wynona tucked Angela in bed that evening, the open sore was healed. No scar. No sign of the skinned knee."

Nick grinned. "I need some of that stuff in my fridge. I'm always getting cuts and bruises workin' on the boat and around the docks. But you said it only lasts in the bottle for seven days, and the good stuff in the water is from the mouth of the spring out thirty-three feet into the pool, right?"

"According to Gideon, yes."

"Maybe it's divine water. God rested on the seventh day. Jesus only lived in the form of a man for thirty-three years. What if it's the *true* holy water? Every year, I ask Father Rodriguez to bless my boat. It's sort of a blessing for the fleet, even if my boat's the only one. The priest comes here to the docks, sprinkles holy water on the bow of *St. Michael,* and says a prayer. That's the way they do it in Greece at the beginning of the fishin' season. Maybe Gideon's spring comes from the real holy water, never touched by man, and flowing from one of the purest places left on earth, a womb that leads to the source of life."

I nodded. "Unfortunately, death now has become part of the equation, and I believe it's just a matter of time before murder charges are filed against Gideon unless I can help him." I looked over at Dave. "What else did you find on the others?"

He finished his water. "It may be classic good and evil at its best or worst, depending on your point of view. The good, bad, and ugly. And from what you shared with me, it's the beauty of the spring, with its enormous potential, that makes it even uglier. We'll talk about it after I hit the head. I'm almost hesitant to pee with this miraculous water in my aged bladder. When I return, there is something you need to hear."

FORTY-NINE

Dave came back to the table and looked at the remaining water in my bottle, as if it held a secret message. He sat down, pulling up the notes on his laptop. "Nick, you put it aptly, suggesting the water is coming from a limestone womb that flows out of darkness from a hidden source of life. I'm not sure a hydrogeologist would analyze it quite that way, but you have a point. To expand on that point, a product like that, even with a short shelf life in terms of the water's most effective use, could be a marketer's dream."

"How's that?" Nick asked.

"What Sean alluded to in an earlier conversation and again today—the Fountain of Youth. Imagine how a large international water bottling company would market water ostensibly from the lost and legendary Fountain of Youth. Even as a tongue-in-cheek ploy, the publicity value could build international brand awareness, especially since the water does have that smooth and crisp taste that you said it has, Sean."

Nick glanced down at his hands, stretching his fingers, clenching his fists, and repeating the exercise, looking at both of his big, scarred hands. "I pulled nets and rods two days ago at sea. My knuckles were sore. Now, it feels like the soreness is easing up some."

Dave grinned. "I hope it will lessen my heartburn after a plate of Mexican food."

"My joints feel better already. Sean, what's really in that water?"

"Gideon says it's infused with magnesium, potassium, calcium, electrolytes, and all the rest to create a perfect alkalinity or pH balance. On the subatomic level, it has an unspoiled molecular balance of hydrogen and oxygen."

Dave cleared his throat. "Apparently, the stuff of life. It's equivalent

187

to a liquid genie in a bottle. A big water company's three wishes would be *exclusive, sole,* and *absolute* rights of use for decades … or until they pumped the spring dry. To obtain those rights, what are they willing to do? How far will they go, Sean?"

"Try murder."

"But, right now, you don't know for sure that they are behind the murder on Gideon's land. Could there possibly be someone else who'd like to shift the suspicion to Gideon or to a global water bottling company? We do know bottled water has one of the highest profit margins of any product. On an annual basis, it is a 400 billion-dollar business. That can spell motive."

I nodded. "When deputies found the body, that showed how far *someone* is willing to go. Will they go further? If Gideon is arrested and convicted, will they find a way to kill him and make it look like an accident? A suicide? A jailhouse death while in custody?"

Nick shook his head. "You said Gideon gives away as much of the water as he can, because he knows it has a short shelf life. It's too bad that an old man, trying to do the right thing, is in somebody's sights because they want what he has—his spring." He looked at Dave. "It's not the three wishes from a genie in a bottle, but the three wishes or the deal somebody makes with the devil. Greed, greed, and more greed. Sean, are the cops hunting down the perp? You handed 'em all that stuff."

"Let's hope they can. The body found on Gideon's land tells me of the enormous profit margins from the spring if it can be taken out of his hands. Dave, what else do you have on the known players?"

"You have the data on the guy you spotted watching Gideon at the farmer's market, Floyd Shaw."

"Do you have anything else on him?"

"No."

"Who is this Shaw fella?" Nick asked.

Dave glanced at his notes. "He's anything his employer wants, from a man hired to surveil someone to a guy who would use a tire iron across your knees. The mob used to call those guys enforcers. Is he a hitman? Probably."

I leaned forward. "We don't know who hired him. Maybe it was the man who met Gideon for lunch and tried to convince him to sell water rights to one of the world's largest water bottling companies, Glacier Artesian Springs. That guy is Roger Heller. What did you find on him?"

Dave looked through his bifocals at his computer screen. "Heller works for Glacier Artesian Springs as their senior VP of mergers and acquisitions. From what I found, he lives in Manhattan, has a business degree from the University of Texas, and a law degree from Penn State. He was an acquisitions' attorney for a large soft drink and water bottling company before working as an attorney inside one of the top Big Pharma companies. He left the company after three hospitals became embroiled in a class action lawsuit for allegedly falsifying documents used in underreporting deaths in a clinical trial. Glacier Artesian Springs evidently instructed Heller to fly down to Florida and begin negotiations with Gideon."

Nick chuckled. "So, he's here to prime the pump, so to speak."

Dave nodded. "Yes, something that he's apparently good at doing. According to data I've pruned from business journals, Heller has an impressive batting average. He was involved in more than a dozen acquisitions of natural springs across the nation, from Michigan to California. And now he's in Florida."

Nick said, "He's the guy that hits towns before the circus and becomes the deal closer."

"Indeed. He's often the representative to field questions at the public hearing before a water district or a county commission decides. I pulled this video from a heated public hearing in Mulberry, Arkansas. Most of the public in a rural area was incensed that Glacier Artesian Springs was negotiating water rights for part of the small town's only spring and its primary water source. Heller was answering a heated and accusatory question from one of the residents."

Dave turned his computer screen so that Nick and I could see it. It was a packed public hearing. A woman in a ponytail stood at the speaker's podium. Roger Heller was standing in front of a five-member county commission seated behind a U-shaped dais. He wore a denim shirt with the sleeves rolled up and held a microphone. Heller flashed a Hollywood smile, taking the posture of a pitcher on the mound before winding up to throw a ball, measuring the batter.

"I understand your reluctance, Ms. Jackson. I'd feel the same way if I were in your shoes. Your points are all well taken. Unfortunately, there is no scientific data or study to back up your claims. I assure you that they are unfounded, and here's why. Bolder Springs is a magnitude four spring. It produces more than four million gallons of water each day. Even with what the town takes out every day, more than ninety percent of the remaining water flows into the Arkansas River. Our proposal is to only bottle ten percent of the water that flows away from the town. Water you will never miss, and water that will be shipped to people all over the world."

As he continued, explaining the data, Nick looked up from the screen. "That guy could sell butter to a dairy farmer."

When Heller concluded, he scanned the audience. "To become members of the community and to make a commitment to be good neighbors, Glacier Artesian Springs is making a pledge today to build two parks—one in the city and a three-acre park on the river. And we will pay down the city's bond that was issued to fund a series of hiking trails. This financial commitment, according to your city attorney, James Bigelow, will lower your property taxes. The average family will see a ten percent reduction in taxes during the next five years."

Silence fell over the crowd. The woman at the podium, visibly uncomfortable, used the palm of her hand to smooth the fabric of her blue dress. After a few seconds, the council chairman, a balding man with a heavy pink face, dismissed her and said, "Unless there is further discussion, I move that we take a vote."

Dave hit a button on his keyboard, stopping the video. He looked over his bifocals. "Care to guess how the city council voted?"

Nick snorted. "Bet it was a slam dunk in favor of the water company."

I stared at the frozen image on the screen for a moment. "Was it a unanimous yes decision or a split vote, the majority voting yes?"

"Unanimous. Heller looked like a conquering hero. That was last year."

I looked back at the screen. "Dave, zoom in as close as you can to Heller's face." I stared at the image for a couple of seconds. "I've seen this man before."

FIFTY

My phone buzzed on Dave's table, the vibration causing the water in the bottle to quiver. I looked at the screen. Gideon was calling. I answered, and he said, "Sean, you told me to call you if or when something occurred."

"What's happening?"

"Detective Lofton called. He's asking me to come down to the sheriff's office for additional questioning. I answered every question that they asked when you and Margaux were sitting on the front porch with me."

"Where's Margaux?"

"She spent some time here before driving back to the place she's renting in New Smyrna Beach. She swam in the spring, ate honey from the hives, and told me she was more relaxed than any time in her life. She's a thoughtful woman who's been through a lot of struggles. I think those challenges made her strong."

"Call her. Don't go into an interrogation room without your attorney there. In this case, since you never officially hired Percy King, Margaux is your lawyer, unless you've changed your mind."

"Oh, no. Margaux's excellent. She seems very competent. And the fact that she's family—the only one left—makes me feel like she'll pour her heart into this if need be." He paused. I could hear his breathing over the phone. "Why would they want me in their office for more questioning?"

"Maybe there are some new developments in the case. It could be a good thing, Gideon. Your insight might help them with whatever they have."

"I don't feel like I have much of an insight any more than what I told them."

"I understand. I'm hoping that they're honest investigators simply trying to do their job. And part of that job should be to eliminate you as a suspect."

"I'll call Margaux. We'll let you know what happens."

"Thank you." I clicked off and looked over at Dave and Nick.

Dave removed his bifocals and used a lens cloth to clean them. "Do you believe the police have any additional information on Gideon? Something that might have been planted, like the body on his land?"

"I doubt it, at least nothing that severe. Let's hope the questions are to clear up some loose ends."

Nick shook his head. "Imagine living a long life and being kind to people. Then, when you turn ninety-nine, you're a suspect in a murder case because one of the most valuable springs in the world runs through your property."

Dave grunted. "Becoming the fall guy, the innocent victim, has no expiration date when evil people are pulling strings." He looked over at me. "You said that you recognized Roger Heller's face. From where?"

"From him driving by Gideon's property the day that I found the shoe prints in the mud and the car that turned out to be Darnell Reid's vehicle. I saw Heller for about two seconds behind the wheel of a black Lincoln Navigator, probably a rental car. Although I saw him briefly, I do know that the photo you have here, Dave, is the same guy."

Nick said, "Maybe it's coincidental, or it could be he was checking out the crime scene."

"At that time, it was not a known crime scene. It was a parked car off the shoulder of a county road."

Dave looked up from his notes. "Heller's here on business. He knows where Gideon's land is—where that sought-after spring is located. Maybe he was checking out the property."

"And he could have hired whoever abducted Reid. Arsonists return from time to time to observe the chaos they caused as firefighters try to save lives and a building. What do you have on Margaux Brennon? Do you think she's Gideon's great-granddaughter?"

"Possibly. You brought the swab samples. I am expediting DNA testing for Gideon and Margaux. In the meantime, let's look at who she is and where she's been. Margaux grew up in Ashland, Oregon, not far from the California border. She earned her undergrad from Reed College and graduated from Stanford University's law school, finishing top in her class. She worked as a prosecutor for three years before becoming a criminal defense attorney for a Seattle firm, Hotchkiss & Goldberg. After a few years, she left to open her own practice. She's divorced. No children. Her parents died in a car crash when she was in college. No siblings."

"Could you trace her family roots?"

"Yes, on both sides. Are you looking for a specific ancestor, someone connected to Gideon Wright?"

"Did you find the name Tiffany Harper?"

Dave looked at his notes. "Indeed. Tiffany Ann Harper. She is Margaux's great-grandmother, having given birth to her grandmother, Lily."

"Margaux showed us a diary, which she said had belonged to Tiffany Harper. In it, Tiffany writes that Gideon was her true love, and she was pregnant with his baby when her family moved from Florida to San Francisco. Gideon never knew she was carrying his child."

"Oh boy," Nick said, leaning forward. "At the time, Gideon's girlfriend had been whisked away across the country to have his baby, and he was here, almost three thousand miles away, with no communication. That's sad. Back then, though, I'm sure a lot of it was letter-writing. Telephone use was not everywhere."

I looked over at Dave and asked, "Was any of Margaux's law practice in real estate or representing large companies in mergers, acquisitions, mineral rights, or imminent domain?"

"No, I couldn't find any reference to that type of law practice for her. She appears to be who she says she is—Gideon's only living relative. DNA analysis should nail it."

"Do you have anything else on the players?"

"Clifton Price, the CEO of Glacier Artesian Springs, is like a character from the movie *Wall Street*. He graduated from the Wharton School of Business. Hard-charging guy. Price participated in two hostile corporate takeovers of food processing companies before becoming Glacier's CEO. He's known for orchestrating water rights' deals that pay counties or landowners pennies on the dollar while Glacier ranks in the billions worldwide in water sales. He's twice divorced. His last wife filed domestic abuse charges against him. She alleges he tried to strangle her. It was settled out of court, the terms locked in sealed documents."

Nick pursed his lips, making a slight whistle. "He sounds like a peachy fella—a guy who ought to go into anger management therapy before he breaks a nine-iron over someone's head at the country club golf course."

Dave nodded. "The question is, though, is he too far up the ladder to participate in nefarious criminal activity that results in murder? Sean, what do you think?"

"I think I need to call Gideon. Can I borrow a pen and paper?"

"Of course." Dave shuffled over to a desk in the far corner of the salon. He returned with a pen and paper, setting them in front of me. I closed my eyes for a second, remembering what I'd seen on Gideon's porch, wrote out a number, and called him.

FIFTY-ONE

After the seventh ring, I thought Gideon wasn't going to answer his phone. Maybe he was speaking with Margaux, getting ready for further questioning with detectives at the sheriff's office. He answered. "Hello, Sean."

"Gideon, when we were talking on your front porch, you mentioned that Roger Heller gave you his business card."

"Yes, he did."

"Do you still have the card?"

"Yes. It's in my house. I just finished tending my winged friends, the bees. Hold on a minute, and I'll find the card."

Dave and Nick were silent. Max was sitting on Nick's lap. I looked at the number I'd written on the piece of paper. I put the call on speaker. Gideon returned. "Okay, I have his card."

"Please read the number to me."

"Okay. The area code is 212.

As he read the phone number, I looked at what I'd jotted down. When he read the last digit, a five, I pushed back in my chair. "What else does it say on the card?"

"Just his name and a title: Roger Heller, VP, Mergers and Acquisitions, Glacier Artesian Springs, New York. Maybe he's gone back to New York. Why do you ask about his phone number?"

"Because I think Heller is the type of guy who never learned to take no for an answer. He's used to leveraging his charm and barrels full of money to convince or buy people. Gideon, that day on your porch, Percy King arrived after police found Reid's body on your land. I don't believe that was coincidental. I think he knew you'd be anxious for legal help in view of what was happening and be ready, eager, and desperate to sign the agreement. And then he met Margaux and me."

"He certainly wasn't expecting to see anyone but me."

"When you brought King a glass of your honey-sweetened tea, he set his phone on your porch table. He received a call. Although his phone screen was upside-down from where I stood, I memorized the number."

"That's impressive. I didn't know you did that. What made you want to memorize it?"

"Because of the area code. It was a New York number. It was the number you read to me from Roger Heller's business card."

"That's rather curious."

"It's more than curious. That means that Heller and Percy King know each other. And it probably means that they are doing business together. I believe that Heller or the company he works for, Glacier Artesian Springs, hired or was in the process of retaining King."

"That doesn't make sense. Percy met with me and had drawn up papers to be my attorney."

"It does make sense if he's a shady attorney. He calls himself a simple country lawyer. Try to find a straight country road for a mile. Some are crooked. Is Margaux coming to pick you up for the trip to the sheriff's office?"

"Yes. She ought to be here within the hour."

"Ask her to call me. I need to go over this with Margaux and ask her a question."

"All right. I'll tell her." Gideon's voice sounded tired, not like his typical self.

"Are you okay? Are you nervous about speaking again with the detectives?"

"No. I reached a point in my life, long ago, in which someone's opinion of me didn't matter in the big picture. As a geologist, I've learned about nature's truths. They are absolute. Water doesn't flow against gravity for any real length. Empirical truths, though, can be manipulated by faulty science, negating the meaning of truth by creating false assumptions."

"Unfortunately, it happens."

"I know I did not kill and bury that man in a grave on my land. But I also know the criminal justice system can be swayed by made-up science. It's my hope, Sean, that between you and Margaux, the absolute truth will be the bellwether and lead me home."

"I'll do the very best I can. Hang in there." I clicked off.

Dave glanced at the slip of paper in front of me. "It sounds like Gideon's situation is becoming more complex. Perhaps ominous is a better word. You've established the Roger Heller-Percy King link. The spider's web just got stickier. Maybe now it's about catching a mosquito in the breeze. Is Heller the spider or the mosquito? And what role is King playing?"

I said nothing, listening to a halyard rattling against the steel mast on a Catalina sailboat in an adjacent slip. Nick set Max on the salon floor, got up and walked behind Dave's bar. "Anyone feel like a cold beer?"

We both declined. Nick popped the top off a bottle of Corona. He looked at the water bottle on the table. "I think Gideon has some great water, maybe it is the freakin' Fountain of Youth. I also believe a beer from the land of the Aztecs will lower your stress level, and maybe that means you'll live longer." He grinned, looking down at Max. "Right, Hot Dawg?"

She barked, glancing up at me, maybe seeking a Nick translation.

Dave closed his laptop. "What's your next move, Sean? Do you wait for the local police to weave their way through the case, perhaps indicting Gideon, or do you step in to prevent that? If he's arrested, the news media will descend on the location, putting the old spring and the old man in the spotlight. There is no limelight in that scenario."

Nick placed his bottle on a cork coaster labeled *Tiki Bar - Ponce Inlet.* "You gave the cops the photos and video of the tire and shoe tracks in the mud. What more can you do?"

"I can pay a visit to Percy King's office. Unannounced."

Nick shrugged his wide shoulders. "Cops can do that, too."

Dave shook his head. "They can, but will they? Even if Sean tells the detectives about Roger Heller's number popping up on King's phone, that's not a crime. It's nothing unless you start connecting the dots—dots that could lead you all the way up the corporate ladder."

Dave picked up his legal pad, looking at his notes from top to bottom. "Percy King practices law in a small town of DeLand. He knows many members of the local police and sheriff's departments. He does criminal and civil trials. He's probably helped some cops with their divorces, wills, probate, and so on. Not that the personal connection will influence a murder investigation, but will he be on their radar just because of a phone call from a water bottling company rep? I doubt it."

I nodded. "That's a good way to sum it up. After I spent twenty minutes with Percy King on Gideon's front porch, I felt like I should have hosed the deck off when King left. After I speak with him, depending on what he says or doesn't say and the way he reacts to my questions, it will determine whether I go find the guy who was initially following Gideon. And that guy is a habitual criminal known as Floyd Shaw."

FIFTY-TWO

I needed a quiet place to put together plans A and B. An hour later, I left Dave's boat, and walked to the end of L dock, boarding my boat *Jupiter*, a 39-foot Bayliner. I unlocked her salon, letting the warm air out, and climbed up the steps from the cockpit to the flybridge. I opened the windows, letting in the breeze, which carried the scent of the sea and marine life. I stood there for a few minutes, looking over the marina and across the water—a view I never get tired of.

I sat in the captain's chair and went over the events, thinking about what Gideon had told me on the phone. *As a geologist, I've learned about nature's truths. They are absolute. Empirical truths, though, can be manipulated by faulty science, negating the meaning of truth by creating false assumptions.* Gideon knew the noose was tightening, and that he was being framed. He understood the fate of his spring and land, with human nature and the balance of life now in danger.

I thought about calling Percy Wright's receptionist and making an appointment. But he may answer the phone. Having met me on Gideon's porch, would King meet me in his office? Probably not. He knows I'm a PI working for Gideon. So, to poke the teddy bear, I needed to get him out of his cave in a more open setting.

I used my phone to find his website. His picture was on the home page. He was wearing a dark suit and standing next to his desk. I found a photo of his office assistant, Gladys Nelson. She appeared to be about forty years old, her black hair coiffed, as if she'd just left a beauty salon. I made the phone call.

A woman with a southern drawl answered. "King Law Offices, how may I help you?"

"Hi, is this Gladys?"

"Yes, sir."

"I'm on Percy King's website, and I saw your picture. You have a nice smile."

"Well, thank you."

"I'm searching for an attorney to do my will and estate planning. I have property I'd like to leave to the right person in the event of my death. I'm looking at attorneys in Deland. I'm surprised there are at least five lawyers in town who do wills and probate. Is this in Mr. King's area of practice?"

"Yes, sir. He's good at wills, trusts, and probate. Would you like to make an appointment?"

"That might work. I'm going to be in town tomorrow."

"Hold on a sec. Can you come in the following day, say, at 2:00? His calendar is full tomorrow."

"Darn, I'm sorry to hear that. Even though there are no appointments in his office, I bet he takes time for lunch. Does he have a favorite restaurant on Wednesdays?"

"As a matter of fact, he does. He likes the Stetson Café. They have the best catfish specials on Wednesdays. I do know he sometimes meets with clients for lunch. But you don't know how to recognize him, do you?"

"I believe so. His picture is on your website. He looks like a lawyer people would want to represent them—a man to keep people out of court."

"Yes, sir, he's sure good at that. He has one client, an older fella, who's a property developer. Percy has never seen him. Imagine that. Does all his business by telephone. This client was being sued for a slip and fall in one of his businesses. I remember that he told Mr. King to work with the insurance company and to do what it took to keep him out of court. I think it's because this client is so busy, his time is better spent elsewhere rather than in court."

"That's what I want, too. Percy sounds like my kind of lawyer. Thank you, ma'am. Bye." As I was clicking off, she was asking my name.

In less than a half minute, my phone buzzed. I thought it might be King's secretary. I looked at the screen. Margaux Brennon was calling. "Hi, Sean. Gideon and I are on our way to the sheriff's department. He said you wanted me to call you."

"Yes. Thanks. Chances are that the two detectives we met, Lofton and Ortega, will play the roles of good cop – bad cop. One trying to pressure Gideon, the other expressing empathy, both seeing if they can get him to suggest that the killing of Darnell Reid was either an accident or maybe a self-defense, stand-your-ground position."

"I assumed they'd work in that manner. As Gideon says, he comes to the table with me and the absolute truth on his side. I'm a pretty good attorney, but the truth surpasses me."

"After they finish with their questions, maybe you can ask one of them."

"What's that?"

"Ask them if they have the forensic results on the shoes Reid wore when he was killed. Does the tread pattern on one of those three sets of prints next to Reid's car match what he was wearing?"

"I'll ask. I've found that police often hold their cards close. Under the guise of the terms *an active investigation*, they don't offer too many facts unless they will help nail a suspect. But I don't mind asking."

"Good." I shared with her some of the information Dave had found, adding, "Enviro Resources lab was hired by Glacier Artesian Springs. This goes to the top of the corporate ladder."

"Interesting and not surprising in the least."

"Please let me know how it goes." I clicked off and stared at the wide Halifax River, which flowed to Ponce Inlet and the Atlantic, watching three pelicans sail over the mangroves, Gideon's words swirling in my thoughts. *I reached a point in my life, long ago, in which someone's opinion of me didn't matter in the big picture. As a geologist, I've learned about nature's truths.*

While truth in nature is one thing, the manmade version is subject to change, manipulation, and interpretation. Gideon Wright's values and beliefs came from the natural world, where beauty and truth were in a cycle of balance and harmony. Both are necessary for coexistence and are absolute. In the dark world of the criminal mind, evil is not so much necessary as it is compulsory. There is no coexistence there with good, only a shadowy conditional mingling. It is a parasitic relationship where the blood of good and innocence is fair game in an unfair world.

The night Darnell Reid was killed, evil left two sets of shoe prints in the mud. I knew it was a matter of time and circumstances before the trail would lead back to Gideon. I would do my best not to follow evil but to be there before it arrived.

FIFTY-THREE

Gideon and Margaux sat at a square table in one of the interrogation rooms within the sheriff's department. Detectives Richard Lofton and Sylvia Ortega entered, taking seats on the opposite side of the table from Gideon and Margaux. Lofton was the first one to speak. "Mr. Wright, thank you for coming down to the office today."

"Happy to help if I can."

Lofton nodded, his eyes revealing nothing. "Mr. Wright, although we couldn't find any record of criminal behavior in your life, we couldn't find much else either. It's as if you've been off the grid for many years. No social media presence. No military records. You use a post office box for correspondence, and there is no family history that we could find. It looks like you had a career as a geologist that took you around the world."

"I did. I can't be off the grid when I've never been on it." He smiled.

"How'd you wind up on that land in the national forest?"

"I didn't wind up there. The land and home have been in my family since 1869. I came back to it after there was no one left in the family to be a caretaker of the land and spring. That was many years ago, after my brother died."

"In your role as a caretaker, it looks like you're very passionate. Although we couldn't find a criminal record, we did find a complaint filed against you by a man named John Robinson. In it, he states that he and his family were hiking in the forest when they came upon the spring. They spent time there enjoying it—swimming, picnicking—until you ran them out. In the complaint, the family says they feared for their safety." He looked down at an open file folder. "Mr. Robinson called you a crazy, dangerous old man with a bad attitude."

Gideon shook his head. "The truth behind those claims is that the family spent an entire day there. They had two girls and four teenage boys. I gave them permission to swim in the spring. But as they were leaving, they left trash and garbage, even leaving two beer cans at the bottom of the spring. I handed out trash bags and asked them to clean up the mess. The father, Robinson, was drunk. He became belligerent and said the clean-up was my problem. I told them to leave, and if they didn't, I would call the sheriff. They begrudgingly left."

Margaux leaned forward. "Detective Lofton, my client has been and is an extraordinary custodian of his land and spring. The nature of your question implies that he's some sort of curmudgeon, someone who yells at kids to get off his lawn. That's not the case, and I don't see why you feel it's germane to your murder investigation."

Lofton shifted his eyes from his file to Margaux. "Ms. Brennon, if I were in court, I wouldn't tell you how to question a witness. Please, let us do our job."

"This witness happens to be my client. More than that, he's my great-grandfather." Both detectives exchanged glances. "We came down here as a courtesy, but not to be part of a fishing expedition where you try to set hooks in him, implying an elderly man is a threat to everyone trespassing on his land. What questions do you have related to your case?"

Detective Ortega, nodded. "We understand your defense of your great-grandfather." She looked at Gideon. "Mr. Wright, as the population of the area grows, it's inevitable that people will seek out your spring. Each time people arrive trespassing, I'm sure it's just another thing for you to deal with. Especially when they don't respect the spring. After a while, anyone's patience would grow thin. When Darnell Reid came on your property unannounced, taking water samples, that must have been the ultimate violation."

"It was not when he came onto my land the first time, Detective. It was the third time. Each time, I asked him and whoever he was with to leave. He became indignant on the last encounter, getting into my personal space."

"What was your reaction?" asked Lofton. "Did he push your buttons so hard that you wanted to retaliate by making him leave and never return?"

"They waved me off like I was a fly in their faces."

"And that angered you, as it would anybody, right?"

Ortega asked, "Did Reid come back later, by himself, and threaten you? Did you have to come out of your home and confront him, or was he trying to enter your home?"

"Neither. I never saw him again."

Lofton said, poker-faced, "Until that night, he died."

Margaux leaned forward. "Detective, you are leading my client into a pasture filled with weeds and cow pies. How is someone Gideon's age going to retaliate? He's not going to engage in a fight. He will demand that the water techs leave once again and never return. That's exactly what happened. Perhaps you might ask Enviro Resources Corporation in Tallahassee why they've sent water testing people onto land that's posted as no trespassing."

"We can do that," Ortega said.

"Even further, you can ask the Glacier Artesian Springs bottling company why they hired Enviro Resources. What's water from Gideon's spring worth to a global company—a company with a reputation for paying pennies on the dollar and then reaping billions in profits? This is a classic David versus Goliath battle, detectives. Some very wealthy people want to pump water from Gideon's unique spring. He's the only one standing in their way. If you look hard enough, there's motive here, and it's not coming from Gideon."

Detective Lofton jotted something down on his notepad. He looked up at Gideon. "Mr. Wright, the night Darnell Reid went missing, most likely the night he died, you told us you were home. The national forest adjacent to your property is so thick with trees and jungle-like terrain that it would be hard for kidnappers to traipse through the woods at night with Reid in tow. They probably walked across your land, past your cabin and barn, to head back to the end of your property, where we found the body. Are you sure you didn't see or hear something that night?"

"Yes. I go to bed early and rise before the sun comes up."

"Did you hear anything that sounded like gunfire?"

"No."

"Did you hire people to teach Reid a lesson, but they went too far and killed him? You didn't order it. Stuff happens, though. Doesn't make it directly your fault."

"No. I never did, nor would I hire someone to kill a human being. That violates a sacred tenet of my beliefs in God."

Detective Ortega set her pen down. "Mr. Wright, who do you think may have killed Darnell Reid?"

"I don't know."

Margaux interlaced her fingers. "Detectives, my client is not the killer. He, too, is a victim. He's a victim of controlled circumstances. Someone wants to frame him for the murder of Darnell Reid. Let me ask you a question. We know there were three sets of shoe or boot tread prints in the mud the day Reid's car was found on Gideon's property. Did one pair match the shoes on Reid's body?"

Lofton looked at Ortega and said, "Yes."

"So, all you must do is find the two people who wore the other shoes or boots. Maybe you'll find the car they drove, too."

"And maybe we'll find something else on Mr. Wright's property. Our search warrant is still open. If you don't mind, Mr. Wright, I want a couple of my deputies to conduct an additional search using a canine."

"I don't mind at all."

Lofton looked across the table at Margaux. "Counselor, we are searching for matches to the shoe and tire tread prints, and we're searching for the murder weapon."

***

I was in my home office when Margaux called. "Sean, Gideon, and I are driving back to his house." She told me what happened when the detectives questioned Gideon and added, "When I asked them if one set of the shoe prints matched the shoes on Reid's body, they said it did. I was surprised they'd be that forthcoming."

"For them, that narrows the suspect list to two."

"Make that three. As I mentioned, some of their line of questioning had to do with the possibility of Gideon hiring two thugs to take out Reid, assuming the buried body wouldn't be found in a remote section of Gideon's land."

"They could have dumped or buried the body anywhere in Florida. To do it on Gideon's property shows planning and intent, with the goal being to frame him."

"No doubt. Something else, too. They're using the open warrant to come back and search his property."

"Search it for what?"

"A murder weapon."

"They should search the trunk of the vehicle that was parked in front of Reid's car that night."

"You think they'll find it?"

"Maybe."

"If not, what then?"

"I will."

FIFTY-FOUR

The scent of ground coffee beans, biscuits, and sauteed potatoes with onions greeted me at the door. It was the next day, and I was arriving at the Stetson Café before noon. I walked around the tables over the cypress-planked wooden floor to sit in a booth with a clear view of the front entrance.

The café was a Norman Rockwell painting come to life. The Americana was as thick as the apple pie under a glass dome on one side of the countertop. A police officer sat on a stool at the counter. Next to him was a college student wearing earbuds, researching something on his laptop. The café attracted a mix of working people—electricians, plumbers, and truck drivers.

Scattered among the mix, sitting at the tables, were lawyers, accountants, and what looked like a group of four bearded professors from nearby Stetson University. When I walked by their table, they were discussing changes to the curriculum. "Glad I'm retiring from academia next year," one said.

I sipped coffee and waited for Percy King to enter. I didn't have to wait long. He came through the door in a wash of sunlight, wearing a blue sports coat, a pale blue shirt, and no tie. His veiled eyes swept the place like disguised radar. He walked over to what appeared to be a table of four lawyers. All of the men were in their forties. Sports coats hung from the back of their chairs, ties neatly notched at the collar. One wore monogramed cuffs.

After a minute of small talk, King walked to a corner booth and took a seat. A blond waitress brought him a cup of coffee and took his order. She laughed at something he said before heading back toward the kitchen. I got up and moved toward him. At his booth, I stopped. "Mr. King, how are you today?"

208

He looked up at me, the sunlight through the window reflecting off the shiny table and highlighting the soft flesh under his double chin. "I'm fine, sir." He looked at me with a mix of amusement and curiosity. He grinned. "I remember you from Gideon Wright's home. Sorry, but your name slips my mind."

"It's Sean O'Brien. Do you mind if I sit? I hear you'll get hooked on the fried catfish."

Before he could answer, I sat in the booth across from him and sipped my coffee from a thick mug.

He nodded. "Are you a resident here in DeLand?"

"No. I live in the country."

"You and Gideon seem to have a common domain. He lives in the country—in the Ocala National Forest. Quaint. How is Gideon?"

"He's fine, thanks."

"I assume his lady lawyer is taking good care of his legal needs."

"He doesn't have any immediate legal needs, but she is there in the event he does."

He made a mock smile. "That's not what I hear. The way I hear it is Gideon could be indicted or charged with premeditated first-degree murder any day now. That'd be a shame, considering his advanced age and all."

"It would, considering the fact that he's innocent and all."

"I suppose the burden of proof will be on the lady lawyer, should that come to fruition."

"The lady lawyer, Margaux, is Gideon's great-granddaughter. They're family, and they're a team. Despite his *advanced* age, Gideon is confident that the land and spring will remain as they are in perpetuity now that his rightful heir has arrived." I watched King's eyes. They were like a toad's eyes, unblinking, as if waiting for an insect to crawl by. I sat in silence.

After ten seconds, he moistened his lips, looking from me to the café's counter across the restaurant. Then he eyed me. "Why are you here today, Mr. O'Brien? If you are a licensed private investigator, why aren't you out there investigating on behalf of Gideon?"

"I am investigating on his behalf. That's why I'm here."

"What are you implying?"

"What are you inferring?"

He sipped his coffee, setting the cup back on the saucer. "My granddaddy used to pour coffee from his cup into the saucer. He said it cooled down quicker. Then he'd lift the saucer up and sip. He did it often while eating cornbread. I think it's a southern thing, unique to southerners. Are you one?"

I sipped my coffee, set down the mug, and placed both of my forearms on the table. I wanted to watch King's eyes closely. Even a sociopathic liar can't control the pupils of his eyes. "What's your relationship with Floyd Shaw?"

He stared at me as if he were waiting for an echo. His pupils opened slightly wider. His brain was calculating. Maybe misfiring. He glanced to his left. But there was nothing to see through the window except the other side of the street. "Floyd Shaw? Who might that be? He's not one of my clients unless he goes by another name."

"Are you denying that you know him?"

"Who is he?"

"Why don't you tell me?"

"Sir, just the way you phrased that question suggests that I'm a liar."

"Are you?"

"I don't know someone named Floyd Shaw. He's certainly not a client."

"But Roger Heller is a client. Maybe your biggest, paying you a large retainer fee."

"I will not justify a response to that ludicrous statement."

"I know you're working for him and, all the while, trying to get Gideon to sign a one-sided agreement. Heller called you that day you slithered up and onto Gideon's porch, when you met Margaux Brennon and me. I saw Heller's number pop up on your phone screen. Maybe it was just a wrong number. What are the odds, counselor?"

"You've worn out your welcome at this booth, Mr. O'Brien."

"Shucks, I wanted to stay through dessert. I hear they make a great apple pie."

"If you do not leave my immediate premises, I shall walk over to that lunch counter and let Officer Doug Henderson know that you are harassing me. They'll haul you away."

"And I'll let the homicide detectives know that you know Floyd Shaw, your go-to guy with a long rap sheet. As a suspect in two murder-for-hire jobs, I'm sure they'd be interested in your connection."

As his food arrived, I stood from the booth. His brow was furrowed, as if his brain hurt. He looked at the waitress. "Thank you, Sheila."

I left the café and walked down the opposite side of the street. About fifty yards from the café, I ducked into a coffee shop. I stood at the window and watched. Seconds later, Percy King came out of the café. He was in such a hurry that his paper napkin was still tucked into his open shirt. He reached for his chest, ripping the napkin off, dropping it in a trashcan, and waddling like a penguin toward his office.

I knew I'd touched a nerve. Now it was time to find Floyd Shaw.

FIFTY-FIVE

Percy King entered his office in a huff, his mind moving in a dozen directions. His secretary, Gladys, looked up from her computer screen. "Mr. King, Roger Heller called. He said it was urgent." She handed him a slip of paper with his name and number on it. "Mr. Heller said he tried your cell phone, but you weren't answering. I told him you were at lunch and probably with a client. Did a nice man with a deep voice meet you at the Stetson Café?"

"What nice man?"

"He called yesterday and said he was shopping for attorneys, looking for someone who can do estate and probate work. I told him you're the best in town."

"What's his name?"

"He didn't say, but he did say he might be in town today, and if so, he'd get lunch. I recommended the Stetson Café. Figured you could at least give him your card if he showed up."

"Gladys, always get their names."

"Okay. Sorry. I was asking for his name as he was hanging up. I think I'll go to lunch. Did the fella show up?"

Percy was halfway down the hall, walking to his office. He sat behind his desk, turning through a rolodex, stopping when he found the name and number he wanted. He took out the card, setting it in front of him. King looked at the number on the slip of paper that Gladys had given him. He made the call.

Gladys stood, reaching for her purse, stopping near the front door. Even from there, she could hear King cursing as he returned the call.

Heller answered. "You're a hard man to find, Percy."

"With all due respect, I do have other clients."

"But they're not paying you the kind of retainer that we're advancing. In other words, when I say jump, you inquire as to how high. Why hasn't Gideon Wright been arrested?"

"The detectives are getting closer. I'm sure the arrest is looming."

"If this plan does not actualize, you're out. We will hire other lawyers and pursue an eminent domain action, working with pay-to-play politicians to seize Wright's land and spring. You'd be surprised how far words like *in the best interest of the public* go in state government via political action committees."

"That would take a long time. And now that Wright's great-granddaughter is in the picture, a woman with a legal background, your chances of obtaining eminent domain are greatly diminished. I need cash to manage a couple of issues. One is the great-granddaughter. The other is a PI named Sean O'Brien. If you want this handled and done right in a courthouse, which I know like the back of my hand, then you retain soldiers and provide cash for removing obstacles."

"How much?"

"I'd say that two-hundred-fifty grand in cash will take care of that and another potential problem."

"What other potential problem?"

"Somehow, O'Brien knows the name of one of the associates I use from time to time."

***

Hank Marsh was leaving the moored shrimp boat, *Miss Marla Jean*. Marsh, in his early forties, had blond hair like windblown straw, and was lanky with muscular arms under his white T-shirt. His thin face was weather-beaten from years working as a shrimper and commercial fisherman. His jeans were stiff from salt spray and spotted with grease. He wore orange rubber boots. He'd take them off after he walked across the lot and got to his ten-year-old pickup truck.

The phone in his pocket buzzed. He looked at the screen and thought about not answering the call from Percy King. Maybe it was urgent, like something about back child support or a warrant for his arrest. "Hello?"

"Hank, it's Percy. How's shrimpin' this week?"

"Same as last week. Shitty. Asian markets and farm-raised shrimp are killin' us. It takes all I can do to make the payments on the boat."

"The economy doesn't look like it's going to improve anytime soon. You need to pay off what you owe on *Miss Marla Jean.*"

"I need the price of diesel fuel to come back down, but that ain't gonna happen either."

"Is Miguel Morales still working on your crew?"

"You mean Mutt? That's what we call him. He's off and on. He works on three boats. The guy likes stayin' out at sea 'cause he's got so many outstanding warrants against his ass. He's at the docks now, just came back with me. He ought to be here a couple days before he ships out."

"I need some personal work done."

"What kind of work?"

"The kind that'll pay off your boat and buy you a new Ford F-250. You'll probably need to use Mutt or Carl Lee. Maybe both. I don't care who you use, as long as the law can't trace it back to me and my clients. This is a cash job. It'll be done when you take the collateral far out into the Atlantic, at least to the Gulf Stream, and dump 'em where the sharks feed."

***

Gladys Nelson, distraught from overhearing some of King's conversation, quietly tiptoed from near her desk to the law office's front door. She opened it, the hinges squeaking. As she was going out the door, King appeared in the hallway. "I thought you'd gone to lunch."

"Forgot my phone. I'm leaving now." She closed the door, walking out into the sunshine, her heart beating faster.

***

As I was leaving DeLand, I called Detective Lofton. The receptionist put me through, and Lofton answered. "Mr. O'Brien, what do I owe the honor of this call?"

For some detectives, a PI is like a gnat in their face. Some look at a PI as a person who was hired because the cops did shoddy work and the victim, or his family, is looking for justice and some form of closure. I think, in Lofton's case, he was an investigator who would take cards from a PI's deck and not reciprocate. Gideon Wright wasn't a victim yet. But he was in someone's crosshairs.

"Detective, I just wanted to give you something that I learned, something you might find useful."

"And what would that be?"

"Do you know a local lawyer by the name of Percy King?"

"I know of him. He's never been involved in a homicide case as the defense."

"He may be involved, but not as a defense attorney. He could be an accessory in the killing of Darnell Reid."

"Why is that?"

"Because King was working with Gideon Wright, trying to coax him into signing an agreement that would have made King not only the executor of Gideon's will but the guy who determined the eventual fate of the land and spring. When Gideon's great-granddaughter, Margaux Brennon, came on the scene, that put an end to King's legal opportunities with Gideon."

"O'Brien, all that sounds like is an heir showing up and canceling out a local lawyer who was courting the elderly man for business."

"As a detective in a murder case, do you ever feel that coincidences play a role in your investigation?"

"I'm not sure that I understand your line of questioning."

"When I worked as a homicide detective, anything that appeared coincidental was not. Whatever happened, it happened for a reason. I had to push back the fallen dominos to figure out how each piece interacted with the others. When I was on Gideon's porch the day that we met you and Detective Ortega, I saw a phone number pop up on Percy King's phone. It was the same number from a business card that was given to Gideon. The card came from the man representing Glacier Artesian Springs. That man is Roger Heller. I think King works for him. I'll leave it at that. The ball is in your court."

FIFTY-SIX

The following morning, I strapped on a holster above my left ankle before walking to my mailbox. A compact 9mm Beretta was in the holster under my pant leg. I rarely leave home without it. After breakfast with Wynona and Angela, I'd head out to find Floyd Shaw. I wanted to ask him why he had an interest in Gideon Wright. And I wanted to see if he knew or had known Darnell Reid, Percy King, or even Roger Heller.

The sun was coming up over the cypress tree line in the east, and a mourning dove was cooing from the woods across the road. The sunlight was glinting off the dew that covered the grass. Max trailed me down my long driveway, the gravel and crushed shells beneath my feet, the sweet scent of honeysuckle in the air.

Max, as she always does, sprinted ahead of me. Ever the watch dog—all ten pounds of her. The driveway made a long, partial S shape, almost a hundred yards from the county road down to our home. There was a gate at the end of our driveway. The ancient shell mound, built by the Timucuan a thousand years ago, was the highest point on the property. The mound's apex was thirty feet above the surrounding terrain of moss-draped live oaks, palms, and thick cypress.

I carried a handheld remote switch to send a signal to the gate motor. Max sat, waiting patiently as the gate swung open. I thought about the gate over Gideon's driveway, how he locked it with a chain and padlock. Max trotted out before me. As I approached my mailbox, I noticed fresh tire tracks in the damp earth near the mailbox. I knelt, using the tip of a finger to touch one of the tread marks.

I stood, pulling out my phone, listening for cars in the distance. I found the pictures of the tire tread impressions I had photographed on Gideon's property. I looked at one of the closeups of the tire treads that were not from Darnell Reid's car. From the same perspective, I took a picture of the tread tracks on my property. I studied both photos, side-by-side on the screen. They were identical.

I looked around, listening, wondering if someone was watching as I was about to check my mailbox. A large crow flew to the top of a lone pine tree in my front yard. The bird looked down at Max and me before angling its head toward the east. It cried out, making three quick caws in the still morning air.

Max looked up at me, her face inquisitive, curious as to why I stood so still. "Is that crow bidding us a good morning, Max, or is the wise old bird telling us to be on the lookout? What do you think the crow sees from way up there in the top of the pine tree?" I spotted something else in the wet, black earth. It was a cigarette butt. As I squatted down to examine it, my mailbox exploded.

I grabbed Max and rolled back behind my fence and the thick wax myrtle shrubs. As I reached for my Beretta, I simultaneously hit the remote to close the gate. I looked over at the bullet hole in one side of my mailbox, watching as bits of mail fluttered in the air like confetti. I knew, from the trajectory, that the initial impact was on the opposite side of what was left of my mailbox. I was looking at the exit hole. I had no doubt that it was from a high-powered rifle.

I held Max in my left hand and the Beretta in my right. In the distance, I could hear a car's engine. I crouched behind my wrought-iron fence and shrubs, listening to Max growl at our unseen enemy. My phone buzzed. Wynona calling. I answered. "Sean, we heard a gunshot. I looked out our bedroom window and couldn't see you or Max. Where are you?"

"Stay inside! A sniper just blew a hole through our mailbox. The gunman was aiming at me. Keep Angela inside the house."

"We have a rifle here. Can I do anything to help?"

"No. Just stay inside. I have Max. We're behind shrubs to the left of our driveway. Gotta go. Someone's coming." I clicked off and waited. The engine was growing louder. Around a bend in the road was a dark red SUV. As it came closer, I could tell it was a Ford Expedition. The way the vehicle was coming meant that the passenger side of the front seat would face me. The windows were dark as midday shade.

I had to decide fast. At this point, I didn't know for sure that whoever was in the SUV pulled the trigger that destroyed my mailbox. If I emptied my Beretta into the side of the vehicle, I could kill or injure an innocent person. I assumed the SUV was the same one I'd seen in the farmers' market parking lot and the same one I'd seen a few days ago driving slowly by my property.

But I didn't know for sure.

I'd have to hold back any return fire. Maybe they didn't see me roll behind the shrubs. Maybe they'd drive by without even hitting the brake pedal. In seconds, the SUV was within fifty feet of my driveway. Like a slow-motion scene in a movie, the passenger-side front seat window came sliding down. The muzzle of an AR-15 rifle stuck out like a coiled snake. I recognized the black shape of the barrel and stock. But I didn't recognize the man holding the rifle. He wore a baseball cap. Both hands gripped the gun.

I held Max and ran to my left just as a half-dozen rounds tore through the gaps in the fence, the wax myrtle limbs and leaves shredding like pulp. As the vehicle went by, I ran behind the cover of bushes to the shell mound, climbing halfway up. I set Max behind me as I fired down on the SUV, shooting three times. The rounds shattered the rear window.

The man with the gun tried to lean out and turn in my direction. I aimed and squeezed, firing. I saw a pink mist as his head exploded. The driver pulled the man's body back into the front seat and hit the accelerator. The SUV was now speeding away, pieces of glass falling from the shattered windows as the Ford vanished around a curve in the distance.

I looked down at Max. She glanced up at me, snorting and making her dog nod, as if to say *we won.*

But I knew we didn't win. I only managed to slow down the inevitable pursuit of an old man and his billion-dollar spring. I scooped up Max and walked down the driveway back to our house, my heart pounding, adrenaline pouring through my veins, and the odor of spent bullets in the morning air. I was on the receiving end of an attempted murder—a hit. A bullet had just missed my head and destroyed my mailbox. I'd emptied all six rounds into the SUV. I knew I probably killed the man holding his rifle.

It was only 7:30, and the day had just begun.

The crow flew from the pine tree, over my house, and across the river.

FIFTY-SEVEN

As Max and I returned to our screened back porch, Wynona and Angela were there to greet us. We walked up the three steps and entered, Wynona wrapping her arms around me. "Are you hurt?"

"I'm okay. So is Max."

Angela picked up Max, hugging her. "Daddy, it was like fireworks, those sounds."

"I wish it was fireworks, sweetheart."

Wynonna straightened, using one hand to touch Angela on her shoulder. "I explained to Angela what made those sounds and how you had to defend yourself."

I bent down and kissed Angela on the top of her head. "Sometimes bad things happen because of bad people. But good people get through it and become even stronger. Even brave dogs like Max. Why don't you take Max in the kitchen and give her some water—maybe a little breakfast, okay?"

"Okay." She turned and entered the kitchen, Max in her arms, staring back at me.

Wynona glanced down toward the river and then looked at me. "This is getting too close to our home. It must be stopped. Are you going to call the sheriff's office and report it?"

"Yes. But to stop it, I'll have to make it stop. Remember, I gave the detectives the information I found about Roger Heller calling Percy King. Are they following that lead? The SUV that I saw in the farmers' market parking lot is probably the same one, but this time with two killers in it. I couldn't make out the license plate because a guy was shooting at me. When I walked to the mailbox, I spotted fresh tire tread marks. The tracks matched those near Gideon's land the night Darnell

Reid vanished. When the killers saw me at the mailbox, the guy in the front passenger seat took a shot at me. They came barreling down the road seconds later, opening fire."

"Who's paying these hitmen? Is it someone from Enviro Resources, Glacier Artesian Springs, the lawyer Percy King, or someone else? Could it be Margaux Brennon?"

"Regarding Margaux, I don't think so."

"You shared with me the conversation you had with Percy King and how he left the restaurant without eating his food, almost jogging back to his office. Who'd King see or call?"

"I'd like to know that. I'm going to track down that SUV and its owner. In the meantime, I want you and Angela to stay at the marina on our boat or spend a few days with your mom on the res."

"I can't run my antique store from the res down near the Everglades. I can do it by commuting from the marina. I don't believe the perps are after Angela and me. It's you that I worry about, Sean. You are the thorn in their side."

"Yes, to some extent. But the real and permanent thorn is the woman who stands to inherit the land and spring after Gideon's death. That's Margaux Brennon."

"Do you think she's in danger?"

"Yes."

"Is that because someone has estimated the spring's value in the billions of dollars?"

"Yes. The spring run is short before it merges with the river, therefore, the curative value of the water has been overlooked or hidden for decades. And now, with droughts in America and around the world, pure spring water is liquid gold. Margaux, metaphorically speaking, is the dam keeping the water rights in the family."

"Not a good place for her to be."

"Not at all. If you do the math, she's the odd number. The spring flows with a high-magnitude discharge, maybe up to thirty million gallons a day. You can see how much money can be made if a large water company acquired pumping rights for ten years with the option to renew for another ten. It's like a massive lottery flowing with cash day and night."

"Did you know that the Garden of Eden was watered by a spring that flowed out to meet four rivers? With Gideon's spring, you just have to figure out who's the serpent in all of this." Wynona managed a smile.

"Well, thanks for that piece of trivia and the serpent-like evil foe comparison. I'll be sure to look for snakes in the grass the next time I'm out at Gideon's." Sean laughed.

"You're welcome—just helping with the visuals."

"If the water techs taking samples from the spring got close to the mouth or the boil, they might find what Gideon knows—water of unparallel healing potential. However, they may not know, like most things in life, that it has an expiration date."

***

A half hour later, I met with two deputies who'd been dispatched to investigate my call. I used my remote control to open the gate and approached them as they stopped their cruiser near my home. One deputy was a woman with reddish hair worn up, pastel skin like candle wax, and black dots in her earlobes where earrings were removed. No makeup. Her partner was a deputy with the body of a football linebacker—at least 225 pounds, a wide chest, and a dark face filled with wariness.

"Are you Mr. O'Brien?" asked the man.

"Yes. Thank you both for coming out here. You can call me Sean."

The female deputy pulled out a small notepad and a pen. "We were told there was a shooting at the end of your driveway. What happened, Mr. O'Brien?"

I gave them the details and added, "I was forced to return fire."

"Did your rounds strike anyone?"

"Maybe. It happened in seconds. The hitman was hanging out the passenger-side window and firing an AR-15 at me. I do know that I shot out their back window."

"Why would two guys in an SUV do a drive-by shooting at your house—at you?"

"Maybe they think I'm in their way."

"Why is that?" asked the man.

"I'm a PI investigating a murder. A body was left on an elderly man's land back in the woods. His name is Gideon Wright. He's my client. I've tried to work with Detective Lofton in your homicide division."

"Both deputies exchanged glances. The man nodded. "We're familiar with that case."

I said nothing.

The female deputy pursed her thin lips. "You said you *tried* to work with Detective Lofton. What do you mean by that?"

"I've given him leads that I've found. I'm hoping that he and his partner, Detective Ortega, find that information valuable."

"Did anyone witness the incident at the end of your driveway?"

"Only the two guys trying to put a bullet in my head. My wife and daughter heard the gunfire."

"Do you have a gun carry permit?"

"Yes." I'd anticipated that question and had removed my permit card from my wallet and placed it in my shirt pocket. I reached in and gave the card to them.

The man looked at it for a second. "Where's the gun you used?"

"It's above my left ankle. Would you like for me to pull up my pant leg and hand the Beretta to you?

"No. Lift your pants, and I'll get it."

"No problem." I did as he requested. He removed it from my holster, took a cursory look, checking the clip, and put the gun back. I lowered my pant leg. "It holds six rounds. None left."

"I see that."

"Is there anything else I can help you with, deputies?"

The man shook his head. "We'll stop at the end of your driveway and canvas the immediate area to see if we can spot blood. We noticed pieces of broken glass on the road."

"You'll probably notice the tire tread impressions in the dirt near my shot-out mailbox. They are the same tracks in the photos that I gave to Detectives Lofton and Ortega. You're welcome to take pictures and add them to his collection."

"Without pouring casts, how can you be sure the tire marks are the same?"

"Because the close-up photos of the tread easily match the details in the photo that I took of the tire tracks in the mud on Gideon Wright's land. Same tires, probably the same car. And now for the same reason … murder."

"Anything else you'd like to add, Mr. O'Brien?" asked the female detective.

"My wife and daughter are inside this home. I protected them from whoever was shooting out of that vehicle. Had those men come through the gate and down to my house, you'd be here with the coroner and two body bags. You can add that to your notes."

The female deputy looked up at me, not sure what to say, almost like she was watching a gnat between my face and hers. She cleared her throat. "Thank you, Mr. O'Brien."

The male deputy nodded, tilting his head slightly in the late morning sun as it peered through the oaks. As he started for his cruiser, he turned back to me. "It's one thing to be a PI. It's another thing to be a vigilante. Hope you know the difference."

I said nothing.

FIFTY-EIGHT

Gideon was listening to the buzz of bees when he heard the barking of a dog. He was tending the beehives behind his home. Except for a long-sleeved shirt, he wore no protective clothing. No beekeeper's veiled hat, no hazmat-like suit. The bees flew around him. Some crawled over his hands. None stung him. He spoke to them like he was speaking to a group of people.

"You guys and gals work so darn hard. I'm thankful that you share your honey with me. I promise not to take too much. Just enough to fill a few jars for me and some of my friends at the senior care facility."

As he was removing the top off the bee box or hive, movement to his far left got his attention. He stopped and stood erect. Four deputies in uniform and one German shepherd dog were coming his way. When they got within fifty feet, they came to a halt. "Mr. Wright," said the deputy holding the dog's leash.

"Yes?"

"We're continuing our search of your property in reference to the body we recently found." The deputy looked at the taller officer. "Larry, why don't you give Mr. Wright a copy of the warrant?"

"Okay." He started to walk closer to Gideon but stopped after twenty feet. "Sir, you have an open beehive, and bees are flying all around you."

Gideon nodded. "That's what generally happens when I take the top off a hive."

"Why aren't they stinging you?"

"Because they don't perceive me as a threat."

"Would you walk this way? I'd rather not get stung. I'm allergic to bee stings."

"I'll do that after I put the roof back on the hive." He put the top on the vertical wooden structure and walked toward the deputy. Gideon reached out and looked at the copy of the search warrant. It was the same one that had been presented earlier. "You folks have been here searching. You didn't find anything then. May I ask why you fellas are back here?"

The deputy standing next to him answered. "Because we have a dog, one trained for different search techniques, and we have a reason to continue the search."

"Where would you like to look?"

"We'll start in the barn and then go back to the area where we found the body."

"Okay. I was about to go into the barn to spin some honey from the bee frames."

"Give us a few minutes. This dog doesn't take long."

The deputies didn't wait for Gideon to respond. They turned and headed toward the barn a hundred feet away. Gideon walked across the yard to the massive live oak. He sat on the wrought-iron bench. A breeze moved through the limbs and leaves, the gray beards of moss swaying like pendulums on grandfather clocks. He leaned back, resting his head on the tree's trunk, looking up into the gnarled limbs. "Hello, Seth. As you can see, we have visitors. I often wonder what and who you've seen walking this land. When the Spanish came through here, were you just a young oak? When the last Timucuan vanished, did you see that? When our ancestors fought on this hallowed ground during the Civil War, did you witness the bloodshed? What have we learned in the centuries that you've stood here?"

There was a rustle in the branches. A squirrel came down the trunk, scampering to the ground. The squirrel leaned back on its hind legs, staring at Gideon. "Hello, my friend. Let me see if I happen to have a treat." He reached in his pocket and took out a shelled peanut. Gideon held the peanut in his outstretched hand. The squirrel hopped over to him, taking the nut in its mouth and climbing back up into the boughs of the tree.

Seconds later, shards of peanut shell fell like confetti through the limbs. Gideon held out his hands, palms up, smiling as the bits of the peanut casing dusted his hands and shoulders.

***

Inside the barn, the deputies stood near the wide-open front entrance. The canine handler unclipped the dog's leash. "Okay, Rex, the place is all ours. Get at it." The dog moved through the barn, stopping to sniff hidden odors, doing so more than a dozen times as the animal worked its way in and out of the many nooks and crannies.

The deputy looked at his partners. "If there's the slightest hint of blood, Rex will smell it unless it's bagged and buried under ten feet of dirt."

One of the deputies nodded, his gaze scanning the barn, sunlight filtering through the cracks and worn knotholes. "Man, this place feels like it was built a hundred years ago. That steel sickle on the wall looks like something farmers used in the late 1800s."

A round-faced deputy shook his head. "That's more like the kind of tool the Grim Reaper carries. I think it's called a scythe. If we find a dark hooded cape in here, we need to put the cuffs on that old man." He feigned a chuckle. No one laughed.

The dog vanished to the back side of one of the three horse stalls, barking twice. The canine handler pointed. "Rex found something." The deputies followed his lead as he turned on a flashlight, walking toward where the dog stared up at more than a dozen tools on a rough-hewn wall. The dog snorted, looked down at the tools, and was eyeing a shovel in one corner, not looking away as his handler and the others came up to him. "Whatcha got, Rex?"

"He's staring at that shovel," said one of the deputies.

The handler nodded. He stepped closer, using his flashlight. He stopped moving the beam when he spotted a tiny, dark stain on the blade. "Take a look. I'd bet that's dried blood."

"Let's bag it," said another deputy, putting on latex gloves. "Why would the old man bring it back in here if it's something that was used to crack a man in the head? Why not toss it in the swamp or the river?"

"Maybe he ought to have hung it up next to that old sickle," said the canine handler. "Let's take it to the lab. In the meantime, we'll lead Rex back to the burial site to see if he can find anything else."

***

From where Gideon sat under the old tree, he could see the deputies and the dog leaving the barn, heading for the woods in the west. One of the deputies was carrying something in a paper bag, the kind of bag often used at grocery stores. A wooden handle protruded from the bag. Gideon knew they'd found something—a tool. Had someone entered his barn that night, when Darnell Reid was killed and buried? If so, what had they left?

He put on his bifocals, taking his phone from his denim overall pockets. He called Margaux.

"Hey, Grandpa. Are you okay?"

"I'm fine. Some more deputies from the sheriff's office came back here with another dog, and they just looked inside my barn. Now they're heading to the back section of the property where they found the body."

"What did you say to them?"

"Not much. I was tending my bees, getting ready to spin some honey, as they approached me. When they left the barn just now, they were carrying something in a paper bag."

"That's often used in the field as an evidence bag."

"It looked like it was covering a tool, maybe a shovel, since a wooden handle was sticking out of the bag. If they found something linked to the murder, somebody put it there."

"I'm leaving New Smyrna. I'll be there within the hour. Don't agree to be questioned anymore until I get there."

FIFTY-NINE

Floyd Shaw was used to seeing death, but he was not used to carrying a dead body in the front seat of his SUV. As he drove southwest on a county backroad, he glanced over at Jack Rizzo's body. The round from the pistol had gone through Rizzo's left eye, exiting at the back of the head. The body was slumped against the dashboard, with blood spattering over the seat, dashboard, and windshield.

Shaw scanned the countryside, searching for someplace to pull into and dump the body. Perhaps a remote lake or deep in the woods. He fumbled for his phone and made a call. When it was answered, he said, "Shit's hitting the fan!"

"How?"

"I got a dead body in my car. Jack's been shot in the head. Somehow, that guy, O'Brien, made a shot with his pistol from a good distance during our drive-by. We were in a speeding SUV. He did it after we drove past his place, Jack firing out the window. O'Brien made a shot that very few people could make. Trust me on that. Who the hell is he?"

"He's a problem."

"Man, I gotta dump the body—gotta lot a blood in my Ford."

"Where are you?"

Shaw looked at the GPS map on the screen built into his dash console. "County Road 445, heading southwest. Plenty of woods on both sides of the road. I see a lake a little further south, Lake Dorr. It's probably full of big gators. All I gotta do is drag the body to the water in a remote part and drop it in the lake."

"Wait a minute. Just think. Somebody—a fisherman, game warden, whoever—might see you at that lake. It's too risky. Also, blood from the body can be traced to your vehicle. You told me that you live in a rural area of Hillsborough. No neighbors, right? You have a storage shed, correct?"

"Yeah. The place I own is on three acres. The doublewide is in the center. It's private."

"Go there. Take the body out of your vehicle. Stash it in the shed. Take your car to a carwash, a place where you can do it yourself. Clean out the blood. Do you have leather seats in your vehicle?"

"Yes."

"Use lukewarm water and a soap like Dawn. You can mix a touch of ammonia, too."

"How about the body? I can't leave it in the shed very long."

"Leave the shed unlocked. I have cleaners. They'll come pick up the body tonight."

"What the hell will they do with it?"

"If you don't know, you can never say in case you're ever questioned. Let's just put it this way: sharks are more effective than alligators in terms of body disposal."

"Wicked. Are you sure you were never a lawyer for the mob?"

"They'll be at your place tonight. Come nightfall, leave the shed unlocked so they can remove the body. Understand?"

"I'm not stupid. Hell, yeah, I understand. If they aren't here tonight, I know a gator hole in Hillsborough County where I'll take it. I ain't gotta boat to go drop shit in the ocean."

***

I wanted to be at Floyd Shaw's house under the cover of darkness. Before leaving my house, I studied satellite maps of the house and property. I looked at ground-level maps, reviewing the topography and the nearest homes or buildings to where I believed Floyd Shaw lived. I was relying on the property records that Dave Collins found. I was in my home office, preparing for the clandestine trip. I had no idea whether Shaw would be there. But, based on the maps I studied, I knew how to approach his place in the country.

I pulled out my 12-gauge Mossberg tactical shotgun from where I keep some of my weapons locked in the office. I loaded it along with my Glock and the Beretta. I assumed it would be Floyd Shaw at home alone, but I wanted to be prepared should he be there with like-minded criminals. Never go to a knife fight with only a knife.

From the kitchen, I could hear Wynona and Angela talking and laughing. Max chimed in, barking twice. Wynona had packed some clothes for them to take to the boat. I had enough clean clothes on *Jupiter* to get by for a few days.

A text came through on my phone. It was from Margaux. She wrote: *Deputies and a canine are back at Gideon's home. They've searched his barn and are now heading to where the body was discovered. I'm driving to Gideon's home to help him.*

I looked up at my whiteboard above my desk, staring at her picture. As I started to return her text, my phone buzzed. Dave was calling. I answered, and he said, "I received the results back from the DNA tests on Gideon Wright and Margaux Brennon."

"Great. Do I have to guess the results, or are you in a sharing mood?"

SIXTY

I stood from behind my desk, reaching up to the whiteboard, staring at the photos of Gideon and Margaux as if they were about to speak. I looked closely at the motionless images, which looked back at me with a resemblance that is not as apparent in person. Between Gideon's age, his full beard, and Margaux's animated style of speaking, often using her hands, the similarity in their eyes is much more obvious in side-by-side photos.

"Sean, are you there?" Dave asked.

"Yes. I am at the whiteboard in my home office, planning my approach to Floyd Shaw's trailer, and looking at pictures of the known players."

He chuckled. "Your initial deduction was accurate. Gideon and Margaux are most definitely related. From what you told me, he'll be happy to know he does have a great-granddaughter."

"She'll be excited, too." I stared at the two pictures of Gideon and Margaux. "Thanks, Dave. I'll let them know. Although, in my heart, I believe they already do. But the confirmation will give Gideon peace of mind should he be thinking about leaving the land and spring to her. She is his legitimate heir. What he chooses to do will be up to him."

"What's the status of your investigation? Have the police made any arrests?"

"No. Margaux just texted me. She said that deputies and a canine are back on Gideon's land for a second search."

"They usually don't do that unless there is a compelling reason."

"A body was planted there. Maybe something else was as well. Police are searching Gideon's property while hit men are trying to kill me."

"Okay, I'm sitting in *Gibraltar's* salon, sipping Greek coffee that Nick ground for me, and waiting for an explanation. What the hell happened?"

I told Dave and added, "I'm going to find Floyd Shaw tonight, or at least I'm going to the residence you found. Let's hope he's home."

"You think you killed the shooter?"

"Probably. If so, Shaw most likely dumped the body somewhere not too far from the scene and then sped away. I gave the deputies all the details and suggested that they let Detectives Lofton and Ortega know just in case they were keeping score."

Dave chuckled. "Based on what you've told me, it's apparent that the rep from Glacier Artesian Springs, Roger Heller, is playing in the same sandbox as the lawyer, Percy King. Do you think there's an implied consent from the company, as part of King's retainer, to hire a hit man— sort of the unwritten terms of the contract?"

"Maybe, considering the potential profit margins. Right now, as far as we know, two crimes have been committed. The killing of Darnell Reid and the attempted murder of me. I think my meeting with King was the leverage behind the shots fired at my head. To prove it, I need to find my would-be assassins—or the lone assassin, since one is probably dead. The driver, Floyd Shaw, could be so shaken up after pulling the body back inside his SUV that he's renegotiating his contract with King, if in fact, that attorney hired him."

"I've spent a little more time studying Roger Heller's track record."

"What'd you find?"

"He enters new territory like he's rehearsed chapters from the book, *The Art of War.*"

"How's that?"

"In a small town northeast of Nashville, Heller was trying to sway a county commission to go along with the water district's recommendation to allow Glacier Artesian Springs exclusive pumping rights to a lovely spring that's within a county park. There was some very vocal opposition. More than fifty protestors. Heller hired bodyguards or mercenaries, the latter being the more accurate term. Four ex-military personnel, locked and loaded. They attended every public hearing. In one case, they pushed a half dozen mom and pop demonstrators to the ground as Heller was escorted to his chauffeur-driven car."

"It almost sounds like someone is hiring muscle to handle labor union disagreements."

"The bottom line is that Heller can find and pay people to do his bidding. But that doesn't mean he hired those guys to kill you, and it doesn't mean he'd harm Margaux should he be unable to buy her out if she inherits everything. However, he is used to going into towns with pockets full of cash to buy politicians and people on water district boards or to do whatever it takes to open the tap on millions of dollars in profits from natural spring water. There aren't that many of these springs left, and one like Gideon's could be Heller's crown jewel if he can get it."

"I look forward to meeting him."

"I bet you do. I know that before you meet him, you'll have evidence to leverage against him if Heller is indeed the man behind the curtain pulling the strings."

"I'd like to see if he knows Floyd Shaw."

"Sean, I know you have no plans to tell the police that you are hunting for Floyd Shaw. He seems like a bit player to them and is off their radar. Just do me, your friend on the sidelines, a favor when you leave Shaw's place. Text me so that I know everything is fine because it sounds like the excrement is about to hit the fan."

"Yeah, it is. Wynona and Angela will be staying on *Jupiter* for a few days. I'll join them when I can. Please let Nick know they'll be at the marina. Between you two, there is no other neighborhood watch that is more secure. Thanks, Dave." I clicked off.

I didn't know the name of the man I thought I'd shot in the SUV. But I would remember his face if I ever saw it again, dead or alive. I looked at the pictures of Roger Heller, Darnell Reid, Clifton Price, Percy King, and Floyd Shaw. I was hoping that Shaw, after our chat, would be amenable to pointing me toward the person who hired him. I thought it was King, but who hired King and for how much? Was it Heller or one of the internal corporate attorneys employed by Glacier Artesian Springs and taking orders from the top, CEO Clifton Price?

I looked at the pictures of Margaux and Gideon. The color of the irises was identical, a bluish-green hazel. If the eyes are the windows to the soul, there was a connection in the perception of the moment that was shared by Gideon and Margaux. They both looked back at you with an intelligence that seemed to absorb the molecules in the air. In Margaux's eyes, there was a controlled astuteness that waited for the next move on the chess board. In Gideon, understanding could be seen in his eyes, and he viewed something or someone with a gentle acceptance rather than harsh judgment. He was truly an old soul, and, like a chip off the old block, Margaux seemed wiser than her years.

As I looked into their eyes, my phone buzzed. It was Margaux calling. I answered, and she said, "Sean, I wanted to give you an update on what's happening to my grandfather."

"Okay."

"The deputies found a shovel in Gideon's barn with what appeared to be blood stains on part of it. Nothing more than a few specks, but that's what their dog allegedly discovered. Their forensics lab will run tests on the blood. If the planting of the body on his land wasn't enough, someone has placed fake evidence inside Gideon's barn in a further attempt to frame him."

"Is it Gideon's shovel?"

"Yes."

"And probably the one I found not hanging up with the rest of the tools, but rather in a corner by itself. The killers used it, leaving the prop in the barn for police to eventually find. That does not mean Gideon used it to kill Reid."

"I know that, but it gives a prosecutor what appears to be additional physical evidence. Investigators need to look at it as a planted smoking gun rather than the real thing. But will they?"

"I'm not going to wait to see how they answer that question." I gave Margaux a quick rundown of what happened at the end of my driveway and added, "I want to track down Floyd Shaw to see why he and his pal wanted to take my head off. Maybe they left the shovel in the barn. If I wait until the police get around to asking him, Gideon will be facing murder charges."

"No doubt."

I could hear birdsong in the background. "Are you on Gideon's porch?"

"How'd you know? Gideon's out here with me. Would you like to speak with him?"

"I want to speak with both of you. I'd tell you over the phone, but this information needs to be delivered in person. If the deputies are still there when I arrive, I have a question for them."

SIXTY-ONE

Floyd Shaw had a plan B. If Percy King's "cleaners" didn't show up and take care of the disposal job, he'd do it at first light, driving fifty miles north to the Green Swamp Preserve, down Hog Back Road to a hidden lake. He'd fished the lake last summer and saw more gators on the shore and in the water than any place he'd been in Florida. The gators would take Rizzo's body down into a muddy hole and tear it apart. Catfish would pick up the pieces.

Shaw drove his SUV slowly down the rutted dirt driveway that led from the county road to his double-wide mobile home. *Mobile* was not the case, he thought. The trailer hadn't moved in twenty-two years. He parked near the shed in his back yard, got out, and looked around. There was no sign of another human being for miles. Shaw unlocked the shed door before dragging Rizzo's body from the vehicle and placing it inside the shed. He lowered the body in the center, next to a push lawnmower and a wall full of hand tools.

A blowfly followed Shaw, alighting on Rizzo's bloodied face. Although Shaw had seen death many times and caused it a few times, he never liked to look at their dead faces, especially if it was someone he knew. That was what he'd remember on those lonely nights when he would curl up with a bottle of Jack, feel the liquor seep into his pores, and drift away to the edge of false validation or nightmares. The morning light always delivered the harsh reality of consequences. It was during these times that he realized vengeance literally would be hell.

"Screw it and judgment day," he mumbled, pulling a crinkled blue tarp from one corner of the shed and lying it over the body, now stiff from rigor mortis. The blowfly buzzed from somewhere under the tarp.

Shaw left, closing the shed door behind him, remembering what King had said. *Leave the shed unlocked. I have cleaners. They'll come pick up the body tonight.*

He opened the door to his SUV, lowered the driver's side visor, and picked up two hand-rolled joints. The weed was called Purple Haze; it was his favorite brand, sold at a medical marijuana store in a strip mall next to a vitamin shop.

Shaw walked toward his trailer, lit a joint, and inhaled the thick smoke deep into his lungs. He exhaled and sat on one of the wooden steps leading up to his small porch. He took a second hit, and after eight seconds, his mouth, forming an O, puffed a creamy smoke ring in front of his face.

A pumpkin orange and black cat came out from beneath the porch carrying a mouse in its mouth. The cat stopped a few feet in front of Shaw, setting the mouse on the ground. The mouse was lying on its back, trembling paws, blood oozing from the chewed neck.

***

When I arrived at Gideon's home, two sheriff's cruisers and a canine unit were leaving. I waited in my Jeep at the open gate as they drove off the property and down the road. I pulled in, stopping to lock the gate before driving up to Gideon's cabin. I spotted Margaux's car next to Gideon's Land Rover. They waved from his front porch as I parked and approached them.

Gideon smiled. "Hey, Sean, would you like some sweet tea, coffee, or water?"

"I may take a bottle of water for the road. I never know when I might get a scratch or two and need something to help it heal." I climbed the steps to the porch.

Gideon cleared his throat. "Margaux told me what happened to you at the end of your driveway. I thank God that you're alive. Do you know who did it or who's behind it?"

"It's probably two different people or sets of people. I believe the stalker from the farmers' market, Floyd Shaw, was driving. I don't know who the guy hanging out the passenger-side window is or was. I returned fire."

No one spoke for a long moment. The only sound was from the breeze tinkling the windchimes hanging from one of the eaves on the porch. Margaux smiled. "Sean, I told Gideon what you mentioned on the phone—that you had information for us. Thank you for coming out here to deliver it. I hope it's not a good news or bad news scenario."

"It could be, depending on how these events shake out. Before I get to that, did the deputies find anything more than what you told me?"

Margaux shook her head. "No. Just the shovel. They didn't have much to say. You said that you had a question for them. What was it?"

"I wanted to know if the shovel was in plain sight, easy to find, or was it hidden? Did the dog have to work to find it?"

"We don't know."

"If they expedite the lab work, since they already have blood from the body, they can know very quickly if it's a match. Because the shovel is Gideon's, his prints may or may not be on it. They cannot prove Gideon had any connection except for the fact he owns it, just like dozens of other tools in his barn."

Gideon didn't respond. He stared at the old oak, his wind chimes barely tinkling. I looked at him. "Here's the good news. Speaking of blood work, the DNA results are back. Gideon, you and Margaux are very much related, as in great-granddaughter and great-grandfather. Congratulations."

Margaux clasped her hands together, her eyes watering. Gideon smiled. "I knew it all along. Give me a hug, grandkid." They stood and embraced, Gideon patting Margaux gently on the back.

When they parted, Margaux opened her purse, took out a tissue, and dabbed tears from under her eyes. "This is a day I will never forget. It's not often that a girl can find her long-lost great-grandfather. And I got lucky because my grandpa is a sweet and loving man."

Gideon grinned. "Aw, shucks. Don't make me blush, kiddo." He looked over at me. "Thank you, Sean, for working the science to corroborate what I felt in my heart."

"You're welcome."

Margaux smiled. "I feel the same way." She looked from me to Gideon. "After spending our first half hour together, I somehow knew in my heart that you were my great-grandfather. From this moment forward, unless I'm in a formal situation, I will call you Grandpa because that is who you are."

"And you are my granddaughter. Let's just remove the word *great* in front of it because it's a tad long. But getting to know you, Margaux, I believe that you are great because you are a woman of noble character."

"Don't make me cry again." She took a deep breath and looked up at me. "Sean, when I asked you if it's a good-news-bad-news scenario, you said it depends on how events shake out. You gave us the good news. What might the bad news be or become?"

A phone vibrated on the table in front of their chairs. I recognized the number because I had dialed it when I first called Percy King's office.

SIXTY-TWO

Gideon put on his bifocals, but I still could read his eyes as he looked at the phone screen. He displayed no reaction to the incoming call. "It's Percy King. Why would he be calling me?"

Margaux gestured to the phone. "The only way to find out is to answer it. Please put the call on speaker, okay?"

"Okay." He pressed the speakerphone button and answered. "Hello."

"Gideon, it's Percy."

"Hello, Percy."

"Over coffee at the café this morning, I was thinking about our last conversation. I don't blame you for wanting to have the lady lawyer work with you. If she's kinfolk, and that's a big if, considering her showing up out of the blue and from a place like Seattle. Folks there don't share our southern values 'cause they never had them in the first place."

As King spoke, I looked at Margaux. She kept her composure and was silent. King continued. "I was thinking about what the fella from New York City said to you that day in the Wagon Wheel."

"What about it, Percy?" Gideon's voice had a straightforward tone.

"Well, I think, with the right representation on your side, someone like me who has a successful track record of working between landowners, environmentalists, and big corporations, we could come up with a win-win deal."

"What do you mean?"

"I have a gut feeling that Mr. Heller has been authorized to offer you an extraordinary amount of money. But only if you have a seasoned, experienced lawyer, which is me, workin' like a bulldog on your behalf. Should you be indicted in this god-awful mess, you're gonna need a boatload of money to hire a hell of a defense team."

"I don't think it will come to that."

"That's where you're wrong. I got my ear to the legal machine in the tri-county area. They're coming for you, Gideon. No disrespect to the lady lawyer. I can be the quarterback and put together a top-notch defense team from Orlando that will keep you out of prison. I'd start with Robert Jenson. He defended Carolyn Lewis in the double murder trial of her ex-husband and his whore, the stripper. Robert convinced the jury that it was self-defense. Carolyn is back home with her babies. This isn't Seattle. You're gonna need me and what I can offer you."

"Thank you, Percy, but no thanks. At this point, there is no reason to continue communication with you. I appreciate your offer, but not this time because …."

"Gideon, sir. Please listen to me. You're gonna be arrested. That lady lawyer who mysteriously appeared in your life is bad news; she is pure evil. Mark my words. She's after your land and spring." As he continued berating Margaux, she motioned to Gideon to hand her the phone.

"Mr. King, this is that evil lady lawyer, Margaux Brennon. I'm tired of your impotent assertions that I somehow dropped into Gideon's life. We have irrefutable DNA proof that we are blood related. Gideon is my great-grandfather. We *are* family, and family sticks together. I will represent my grandfather in all legal matters. You need to understand that. If you continue to bother my grandfather, I will file harassment, stalking, and elder abuse charges against you. This, in front of witnesses, Sean O'Brien and Gideon Wright, is an oral demand for you to cease and desist all contact with Mr. Wright. Do you understand?"

"I didn't know we had an audience." King's voice changed to a mock sweetness flavored with the sour edge of disdain. "I understand more than you realize. However, for the record, your message is clear, Ms. Brennon. I will stop all congenial efforts to help a gentle old man enjoy his life free from the iron constraints of prison. Have a good day, y'all." He clicked off.

Gideon made a low chuckle. "I wish Percy King well."

Margaux leaned forward in her chair. "I hope you're okay with what I said to him."

"Yes. It needed to be said."

Margaux looked up at me. "Sean, before we were interrupted, you mentioned bad news in the good news and bad news situation."

I said nothing for a moment, listening to the sound of an acorn falling from the old oak and rolling down the cabin's tin roof. "The good news is what already exists. For example, the fact that you two are family, all the family that you have left on earth. That news isn't bad until something happens to make it that way or to start the process. In your case, bad things are shifting and attempting to gain traction. I'm trying hard to keep the moving tectonic plates from becoming an earthquake. Margaux, because you're Gideon's granddaughter, it could accelerate the seismic shift. In addition to Gideon, that puts you in danger. Do you know how to use a gun?"

SIXTY-THREE

Wynona stood behind the counter of her antique store, opened a drawer, and stared at the Ruger .380 pistol in a leather holster mounted to the inside of the drawer. It was closing time, and two female customers were still browsing the antiques. Max napped on a soft cushion behind the counter, near the cash register. Angela was in the back office, playing with one of her favorite dolls. Piano music came from a Victrola record player in the corner.

The women approached the register, one carrying a vintage book, the other with a small, framed painting of a sunrise over mountains. The customer carrying the book, a tall woman with blond hair that shined under the store lights, set her new treasure on the counter. "I'm so glad I found this book. It's Great Expectations by Charles Dickens. This was one of my mother's favorite novels. This book looks very old."

Wynona picked up the book. "It is old. This edition was printed a few years after the Civil War. The cover, spine, and pages are in remarkable shape."

"Yes, they are. It's so hard to find a copy like this. Where'd you get it?"

"From an estate sale."

"I love the story because it deals with something close to my heart: orphans. I was adopted as a little girl. I could relate to Pip in the story. He was a survivor, and he was kind."

"Yes, he was." Wynona rang up the sale. "Not only is it an excellent coming of age story, but the book also addressed social issues in England at the time, such as the class system and human worth." She chatted with the second woman as Wynona finished the sale of the small painting.

When the women were leaving, Angela came out of the back office, approaching the counter. "Mama, can I have a snack?"

"It's getting too close to dinner."

The woman with the book smiled. "Your daughter is beautiful. What's your name?"

"Angela."

"I like your dress, Angela."

"Thank you."

As the women left the store, Wynona walked to the front door, flipped the sign from *Open* to *Closed,* and locked the door. She looked through the glass window, spotting a man in a pickup truck parked next to the curb across the street. When Wynona stared at him, he turned his head. She went back behind the counter, where Max, now awake, was wagging her tail.

"Max, are you ready to call it a day?"

She barked once.

Wynona removed the cash, checks, and credit card receipts from the register and secured everything in the office safe. When she returned to the store area, she noticed a man standing outside the door, fidgeting with the door handle. Although he was there for only a few seconds, Wynona thought he was the man she'd seen in the truck.

"Angela, you and Max come back from the front door."

"I thought we were leaving, Mama."

"We are, but in just a minute." She walked behind the counter, taking the pistol from the drawer and placing it in her purse. When she moved back to the front door, the truck was leaving. Wynona could make out two bumper stickers on the rear-left side. One was an image of a great white shark in the colors of the American flag. The other was a cartoonish-looking shrimp with raised fists and barred teeth. She barely made out the two words below it: *Bubba Grumps.* Wynona glanced back at Angela. "Let's put Max on her leash."

"I can do it." Angela took the leash and fastened it to Max's collar. "Okay, we're ready."

"How would you like to spend a few nights on our boat at the marina?"

Angela grinned. "Yippee! Will Dave and Nick be there?"

"Dave will. Nick might be fishing in the ocean."

"Let's go see."

"Okay. Where's Daddy?"

"He'll meet us here." Wynona stopped at the front door. She looked outside again. The truck was gone and hadn't returned, but the memory of the scruffy man standing outside the store's locked door was fresh.

SIXTY-FOUR

Margaux rummaged through her purse for something. Seconds later, she removed a laminated card and smiled. "Not only can I handle a gun, but I also can legally carry one. I got a permit after living in Seattle. Crime's out of control. My Sig pistol is back in my condo."

I nodded, and Gideon smiled. Margaux continued, "Sean, I know what you're saying. Percy King's veiled threat is an example. I just wonder why he'd call Gideon, trying to put together a deal and hire a legal team. If he's part of those who hired hit men to target you, why is he coming back with alternate moves?"

"Because that's what he does. Gideon, you saw it when King overheard your conversation with Roger Heller in the Wagon Wheel. As King was drawing up an agreement for you to sign, he was soliciting Heller and those he represents. King figures out all the angles and tries to be two checkers moves ahead of everyone. But his poker-faced, banal transparency ends at his dark heart."

"What can you do, Sean?" Gideon asked.

"I stay as proactive as possible. As a PI, I walk a tightrope over traditional law enforcement. They are, by the definition of the word *investigator*, examining a crime. I try to prevent it from expanding. Margaux, as Gideon's granddaughter, you will be perceived as a roadblock to this land and its spring falling into the greedy corporate hands of an international company. That means you may have stepped into someone's crosshairs. If they think I'm in their way, imagine what they might do to you as his only possible heir."

She looked from Gideon to me. "I've had challenging and even dangerous cases in my legal career. I try not to worry about the what-ifs and focus on how to get results for my clients who usually are legitimate victims."

245

I nodded. "But it's hard to be a director and actor. That is, you may lose sight of helping Gideon while defending yourself."

"What are you suggesting?"

"Nothing. What I am saying is that, unlike most cases, any nefarious activity could be happening in *real time* to you and Gideon simultaneously. So, your greatest defense might be staying alive."

Gideon shook his head. "I don't like the sound of that. Do you really think these people would go that far, Sean? I can't risk losing my granddaughter, whom I've come to know and care about."

"I understand. If those responsible for killing Reid and trying to shoot me can hide behind untraceable layers of complicity, the answer is yes."

Gideon sipped water from a glass canning jar. "I've been all around the world and always have felt that most people are basically good. They try to do what's right. But I've seen the other side, too. Situations so heinous that you walk away feeling the need to take a shower because you know some of the evil was slung on you like a dog shaking dirty water out of its fur."

I glanced at my watch. "I need to be going."

Gideon stood. "Before you go, let me give you some more water and honey." He left.

Margaux said, "Thank you for being so proactive, Sean. Most private investigators I've met work cases involving spousal infidelity or business fraud. You, though, dive into the hard stuff. And you do more than that, you try to contain the crime if you can. I know that must be very difficult, because once the genie is out of the bottle, it's hard to put him back. You have to catch him first. How do you find cases or clients?"

"They find me, mostly word of mouth. I only take a few cases each year. Those that are unique and hard to solve. Sometimes it's cold cases, and sometimes it's situations like Gideon's—someone trying hard to do the right thing and help others while fending off predators. When Gideon told me his story and asked for assistance, I couldn't walk away. I've always felt a personal obligation to help people if I can."

"Your wife must be very proud of you. But I'd guess you're fearful for your family."

"It's an ongoing balance. My wife is a former FBI agent. So, she is acutely aware of the dangers I frequently face in the field. I don't work a lot of cases."

"But the ones you do work on seem to be the most dangerous."

Gideon returned with two bottles of water and a jar of honey. "Sean, take these to Wynona and Angela. The best potential from the water is good for seven days. The honey is good for a lot longer."

"Thank you. I'll see them later in the day before I leave for the night shift."

"We know you're hunting for the men who tried to kill you. When I saw you and your family at the farmers' market that day, when you first spotted the man with the camera, I had no idea what would occur after that. That's where this thing started. Hopefully, with him is where it'll end."

"Maybe." I smiled and left, driving past the massive oak and the spring toward the gate. I didn't want to sugarcoat Gideon's illusion. But I knew this situation wouldn't change when I found and interrogated Floyd Shaw. He was a cog, a dangerous cog, but one in a machine with deep pockets and roots that reached into an old man's waterhole for its soul.

On the way to Ponce Marina, Wynona called my phone. Her voice sounded anxious. "Something odd happened at the store today."

"What was that?"

"As I was closing, I glanced out the front window and spotted a man in a pickup truck parked across the street. At first, I thought he was waiting for someone, but he didn't look like a man who had a wife or girlfriend shopping for antiques. After I locked the door and was coming back from putting the cash drawer in the safe, he was standing at the door rattling the handle. He peered inside, then left. I don't want to sound judgmental, but he looked like he had been living out in the woods for a couple of weeks."

"What kind of truck?"

"I believe it was a Ford. Black. It looked at least ten years old. Oh, something else. As he was leaving, I could see the rear of the truck. The license plate was muddy. I only could make out the first two letters: L and D. The truck had two bumper stickers. One was of a cartoon shrimp with its fists raised, teeth bared, and an angry expression. The caption read: *Bubba Grumps*. The other sticker depicted a great white shark, grinning, with its body painted in the colors of the American flag."

I couldn't help but think of Percy King—the man with the toothy shark's grin swimming toward you.

SIXTY-FIVE

The evening sky was streaked in shades of deep purple and mauve, and the clouds in the west were backlit with an orange tinge of sun flare as twilight crept over Ponce Marina. I stood at the end of L dock, watching the weather and plotting my night attack on a man who had crossed my path twice. The first time was with a camera. The second time was with a rifle.

There would not be a third time.

I had no intention of killing Floyd Shaw. But after our chat, I felt certain that he'd say enough to give police reason for a follow-up arrest. Or he would vanish into the night and head for another state. I hoped he'd want to cut a deal with a prosecutor, putting the cards on the table—the faces and names of the people who hired him. After our conversation, he might be in a more receptive mood to negotiate.

Maybe not.

He could try responding by putting a bullet through my head or a knife in my chest. I'd packed my Jeep with the guns I thought I'd need. I knew Shaw's address. He was about two hours away, his trailer isolated in a remote section of Hillsborough County. Tampa would be his closest large city. He could have taken his SUV into an auto body shop for repairs, but only after cleaning any blood from the front seat. Or he might be home, lying low, and waiting for his next order.

I walked back to *Jupiter,* hearing Angela in the boat's salon trying to teach Max a new trick. "Roll over, Max," she said. "You can do it." Angela held a dog treat in her hand, with Max patiently sitting and watching.

The boat still had the slight scent of garlic shrimp, a gift from Nick earlier in the day. Wynona came into the salon from the galley, carrying something in her hand. It was a small rubber bone, one that squeaked when squeezed. She looked at Angela and Max. "Since Max is a doxie, it's not easy for her to roll over because of her short legs and tootsie-roll back. But she loves to go fetch a new toy. I bought this one yesterday." She handed the toy to Angela. After a squeeze and a squeak, Max was primed.

Angela tossed the rubber bone across the salon. Max scrambled, retrieving it. The exchange was promptly made. Angela handed Max a treat. "Here you go, Tootsie Roll." Angela giggled. Max dropped her new toy, and Angela picked it up for round two.

I motioned for Wynona to join me in the cockpit. We stood near the transom, the marina drenched in a sepia tone that pulled the real colors from the sky, water, and even the boats. Even the air was heavy, as if it had a negative electric charge in the atmosphere. I felt like we were caught in a photo of yesteryear—a postcard from the past, framed by the reflective borders of hesitation because of what I was about to do.

Wynona looked up at me, her face pensive yet accepting. The warmth of her eyes cut through the colorless feel of an antique photo. She didn't have to ask, yet I could tell that she wanted words of assurance as I was leaving. She touched my forearm. A passing boat's wake slapped against the dock timbers. I could smell rain coming in from the west, promising an early morning shower.

I leaned down, cupping her face in my hands, kissing her. After a moment, she looked toward the revolving light from Ponce Lighthouse and then back at me. "The old lighthouse has saved a lot of mariners. Tonight, Sean, follow that light back to us."

"Leave a light on for me." I smiled and touched the tip of her nose.

"If I tell you to be careful, it has a hollow sound. Be who and what you always are: cautious, keenly alert, and vigilant. And be home as soon as you can."

"I should be home before dawn."

"Call me when you're headed back. I don't care what time it is."

"Okay."

She looked at the sky, charcoal clouds floating like giant jellyfish in the atmosphere.

I hugged her, the sound of a shrimp boat's diesel engines in the evening air as the boat headed from the marina toward Ponce Inlet. I walked back into the salon and kissed Angela on her forehead. "That's your goodnight kiss, pumpkin."

"But it's not my bedtime yet, Daddy."

"I know. I need to be gone for a little while, and I won't be here to give you your goodnight kiss at bedtime. So, I'm giving it to you a little early tonight, okay?"

"Okay."

"Max, you're now the watch dog."

**

As I walked by *Gibraltar*, I heard Dave's voice. "If you need an eye in the sky tonight, I can do that for you."

I stopped as he came down the port side gunwale to the bow. "I appreciate that, Dave. But I don't think I'll need any real-time satellite surveillance. Shaw is either there or he isn't. I hope to catch him after he's knocked back a shot or two of whiskey, maybe smoked some weed, or whatever he does after a gunfight."

"I'd bet he'll be alone since you think you may have tagged his passenger shooter."

"That guy could be alive. If not, maybe after our chat, Shaw will tell police where he dumped the body."

"Nick and I will take care of Angela and Wynona, although I'm certainly aware Wynona can take care of herself. I happen to know that when she graduated from Quantico, she was tops in her FBI class at the gun range."

"I'm not even going to ask how you know that."

"The real story is that she told me, but only after I asked last year when we were all having dinner." He chuckled. The dark clouds parted, and stars appeared like diamond flecks in the inky sky. "Just for grins, and because I enjoy living vicariously through your covert work, I might access a real-time satellite feed over the destination property."

"With a safety net like that, I might let my guard down and not be on my A-game."

"Hardly. I'll see you when you get back."

**

Two hours and twelve minutes later I was driving slowly up to a dirt road, which according to my digital maps was Blackwater Road. I turned.

It led down to the trailer owned by Floyd Shaw. I passed the rusted mailbox and noticed there was no name on it, only a house number: 97310. I drove another fifty feet before turning around. When I came back to the driveway entrance, I shut off the Jeep's headlights.

I turned into the dirt drive, lowering the Jeep's side front windows. In a nocturnal strike, when the visuals were at a minimum, all five senses were needed. Hearing was a big one, like radar. I drove a hundred feet, stopping and listening. Cicadas screamed from the slash pines and scrub oaks. I drove on, knowing that sometime tonight, my five senses wouldn't be enough.

I'd need a sixth sense. It was the one sense that had repeatedly saved my life.

SIXTY-SIX

When Wynona and Angela were returning from walking Max, they made an unscheduled stop along L dock. Nick, smoking a cigar in the open air of *St. Michael's* cockpit, said, "My favorite three ladies. Wynona, Angela, and my gal pal, lil' Max."

Angela grinned. "You always call her Hot Dawg. Mama called her a tootsie roll today."

Nick laughed. "Yup, she's the special pup. I was just about to head over to Dave's boat for a nightcap. Why don't y'all join us? I know Dave's got some Italian gelato—chocolate and vanilla."

Angela wrinkled her noise. "What's gelato?"

"It's like ice cream. I think it's better than ice cream."

She looked up at Wynona. "Mama, can we go?"

"Maybe we should ask Dave first."

"You never need to ask permission to board *Gibraltar*," Dave said, walking port side on the trawler toward the bow. "Wynona, I was just about to pull the cork on a fine Spanish cabernet. Let's have a glass. You two probably could use some company right about now. It was remiss of me not to have invited you over earlier. Some conversation and company may take your mind off life's what-ifs."

Wynona nodded, smiling. "Yes, we could use a little diversion."

"Come aboard."

Nick winked at Dave and said, "Angela's curious to know what gelato is."

"Well, Angela, I think we should go find out."

A few minutes later, three glasses of wine were poured, and Angela had a bowl of chocolate and vanilla gelato as they sat around the table in *Gibraltar's* salon, the doors open, the night sky clear and full of stars. Nick said, "Let's toast to this fine Florida evening and to when Sean will join us."

252

Dave lifted his glass. "I'll drink to that."

Wynona smiled and sipped her wine. "This is very good. Yes, Nick, it'll be nice when Sean can be with us in a casual setting. Unfortunately, that's not in the cards for the immediate future."

"Look!" Angela pointed up at the night sky. "It's a shooting star. Daddy said you can wish upon a shooting star, but you must be quick."

Nick chuckled. "Yep, you gotta have a fast reaction. Quick draw."

Angela nodded and put a spoonful of gelato in her mouth. Nick picked up Max and set her on his lap. She sat up like the boat's captain. Angela said, "Max loves you, Uncle Nick."

"That's 'cause she knows I'm a loveable guy. Hot Dawg is my lil' buddy."

"Am I your buddy, too?"

"Of course, you are."

As they chatted, Dave motioned for Wynona to join him on the aft deck. They walked toward the transom and stopped. Dave looked over at Wynona. "I can see the worry in your face. Sean's a survivor. He uses every tactical stealth concept in the book and then some that I believe he invented."

"I try hard not to worry. All my FBI training and experience in the field tells me what you just said is true. But, as his wife, I feel anxious until I hear his voice. Maybe nervous is a better word. Either way, I'm certainly concerned for his safety."

"You walk a fine line, never looking at what Sean does as routine investigative work while trying not to be the wife who bites her fingernails when he is on a surveillance operation."

"You're right. It's a difficult balance. I want to support Sean in his work, God knows he's good at it, but I don't want to feel like he's playing a deadly game of Russian roulette when he's out there in the dark. Absolute evil, the kind that Sean takes head-on, fights back very hard. He does what very few people do because not many have the intuitive instincts he has or gets when he probes a crime or even the potential of a crime. It's always a double-edged sword."

"I don't know if he learned a lot of that by surviving combat in the military or working as a homicide detective when he left the service. Maybe he was born with it."

"In my eight years with the Bureau, I never saw an agent work a case like he does. It's as if Sean enters the criminal mind. I'm not sure what mysterious portal he uses to go there."

"Life moves in cycles and patterns. He has an innate ability to recognize and quickly decipher patterns in the environment, people, their actions or inactions, places, and things. He's quick to detect objects that are out of sync or not part of the pattern, and he's able to assimilate that information into something sensible. He does this by moving from a biological to a deep psychological level, like it's an acute sense of perception—a radar, if you will."

"I always pray that his radar, as you call it, is the early warning signal that gives him an edge in places where evil lurks because those corners in the world are designed by deception."

"Do you miss your time in the FBI?"

"No. Not anymore." Wynona looked at the moon over the marina. "Dave, thank you for being such a good friend, and thank you for caring so much about Sean."

"Absolutely. Wynona, both of us can draw comfort by knowing that Sean's radar usually turns into something reasonable and conclusive."

***

I drove by the light of the moon, following the narrow drive, dodging ruts as the path zigzagged between tall pines. My Jeep was earning its off-road reputation tonight. I glanced at the digital map on the console screen. The trailer appeared to be about fifty yards away. From the digital images, I knew there was a shed to the left of the trailer.

I could see horizontal man-made light coming through the gaps in the trees. I stopped and listened for the barking of a dog. The cicadas were the only sound. I was glad they were in full crescendo form tonight. Their chanting would mask some of the sounds of my engine.

Half a minute later, I came to a clearing. In the moonlight, I could see the doublewide mobile home and the SUV parked to its left. I didn't want to drive too close, but I also didn't want to leave my Jeep near what appeared to be the only exit. In the unlikely event that any of Floyd Shaw's friends showed up, they could easily block me from exiting. And, in situations like this, my exits are usually fast.

Get in and get out.

Typically, getting in is the easiest part. Getting out alive often is something else. I felt that tonight would be no exception.

SIXTY-SEVEN

I needed a spot to hide my Jeep—a place in the woods to tuck it away. I drove along the tall weeds and scrub bush bordering the property. I found a short nook, a honeysuckle choked alcove that led about thirty feet away from the cleared land. I parked there, walking toward the trailer, staying in the moonlit shadows of the trees as much as I could.

I carried my Glock in one hand and the Beretta strapped to my leg above the ankle. Had there been another vehicle or two, I would have been carrying my 12-gauge shotgun. Maybe Floyd Shaw would be alone. Maybe not.

There was no sign of movement in or around the trailer. I ran up to the parked SUV, kneeling at the left rear tire, out of the direct line of sight from the trailer. I touched the tread on the tire. From just the feel, I could tell it was the same tire track pattern I'd been following.

I used my camera to take a picture of the tread, then sprinted from the vehicle to the shed. Walking by the door, I wasn't going to look inside, but it had no lock, and the door was ajar. When I opened it, the smell of death greeted me. I used the flashlight on my phone.

A large rat came out from under a dirty blue tarp. I knew what was under the tarp, but I didn't know why Floyd Shaw hadn't dumped the body somewhere in the deep woods or a lake. I put on latex gloves, pulling back the tarp. Another rat bolted out, running between my legs to a far corner of the shed. I didn't recognize the man's body. My last round had hit him slightly above his left eye. I hoped his death was quick.

I walked to the other end of the tarp, lifted it, and looked at the soles of his shoes. They were military-style tactical boots. I recognized the tread pattern from the pictures I had taken in the mud on Gideon's land. I squatted, using my phone to take a picture of the tread design on the boots. I stood there listening to rodents shuffling through junk in the shed and a mosquito buzzing by my ear. The choking stink of rat urine and death caused me to hold my breath.

I left, heading to the trailer. As I walked around Floyd Shaw's home, I looked for cameras, wondering if Shaw had a doorbell camera. Considering the age of the trailer, I wondered if he had a doorbell. There was a light to the left of the front door. Moths circled it. Soft light came from a window. I could hear sports announcers at an NFL game on a TV somewhere in the trailer. I walked around the mobile home to the backyard. In the moonlight, there was a small tractor with a bush hog mower coupled to the back of it. Weeds grew around the mower and the tractor tires.

I spotted a satellite dish on one corner of the trailer as Dave's words moved through my head. *If you need an eye in the sky tonight, I can do that for you.* I sprinted to a small back porch, climbed the steps, no handrail leading to a wooden deck. I stood on the porch and looked through a gap in the curtains behind the sliding glass doors.

Floyd Shaw was standing twenty feet away in the kitchen, his long-sleeved shirt hanging out and unbuttoned, and his jeans ripped at one knee. A week's worth of whiskers sprouted from his lean face. I saw the tat of a blue lightning bolt on his neck.

He used the edge of the kitchen counter to knock the top off a bottle of beer, turned it up for a long pull, and then walked out of the room, heading to where the game was playing on his TV.

I pulled out my knife, easily popping the lock. I opened the sliding glass a few inches and listened. The announcers were calling a football play. In seconds, I heard the roar of the crowd in the stadium. I gently pulled back the door far enough for me to step inside, closing and locking it.

I held my Glock, following the sound of the game. I walked down a short hall, peering around the open door. Inside the small living room was a large TV. The seventy-inch screen was mounted to one wall, overpowering the size of the room. Shaw's back was to me. He was in a recliner, watching the game.

The leftover stench of smoked weed, fried meat, and body sweat was in the room. I pressed the audio record button on my phone and placed it with the microphone end up, just inside a front pocket on my jeans. I walked softly, coming up directly behind his chair.

As he took a long drink from his bottle of beer, I pushed the muzzle into the tat on his neck. "Game over, Shaw."

He spit out the beer, choking on a swallow that went down the wrong pipe. "What the shit!"

I stepped out in front of his recliner, the Glock pointed at his chest. "You and your pal came by my home. I thought I'd return the nice gesture."

He stared at me, the whites of his eyes like strawberries, pupils wide, and scattered thoughts numbed from alcohol and weed.

SIXTY-EIGHT

He pretended to be unfazed. But there is something unnerving about holding a gun on a man and not saying a word. The open, dark end of the muzzle is the most real black hole in any person's universe. It evokes fear and frenetic conversation. He looked from the Glock to me. "What do you want?"

"The truth. I know it'll be difficult for you. But if I don't get it, you'll join your pal in the shed. Give the rats some fresh meat."

"Kiss my ass."

"Bad answer. In life, there is something called the *moment of truth*. What you do or don't do during this brief time, what you say or don't say, will affect your consequences."

He made a dry swallow, beer dripping from one nostril, his carotid artery jumping where I'd wedged the muzzle. Shaw pushed back in his chair. "I didn't shoot at you. That was Rizzo. I was just the driver."

"That's semantics. Shaw, it doesn't matter if you pulled the trigger or drove the getaway vehicle. What matters is that you not only participated in a murder for hire, but you also orchestrated it. You were calling the shots even before that day, when I first saw you at the farmer's market, where you were stalking Gideon Wright."

"You can't prove that. Lots of people were at the farmers' market."

"But none of them were using a long telephoto lens to take photos of Gideon. And none of the other people there have the tire tread that you have on your SUV. It matches the tread in the mud near Gideon's driveway. The groves and pattern on the dead guy's boots in your shed match those in the mud next to your tracks and those from your tires. You and your pal marched Darnell Reid into the woods, killed him, dug a shallow grave, and tossed dirt over him. You knew police dogs would easily find Reid's body."

259

"Bullshit!"

"Really? The evidence is there. But you two guys, scumbags that you are, aren't entirely to blame. The question I have, and one that prosecutors will want to know, is this: Who hired you to kill Reid and frame Gideon Wright?"

He looked down at his beer bottle on the table. "I got no idea what you're talking about."

"Shaw, you don't have to take the fall. Your pal, Rizzo, is dead. And right now, that means that you, all alone, are looking at lethal injection for a crime in which you played a part. Who's the quarterback? Who's calling the shots?"

Silence.

"This is the last time I'll ask. Who hired you?"

He looked up at me with eyes filled with hate and contempt. "You ever heard of the Dixie Mafia?"

I said nothing.

"I've got a question for you, smart guy. What happens when you combine today's version of the Dixie Mafia with more money than Fort Knox and with people who always get what they want? I tell you what happens. They can buy anybody. Me and Rizzo, who's lying out there in the shed, are just the first foot soldiers. They're already coming for you. I might have missed the first round. But I guarantee you, they've got a deep bench of pros."

"What's Rizzo's first name?"

"Jack."

"Did Percy King hire you two?"

He looked up at me, his nostrils flaring. He glanced away, his left fist clenching. "Never heard of him."

I now knew that King had hired hm. "Really? Shaw, if you work with the police and with the prosecutor, there's a good bet they'll cut you some slack if you can give them evidence that you take orders from King and the people who hired him."

"*If* is a shitty little word. If I go back into prison, especially Raiford, I'm a dead man. They'll have somebody shank me when I'm takin' a piss."

"Who are *they?*"

"People with a hell of a lot of control, both in and out of prison. Either way, I'm screwed."

"Did they tell you why they wanted to frame an old man for a murder he didn't commit?"

"I got no idea what you're talkin' about."

"Yes, you do. Remember me mentioning the moment of truth. For you, that's either telling what really happened or taking the fall for wealthy people who buy their way out of court. You want to give them a pass while the state straps you down and shoves three different needles into your veins, the last shot of potassium chloride squeezes like a vice grip on your heart. Imagine your heart in the hand of a gorilla as the animal starts to grip. It is compressed down to the size of a plum. Are you willing to go there?"

He looked from the TV screen back to me. "This is a big decision on my part. I need a smoke to calm down and get my shit together. You mind if I stand outside for a smoke, right next to the door? I got no guns out there. I need fresh air to help clear my head and a smoke to settle my nerves."

"Where are your cigarettes?"

"On that table to the left of the door. Right there with my car keys."

I glanced at the pack of cigarettes. I didn't see anywhere that he could easily reach for a hidden gun if I let him get a cigarette. "Stand slowly. If, for one second, I can't see your hands, I'll shoot you between your eyes. Is that clear?"

"Yeah, man. Sure, you got the gun, and you got issues. I just wanna smoke."

"Walk to the table and pick one out of the pack. I see there is a lighter next to the pack. Pick it up and light your cigarette."

"After that, can we step out on the porch so I can smoke it? I might do weed in here, but I like to have a cigarette outside. Listening to the hoot owls and stuff helps me think."

"All right. We'll step out on your porch in the center of this remote place in the woods. You will smoke your cigarette. And when you are done, we'll come back in here, and you'll tell me who hired you and how much you were paid. Is that clear?"

"Sure, pal. I'm not gonna be anybody's chump." He stepped outside with his cigarette and lighter. I was right behind him. He lit the cigarette and took a deep drag, the smoke looking dragon-like as it exited his nostrils under the yellow glow of the porch light. He eyed me. "Are you workin' for that old man?"

"Yes."

"Why bother? The old fool will be dead as a cockroach soon. All your work will go to the grave with him."

I said nothing. My phone vibrated in my pocket. I kept my gaze on Shaw, the Glock aimed at him as I slid the phone from my pocket with my left hand. Dave Collins was calling. Holding a gun on a man like Shaw meant I couldn't answer. I lowered the phone back into my pocket, the audio recording still running.

Shaw took another long drag, blowing smoke through his lips at a mosquito, flicking ashes onto the wooden porch. He looked up at me. In the glow of the yellow light, I could see the change in his eyes. It was as if a mask melted, and evil was staring at me with unblinking eyes. "No matter what I tell you tonight, before this is said and done, there will be three graves dug. For the old man, the bitch who's his lawyer, and for you."

As Shaw turned to flick his cigarette butt off the porch, his head exploded. I was hit with blood spatter and bits of his skull and brain. The round entered his left temple, exiting out the other side. I dove off the front porch as a hail of bullets chewed up the aluminum siding on the trailer. I ran behind a clump of willow trees.

Muzzle flash was coming from three guns. The rounds slammed into the trailer, causing pieces of limbs and leaves to fall in a torrent. A cloud parted. In the moonlight, I could see a pickup truck. The gunmen stood on the opposite side of the truck bed. I thought about the 12-gauge in my Jeep. It was too far to sprint and risk a bullet.

I crawled in the dark shadows between the willows and scraggly azalea bushes, finding a rock about half the size of my hand. I slowly stood behind one of the willows and threw the rock toward the bushes on the right side of the trailer. The men begin firing toward the sound.

I bolted to Shaw's SUV, taking a position behind it. I used one hand to wipe Shaw's blood out of my eyes and aimed my Glock toward the silhouettes moving behind the pickup, opening fire. Eight rounds. Eight seconds. I heard some of the bullets strike the truck.

Seconds later, they returned fire, blowing the front windshield out of the SUV. I slapped another magazine in my Glock, pulling the Beretta from the holster, slipping it into my left pocket. I crouched low, moving to the back of the SUV, where the window was already shot out. From there, I could shoot through the open space and the gap in the front windshield.

I fired four rounds from my Glock.

"Shit!" One of the men yelled. I could hear muffled cursing.

I fired two more rounds through the blown-out windshield. I saw the red blink of brake lights and the headlights coming on as the truck's engine roared. I ran toward the moving vehicle, firing from my Beretta, a round shattering one of the taillights. Near the other taillight, I could barely make out two bumper stickers. One was a shark in the colors of the American flag. The other was a caricature of an angry shrimp. Fists clenched. I could just make out the words *Bubba Grumps.*

SIXTY-NINE

I needed to get Shaw's blood and brain slivers off my face. I jogged to the Jeep, using water from a plastic bottle to rinse my face and hands. I stood there for a second in the swath of moonlight, looking back at the trailer and the bullet riddled SUV. In the porch light, I could see Shaw's body lying face down in a prone position, the door open, and images from the TV flickering across the glass door.

I looked at my phone; the audio recording was still going. I stopped it. The phone had recorded the gunbattle and Shaw's last words on earth. *Before this is said and done, there will be three graves dug. For the old man, the bitch who's his lawyer, and for you.*

Only three people knew Margaux was Gideon's new attorney. Detectives Lofton and Ortega … and Percy King. I doubted that the detectives were in any way connected to Floyd Shaw. King, though, had motive. And if he was receiving a huge amount of money from Roger Heller and Glacier Artesian Springs, the motive was combined with a financial incentive. Suspecting it is one thing, while proving it is quite another.

I thought about the men who'd murdered Shaw and tried to kill me. Was I the initial intended victim? Did one of the shooters accidentally hit Shaw? I didn't think so because it was a perfect headshot, designed to instantly kill. Someone didn't want the risk of shooting him in the chest and possibly not killing him, allowing Shaw to testify against them. Floyd Shaw was a liability.

Not anymore.

Whoever it was, they knew me. They knew that Wynona was my wife and where she worked. I thought about the bumper stickers on the back of the pickup truck: a grinning shark depicted in the stars and stripes of the American flag and an angry shrimp, ready to fight. If these

264

men were hired by Percy King, who were they, and where did they come from? Locals or out-of-town thugs?

Wynona was right. The pickup truck was at least a decade old. The license plate was a Florida tag. Below the number, I could make out the county—Volusia. Most likely, they were local-hired guns. And most likely, at least one of the three men is or was a client of King's. Perhaps someone who owes King a favor. *Dixie Mafia.* A perp who might need a large infusion of cash.

With two dead bodies, I didn't want to be on the property when the police arrived. Even though every word and gunshot was captured on audio, the thought of spending time answering questions at the local sheriff's office was not in my immediate plans.

I could let Detective Lofton know that I'd tracked down Floyd Shaw, what I found, and what I left behind. Maybe he'd work with the Hillsborough County sheriff. Or simply, he'd take the information—two dead men allegedly connected to Percy King—and then move forward. But would he move fast and in the right direction to stop three guys in a truck from killing Gideon, Margaux, or harming Wynona and Angela? It's easier to investigate after the fact than to work to prevent a possible crime from happening.

My phone buzzed. Dave Collins was calling again. I answered, and he said, "I tried to reach you earlier. Are you okay?"

"Define okay. Considering what went down, I'm okay."

"I called because I used a live satellite feed and saw a vehicle arriving on the suspect's property after you got there. I was trying to alert you to a possible ambush."

"Thanks, but I had a gun aimed at Floyd Shaw at the time, so I couldn't answer my phone."

"What the hell went down?"

I told Dave what happened and added, "My options are to walk away, call it in to the locals, or let Detective Lofton know what occurred here tonight."

"What's your gut telling you to do?"

"Lofton and his partner, Detective Ortega, never followed up the Floyd Shaw lead that I gave them. Tonight, Shaw was cagey, never admitting to participating or even knowing Darnell Reid, and never admitting to knowing Percy King. He danced around names, using vague references to a new version of the old Dixie Mafia, and talking about wealthy, powerful people. Anonymous people."

"It sounds like he was giving you a threat before he was killed."

"No doubt. He did ask me if I was working for, to quote him, the 'old man.' When I said yes, without acknowledging Gideon Wright's name, Shaw said that Gideon would be dead soon. Right before Shaw's head exploded, he said they'd be digging three graves. One for the 'old man,' one for the 'bitch lawyer,' presumably Margaux, and one for me."

"Did you see security cameras around Shaw's trailer?"

"No."

"Then there's no evidence that you were there tonight. Maybe you should walk away, Sean. Two perps, one of whom tried to kill you at your mailbox, are eliminated. All that is left is a global corporation with billions of dollars in assets, a wary and secretive country lawyer who appears to be the go-between—the man behind the curtain, if you will—and some shady characters, people who may or may not be linked to a modern-day version of the Dixie Mafia. Sounds like you have your work cut out for you."

"Yeah, I do. In my Jeep, I have a burner phone. I'm going to call this into the local sheriff's office. I want it on police records that Floyd Shaw, the perp I first spotted stalking Gideon at the farmers' market, is out of the game, along with his accomplice, a man he said was Jack Rizzo. Detectives in Volusia County eventually will be able to connect the dots."

"That's only if you help them. The difficult part will be connecting this to a small-town, savvy lawyer who covertly delegated the knee-breaking to enforcers he keeps in his pocket. They may not be a retooled version of the Dixie Mafia; however, if King is acting as a mob boss, he apparently knows who to call when the team owners want a change in play or need new players. Because he has a keen and analytical mind and knows the law and its loopholes, he's going to be a tough one to catch."

"I need to get out of here. I'll call you when I'm on the road, right after I talk with Wynona." I clicked off and switched to my burner phone to place the call.

"9-1-1. What is your emergency."

"I want to report a shooting. Two people are dead."

"Did you say two people are deceased?"

"Correct. The address is 97310 Blackwater Road, the home of Floyd Shaw."

"Are you a family member, sir?"

"No. I was just visiting. Shots were fired at me, too. The assailants were three men who showed up in a pickup truck with guns blazing. The second body is in Shaw's shed near his house."

"What is your name, sir?"

I clicked off, picked up my other phone, and ran to where I had crouched behind Shaw's SUV to return fire. I scanned the ground with the phone's flashlight, picking up the spent casings from my Beretta and Glock.

I started the Jeep's motor and drove as fast as possible back down Shaw's gravel driveway, turning onto the county road and heading northeast. I was less than a quarter of a mile away when I saw headlights in my rearview mirror. The lights were cutting out seconds later, with the vehicle leaving the road and entering Floyd Shaw's driveway. I didn't know if the vehicle was the same truck—the same killers that I'd just faced—or someone else.

Whoever it was, I made the decision not to go back. I was ambushed once by them. I wanted to make sure the tables were turned the next time we met.

SEVENTY

Ponce Marina late at night has a surreal feel to it. Daybreak was still a couple of hours away. Maybe the darkest hour is just before dawn. As I walked down L dock toward *Jupiter*, moonlight glistened off the black water. The tide was rising, which was causing the mooring lines to become taut and the rubber bumpers to creak as the high water pushed the boats closer to the dock posts. Although the storm had held to the west, the night air was heavy, the luster of dew beginning to form across the dock planks.

The events of the last few hours played back in my mind. If evil had a smell, the odor would be following me, and its stench would now be drifting toward my wife and daughter. I was no longer only investigating nefarious people and events surrounding Gideon Wright. I was also protecting my family from those who wished me dead.

The threat from Shaw wasn't veiled any more than the appearance of the truck with the bumper sticker parked near Wynona's store. *Before this is said and done, there will be three graves dug. For the old man, the bitch who's his lawyer, and for you.*

I had no idea how many thugs Percy King has at his beck and call. But I did know that the three guys in the truck were working for him. What if one or all three of them became liabilities because they needed a plea deal and were about to tell the police just who and what King is? Would King have his next level of goons take them out?

King was a lot more than he pretended to be—a simple country lawyer. He was a devious power broker, and a man with an intimate knowledge of water resource laws that can be enforced by any of the five water management districts in Florida.

King manipulated the legal system, walking the fine lines of criminal behavior, finding ways and excuses to cover his tracks by playing upon

268

the naivete of others. He added them to or removed them from whatever illegal scheme he engineered. He moves from local courthouses to the halls of the Florida legislature with a swagger of near impunity.

Working for lobbyists and powerful multinational companies, King doesn't blatantly steal taxpayers' money. Instead, he helps to divert it into special projects lined with fat, like the money lined in his pockets. Through his engagement in greedy, pay-for-play politics, he's the frenetic little man behind the curtain, pulling the levers.

When you combine his underhanded expertise with his skill in areas of law, including estate probate and eminent domain, he's managed to carve out some very lucrative territories for himself. King is the quintessential pompous king, the big man in a small town, or, as Shaw alluded to, the mob boss. He can disguise anger like a bullfrog swallows a bug—no change in expression.

Had Floyd Shaw lived, I was hoping that he would have cut a deal with the prosecutor to take King down, and maybe reach into the lair of Roger Heller and his superior, Clifton Price—people who believe they're better than you, above the law, and untouchable. With Shaw dead, to nail King, I had to hunt the guys in the truck, and I had to do it before they struck again.

As I walked closer to the end of L dock, I stopped and stared at the Ponce Lighthouse above the tree line and at the mouth of the inlet, which too bore the name of the man who sought eternal youth, Ponce de Leon. The rotating light swept across the face of the sea, guiding mariners 150 years before GPS and radar.

What had guided Ponce was a burning desire to find gold and a legendary fountain—a source of water that was said to possess the magic or a mysterious elixir to keep people from aging. That was his moral compass and compulsion. In the end, he was hit by an arrow dipped in poison and sailed back to Cuba, where he died an agonizing death. If he had found the mystery water, would it have saved his life?

Ponce de Leon's legacy is that he stepped onto the gangplank of infinity, trying to postpone or deny the inevitable—the progression of time and the assurance of death. The universe has its own rules. Maybe people like Gideon can somehow bend them a little for the good of others. But in the end, as he said under his old tree, *We're all just passing through, like the brevity of a comet in the night sky, not even a grain of sand in the hourglass of time. But never think you don't matter, because you do.*

Had Ponce sailed into this inlet five hundred years ago looking for the fabled Fountain of Youth? Maybe. And, maybe, if he and his Spanish conquistadors had marched another fifty miles west into the heart of an old forest, they might have discovered what I think Gideon knows.

I was tired. Misty spheres appeared around the low-wattage lamps elevated fifteen feet above the docks. The moths circling in the orbs of light captured my attention. I watched as the bats darted in and out of the soft light, silently capturing the moths. The circle of life was playing out around the glowing globes above the dock. I looked forward to a few hours of sleep before I began hunting for the three men who tried to take off my head.

A shadow moved near a dock post.

There was something in the man's hand.

I reached under my shirt, pulled the Glock, and pointed it directly at the man's chest.

SEVENTY-ONE

He grinned, and I lowered the pistol. Dave stepped into a cone of light cast from one of the dock lamps, a cup of hot coffee in his fist, the steam drifting up in the motionless air. "Good morning, Sean. It should be dawn in about an hour and eleven minutes. I assumed that I might see you about this time. Delighted you didn't pull the trigger before I sipped my coffee. I'd hate to waste Jamaican Blue Mountain."

"Why aren't you in bed?"

"I have been. I got what I needed. Usually, I sleep a little longer, but sometimes my internal alarm clock tends to nudge me."

"Just as long as it doesn't alarm you, all will be better in the world." I put the Glock back under my belt in the small of my back.

He smiled and took a sip of coffee. "Indeed. One of the reasons I'm standing here is because Nick and I took shifts, each of us keeping an eye on *Jupiter* and your sleeping family. It's my shift."

"Thanks, Dave. You and Nick are true friends. I'm lucky to have both of you in my life."

"Who needs the Fountain of Youth when I have you as a friend to keep me young? When I assist you on some of your cases, it keeps my cranium lubricated. No need to work crossword puzzles when I can stand on the sidelines and analyze your plays and that of those you are hunting. I trust that you spoke with the police in Hillsborough County."

"I left a message with the 9-1-1 dispatcher. I assume that sheriff's deputies are working the case by now. After I left Shaw's property, turning west onto the county road, I spotted headlights in the distance behind me. I watched the lights approach in my Jeep's mirrors, then the truck or car turned into Shaw's drive. I started to go back but decided I might not have the advantage I needed if it was the same three guys in the truck."

271

"Maybe it was a sheriff's cruiser with the emergency lights off until deputies could assess the scene, perhaps approaching in stealth mode."

"I don't think that's the case. They'd come in a conga line of police cruisers and ambulances. It was somebody else."

"Who'd be turning into Shaw's drive at that late hour?"

"Maybe the same guys who had left earlier, the guys in the truck."

"But why? You had a shootout with them. You may have shot one of the three. They left the scene. Would they come back with reinforcements? They should have figured that you would have left quickly after they left unless you chose to wait for the police."

"Maybe they left something behind that they had to go back and get."

"What? Could it be evidence of some sort linking them to Shaw's murder?"

"I don't know."

"Or maybe they're planting evidence to point at you, as Shaw and his partner-in-crime did by burying Reid's body on Gideon Wright's land."

"They have nothing that would connect to me."

"Then, what did Shaw have? And what can you find that will directly connect them to the lawyer, Percy King? You believe he is the equivalent of a southern mob boss tucked away in a serene and idyllic town, DeLand. If he is indeed running his own little corner of a modern Dixie Mafia, how deep do the roots penetrate? And who does King influence in law enforcement or within the courthouse legal system?"

"All good questions, and they are questions I can't answer yet."

"What's your next move?"

"Sleep. After that, I need to find those guys in the truck with the cartoonish bumper stickers. One decal is of a great white shark in the colors of the flag, and the other is of an angry shrimp, fist clenched and raised for a fight."

"It's not even a needle in the haystack, because you don't have a haystack in which to search."

I said nothing.

"Get some rest, Sean. I'll retreat to *Gibraltar's* aft deck, where I'll watch a sunrise with my pot of coffee. I shall think about the pickup truck's unique bumper stickers. Maybe I can come up with an idea as to where a shark like that might be found swimming, or the caricature of a fuming shrimp might stand his ground."

I unlocked *Jupiter,* moving quietly through the salon, then went back to the berth where Angela slept. I opened the door, and in the moonlight coming through a porthole, I could see her silhouette lying on the bed. Her dark hair was cascading over the pillow, and her favorite teddy bear was under the covers, the bear's face just visible. I kissed her on the forehead.

When I entered the master cabin, Max, who was lying next to Wynona, lifted her head. I held one finger up to my lips, gesturing silence. Max made what looked like a slight nod. I was beginning to think she could understand sign language. I quietly undressed and got into bed. Wynona reached for me, holding my hand in the dark.

In just a few hours, I would leave again. I closed my eyes, and in my mind's eye, I could see the headlights from the unknown vehicle turning into Floyd Shaw's driveway. If it was the killers in the truck, I didn't think they were going back to plant evidence against me. They might be removing evidence that could be linked to Percy King, such as two dead bodies. Where would they take the bodies at that time of the morning? I thought about the truck, the bumper stickers, and the name of the Florida county barely legible on the license plate.

I had an idea where to look. I believe I've found the haystack.

Now I had to find the needle.

SEVENTY-TWO

A pewter gray morning was breaking as Captain Hank Marsh left the docks in his shrimp boat, *Miss Marla Jean*, piloting a course toward a watery graveyard. He stood in the wheelhouse, a cigarette in a corner of his mouth, a cup of black coffee in one hand. He thought about the two bodies on ice in the cooler where he usually kept his catch of shrimp. He felt disdain toward Percy King, a man Marsh considered to be the devil in a suit.

More than that, he hated himself for ever getting involved with King. One small job led to the next, and then the next. And now murder. *It was like quicksand*, he thought. *The harder you struggle to get out, the more that bad shit pulls you down.* But, with the cash infusion, he'd sell *Miss Marla Jean*, buy a new identity, and head for Costa Rica.

"Cap, how far out we gonna go?" Deckhand Miguel Morales stood at the open door, the sun a pink sliver where the Atlantic met the sky. Morales, or Mutt as he was called, was a bulldog of a man, with cantaloupe-sized biceps, a short and stocky build, and eyes set far apart. Spiky hair. Part of his left ear was jagged, the result of a knife fight three years after his last release from prison.

Marsh took a drag from his cigarette, exhaling smoke from his nostrils, his nose pitted with pockmarks. "We're goin' all the way out to the Gulf Stream. Where's Carl?"

"He used the first-aid kit to put a bandage on the side of his arm that was hit with a bullet."

"He just got grazed. I've been hurt a helluva lot worse. I'm still carrying shrapnel in my right leg from the combat I lived through in Yemen. The damn infection that came later was worse than the bomb."

Carl Lee came from the deck to the wheelhouse wearing jeans, orange rubber boots, and a T-shirt. His left forearm was bandaged in

274

white gauze. He had aloof black eyes, like those of a drifter who carried secrets as he hopped into box cars and rode the rails from one town to the next. A week's worth of whiskers sprouted from his thin face; a small hoop earring was in one earlobe. On his head he wore a blue bandana with images of skulls imprinted into the fabric.

Marsh looked at the bandage. "How's your arm?"

"It'd be better if I had a smoke. Left my pack in the truck."

Marsh shook out a cigarette from his pack, handing Lee a Zippo lighter. Lee lit the cigarette with cupped hands. A tat, in the image of a dagger, was on the middle finger of his right hand. He looked at Marsh. "The bodies are stiff now. Don't take long at that temp."

Mutt nodded. "Out there in the Gulf Stream, they'll thaw quick. The temperature of that water always is warmer than the other parts of the ocean."

Marsh finished his coffee, his mouth tasting like swamp water. "Before we dump 'em, y'all need to chain a concrete block to the leg of each dude." He lit another cigarette, looking at the radar for boats in the area. He spotted a freighter at the horizon line. Marsh adjusted the shrimp boat's path and watched the sun rise from the edge of the world.

***

Captain Hank Marsh had *Miss Marla Jean* in the center of the Gulf Stream in the Atlantic, fifty miles off the coast of Florida. At this point, he knew the water was more than 3000 feet deep. He used his binoculars to scan the area in all directions. No vessels were in sight, not even a gull overhead. He put the diesels in an idle position and climbed from the wheelhouse to the deck. Let's do this and get the hell outta here."

Lee grinned. "You know, this could be a business. People who don't wanna get buried or cremated. Funerals at sea could be the next big thing. Screw the scattering of ashes. Lots of tree huggers and new green deal people would give their bodies back to mother nature. They just might be okay with sharks gnawing on their bones."

Mutt laughed. "Dude, you might be onto something. With all the people in Florida, lot of them old, business would be steady. Hell, cut a deal with the area funeral homes and call it Sail Away Wakes. Shit, that's freakin' genius."

Marsh shook his head. "Y'all are screwed up. C'mon, let's dump those bodies. We'll head to some shrimpin' grounds after that. Got to cover our asses. We're out here because it's what we do. We're just shrimpers tryin' to earn money at sea." He motioned to the freezers.

The men opened the large stainless-steel door, and frosty air billowed out like fog in the early morning. Seconds later, the two bodies, stiff from rigor mortis and the cold, were dragged onto the deck. Mutt and Lee ran the chains through concrete blocks and attached one to a leg of each body. Lee looked up at Marsh. "Let's toss this one over first. It was ripe when we found it. Rats done ate off the soft parts. Can't stand looking at what's left."

Marsh nodded, folding his arms across his chest and glancing around the horizon. The men set a concrete block on the chest of Jack Rizzo's body, carrying it over to the gunwale. Mutt blew out a breath. "On three. Ready. One … two … three." The men threw the body overboard. The frozen corpse twirled for a second, one stiff arm pointing skyward as the body slipped beneath the water.

They picked up Floyd Shaw's remains and did the same thing. Marsh grunted. "All right … one … two … three." They slung the body overboard. The men stared at it like they were watching the final play of a tied football game. The chain snaked around one stiff leg, spinning the body on the surface for a moment before pulling it down. They watched it descend for twenty feet of clear water before becoming lost in the abyss of turquoise.

Carl Lee grinned, his dark eyes amused as if he'd just walked into a county fair. "This is easy money. Is the big boss man done, or are we gonna be working the disposal service on more of 'em?"

"From what I hear, there might be another one. Could be two, depending on how this whole thing plays. I'd like one of them to be the dude who returned fire on us. Just gotta figure out who he is."

Lee glanced at the wound on his arm. "I look forward to another run-in with that prick. Maybe we can chum for sharks with his body parts. It'd be a shame to see him slip away so far down."

SEVENTY-THREE

They came at dawn. Eight sheriff's deputies, all heavily armed. After cutting the lock off Gideon's gate, the deputies and two detectives proceeded to the rustic cabin. Two deputies moved into the backyard area. The remaining officers and detectives came up the front porch. Three had their guns drawn.

Detective Lofton looked at his partner, Detective Ortega, as the morning sun poked through holes in the branches of the live oaks. Lofton blew out a breath. He spoke in a whisper. "Odds are that he's asleep in bed. But he could be sitting behind the door with a loaded shotgun."

She nodded. "When we serve an arrest warrant, we never know what we'll find. Do you want to break the door down?"

"If there is no response in a reasonable period of time, yes." He turned to the front door, pounding on it with his fist. "Gideon Wright, this is the sheriff's department. Your house is surrounded. Come out. We have a warrant for your arrest."

No response, only the abrupt end to a mockingbird's morning serenade. After thirty seconds, Lofton pounded again. "Mr. Wright, open the door. Now!"

A thick-bodied deputy with an iron battering ram asked, "Detective, want me to open it?"

As Lofton was about to answer, Ortega held up her left hand. "Hold on a second. I hear something inside."

A few seconds later, there was the sound of a deadbolt lock turning and the door opening. Gideon Wright stood just inside his front entrance. He was dressed in flannel pajamas; his hair was matted, and he had sleep lines on the left side of his face. He nodded. "I heard you the first time. I can't jump out of bed like I used to. What is this about, detectives?"

277

Lofton cleared his throat. "Gideon Wright, you are under arrest for the murder of Darnell Reid." He read Gideon his rights and added, "You need to come with us."

"Do you mind if I change my clothes?"

"Under supervision. We don't know if there is a firearm in your home."

"There isn't one."

Lofton motioned to one of the deputies. "Jenkins, go with him."

The deputy nodded, holstered his pistol, and walked inside, following Gideon to his bedroom.

After he dressed, Gideon and the deputy returned to the porch. Detective Ortega said, "Mr. Wright, please come with us, sir."

"Okay. May I call my lawyer?"

"When you get to the station and are booked, we'll make arrangements for you to speak with your attorney."

***

An hour later, right before Gideon was fingerprinted, photographed, and booked into a holding cell, he was given the opportunity to make a phone call. He was told to use the phone on the wall in the hallway leading from the sheriff's department to the criminal justice building. He called Margaux and told her what happened. "I didn't think it would come to this. The police said Darnell Reid's blood and DNA were found on a shovel in the barn. Someone put it there."

"I know." Margaux, dressed in a T-shirt and shorts, stood inside the kitchen of her condo. "I'm getting dressed and heading to the sheriff's department. I'll be there through your arraignment and the rest as we prove that you had nothing to do with Reid's murder."

"I'm glad you showed up in my life when you did. If you weren't here, I suppose I'd be on the phone with Percy King, and now I believe that would not have worked out well. At least not for me."

"I'm on my way."

"Before you go, can you call Sean O'Brien and tell him what happened?"

"Absolutely. No one is going to frame you and take you down to steal everything that you've worked so hard to build and maintain. I'm a fighter, and now I really have something worth fighting for—my grandpa."

"Thank you. When we hang up, they say they're going to put me in a holding cell. In all my long life, I've never been locked in a jail cell. Please hurry."

SEVENTY-FOUR

I sipped black coffee on *Jupiter's* flybridge and thought about the elusive trail I was trying to follow. After three hours of sleep, I'd showered, made coffee, and climbed up to the bridge to think—to gain a better perspective on what I faced. There were thousands of pickup trucks registered in Volusia County. But how many had shark and shrimp bumper stickers? I'd bet on only one.

My phone buzzed. It was Margaux. "Sean, detectives arrested Gideon and are charging him with the murder of Darnell Reid. Apparently, one of the tools in Gideon's barn allegedly had blood on it. Detectives say their forensics lab matched the blood to Reid's DNA."

"The shovel."

"Yes. When you were on Gideon's porch, you asked him when he'd last used his shovel. He said it had been at least a few weeks."

"The shovel wasn't hanging from a spot on the wall. It was in a corner."

"And that stood out to you—something in a corner of a dark barn?"

"That setting was inconsistent with how Gideon stores his tools. Somebody put it there."

"Who?"

"Maybe Floyd Shaw or his accomplice, Jack Rizzo."

"The police need to question them."

"They can't."

"Why, Sean?"

I thought about not sharing the information, but because Margaux was Gideon's defense attorney, she was going to need everything she could muster to win a case in a courtroom that Percy King knew like the back of his hand. "Because they're dead. After Shaw and Rizzo tried to kill me at my mailbox, I tracked them to Shaw's trailer in Hillsborough County, hoping that at least one of the two would turn state's witness and cut a deal with the prosecutor, revealing the role that King is playing. But Rizzo was already dead, and Shaw was about to be."

"What do you mean by about to be?"

"Some guys showed up and killed Shaw while I was talking to him on his porch. It led to an exchange of fire, allowing me to escape."

"And you think that the new killers are working for that crooked lawyer, Percy King?"

"Yes."

"It's like they eat their own, the law of the jungle on steroids, because they have guns rather than claws and fangs as weapons, and they have greed as a motive. It's an age-old story."

"If I can hunt down Shaw's killers, I might be able to give you the evidence you need to keep Gideon out of prison. Where are you now?"

"I'm arriving at the county jail. I want to get Gideon immediately in front of a judge for a first appearance bond hearing. He's strong for his age, but Gideon might not stand up to the rigors of a drawn-out murder trial."

"It's my goal to keep that from happening. Call me after the hearing. Thanks." I clicked off, leaning back in the captain's chair on the flybridge, three white pelicans soaring over the masts of moored sailboats. I could hear Max barking as she came down L dock with Wynona and Angela. Max had led the way on their walk, leaving and returning to *Jupiter.*

They stopped at Nick's boat, *St. Michael.* I could see his hand gestures as he talked, standing in the cockpit, with Angela laughing at something he said. Dave joined them, a cup of coffee in his hand. He and Nick treated Wynona and Angela like close family. And they were.

I spotted Dave taking a phone from his back pocket. He held it up to his ear and looked my way. I answered, and he said, "Good morning. I know you are up in your loft of solitude, but you must descend to eat. Your family is coming over to *Gibraltar* to dine on a fine breakfast. Nick's going to make shrimp 'n grits, Greek style."

"I need to hit the road. I have time for a cup of coffee."

"You barely sleep and don't eat. You can't slay dragons if you aren't ingesting fuel." He chuckled. Max looked my way and barked. "Hear that, Sean? Even Miss Max is calling you down from your morning perch. Come smell the shrimp 'n grits."

Across the marina, I watched a shrimp boat head out to the Halifax River and then through Ponce Inlet and the Atlantic. The boat was called *High Life,* and its captain, Drew Sullivan, was someone I'd met. At that moment, the haystack wasn't looking quite as formidable as it had been. And the needle was getting closer.

I joined my family aboard *Gibraltar* as Nick finished cooking in the trawler's galley. Max and Angela followed him around. I told Dave and Wynona what Margaux had shared with me and added, "She will be there for Gideon's first appearance bond hearing. He's in good hands with her, but she is only as good as the evidence available to prove Gideon is not the killer. And right now, that evidence is thin. I must find it because the police have gone down the path of least resistance."

Dave grunted. "Indeed. I'm not making excuses for them, however, when forensic evidence points to a tool in Gideon's barn that may have been used as a murder weapon, most cops will follow that path."

Wynona lifted her coffee cup, holding it in both hands. "But it's their job to *prove* that it was Gideon who swung the shovel at the man's head, causing the death."

"Yes, but forensic evidence trumps circumstantial evidence, at least in the eyes of a prosecutor and in the collective consciousness of a jury as well." He glanced across the table at me. "Half an hour ago, I went online to see if there was any news coverage of what occurred in a trailer on a remote piece of land in Hillsborough County after someone called 9-1-1 to report a crime."

"Did you find anything?" Wynona asked."

"Indeed. There is coverage on two of the three TV stations in the Tampa area and on a local blog news feed over there. The most thorough story, though, is coming from Channel Two. I saved it on my computer." He set his laptop on the table and pressed the keys. The video started playing.

I wanted to hold my breath as the first image faded up on the screen.

SEVENTY-FIVE

I didn't want Angela to see or hear the news story. I hoped she would remain in *Gibraltar's* galley with Nick until the news clip ended. On Dave's laptop screen, a TV news anchorwoman with auburn hair and wide eyes said, "This morning the investigation continues into what detectives say is a bizarre crime scene. Last night, a tip came into 9-1-1, with the caller saying there were two dead bodies at a home in a rural section of Hillsborough County. When police arrived, the bodies were gone, but other things of interest were found. Janice Stevens has more."

The video cut to a wide shot of Floyd Shaw's trailer. The report began. "County property records indicate that this is the home of Floyd Shaw, a forty-year-old man whom neighbors describe as a loner. Sheriff's deputies spent the morning looking for Shaw, or his body and that of another person. So far, they've discovered forensic evidence but no bodies."

The video showed images of blood on the porch and bullet holes in the trailer. "CSI techs are analyzing the blood and skull fragments of what detectives found here on Shaw's porch. Also, police discovered human blood in a shed close to the trailer. Detective Mark Sutton told us that it looks like there was quite a shootout on the property."

The video cut to an interview with a man wearing a dark brown sports coat and an open shirt. His black hair was cut short, military-style, and he had a slender nose and a thin face. "We found where eleven rounds had been fired into Mr. Shaw's trailer, and its front and back doors were unlocked. An SUV registered to Shaw is in poor condition. The front and rear windshields are shot out, there are bullet holes in the body, and there are dings where they hit the motor. However, we could not find spent bullet casings near the SUV, yet there were more than two dozen about eighty feet away, where we believe another vehicle was parked."

"What do you think happened to the bodies?"

"Someone moved them, and that's very odd. Most homicides I've worked on have a body or bodies. Usually, the only reason someone moves a body is to hide it or make us think the murder occurred someplace else."

"Do you think that's the situation here?"

"We don't know."

"Do you think the person who called 9-1-1 moved the bodies?"

"That doesn't make sense. Why call law enforcement if you're going to remove the bodies? My guess is that whoever called it in may have been an intended victim who somehow survived the shootout."

The video cut to parked police cruisers, two ambulances, and one coroner's van on the scene. Emergency lights flashed behind the reporter as she looked into the camera. "Police will run forensic tests to see if the blood found in the shed matches that on the trailer's front porch. Without bodies, it doesn't mean there were no homicides here. All indications are that this is a brutal crime scene, and there's an unknown witness out there. Other than that, there's nothing left behind but blood, bullet holes, and shell casings, all pointing to a crime. Police say the caller left no name and is believed to have used an untraceable phone to make the call. Reporting live from the scene, this is Janice Stevens. Now back to you in the studio."

Dave leaned forward in his chair. "Now you know why that vehicle was turning into Floyd's driveway as you left the scene. They also could have been waiting to find out what you drove as a future identifier."

Wynona nodded. "It appears they were the cleaners. They arrived and removed the bodies. Often, cleaners for the mob will scrub the scene, erasing as much evidence as possible. In this case, it appears that the bodies were all that they wanted, or they didn't have time to clean. Where would they take them and why, Sean?"

"Why? Because the bodies can be linked to Percy King. Had Shaw or Rizzo lived, one of them might have implicated King and others in the murder of Darnell Reid, exonerating Gideon. But dead men don't talk. To answer your question about where they might take the bodies, Ponce Lighthouse could point the way."

Dave angled his head, his eyes inquisitive. "At sea? You mean in the deep blue sea?"

"Let's eat!" Nick barked, bringing out plates of food, setting everything on the round table in the salon, the aft-doors wide open, the morning sky a deep blue. He grinned, sipping a bloody Mary. "Angela was my lil' helper in the galley. Hot Dawg was there for clean-up duty." He laughed. "Bon appétit. You too, Sean. You can make time for a breakfast like this."

As we all sat around the table, Wynona was the first to sample the food. "Nick, this is very good. How'd you make it?"

"It's the old Greek way. Today, I used rock shrimp. They're small shrimp, but they're a delicacy. They come from the waters off Daytona down to Port Canaveral. And shrimpers can only catch 'em certain times of the year. I sauteed 'em in my cast iron pan, mixing in a light tomato sauce, basil, parsley, black pepper, and a dash of sea salt. Then I ladled the shrimp onto the buttered grits that Angela and I made and added feta cheese."

Dave took a bite and closed his eyes. "This dish is a culinary creation that must have been food for the Greek gods and served on Mount Olympus."

Angela scrunched her nose. "Dave, where is that place?"

"Only Nick knows. It's his happy place."

Nick laughed. "Don't let my priest friend hear you say that."

"I want to go there." She smiled, staring at a shrimp on her plate.

"One day, I'll take you and Hot Dawg there in a cool adventure story. That way, we can go there in our imaginations. It'll be fun." Nick winked at Wynona.

I looked at the shrimp on a bed of grits. "Nick, you said rock shrimp are seasonal. I just saw one of the shrimp boats moored here heading out to sea. The boat was *High Life*. Do you know the captain?"

"Yep. Cap'n Drew Sullivan. He's a good man. Damn hard worker. I buy my shrimp from him. He buys his fish from me. Works out well. He's the only shrimper that still calls Ponce Marina home. Most of the fleet is based outta Daytona Harbor Marina. It's about three times bigger than this place."

"Do you have Captain Sullivan's number?"

"Yeah. It's here on my phone. Why?"

"Once he clears Ponce Inlet, it won't be long before he's out of cell phone range. Can you call him for me? I'd like to ask Captain Sullivan a question."

SEVENTY-SIX

Nick made the call from *Gibraltar's* cockpit. I stood next to him as he put the call on speaker and said, "Hey, Drew, it's Nick. You headin' out today? Thought I saw your boat."

"Yeah, got to catch the rockers before the end of the season. Got customers waitin' on 'em. Those lil' buggers are deep down. We're using a reinforced net to catch what we can. Tore up a net on coral last month."

"Good luck. I'm sure I'll see you in a few days. One reason I'm callin' is because my good friend, Sean O'Brien, has a question for you. You might remember Sean. He bought a few pounds from you at the beginning of the season."

"Yeah, I remember him. He's a big fella. A private eye, right?"

"Something like that. He takes on unique cases from time to time."

"Put him on the phone. I'm goin' through the pass now."

I took Nick's phone. "Hi, Captain Drew. I know you have your hands full in the wheelhouse heading through the inlet on an incoming tide, so I'll make it quick."

"Sure. No problem."

"I figured you might know some of the players in the Daytona area shrimping fleet."

"I know a lot of them. Why?"

"Do you know anyone who owns a black Ford 150 pickup with a couple of unique stickers on the back bumper? One is of a great white shark in the colors of the American flag, and the other is of a cartoonish shrimp. The shrimp looks angry. Big eyes. Its fists are clenched, and it's in a boxing stance, with a snarl on its face and baring its teeth. There was no caption below the shark sticker, but below the shrimp sticker are the words *Bubba Grumps.*"

He chuckled. "I know a captain whose nickname is Sharky. His real name is Hank Marsh. As far as the shrimp sticker goes, Bubba Grump's is a dive bar on the strip in Daytona. It's a place where Sharky likes to hang out 'cause his brother-in-law is part owner. Sharky gets free drinks."

"What boat does Marsh or Sharky own?"

"It's called *Miss Marla Jean.*"

"Thanks."

"No problem. If you don't mind me asking, why are you interested in Sharky or his truck? Did he do a hit 'n run?"

"That's a good way to phrase it. Something along those lines."

"Gotcha. Be cautious if you go messing with him or some of the scum he hires to go shrimpin'. I know some of them. I wouldn't hire those guys to take out the trash. And be damn careful if you approach them. I'd advise you to do it in daylight and in a public place."

"Thanks, Captain. I hope you catch plenty of rock shrimp." I clicked off.

Nick blew out a deep breath and sipped his bloody Mary. "For Drew to say somebody is a bad dude, they really got to be damn low on the human totem pole. He calls it like he sees it. No gray areas with him. He hires guys who love the sea and fishing and work hard. For him to tell you to approach this guy Marsh and his crew in a public place says a lot."

"I need to be going."

"Where are you heading?"

"To find Sharky and Bubba Grump's. Maybe Bubba's not so grumpy."

***

I went back to *Jupiter,* retrieving my 12-gauge tactical shotgun, Glock, and Beretta. I put the pistols under my shirt and pants legs, and the shotgun in a leather carrying case. As I was walking down L dock, Dave caught up with me. "Sean, I didn't want to say anything in front of Angela, or even Wynona, for that matter. But from what Nick shared with me, it sounds like you've narrowed this hunt down to the worst of the worst. Is there anything I can do to help you?"

"There might be one thing."

"What is it?"

"I'd like to see where this guy, Captain Marsh, AKA Sharky, goes when he's in port, assuming he is now. I'm betting he dumped those bodies at sea. Sharky feeding the sharks. Do you have an extra GPS tracker on *Gibraltar*?"

"I still have one left in a box from the last time. I'll go get it. I can help you monitor it, should you perchance be otherwise preoccupied. You constantly must watch your back. I only need to look at a satellite feed to help you find a great white shark and a misunderstood shrimp. Perhaps the Napoleonic attitude goes with the name *shrimp*."

"No doubt. I'll put this shotgun in my Jeep and wait for you there."

***

Ten minutes later, Dave walked up to where I had parked my Jeep in the marina lot. He carried a small box. From where we stood, I could smell bacon cooking in the Tiki Bar restaurant. Its isinglass windows were rolled up, and the vintage juke box was playing Dire Straits' *Single Handed Sailor.*

Dave handed the GPS tracker to me. "I've programmed it into my laptop. You can do the same with your phone."

"Thanks, Dave."

"Where do you hope this guy, Marsh, will lead you?"

"To Percy King, if I'm lucky."

"I try hard not to advise you in the field. Your instincts are better than mine. However, based on what Nick shared with me, don't let these guys back you into a corner. You managed to call your first encounter, or shootout, with them a draw."

"Keep an eye on Angela and Wynona for me. Wynona is going to stay away from her antique store while I'm tracking these guys, because last week she spotted one of them outside of it."

"That's smart, and of course I'll keep an eye out. Wynona is a remarkable woman. The qualities that made her a good FBI special agent also make her a good businesswoman, mother, and wife. You're fortunate."

"I am."

"She tries hard not to show it, but she's very worried that the law of averages will catch up with you. Wynona pushes it back down, out of her thoughts, until the next client needs help."

I said nothing.

Dave nodded and continued. "I think it's because, in her previous life, she's faced similar situations, which gives her a deep insight into what you confront in your unique cases. Often, they're cold cases that were unsolved for a lot of concealed and heinous reasons."

"With my current case, nothing is cold. It is playing out in real time with deadly consequences. Had I not spotted Gideon that day at the farmers' market, maybe he would be dead. A death made to look like an accident. Or maybe he would be tied up in an eminent domain lawsuit trying to protect his land and the spring that flows through it. He doesn't have to face a global corporate giant alone, at least not on my watch. And I won't let him rot in prison for someone else's greed and misconduct."

"Understood."

I turned, got in my Jeep, and headed out of the lot. My next stop would be the Daytona Harbor Marina. I wanted to find that pickup truck. Maybe *Miss Marla Jean* was in port. And maybe Sharky was there.

SEVENTY-SEVEN

Like carrion birds, the news media flocked to the county courthouse. They could smell a story that would boost ratings and garner *likes* and interest on their extended social media platforms. Outside the courthouse were three TV news vans. Gideon Wright was about to make his first appearance before senior Judge Harry Sherman, who was a man with a ruddy face and bifocals perched at the end of his thin nose.

The packed courtroom had ten long pews in the seating area, separated by a center aisle. All seats were taken by curious spectators and a handful of courthouse workers. Reporters with notepads and audio recorders squeezed into the few standing-only spaces while most of the TV news media lined the back wall, with camera operators staking out spots to put cameras on tripods.

They watched Gideon Wright at the defense table to the left of the front area of the courtroom. He wore an orange jumpsuit. On the back were the words: *County Jail.* Next to Gideon sat his defense attorney, Margaux Brennon. She was someone that courtroom observers didn't know, an attorney who had never had a case before Judge Sherman, who ran his courtroom like a military general. If protocol was violated, he had no empathy for attorneys—defense, prosecutors, or defendants.

To the right of the center aisle in the second row sat three members of Darnell Reid's family—his wife, mother, and father. The wife was a petite woman with chestnut brown hair and puffy eyes from crying. She stared to the left, looking at Gideon's profile, her eyes burning.

Judge Sherman opened a file, read silently for a few seconds, and looked above the rim of his bifocals. "State of Florida versus Gideon Wright. Case number 296715, capital murder in the death of Darnell Reid. I assume Mr. Wright is sitting at the defense table."

Margaux motioned for Gideon to stand next to her. He did, and she looked up at the judge. "Yes, your honor. This is Gideon Wight. I am Margaux Brennon, and I represent Mr. Wright."

"Very well. Welcome to this courtroom, Ms. Brennon." He paused and glanced over at the two prosecutors sitting behind the state's table. One was a middle-aged woman wearing a dark suit, and the other was a younger attorney in his early thirties, balding, and wearing black-rimmed glasses.

The door of the courtroom opened. Percy King, dressed in a blue sports coat and wearing a red bowtie, entered, nodding at the bailiff. King tiptoed, walking quietly to a corner of the room on the right side. He folded his arms across his chest, watching the proceedings like a cat staring at a bird through the window.

The judge eyed Gideon and looked back down at the file. "Mr. Wright, you are facing a charge of first-degree capital murder. Do you understand that?"

Gideon nodded. "Yes, Your Honor."

"Based on the information in this file, there certainly is probable cause for the arrest and charge. We'll set a date for an arraignment."

"Your Honor," Margaux said. "We'd like to ask the court to set a bond at this time."

"That's rarely done in a first-degree murder charge."

"I understand that. However, Mr. Wright has lived in Volusia County most of his life. He has a home and more than two hundred acres of land. He's tied to his community with friends and family. He's ninety-nine years old. Your Honor, I assure you that Gideon is not in the least way a flight risk. And considering that he is ninety-nine-years old, being held in jail through an arraignment and perhaps longer will be detrimental to his health. We request that a reasonable bond be set, allowing Gideon to stay in his home through this process. Thank you."

Judge Sherman nodded, looking over at the prosecutors. "What does the state have to say about this?"

The female, who was the lead attorney, stood. "Your Honor, with all due respect to Mr. Wright's age, he appears to be in good health. Certainly, good enough to dig a grave. The state—"

"Objection!" Margaux fired back. "That accusation is purely conjecture and belongs in a summation before a jury and not in a first appearance hearing."

The judge nodded. "Sustained."

The prosecutor glanced at her notes and then looked at the judge. "Your Honor, being elderly doesn't excuse anyone from the protocol in our judicial process. The state does, in fact, consider the defendant a potential flight risk. Our initial check into Mr. Wright's background indicates that he has traveled and worked all over the world. His passport is current. He could get on a plane and never return. We request that bond be denied."

Margaux shook her head. "Your honor, just because my client worked in different countries years ago as a young man doesn't make him a flight risk. And just because he has a passport, like millions of Americans, doesn't mean he's going to pack a bag and jump on a plane. At his age, where would Gideon go? Nowhere but his home, a home that's been in his family since right after the Civil War."

Judge Sherman pushed back in his chair, picking up the file and reviewing notes. After less than thirty seconds, he leaned forward, clearing his throat. "The court concurs that, considering the defendant's age and his long history with the community, he doesn't appear to represent a significant flight risk. Bond is set at five hundred thousand. We'll have an arraignment in two weeks from today at nine a.m. Court adjourned." He slammed down his wooden gavel, got up, and hustled out of the courtroom into his private chambers.

There was a loud murmur in the room as people stood, the news media jockeying for the best positions to shoot video of Gideon as he spoke with his attorney before a bailiff took him away. Percy King left the courtroom the same way he entered: eyes guarded, mixing into the crowd, and not making eye contact to avoid conversation.

Margaux looked at Gideon. "You'll be able to go home soon."

"Thank you. You know your way around a courtroom."

"They all look pretty much the same. I try to know my way around the law, not to break it but to use legal leverage to my client's advantage. There was no compelling reason to deny you bond. I'll make arrangements for the bail money. You just sit tight for a couple of hours, and we'll go home, okay?"

"That sounds fine."

The bailiff, who looked like a human tank, sauntered over to Gideon. "You need to come with me."

As Gideon was led out of the courtroom, he glanced back at Margaux. She smiled. But Gideon knew she was putting on a brave face as they were about to enter an epic battle.

SEVENTY-EIGHT

Outside the courthouse, Percy King looked up at the cupola on the roof. A bronze statue of Lady Justice, blindfolded and holding balanced scales in one hand and a sword in the other, sat atop it. He stood at the bottom of the courthouse steps, puffing a cigar, contemplating what he had just witnessed. He paid little attention to the people coming and going. Moving to the far left of the general foot traffic area, he made a phone call.

A local newspaper reporter, who was wearing a flannel shirt tucked into his jeans, came outside and sat quietly on one of the steps. He opened his notebook to review the notes he'd taken during the first appearance hearing. He was within earshot of King.

"Roger, it's Percy." King held his phone to one ear and his cigar in the other hand. "The legal machine is going to devour Gideon Wright. The courtroom was packed at his first appearance hearing. When people begin to view Wright as an evil and angry old man, comparable to the Golden State Killer, he'll become deplorable in public's eyes. The redemption will come when the sale of a perceived killer's property is done through eminent domain, because the land and spring will go to a better and more equitable use. It'll appear fair and justified in the eyes of the public and the news media. The prime use, of course, will be to siphon off the best water in the world to quench the thirst of people around planet Earth."

"Do you think that will be the PR spin we can get from this, or will there be blowback?"

"No, your team will look like white knights rescuing water usage, allowing the public access to the spring on a limited basis, while Glacier Artesian Springs is the sole owner of the water rights into perpetuity. You'll make hundreds of millions, and you'll come across as a good and responsible neighbor, taking care of people and the environment. It's a win-win."

"We'll see how this plays out. I assume bail was denied, correct?"

"Not exactly."

"What do you mean, not exactly? That old man should be behind bars through this trial."

"The judge granted bond."

"What! Why?"

"Because King's attorney, the same woman who alleges she's his great-granddaughter, is a very good lawyer. She moved fast and on point. The state had a hard time playing her cards."

There was silence on the phone for a few seconds. "This presents a further problem. If she fights for him that well in court, what's she going to do if she gets the deed to the land and spring in her name?"

"We don't know that she'll ever get the deed to Wright's land. He barely knows her."

"But she might become the sole heir. Can you assure me that doesn't happen?"

"Put a half million into the Caymans' account, and it won't happen."

"Your legal fees are becoming more expensive."

"As is the situation here. Consider it a small payment toward a billion-dollar spring. The real Fountain of Youth comes with a price tag commensurate with what it can return. We'll talk soon." He clicked off and turned around, looking at the reporter sitting on the top step.

"Aren't you Percy King?"

"Who are you?"

"Ken Chandler. I'm a reporter for the Daily Beacon. May I speak with you about ...?"

"No." King shook his head. "Were you eavesdropping on my private conversation?"

"I was just sitting here going over my notes from Gideon Wright's first court appearance. But since you asked, I couldn't help but overhear you. That's why I think we should talk. I want to be accurate when I write a story. It sounds like you're working for someone who's doing a smear campaign against Gideon Wright. What's the story?"

"You need to have your hearing checked."

"I could hear well enough to understand that you just asked someone to deposit a half million dollars in a Cayman Islands bank account. What does all this have to do with Gideon Wright? It sounds like it's about water rights to that spring on his land. You mentioned the Glacier Artesian Springs company. Let me do an interview with you to get the facts straight."

"Not now. Maybe later. I must get to a meeting. Give my regards to your publisher, Thomas Townsend. We're old friends." He scurried down the steps and toward the parking garage, his hard soles sounding hollow against the concrete.

***

I parked my Jeep not far from a shrimp fleet moored at Daytona Harbor Marina. The docks were in the commercial area of the large boatyard. There were dozens of charter fishing yachts, deep-sea excursion boats, and a shrimp fleet of a dozen vessels. It appeared that half of them were at sea. Didn't matter. I was concerned only with finding one, *Miss Marla Jean.*

I took my binoculars and the GPS tracker from the Jeep and walked around the parking area, which was filled mostly with pickup trucks and a few SUVs. After five minutes of searching, I spotted a black pickup truck parked away from most of the other vehicles. It was tucked in an alley between a boat repair building and a boat storage facility. Both buildings were three stories high. Even from a hundred feet away, I could see two stickers on the truck's bumper. A few people were walking in and out of the buildings.

I carried the tracker in one hand, the Glock in the small of my back, and the Beretta in an ankle holster. I knew that under the porch light at Floyd Shaw's trailer, the intruders saw my face. But in the shootout, I never saw their faces. They could identify me, but I couldn't recognize them. Any one of the three could walk right by me, and I'd never know whether he was someone who'd tried to take my head off.

I hoped to see and identify my enemies before they could spot me at the docks. Maybe the binoculars would give me that advantage. I walked up to the parked truck and glanced around for security cameras. There were none visible on the buildings or utility poles.

I now had a good look at the bumper stickers: a grinning shark in red, white, and blue with starfish for stars, and an angry shrimp caricature with clenched fists and lips drawn back in a canine snarl. *Bubba Grumps* was written below the shrimp's image.

And in between both stickers was a bullet hole. Another bullet hole was in the tailgate, and the taillight had been blown out. I moved to the opposite side of the bumper and pressed a button to turn on the GPS tracker. I slipped under the truck, slapping the magnetic side beneath the rear bumper, far enough in so it couldn't be seen walking up to the truck bed.

I found the truck. Now I'd try to find *Miss Marla Jean.*

SEVENTY-NINE

I decided to approach the shrimp docks from the perimeter. Why head into a potential battle by marching into the center of the battlefield? I walked parallel to the docks—in profile, not exposing my full face toward the direction of the shrimp boats. The salty air was laced with the smell of drying nets, dead fish, and diesel fuel. Water from bilge pumps splashed on the surface. I heard music from a sports-fishing yacht: Colter Wall singing *Sleeping on the Blacktop*.

I approached some of the buildings facing the docks, passing boats on jackstands and a gull perched atop the mast of a large sailboat suspended in a wooden marine cradle. I walked about fifty yards farther. Height would be an advantage for me, looking down on the area. It works well for eagles. I looked at the buildings, the rooftops, and potential ways to get to a roof.

Across from the commercial docks, where I counted six shrimp boats, there was a three-story boat dry storage building. I spotted steps to a fire escape that led from the outside of the top floor to the ground. I knew from there that I could look back and see all the shrimp boats lined up and tied to the docks.

If *Miss Marla Jean* was in port, I'd assume that Sharky was on the boat since his truck was here. Maybe the other men were there, too. I headed toward the three-story building. The metal fire escape stairs were on the left side. At the base of the stairs, I stepped over a sign that read: *No Entrance*. I didn't plan to enter, only to observe. At the top of the stairway, I turned toward the docks, balancing my back against the handrail and lifting the binoculars to my eyes.

The boat names that I could read included *Clementine*, *Lady Blue*, and *Night Stalker*. I climbed higher, almost to the roof. Although I saw no one on the shrimp boats, I could feel the presence of crew members on two boats. The vessels weren't buttoned up. Pilothouse windows and doors were open, and a mug of coffee sat on the gunwale of a cockpit work area. *Kathy Sue* was written on the stern of one shrimp boat. Adjacent to that boat was *Miss Marla Jean.*

A crewman on *Miss Marla Jean* came from the pilothouse to the deck. He was followed by a second man. They wore T-shirts, jeans, orange rubber boots, and bill caps. One of the men stepped off the boat and went to the dock, where he fastened a long hose to a spigot and turned on the water. He nodded, and the second man released a hand-held nozzle at his end of the hose, shooting out water. He filled a five-gallon galvanized steel bucket.

Both men used stiff-bristled brushes with long handles to scrub the deck, with water and suds sloshing around the work area. From where I stood, I could see that some of the water running off the deck into the harbor was dark red. Was it blood from the spoils of the sea caught in the nets? Sometimes, fish, rays, and even turtles get trapped with the shrimp in the big nets.

Or was in human blood?

A third man came from the pilothouse, pointing to a spot on the deck that a crew member missed with his brush. Through the binoculars, I looked at each man, taking mental notes of their faces, body language, and the way they walked. And now, in a crowd, I would be able to identify each one.

I could see how the captain, Hank Marsh, got the nickname, Sharky. His eyes appeared wide and deep-set, and he had more teeth than his mouth could hold. He walked around the deck, pacing, looking at the movement in the marina, like a shark circling its prey before striking. He lit a cigarette, using hand gestures as he talked to his men, smoke trailing.

They finished scrubbing the deck and poured the remaining sudsy water from the bucket into the marina. Marsh walked over to the port side of his boat. He took a long drag from his cigarette before flipping the butt into the water. He looked up, toward the building where I was standing on the stairway. I froze. No movement. But he'd already spotted me.

I lowered the binoculars. He went back inside the pilothouse, alerting his men. They turned, looking in my direction. I started down the stairs because I knew that Sharky would be using his binoculars or a telescope to get a better look at me. Maybe the fact that they saw me was a good thing, something that would motivate Sharky and his band of pirates to quickly move to the next place. I wanted it to be a liaison with Percy King.

And I wanted to be there when that happened.

***

One of the jailers, a squatty man who walked like a penguin, approached Gideon Wright, speaking in a high-pitched voice. "Hey, old man, it looks like you got your walkin' papers. Someone made your bond. You can get outta here, at least for now. You'll be back." He unlocked the door to the holding cell. "The receiving clerk will return your personal stuff—your watch, ring, whatever. You can change clothes in the room next to the discharge office."

"Thank you."

"Don't thank me too fast. From what I hear, the prosecutors have an open and shut case."

"Do you always judge someone by the opinions of others?"

"Just sayin' if it walks like a duck and squawks like a duck, it ain't a crow, Pops."

Gideon stepped out of the cell and looked back at the man in the uniform. "Do you judge a tree by the limbs it loses in a storm or by the roots that keep it from falling? Is the acorn a seed of life or just a nut? Until you walk in my shoes, don't judge me by the path I've had to travel. I would never judge you, Kenny. I look at your heart, not your scars."

"How'd you know my first name?"

Gideon only smiled, walking to get his clothes and personal possessions before meeting Margaux in the public area.

***

Margaux and Gideon left the courthouse, and they immediately were circled by more than a dozen members of the news media. Crews were shouting questions and holding cameras, microphones, and audio recorders like they were holding fistfuls of money in a frenzied auction. "Gideon, did you bury Darnell Reid on your land?" barked a tall reporter in a sportscoat.

Margaux and Gideon continued walking toward the parking lot, ignoring the questions, the sun like a white torch in the sky. Courthouse spectators watched as if a strange parade was moving down the sidewalk beneath the live oaks scattered across the dark green lawn.

A heavyset reporter in a wrinkled blue dress shirt asked, "Ms. Brennon, were you surprised the judge granted bond?"

They kept walking.

A blond reporter in a dark blue business suit said, "Prosecutors say they have a slam dunk case. They say the physical evidence is more than enough for a conviction. How do you respond?"

They kept walking.

A radio reporter, a middle-aged man, thrust his microphone forward. "Ms. Brennon, since you are representing Mr. Wright, can you tell us why you believe he's not guilty?"

No response.

The Daily Beacon reporter, Ken Chandler, asked, "Is this all about water rights to Gideon's spring?"

Margaux stopped waking. Gideon did the same. Chandler asked, "Would someone want the water rights to Gideon's spring enough to set him up for murder? If so, Ms. Brennon, who do you think that might be?"

Margaux nodded. "That's what this case is all about. Gideon's spring is the last in Florida, maybe the world, with the best quality water on the planet. Because there is an enormous global demand for natural spring water with mineral properties of good health, my client's spring is valuable. Simply put, that water can't be replicated. The healing properties alone are immense. He refuses to sell, rebuffs these big international companies that want to suck the water and life out of the spring and aquifer."

Chandler nodded, holding his audio recorder. "If this is the case, who do you think might be behind this legal deception?"

She smiled. "If it's a deception, which it is, it's not *legal*. It's criminal. Culpability begins in a corporate board room. We are prepared to take this case to a jury if we must because all Gideon Wright is guilty of is being a good steward of the land and spring. He's a gentleman and a gentle man … one who loves nature's beauty and the beauty within people. Gideon is not a killer. The real evidence will prove he did not do what the prosecutor alleges. Thank you."

Chandler handed Margaux his card as they walked to the parking lot. Reporters were still shouting questions as Margaux and Gideon climbed into her car. A minute later, clearing the parking lot and moving onto the road, she looked at the card. On the back side, Chandler wrote, *please call me.*

She glanced over at Gideon. "That reporter wants me to call him. Somehow, he knows more than all the rest of the wolf pack put together."

Gideon nodded. "The feeling I get is that he might know some of the people involved in this nefarious activity. How did he learn that? And could this knowledge put that young man in danger? Are you going to call him?"

"Maybe. I'd like to know what Chandler knows, and I'd like to give him information that could help turn this thing around in the court of public opinion. That's where the battle begins."

EIGHTY

I was in my Jeep and leaving the Daytona Harbor Marina when Margaux called. I answered my phone. "I have a good news, bad news scenario. Which one do you want first?"

I never liked conversations that began that way, especially when I'm on the receiving end. "Give me both barrels. You choose."

"Okay. The judge did grant bond for Gideon. He's with me in the car. Can I put you on speaker so Gideon can hear us?"

"Yes."

"We'll fill you in on some of the details. Suffice to say, the other half of the good news is that we made bond. The not so good part is the general thrust of the media's questions. They're acting like attack dogs, assuming that Gideon is guilty and asking him questions along that premise. Accuracy and presenting both sides of a story appear to mean nothing to today's so-called journalists. There is one exception, though."

"Who's that?"

"A reporter for the Daily Beacon. His name is Ken Chandler." Margaux explained what happened and added, "Chandler is asking if we thought the case was about taking away the water rights and if the murder was a setup to bring Gideon down. I have Chandler's card, and on the back side, he wrote, *please call me.*"

"Are you going to do that?"

"I don't know. What do you think?"

"Call him. Learn as much as you can about his sources. Without libeling yourself, you can name names, at least to set the stage for Chandler to do some old-fashioned fact-checking. Maybe he can dig up more bones in Percy King's backyard. And maybe he can find a criminal link between King and the executives with Glacier Artesian Springs."

"He might win a Pulitzer Prize if that happens. The reality, however, is that there's very little to go on, Sean, until *you* find it. With the police having arrested Gideon, they've dusted their hands and turned it over to the prosecutor. We also don't know what happened to those bodies you left behind at that trailer in the country."

"I do know."

"What do you mean?"

"I tracked down the men who shot and killed Floyd Shaw."

"That's impressive. How'd you do that?"

"Luck and a little deductive effort. They're shrimpers, probably on Percy King's payroll, at least the one he uses under the table and deals in cash only transactions." I told Margaux what I'd seen at the marina shrimp docks and added, "If they did take the bodies out of the state and into international waters, this case can move from local police jurisdiction to the FBI."

"That certainly would give us a better chance of proving Gideon's innocence. But to unveil the full scope of this crime, the FBI would have to prove connections between a global company and a small-town lawyer. Unless they're willing to come in and do wiretaps, with little known physical evidence, you might have to provide that link. Maybe the feds could take it from there, allowing Gideon to stay on his land with his beloved spring."

I said nothing.

"Sean, I will take Gideon home and then call the reporter to learn more."

"Okay. Are you going to stay at Gideon's cabin?"

"My office is set up in a spare room in my condo. I need to work out of there, building a defense for Gideon, sorting through potential witnesses. I'm hoping you will help throw logs on the fire. When I go back into the courtroom for his arraignment, I want to be a torchbearer with evidence that will shine a light on the evil that is creeping all around him."

"If that reporter, Ken Chandler, requests an in-person meeting with you, do it in a public place, like a café or someplace where you both aren't alone."

"So, are you suggesting that both of us are targets?"

"I know that I am a target. As I mentioned, Sharky and his gang spotted me at the marina. I can only assume that King would like you to go away so the case would be in legal limbo, maybe giving him the chance to buy off another lawyer to take your place. What I'd like to know is how this reporter is so far ahead of the media pack with pertinent and real information."

"I guess the only way to find out is for me to call him."

"I'm going to shift the conversation to Gideon for a moment."

"Of course. Go ahead."

"Gideon, I'm sorry you're having to go through this."

Gideon cleared his throat. "Hi, Sean. I'm okay. I listened as you and Margaux brought each other up to speed. Thank you for what you've done."

"Save that for the moment we can shift a murder charge from you to someone else. And save it for the time we can use your special water in our toast to a better future for the land and spring."

"All right. However, I am very appreciative of what you're trying to do. You're putting your life on the line and doing it more than once. I just wonder how many times you can run back into a burning building."

"As many as it takes. But this isn't a case of rescuing you. It's about preventing someone with the mind of an arsonist from setting fire to your life. That's what Margaux and I are trying hard to prevent. In the meantime, considering you're where they want you to be right now—as the prime suspect in a murder trial—I don't think anyone will feel the need to come on your property and hurt you or plant additional false evidence. But don't take any chances. Keep some indoor lights and all your outdoor floodlights on at night. And call the police if you see or hear anything—don't go outside to investigate."

"Okay."

"Always keep your phone near you." I could hear two quick beeps. "Gideon, hold on a second, I need to check something."

I tapped the app for the GPS tracker and saw movement from the marina. The truck was leaving. "Gideon and Margaux, I need to go. Hank Marsh's truck is heading out of the marina. I'm going to follow this land shark to see where he goes."

I clicked off, watching the satellite map on my phone's screen as the dot moved away from the marina, westward toward DeLand. I made a U-turn in my Jeep and drove in the same direction.

EIGHTY-ONE

I'd gone less than a mile when Dave called. I answered, and he said, "I'm seeing movement from the pickup truck. Looks like Hank Marsh, AKA Sharky, is on the prowl. Do you see it on your phone?"

"Yes. I was speaking with Margaux and Gideon when the alert came. Marsh is heading west from Daytona Harbor Marina in the direction of DeLand. Perhaps that's his destination."

"That's a good bet. Do you surmise it's to meet with Percy King?"

"Most likely. I've been surveilling Marsh and his men on their shrimp boat, *Miss Marla Jean,* at the marina." I told Dave what I'd seen.

"Do you think these guys loaded the bodies on their shrimp boat in the dead of night and dumped them at sea?"

"Yes. Probably weighted them down in the water a mile deep. The ocean will eat just about everything in a couple of days. Since the scope of the crime might have expanded into international waters, maybe the feds will get involved." I shared with Dave what Margaux had told me, adding, "Somehow this reporter, Chandler, seems to be holding a good hand of cards in this deadly game. How they were dealt is the question I'd like answered."

"Maybe Margaux can get the answers when she converses with him. I'm delighted that she managed to secure Gideon's bond in a first-degree murder trial. Quite impressive."

"Yes, she is impressive and proving to be very good at what she does. This case, for all the reasons she studied to become an attorney, has reignited her passion for law. It's not only about obtaining justice for an old man but also about exposing the truth for the last living member of her family."

"She's facing a corporate giant. Let's hope the rock in her sling is deadly enough to bring these people to their knees. I'm looking at one of my computer screens, following the GPS movement of the truck, and it appears like the driver is speeding up some. I'll let you get back in the race. Talk soon."

Dave clicked off, and I looked at my phone screen, watching the moving dot. I took a shortcut to where I thought he was going in DeLand. Maybe I'd get there before Marsh parked his truck. Hopefully, I'd see him enter Percy King's law firm.

***

Margaux walked with Gideon as he opened the front door to his cabin and went to the refrigerator to take out a pitcher of water. "Would you like some? It's only been five days since I put it in the refrigerator. However, with the incarceration, it seems longer."

"Even though the water just surpassed the toddler stage and sits under its shelf life, I find it amusing that, deep in the spring, it has been aged by Mother Earth for thousands of years. See, Grandpa, I'm learning from you already. And, yes, I would love some."

Gideon smiled and poured the water into two glasses, handing one to her. He raised his glass. "Cheers … and thank you for helping me. Thank you for your remarkable skills in the court of law."

"Cheers, and you're welcome."

They sipped the water. Margaux smiled. "Even if this didn't have all the essential restorative minerals for good health, it still would be the best-tasting water in the world. I'm going to step out on the porch and call that reporter."

"Okay. I'll take my glass and enjoy it with Seth. He's such a good listener. Before I go and sit, I want to tell you how proud I am of you. Your analytical mind is fearless, and it is fair. That's a great and admirable trait."

Margaux stood on the porch as Gideon walked over to the old oak and sat down on the wrought-iron bench beneath it. She made the call. "Ken Chandler, can I help you?"

"Mr. Chandler, this is Margaux Brennon, Gideon Wright's attorney."

"Yes. Thank you for calling me. I was hoping to hear from you."

"You were the only reporter to ask us pertinent questions about how and why Gideon is facing bogus charges for a murder he did not commit.

307

How'd you get that information, the questions about the fight for water rights and Gideon's spring?"

"Rather than talk over the phone, can I speak with you in person? I'd like to interview you, ask questions that are on the record, and I'll share with you what I know."

She looked across the yard at Gideon sitting on the bench, a squirrel at his feet. "Okay. When and where would you like to meet?"

"Like most reporters, I'm on deadline. The sooner, the better. Can we meet tonight. Say seven-thirty at the Boston Coffeehouse? It's in downtown DeLand."

"Okay. I'll be there. Just answer one question for me, and you can do it without elaborating. A simple yes or no answer."

"What's your question?"

"Is Percy King part of this puzzle?"

There was a hesitation. "Yes."

***

I parked two blocks north of Percy King's office and waited. I looked at the phone screen, watching the dot come within a mile of where I was. I got out of my Jeep and walked down the street past a hardware store, bakery, bookstore, and flower shop. I stood under an awning across the street from his law office. There were two parking spots by the curb.

I glanced at my phone, following the dot, and looked up as the pickup truck came into view. I stepped into the entrance to the flower shop, watching Hank Marsh parallel park about fifty feet past King's office door. I used my phone to shoot video as he got out of his truck and glanced around for a moment, a cigarette in one corner of his mouth. He took a final drag, dropping the cigarette butt to the pavement, walking to the office door, and disappearing inside.

"Gotcha, Sharky," I whispered as he entered the building.

***

It was dark as Ken Chandler was leaving his ranch-style home about ten miles outside of Deland. As a single man, he rented the home, hoping a better job offer would come his way in the next two months before the lease ended. Maybe the Gideon Wright story would be his key to landing a job at a major newspaper.

He always parked his car, a ten-year-old Toyota, in the driveway next to a sidewalk that led to the front door. He stepped onto the porch, locked the door, and walked to his car. Cicadas screeched from the piney woods surrounding his home. There were only a few homes on the rural road, a mixture of brick-and-mortar houses and some trailers. He looked at the house across the street. The lights were off. There were no vehicles in the driveway.

Chandler unlocked his car door and started to get inside.

Cold steel pressed against the back of his neck.

"Don't move!" whispered the man. "The bullet will cut your spinal cord."

Chandler froze. He raised his hands. "If you want my wallet, take it."

"Shut up!"

Two more men emerged from the bushes. Hank Marsh grinned, his teeth glowing in the moonlight. He nodded. "You boys know what to do."

"What do you want?" Chandler's voice cracked. "Do you want money?"

Marsh stepped in front of him. "What we want is your cooperation."

"Okay. You got it."

"Good. Walk into the woods. We've checked it out. Looks like that footpath goes in about a hundred feet. We need to talk."

"We can talk here in the driveway. What do you want?"

"Just your cooperation, and then we'll be gone. It'll be like we were never here."

"I'm not going anywhere with you."

Marsh smiled. The next second, he hit Chandler hard in the jaw. The blow almost knocked him out. "Grab this dude by the scruff of his neck. Let's move."

The other two men, Mutt and Carl Lee, manhandled Chandler, pushing and dragging him into the woods. A dog barked behind the house with the lights off. Thirty seconds later, they were in a small clearing surrounded by tall pines. They threw Chandler to the ground. The phone in his back pocket beeped.

Marsh sniffed. "You can't answer that. But it would give a new meaning to last call."

Chandler stared up at him through bleary and dazed eyes. Marsh looked at the men and nodded. They attacked Chandler, one grabbing his hair and holding his head back as the other used a knife to cut across his neck. Ear to ear. When the blade hit the carotid artery, blood spurted five feet, the spatter hitting Marsh's sneakers. He lit a cigarette and smoked it while Chandler lay dying.

When the young reporter took his last breath, his body making a short spasm, Marsh reached down and took the phone from Chandler's pocket. "You won't be needing this anymore." He turned to his men. "Let's roll the body into the carpet remnant, secure it in the truck, and get it outta here. This reporter has written his final story."

EIGHTY-TWO

It was 7:27 when Margaux walked through the front door of the coffee shop. Less than a dozen customers, mostly college students, sat at tables, working the keyboards on their laptops. Margaux looked around, not seeing Ken Chandler. The place smelled of fresh-ground coffee beans and cinnamon.

She moved through the shop from the entrance to the rear door. No sign of the reporter. She took a seat in the corner, out of immediate earshot, and ordered a cappuccino from a college-age blond server.

Margaux looked at her watch. It was exactly 7:30. She thought about her conversation with Chandler and the last thing she asked him.

A simple yes or no answer.

What's your question?

Is Percy King part of this puzzle?

Yes.

Margaux felt a sudden chill move down her back. The air conditioner in the shop blew cold air from a vent in the ceiling above her table. The cappuccino was served, and she held the warm cup with both hands, sipping. She sat back and looked at her watch. Chandler was now ten minutes late. He didn't seem to her like someone who would be late, especially since he requested the meeting.

She waited another five minutes before picking up her phone to call him. "You've reached Ken Chandler. Please leave a message."

"Ken, it's Margaux Brennon. I'm at the Boston Coffeehouse. It's about a quarter to eight. Please call and let me know if you're still coming. If not, I need to head home. It's been a long day."

***

Hank Marsh and his men were less than a mile from DeLand, heading to the marina, when Chandler's phone rang. Marsh lifted it off the truck's console and looked at the caller ID. After the call went to voicemail, he played back the message. *"Ken, it's Margaux Brennon. I'm at the Boston Coffeehouse. It's about a quarter to eight. Please call and let me know if you're still coming."*

Marsh used his phone to make a call. His men sat silently next to him in the truck. Chandler's body was rolled into a carpet and secured in the truck bed. "Success with the first item," he said into his phone. "The second item, the one you wanted us to handle soon, is in a coffee shop in downtown Deland right now. We can take care of that, strike while the iron's hot, and pick up our shopping money. There's no better time than the present."

"What would you do, handle it in the parking lot or follow her home?"

"Follow. Less chance of being spotted. Too many people downtown to make it safe to do anything, even at night."

"Then do it. Let me know as soon as you're taking both out to sea."

"I'll do that, and I'll pick up the remaining balance owed tomorrow."

Percy King clicked off, sat behind his desk, and poured a thirty-year-old scotch into a heavy cocktail glass.

***

I was back at Ponce Marina, helping Wynona wash and dry dishes in *Jupiter's* galley. Angela and Max were curled up on the couch in the salon and watching a classic animated movie, *All Dogs Go to Heaven*. I shared with Wynona everything that had happened and added, "I'm hoping that this reporter, Ken Chandler, will tell Margaux how he discovered the ruse and deception of how Gideon is being set up."

"It sounds to me like he has an anonymous informant, perhaps someone who called in to the newspaper, asked to speak with Chandler, and told him what's really going on. This person could have hung up without leaving his name or a call-back number."

"Maybe. But who? Percy King covers his tracks very well. He either buys off trouble or has it killed. Then the evidence is disposed of like taking out the trash."

"You think that's the case with those guys on the shrimp boat?"

"Yes. One of them is the same man who stalked your antique shop, and they are the ones who took out Floyd Shaw. I was there to interrupt the job before they could finish."

"But they returned and finished. It's as if King has a dirty dozen, a select group of criminals at his disposal, to hire or bribe into doing his bidding. Since he's entrenched in the legal system, maybe he's represented some of the criminals he hires. As their attorney, he'd know where their skeletons are hidden. And King wouldn't be shy about threatening exposure."

"I think you summed it up well. If the bodies were dumped at sea, this might not be the first time. Chances are that at least one of the three men working on *Miss Marla Jean* might talk if pressured. Perhaps taking a plea deal to help convict Hank Marsh and Percy King if it meant saving himself from the death penalty."

"How would this crew member be pressured?"

"With sincere negotiations." I didn't elaborate.

Wynona finished drying the last dish, using a blue hand towel to dry the plate. "Sometimes I wish you had a partner, someone to watch your back."

"I do. That partner is you. Dave does a good job from the perimeter as well. Your insight has helped me in many of my cases. I rely on your intuition."

"Thank you."

"I know your contacts with the FBI are beginning to dwindle, but do you have someone you could call to see if he or she might look at the information and the criminal motivation behind this? I think the ultimate criminals work for a global company, and since their detached labor force is dumping bodies in international waters, it fits the parameters of an FBI investigation."

Wynona leaned back against the galley counter. We could hear Angela singing along with the characters in the movie, her voice on key. "I do have an old friend that is bureau chief in the Jacksonville field office. Her name is Claudia Ramirez. I have her cell phone number. We've worked together in the past. She's one of the best of the best and won't compromise her work or the law for anyone."

"Can you call her this evening? It's that urgent. You know the complete story and the players. Maybe I can use the Bureau to do two things."

"What, Sean?"

"Maybe hold a key witness in protective custody and help in a sting involving the biggest players. After you speak with Claudia, ask her if I can call her soon to run those two things by her."

"I can do that. And I'll give her number to you. I'd love for you to meet Claudia and her husband sometime."

"Okay." I heard my phone beep. I'd left it in the salon. I looked over at Wynona. "I need to see who's calling."

"Okay, I'll finish."

I picked up my phone. Margaux was on the line. I stepped out and onto the boat's cockpit to take the call. "Sean, you asked me to tell you what happened when I spoke with the reporter, Ken Chandler."

"Yes, what did he say?"

"Nothing. A no-show. I waited about thirty minutes, finished my cappuccino, and left."

"Did you call him?"

"I did, and I left a message. I'm driving to my condo in New Smyrna. I have a migraine. It's odd that Chandler didn't show or call. He was the one who really wanted the meeting."

I said nothing.

"Are you there?"

"Yes. Just thinking. I want to check something. What's your address?"

"It's 9274 North Atlantic Avenue. Why?"

"I'll call you back in a few minutes."

"Okay, I need to walk my dog, though. Lily's been cooped up for far too long. Poor thing."

I clicked off and touched the GPS app. The dot was moving. Hank Marsh's truck was traveling east on the South Causeway. I stared at the dot, watching the image move. The truck wasn't heading north on its way back to Daytona Beach. It was in the heart New Smyrna Beach, traveling from the South Causeway onto South Atlantic Avenue.

***

Gideon called Margaux, "I was just thinking about you. Have you reached your condo?"

"I'm close. The traffic and headlights brought on a migraine. If I get some sleep, hopefully, it'll go away. Are you okay? Did you make dinner?"

"I reheated some vegetable soup and made toast. Now I'm sitting in my favorite leather chair and reading a book. It's good to be home."

***

I was pacing in *Jupiter's* cockpit when I called Margaux. The call went to her voicemail. "Margaux, some very dangerous men are near your home. It's Hank Marsh—Sharky. Do not answer the door. Call 9-1-1 and tell them you saw a prowler. Call me!"

EIGHTY-THREE

In the master berth, I placed the Beretta in my ankle holster and shoved the Glock under my belt, beneath the shirt. I signaled for Wynona to follow me. She came from the galley to the cockpit, carrying a cup of coffee in one hand. "Sean, what's wrong?"

"I think Hank Marsh knows where Margaux lives, and he's heading to her condo. I need to go right now. My shotgun is hidden in the Jeep."

She nodded, set the cup down, and gave me a brief hug. "Be careful. I love you."

I kissed her forehead, jumped off *Jupiter*, and sprinted down the dock. Dave was stepping off *Gibraltar*. "Sean, I was just walking to your boat. I noticed that the truck owned by the guy you said was Sharky is in New Smyrna Beach. Didn't you say that's where Gideon's attorney lives—his great-granddaughter, Margaux?"

"She's at 9274 North Atlantic. Keep an eye on it for me. Watching my phone screen while driving at the speed I need to will be challenging. I called Margaux, but she didn't answer. I left a message, telling her that Marsh and his men were heading toward her condo. Gotta go."

Dave started to say something as I turned and ran hard down L dock, through the alley connecting the marina office with the Tiki Bar, and up to my Jeep. I squealed tires, flinging gravel as I peeled out of the lot, heading from Ponce Inlet to New Smyrna Beach. The destination is much closer by boat than by going over land. But I had no choice.

I drove toward Highway 1, exceeding the speed limit. I hoped I wouldn't see emergency lights flashing in my rearview mirror. If so, maybe I could lead a pack of police to the condo and let them take over.

Maybe not.

That approach might result in Marsh and his men killing Margaux or holding her hostage. I had to do it using stealth and surprise, and I had to do it with no time to spare. I passed cars, crossing the double-yellow lines. Traffic rules are made to be broken when known killers are staking out a potential victim's home.

My phone buzzed. Dave on the line. I hit the Bluetooth button, diverting our conversation through the Jeep's sound system. "Sean, it looks like the truck is within five blocks of that address. Where are you?"

"Heading south on Highway 1."

"Should we alert the local police and have them head over to Margaux's condo?"

"Marsh and his men will be there before the police can arrive. If the cops come with lights blazing and guns drawn, Margaux will be the first to die." My phone beeped. "Dave, Margaux is calling." I clicked off and answered.

"Sean, I heard your message. How would Hank Marsh and his men know where I live? My name isn't on the property records."

"They wouldn't access records if they're following you."

"What! Following me?" She turned off the street and into her driveway, her heart racing. "I just got out of my car, and I'm walking to the front door. There were cars and trucks going down the highway, but nobody exited behind me. How would they know where …."

"Margaux, you told me that you called the reporter, Ken Chandler, and left a message. What exactly did you tell him?"

"That I was waiting for him at the Boston Coffeehouse and that, if he didn't call, I was going home soon."

"If Marsh and his thugs did something to Chandler, they may have his phone."

"What do you mean *if they did something?*"

"If they killed him and saw your call come in, they could have picked up his phone and heard your message. They might have been following you *from* the coffee shop."

"Oh, my God. I'm going in and will make sure the doors and windows are locked."

"Stay inside. They may be following you to see where you live, planning to come back at another time. I'm heading to your place now."

Margaux unlocked her door, stepping inside the ground-floor condo, locking the door behind her, and turning on the porch light.

"Sean, I'm inside. I've always been a strong woman, but right now I would love to see you here. Please hurry. Bye."

Lily, a white Maltese, came scampering into the hallway, tail wagging, and curled over her backside. Margaux set her briefcase down on a living room chair and picked up Lily. "How's my girl doing? I missed you, too."

She held Lily and walked to the drapes across the front window, peeking outside. She watched the traffic for half a minute before looking at Lily. "Perhaps they're casing our home. It happens in this line of work. But we have some protection—a doorbell camera, a small pistol, and our friend Sean O'Brien, who's heading this way. I bought my gun before you were born, baby girl, because I was afraid of my ex. I'm so glad you never met him. But if he ever finds us here, you can bite his ankle." Margaux laughed, her laugh sounding hollow and forced. She placed the palm of her hand on her forehead. "My head aches. I need to take some aspirin and lie down."

Lily barked, paced, and ran to and from the door. "I know you have to pee. I don't want you to get a urinary tract infection. But we can't go out the front door. Maybe we can slip out the back for the time it takes you to go to the bathroom. Tonight's not the time to be persnickety. Just find a spot and pee, okay?"

Lily barked. Margaux unzipped her purse and removed the Sig P30 subcompact pistol. She looked over at Lily. "I've never had to walk you with a leash in one hand and a gun in the other." She picked up Lily, took the leash off the hook by the door, and walked to the rear of the condo, moving through the kitchen and sunroom. Margaux didn't turn on any indoor lights.

She peered between the slats of the wooden blinds to look outside. The yard was small. Lush tropical landscaping provided some privacy between the ground level units. There was only a service road behind the building, mostly used by residents, guests, and grounds workers. Margaux saw no cars—nothing parked or moving. No headlights. She cracked open the door, and Lily bolted outside.

"Hold on, Lily. I don't want you pulling your collar tight around your neck." Margaux followed her little dog outside, with Lily sniffing at the base of the tall canary palm trees. "Come on, girl. Don't be picky.

Find a spot." With the gun near her thigh, she glanced up at the clouds drifting in the moonlight. "Come on, Sean," she whispered.

A man stepped from out of the dark shadows, walking quietly behind Margaux. He grabbed her right arm, shoving it behind her back, twisting the pistol from her hand. In two seconds, his hand covered her face. Lily barked. Margaux fought, kicking and elbowing her attacker.

A second man appeared. He backhanded Margaux, knocking her to the ground. She was dazed, her mouth bleeding. Hank Marsh pushed through the philodendrons. "Get her bound." His men placed duct tape across Margaux's mouth and used it to bind her hands behind her back.

"Sharky, you sure you just don't wanna waste her now? It'll make it easier to carry the bitch," said Mutt.

"Look at that body. C'mon, we can't waste a woman like that 'til we all have turns with her on the boat." He unzipped a small leather case, which was a little larger than his hand, and removed a hypodermic needle. Margaux tried to roll away. Lily was barking and dragging her leash through the landscaping. "Hold her like you would a calf that needs branding."

His men held Margaux, one man pushing hard against her back, Margaux's face in the grass, and the other man holding her feet. Marsh stuck the needle into her thigh, injecting the chemical. Seconds later, he stood, a thin sliver of saliva coming from the right side of his crooked mouth. "I get this stuff from my girlfriend. She's a vet assistant. A full injection would sedate a horse. I gave this wildcat enough to put her to sleep for a while."

Margaux's heart was racing, her palms damp, and her face hot. The conversation the men were having sounded far away, their words coming in layers of reverberation. She lay on the grass, and Lily huddled near the back door, shaking. Within ten seconds, Margaux's world went dark.

Two of the men carried Margaux to the truck, the tailgate facing the backyard. Marsh fished for his keys in his pocket. "Put her in the cab in a rear seat. She'll be out the whole way."

He dropped his keys on the pavement near the left rear tire. "Shit!" He used the flashlight on his phone to find them. As he was reaching for his keys, he noticed something under his bumper. "What the hell is that?"

Marsh snatched the GPS tracker off the underside of his bumper. "Shit! Somebody's been watching us."

"What's that?" asked Carl Lee.

"It's a tracker. GPS from a satellite signal. Somebody's keepin' tabs on us."

"How the hell did that get there?"

"My money would be on the PI, O'Brien. And now he knows we were here. That means he's probably coming. I wish we had time to hang out and put one through the back of his head. We got the woman and the dead body. We can't stay here and wait for him to turn up, especially is he's already called the cops. We need to get out of here. We'll deal with O'Brien and his family on the next go-round. After that, we can all go down to Honduras 'til the heat blows over. Remember, no body, no crime."

They got in the truck and drove away. Marsh tossed the tracker out his window and into a drainage ditch. Margaux lay unconscious in the cab, only a few feet from Chandler's bloody body inside a carpet in the truck bed. Marsh turned up the volume on his truck's radio and sang along with Blake Shelton's *Fire Up the Night*.

EIGHTY-FOUR

I was within half a mile of Margaux's condo. I called her. The call went to voicemail—not a good sign. I glanced at the tracker app; the dot was now moving westward. Dave called. "Sean, it looks like the truck was there, but for less than five minutes. Maybe Marsh and his men were surveilling where Margaux lives, planning a return trip."

"I don't think that's the case. Margaux's not answering her phone."

"The truck is about five miles away, heading west on Highway 44. And now it looks like it's stopped."

"I'm almost at Margaux's condo. I'll check out the place. Thanks, Dave." I clicked off, speeding the remaining few blocks to the condo. I slowly drove by her car in the driveway. Margaux's porch light was on, but the interior appeared dark. She either didn't want to have the lights on or she wasn't home. I pulled to the side of the road, parked, and jogged back to the condo.

I stood next to some tall palms and called her again. The call went to voicemail. I pulled out my Glock and listened. Light traffic and a jet flying overhead in the night sky were the only sounds. I didn't go to the front door but, instead, sprinted toward the back entrance. As I came up to the lush landscaping, I heard the single bark of a dog. Just from the bark, I knew it was a small dog. I thought of Max sitting next to Angela on the couch, watching the movie.

I pushed through the banana plants and date palms into a modest yard. Near the backdoor was a white ball of fur—a Maltese, her leash on, the little dog looking confused and frightened. I didn't need to go inside to know that Margaux was gone. There is no way that she would leave her dog alone in the backyard on a leash.

I approached the dog, whispering. "It's okay, Lily. I'm here to help you." She wagged her turned-up tail. "Where's your mama? I bet she isn't here." I knelt, Glock in my right hand, and petted Lily. She licked my left hand. I stood and tried the door. It opened, and I entered, walking quietly through every room in the condo. Margaux was gone.

I looked at the tracker app on my phone. The truck was parked off Highway 44. I took off Lily's leash, set her back in the condo, locked the backdoor, and ran to my Jeep. Once inside, with the engine revving, I called Dave. "Margaux's gone. They must have abducted her."

"The tracker hasn't moved. It appears to be about five miles from Margaux's condo. Head west. I'll give you directions."

"Okay." I drove my Jeep west in two-lane traffic, holding the phone to my ear. I could hear Dave tapping his keyboard, jazz playing in the background on his boat.

"From what I can determine, it looks like the truck is off to the side of the road. The optimist in me wants to hope they pulled over to let Margaux go. But the realist in me knows that these outlaws are in too deep to turn things around. And if they killed the reporter, all of them could receive the death penalty. But guys like Percy King skate."

"Not this time. How much farther, Dave?"

"Maybe another couple hundred yards. No movement at all from the tracker."

I said nothing, speeding in that direction.

"Start slowing down. You should have a visual on the truck in thirty seconds."

"It's a two-lane highway. Partially industrial. Lots of vacant lots ready for development."

"Maybe they pulled in behind a building. But even dimwitted thugs don't do a pit stop with a kidnapped victim in the vehicle."

"Not unless you're dumping the body off the road." I slowed, searching for a sign of the truck. There were no signs. "I don't see a truck."

"You ought to be very close, within fifty feet."

"I'm stopping and getting out. Maybe Marsh spotted the tracker and tossed it."

"Let's hope not."

I took a tactical flashlight from my Jeep, got out with my Glock in one hand, and used the light to scan the open field. There were rocks the size of cantaloupes, knee-high weeds, and a grocery shopping cart turned over on its side. I walked another twenty feet, toward a drainage ditch. The water in the ditch has a smell of sulfuric gas and burned motor oil. I used the light to scan the ditch, spotting an object that resembled a small turtle. But it wasn't a turtle.

It was the tracker, lodged in dark mud at the edge of the stagnant water. I walked over and picked it up. I thought about the last thing Margaux said to me. *Sean, I'm inside. I've always been a strong woman, but right now I would love to see you here. Please hurry.*

I put the Glock under my belt and took the phone from my pocket. Dave was still on the line, holding, and waiting. "I found the tracker. Marsh had tossed it in a ditch. I got it, and I'm heading out."

"Where are you going?"

"To where I believe they're talking Margaux—to the shrimp docks at the Daytona Harbor Marina."

"Do you think these criminals have plans to take her on a one-way voyage?"

"I don't know."

"If Margaux is alive, how long would she have?"

"I saw no signs of blood in her condo or her backyard. The only reason to abduct Margaux would be to take her out to sea before tossing her overboard with weights on her body."

"Or they could have other intentions for her. They might hold her as a kidnapping victim, trying to extort money from Gideon. If they're going to the marina, and if they're planning a one-way trip for Margaux, maybe you can get there before they untie the mooring lines and shove off."

"I can try. How I approach them on their boat, though, is the unknown factor. Under the cover of darkness will help. If they're not at the marina, time won't be on our side or Margaux's either." I clicked off and sped up, passing cars as I drove west on Highway 44, turning north on I-95, and heading to *Miss Marla Jean's* home port.

I called Wynona and asked, "Did you speak with your FBI friend, Claudia?"

"Yes. She is very interested in your case and said, if these people are killing people on land and traveling into international waters to dump bodies, she'd like to get her field office involved."

"They may get involved tonight." I told Wynona what I was doing.

"Sean, I'll call Claudia back to get her team ready. Jacksonville's about ninety minutes from Daytona, and that's driving at the speed limit."

"Tell her I think these guys have kidnapped Margaux Brennon. That crime is very much in the Bureau's wheelhouse. I think they are or will be hiding her on Marsh's shrimp boat before heading out to dump her body. I'd like Claudia to head that way with a few agents."

"I'll call her and let you know what she says."

"Thanks. Text her number to me." I clicked off and pressed the Jeep's accelerator. I couldn't get there fast enough.

EIGHTY-FIVE

Margaux regained consciousness and stared at a dead man's face. There was tape over her mouth, her hands were bound behind her back, and her feet were tied at the ankles. Ken Chandler's body was less than ten away, his face ashen, with a deep purple cut across his neck. She was lying on a cold, wet floor in a room with one light on the ceiling. She could see her breath as she exhaled through her nostrils. The refrigerated storage room smelled of shrimp and bleach.

She could feel a slight movement. Margaux didn't know if she was suffering from vertigo or if the room was moving.

I'm on a boat, she thought, terror rising in her chest.

She tried to control her breathing, but her heart was hammering, and her hands were numb from the lack of blood circulation. She listened for the sound of the boat's engine. There was nothing but the drone of muffled conversation coming from another area on the boat. Margaux had no idea how long she'd been unconscious. And she didn't know whether the boat was docked at a marina or out on the water somewhere.

She thought of Lily. *Was she roaming around the neighborhood on her leash? Please be safe.* She closed her burning eyes, remembering one of the last things Gideon had said to her. *Before I go and sit with Seth, I want to tell you how proud I am of you. Your analytical mind is fearless and fair. That's a great and admirable trait.*

She pulled at the tape binding her wrists, flexing her numb fingers while twisting her facial muscles, trying to dislodge the tape. The fear in her chest was being displaced by fury. *Why am I here? Why is Chandler's body here, on a boat? It had to be a shrimp boat.* She remembered what Sean had said about Hank Marsh—Sharky. *If they did take the bodies out of the state and into international waters, this case can move from local police jurisdiction to the FBI.*

325

The thought of being tossed overboard into the ocean sent shivers through her body. She'd almost drowned in a lake as a little girl, and, although she'd learned to swim, Margaux still harbored a dread of deep water. She managed to sit up on the floor, scooting her body into a corner with the cold steel of the walls against her back.

***

I pulled my Jeep into the parking lot of the Daytona Harbor Marina and drove to the last place I'd seen Marsh's truck parked. "Be there," I whispered. I figured there were no more than a dozen vehicles in the lot, which was at least an acre in size.

As I came around a boat storage building, I saw the pickup truck. I parked, reaching into my glove box, removing a gallon-sized, resealable plastic storage bag. I didn't know whether I'd need it, but if I did, there probably wouldn't be time to run back to the Jeep to get it. I stuffed the plastic bag in one pocket, placed the Beretta in my ankle holster, picked up the Glock, and slid a tactical knife into the sheath attached to my belt.

I would keep the Glock under my shirt as I looked for security cameras. I figured that might be why Marsh parked his truck in this part of the marina. There are few or no surveillance cameras in the immediate vicinity. As a shrimper, it wouldn't raise an eyebrow if he or his crew moved boxes and crates to and from the boat. No one would ever suspect that bodies were inside those containers.

I walked by the truck, looking at the truck bed and glancing in the windows. I could see nothing but two beer cans and a McDonald's hamburger wrapper. I stayed in the darkest shadows, walking next to the exterior wall of a boat storage building as I got closer to the commercial docks. I looked at the corners of the building and could see no cameras attached. I stood there for a moment, scanning the marina. There was no visible movement.

I called Dave. "I found Marsh's truck. No sign of Margaux. They could have locked her in one of the seafood processing storage facilities here at the dock, or they could have carried her out to the boat."

"What's your gut telling you?"

"That she's on the boat. Maybe the reporter is there with her. Margaux is facing men who sold their souls to the devil."

"Men like that often don't fear death. It's part of their business model. That elevates their resistance when you face them."

I said nothing, listening to the marina sounds.

"Sean, are you there?"

"Yes. I'm moving toward the shrimp docks. Gotta go." I clicked off.

I walked fast, heading toward one of the three docks where the shrimp boats were moored. A mist was rising from the marina's dark waters, and the night air hung heavy with a brackish odor. I looked at one of the barnacle-encrusted pilings and saw the water moving inward with a rising tide. I knew where *Miss Marla Jean* was moored. As I moved down the dock, I stayed on the right side, trying to keep as many boats as possible between me and *Miss Marla Jean.*

I heard an engine crank. It was the unmistakable sound of a big diesel—odd for this time of night. Shrimp boats usually didn't leave or arrive at an hour like this. I knew the sound was coming from Marsh's boat. And I had seconds to decide.

EIGHTY-SIX

Margaux felt the rumble of the diesels. Her heart raced so fast that she thought she could hear blood rushing through her ears. She wanted to stand and bolt through the door. She was very cold and getting colder. Maybe her abductors wanted her to freeze to death. Margaux glanced down at Chandler's body, remembering their last conversation.

What's your question?

Is Percy King part of this puzzle?

Yes.

Margaux took a deep breath through her nose, the air getting colder. As an attorney, whenever she was backed into a corner, she was able to figure a way out. Sometimes, it was a winning strategy. Other times, it was an exit tactic. As she stood in the corner of a cold walk-in, she couldn't come up with a solution. It would have to take someone coming in—a true intervention on the high seas.

Did anyone know she was here? Sean O'Brien knew where she had been—her condo. But that felt like a lifetime ago. For the first time since she could remember, Margaux began to pray.

***

By the time I moved stealthily down to the end of the dock, I could see the exhaust fumes drifting from the stern area of *Miss Marla Jean*. Two crew members were releasing and pulling in mooring lines, keeping the outriggers vertical. In the pilothouse, I could see a silhouette and the red glow of a burning cigarette moving. Hank Marsh was at the wheel. On the port side of the boat, I spotted a rubber marine bumper attached to a rope, maybe two feet above the waterline.

Was Margaux on the boat? Was she stowed aboard like cargo? Was she still alive?

There was only one way to find out.

I opened the plastic bag, put in my pistols and phone, and stored the bag in the small of my back under my belt. I removed my shoes. I was watching two things simultaneously: the crew members and the distance from the dock to the slowly moving boat. I couldn't dive in if they were looking toward the stern. And I couldn't swim fast enough if the boat moved too far away.

The two crew members finished coiling lines, turning to enter the pilothouse. I dove off the dock straight into the water, swimming underwater for a few yards. When I surfaced, I scanned for movement on the boat. I could see none. I swam as hard as I could. The big shrimp boat was puttering its way around the other boats and marina docks. Once it cleared the obstacles, including million-dollar yachts, I knew that Marsh would kick it up a notch, and I'd never catch them.

I was closing the gap and hoping that no one in the wheelhouse looked behind the boat. I swam through the chop churned up by the diesels, the acrid odor of burned diesel fumes heavy in the night air. Now the words *Miss Marla Jean* were right in front of me. I swam to the port side, grabbing the line just above the rubber bumper. I held on tight, the chilly water skimming over my head and shoulders.

I pulled myself up, hand-over-hand, to the gunwale. I used both hands to pull higher, just lifting my head far enough over the side to see the deck and pilothouse. The men were still inside. Now I could see the red glow of three burning cigarettes. I climbed over the gunwale and onto the deck. It was a large boat, at least seventy-five feet long. I darted behind raised structures, either coolers or part of the crew's quarters.

I removed my Beretta and Glock from the plastic bag, slipping the Beretta into the ankle holster and the Glock into my right hand. I waited as Marsh maneuvered out of the dock area and into the harbor. As he kicked the engines up a bit, I stayed in the shadows and moved to the door of what I assumed was a storage area or where they kept shrimp until they got back to the docks.

The door handle was not locked. I opened it, stepping inside and into the dim light. Margaux was huddled in one corner, her feet and hands tied. She made a murmur, trying to say something through the silver tape over her mouth. I looked at the dead man on the floor and knew it had to be the reporter, Ken Chandler.

I removed the tape from Margaux's mouth. She gasped, taking a deep breath. "Thank God! How'd you know they had me here?"

"I didn't. It was a calculated guess." I put my Glock in my belt as I used my knife to cut the tape off her ankles and hands. She hugged me, her eyes watering. "You're wet. Did you swim to the boat?"

"Yeah. I got lucky. I spotted three men on this boat. Are there any others?"

"I don't know. There were three when they attacked me in my backyard. Two held me down while the other used a needle to shoot something into my thigh."

"I got to your home just minutes after they abducted you."

"Lily. Is she …."

"Lily's fine. I put her in your condo. Stay in here." I pulled the Beretta out of my pocket. "Take this. There is going to be a mess on deck. If anyone but me opens that door, shoot him. Their plan is to throw you and Chandler's body overboard at sea. When weighted down, bodies are never found out there." I handed her the gun.

Margaux's eyes opened wide—there was a look of sudden terror in them.

EIGHTY-SEVEN

I knew something sinister was right behind me. I had a millisecond to decide. The Glock in my belt or the knife in my hand? I dropped and rolled over Chandler's stiff body, which served as both a buffer and leverage to bounce to my feet. I quickly stood. A man wearing a black wool knit cap on his head held a fishing knife with a serrated blade. He charged toward me, thrusting the blade.

I brought my knife up and deep into the center of his chest. He looked at me with fury in his red eyes, and his clothes reeked of weed and grease. I pulled my knife from his chest and plunged the blade into the right side of his neck up to the handle. He fell at my feet on his back, staring at the dim ceiling light. Dark red blood began pooling next to his head. He took his last breath.

I wiped the knife blade on his pants and then took the wool knit cap from his head and put it on. I pulled the cap down to just above my eyebrows. I turned to Margaux. She looked pale. "Stay in here until I come back. Is that clear?"

She nodded. "Please come back."

I put the knife in the sheath, held the Glock, and stepped into the night. There was no one on deck. I kept my head low and moved toward the pilothouse, red lights at the top of the outriggers, and the marina lights in the distance. Marsh had the diesels roaring. We'd be through the inlet and into the Atlantic in twenty minutes. I stopped and stood behind another raised structure, maybe the crew's quarters. I cut off two pieces of rope from a coiled stern line.

***

At the helm, Hank Marsh smoked weed, sitting back in the captain's chair, steering the big wheel with the orange rubber boots on his feet. Mutt stood to the right, watching for boat traffic. He drank Mountain Dew from a can, his whiskers like steel wool. He looked over at Marsh. "Sharky, how long do you wanna keep the woman in the cooler? I don't see any boats moving out here."

"As soon as we get through the pass, we'll bring her out. I want her in the captain's quarters for the first hour. I've got plans for that gal. You and Lee can have what's left of her. By the time we get out to the stream, she'll be beggin' to be tossed overboard. Speaking of Lee, where the hell is he?"

"Don't know. Maybe he's in the shitter."

"He was supposed to check on the girl and come right back. If that sorry ass is doin' her in the cooler, I might hang him upside down from the top of an outrigger. That'd teach him. Go tell Lee to get his ass out here."

"Okay."

Mutt left as Marsh took another hit from the burning weed and rubbed his crotch with a calloused hand.

***

The pilothouse door opened. A man stepped out and lit a cigarette, blowing white smoke into the night air. He was short but built like an NFL linebacker, with biceps that looked like hams. I stood in the shadows between the cooler and what I thought might be the crew's quarters and waited.

Under the boat's running lights, I saw his shadow moving. The moment he was parallel to the recess where I stood, I switched the Glock to my left hand and used my right fist to hit him hard in the left jaw. The blow knocked the man to his knees. His eyes dazed, I dragged him into the nook area. I underestimated his endurance. He hit me in the stomach, the punch almost knocking the wind out of my lungs.

I pushed the Glock into his forehead. "Don't move! You raise your hands, and a bullet goes through your sick brain."

"You're the asshole, O'Brien."

"And, right now, I'm probably the last person on earth you'll see while you're alive. Wherever you go after you die, I'd bet your bed is already made, pal." I pulled out my phone, tapping the record button. "Who are you and Hank Marsh working for?"

"Kiss my ass."

"Bad answer." I brought the pistol grip down hard on the bridge of his nose. The blow smashed cartilage, causing blood to stream over his wide mouth and chin and drip onto his T-shirt. I pulled out my knife. "Here are your choices. I push this sharp blade through your brachia artery in your arm, and then I cut through the femoral artery in your leg, letting the life drain out of you within ten minutes—or you answer my questions. With the blood-letting choice, your heart will try hard to pump on empty. Very painful."

He spat blood. I drew the knife back, ready to strike. "Okay," he coughed. "Cap'n Marsh works for that shady lawyer in town."

"Which lawyer?"

"Some dude called Percy King."

"Who shot and killed Floyd Shaw?"

"We did. Carl Lee pulled the trigger. I guess you done killed him, or you'd be dead."

"Who murdered Darnell Reid?"

"Way I hear it, Shaw and some other dude did it."

"Who killed the reporter, Ken Chandler, and why?"

"We did—me, Carl Lee, and Cap'n Marsh."

"Who's *me?* What's your name?"

"Miguel Morales."

"Why'd you kill Chandler?"

"Cause we were paid to do it."

"Who paid you?"

"Probably that lawyer, King."

"Who abducted Margaux Brennon?"

"We did."

"Who's we?"

"Carl Lee, Cap'n Marsh, and me."

"Who hired you?"

"I believe it was King."

"Good night."

"Huh?"

I hit him hard and fast in his left jaw, cracking the jawbone. His head fell back against the steel structure, his eyes fading. I tied his feet together, rolling him over to tie his hands behind his back. I stopped the audio recording.

Two down. One to go.

EIGHTY-EIGHT

I assumed Marsh would have a gun with him in the pilothouse, perhaps more than one gun. Didn't matter. He probably couldn't shoot well with both hands. I kept my head low, wearing the wool knit cap, as I climbed the four steps leading up to the pilothouse. I glanced through the salt-stained windows. Marsh was sitting in the captain's chair, steering the wheel with his boots, the glow of electronic gauges filling the small room.

I quietly opened the door, smelling the stink of burning weed and sour beer in the air. He was listening to a marine weather forecast coming from the radio. There was a pistol, a Ruger revolver, on the console next to a pack of Camel cigarettes and a Zippo lighter. I hit the record button on my phone while stepping inside.

He heard me, turned, and reached for his gun at the same time. "Don't!" I warned.

He didn't listen, scrambling for the gun. I brought the Glock's muzzle down hard across his right wrist. The blow was strong enough to break bones. I grabbed the Ruger, putting it under my belt. "Sit! You get out of the chair, and you'll never sit again."

"What'd you do with my crew, ass wipe?"

"The same thing I'll do to you if you lie to me. How will I know if you're lying? It's because I know the truth. I just want to hear it from you. Let's call this a confession."

"Screw you! Your days are numbered, O'Brien. Same goes for your wife and kid—"

I backhanded Marsh hard across the left side of his smug face. The blow almost knocked him out of the chair. I picked up a ballpoint pen next to his pack of cigarettes. "Listen closely to me, scumbag. When I was a POW in Afghanistan, I had to shove a pen like this through a

Taliban leader's eyeball and into his brain to escape. I won't hesitate to do the same thing to you. On second thought, I have a knife. It will make a wider, deeper cut."

I pulled the knife from the sheath.

Marsh lifted his hands. "You're a crazy motherfu—"

"Yes! I am. Three seconds. Lay your cards down, or you'll become a one-eyed Jack."

"Shit! Okay! Okay! What do you want me to tell you?"

"The truth. Let's start with Percy King. How long have you worked for him, and what do you do for him?"

"I started out doing odd jobs, and then it sorta grew from there."

"Grew into what?"

"Handling clients that wouldn't pay or were slow to pay."

"Define handling."

"Whackin' knees. Poppin' shoulder blades and elbows out of joint."

"When did it lead to murder?"

"About six months ago. We started out just droppin' a body every now and then at sea. King knows some of the shit I got into, like setting fire to an asshole's shrimp boat. I didn't know the owner was aboard sleepin' when I did it. Anyway, King is a man who can put you in prison for a damn long time or keep you out if you do what the hell he says."

"Why didn't you go to the police?"

"King would hire someone to put a bullet in my head. And he knows a lot of the cops. He's like a small-town mob boss. Got his hands into people, property, and other crap."

"Does he pay you for the jobs that you do for him?"

"Yeah, the sonna' bitch pays good money, but you gotta do a lot of sick shit to get it."

"Tell me about the sick shit. Start with Darnell Reid and work your way up to Gideon Wright, Floyd Shaw, reporter Ken Chandler, and Margaux Brennon."

Marsh rambled on and on about how King paid for dirty jobs in cash and under the table. Marsh included everyone I'd mentioned and added, "He wanted us to kill the old man, Wright, and make it look like he fell in his spring and drowned. Everything changed once all the other shit came down, and when that woman with the little white dog got on the scene. Now, it's all about lockin' the old man up and makin' his granddaughter vanish without a trace."

"Okay, you explained it to me. Will you do it for a prosecutor?"

"Only if they work out a deal with me." He shook his head. "But there are two things you don't seem to understand, O'Brien. Ain't nobody gonna arrest King. He owns too many cops. And he's even got at least two judges takin' bribes. Second thing, unless y'all got a damn good witness protection program, I won't live long enough to testify against King."

"Yes, you will. Turn this boat around."

EIGHTY-NINE

I had to work very fast to close the second and final part of my plan to bring down those who would hurt or kill Gideon Wright. Now I set my sights on the top of the food chain. I had started with the bottom feeders—those hired guns who carried out the grunt work while the bosses dined in country clubs. To get to the very top of Glacier Artesian Springs, I had to set a trap with such perceived value that it would entice the corporate rats to venture into uncharted waters. I wanted them to make an unscheduled stop.

As Marsh used both hands to work the wheel in the pilothouse, I watched the vast bay for any sign of moving boats. City lights twinkled in the distance, the glow from high-rise condos dotting the night sky. As he set a direction for the shrimp boat to go, I pointed my Glock at his forehead. "Call King."

"And say what?"

"What you would have told him when you finished: the job was a success, and you'd like the balance of the money he agreed to pay you. Where do you usually receive cash for the jobs?"

"In his office, behind closed doors."

"Tell King that this time you want the money delivered to your boat at the docks. Tell him you are going to lay low. You and your crew are staying on the boat for a couple of days offshore, making sure that everything has blown over. Then you expect to get the remaining balance of the money he owes you."

"King doesn't like taking orders from people who work for him."

"You have leverage. He owes you the money. And you know who and what he is. So, all you are asking is for him to get off his fat ass and bring the money to you."

"Sure, whatever, pal."

"Call him." As he made the call, I held the Glock in one hand and checked the audio on my phone, making sure it was still recording. I stared at Marsh. "Put the call on speaker."

He did, and after a couple of rings, King answered. "I trust all went well and as planned."

Marsh cleared his throat and shot a look of disdain at me. "Yeah, everything pretty much went as planned. We're heading out to deep water."

"Is the girl still alive?"

"For now. We'll have some fun with her out here first. You know, take our time before she becomes crab food."

"Don't let some passing cruise boat or freighter see you."

"How dumb do you think we are, King? After the dirty deed, me and my crew are gonna hang out a day or two offshore. We wanna make sure there's no heat. Shouldn't be, but you never know. Somebody might have seen something, or there could have been a security camera close by. I'll call or text you when we're in port. Do me a favor if you would."

"What's that?"

"Can you bring the rest of the pie to the boat? When were back, I wanna stay at the marina for a few days and away from Deland. You know, just keepin' a low profile and close to my full tank of diesel fuel."

"All right. Let me know when you dock. You and your boys are becoming so proficient in this line of work. I might have one more job for you."

"What are you thinkin'?"

"I'd rather not be specific over the phone. Suffice to say, though, that this last one will bring down a man who is a mosquito in our faces. Talk later." He clicked off.

I kept my audio recording going, gesturing for Marsh to stand. "Let's take a little walk."

"To where?"

"Can you swim? I'd guess it's at least seven miles to shore. Can you make it? Or a better question: Will the bull sharks in the bay rip you apart within the first mile?"

"I may be an outlaw, but you're one sick asshole. You gonna toss me overboard?"

"That depends on you. If you stay on your best behavior, there will not be a permanent timeout. If not, I'll grab you by the scruff of your neck and throw you overboard. Because you smoke weed and cigarettes, I'd bet that in thirty yards, your lungs will give out." I looked at the depth finder. It's eighty feet deep way out here."

"What more do you want?"

"Get up and walk out of the wheelhouse to the deck."

He did as I ordered. I followed right behind him. I didn't know if he had more guns hidden on the boat. I wasn't taking any chances. "Walk to the cooler and stand to the left of the door." He complied. I slowly opened the door and shouted, "It's me. You can come out."

Margaux walked out of the cooler. She was trembling, her body cold, and her knuckles like cotton as she gripped the pistol. I pointed to Marsh. "Margaux, is this man, Hank Marsh, one of the three men who abducted you from your home?"

"Yes."

"His predator friends call him Sharky. If he makes a move, shoot him. The other two abductors are incapacitated. Marsh is the last man standing."

She nodded. "Okay. Where are you going?"

"Right back here." I picked up a coiled stern line and cut two pieces three feet long. I looked at Marsh. "Turn around and put your hands behind your back." He did so, and I tied his wrists together. "Sit on the engine cover." He grunted and sat down. I tied his legs at the ankles and walked back to Margaux. "I need to make a phone call. If he attempts to stand, shoot him in the chest. I'll put the final shot through his small brain."

I walked back inside the pilothouse, turning off the engines, and called FBI Special Agent Claudia Ramirez. I stepped back outside where I could watch Marsh. Margaux stood fifteen feet away from him, pointing the gun at his chest.

After Claudia answered, I told her everything that had happened in the last two hours. And then I added the background information, including the link to Glacier Artesian Springs. "This is corporate greed at its worst, mixing white collar crime with blue collar kidnappers and hit men. That spring water is worth hundreds of millions."

"I was hoping to hear from you. After I spoke with Wynona, I had a team on standby. We can pull a couple of special agents from the Orlando field office. I'm coming down from Jacksonville with three agents. I can be there in about ninety minutes."

"Excellent. I'll keep the shrimp boat in the middle of the bay before heading toward the docks, trying to arrive right after your team gets there. We can text as you get closer."

"Sounds good. I know the police chief in Daytona Beach. As a courtesy, I'm going to let him know. He can dispatch officers, but it doesn't look like we'll need backup. There appears to be no imminent threat, with one perp dead and two others tied up. However, we could use the local PD in terms of checking boxes and maybe using one of their offices as a temporary headquarters. These cases could be tried in federal or state court. I'm so glad that you recorded audio through most of what occurred. See you soon."

"Claudia, the arrest of these guys is the tip of the iceberg. I mentioned the corporate connection and the local lawyer working as a front man for them to set up schemes to beat the legal system. I have a plan to bring them all down. With your help, we can do it, and they'll never suspect the trap door is about to close on them."

There was a pause. "Wynona told me some of your background. When all of this is behind us, I'd like to hear more." She clicked off.

I walked back over to Margaux. She was still trembling. I put my arm around her shoulders and whispered, "Gideon will be proud of you, especially after your role in the next part of this fight."

Marsh stared across the deck at us. The only sound was the chop of black water slapping against the hull of *Miss Marla Jean.*

NINETY

In less than two hours, I maneuvered *Miss Marla Jean* up to the shrimp boat docks. A team of FBI special agents and local police were there to meet us. Margaux tossed them lines as they helped tie the boat to dock cleats. As I turned off the engines, I could see Special Agent Claudia Ramirez speaking with a man, whom I assumed was the police chief. He was in his mid-fifties, his hair graying, and he nodded as she spoke.

The FBI team boarded the boat with weapons drawn. I came out of the pilothouse and met them. Special Agent Ramirez wore black jeans and a windbreaker with the white letters FBI across the back. I pointed to Marsh. "That's Captain Hank Marsh. He's willing to work with your team and the prosecutors."

I pointed toward the alcove between the cooler and the crew's quarters. "Over there is where you'll find the unconscious man, Miguel Morales, aka Mutt, as his outlaw pals affectionately call him. Before taking a nap, his statements matched what Marsh had said about the players in this murder-for-hire and body disposal criminal enterprise. This is Margaux Brennon. She's a lawyer and Gideon Wright's great-granddaughter. She was kidnapped by the guys on this boat and was about to be dumped out at sea along with the body of Ken Chandler, a reporter, who was investigating Percy King and his various illegal projects. Chandler's body is inside that cooler, which is where they were holding Margaux until I managed to find her."

"I had almost given up until Sean opened that door. He was soaking wet because he had jumped off the docks and swam to the shrimp boat as these men were leaving port." Margaux wrapped her arms around herself.

Ramirez nodded. She turned to her team. "Arrest Marsh and Morales." She looked at me. "On the phone, you mentioned a third man here."

I gestured to the cooler. "He's in there. He pulled a knife on me. I got lucky and managed to turn the tables on him. Margaux saw everything."

"The coroner's van is in the parking lot. We'll have them remove the bodies. I've been speaking with Chief Don Weaver. He's up to speed on most of what you shared with me. I didn't go into detail much beyond what you told me about the abductions and what happened on the shrimp boat."

"That's good."

"Don is offering the FBI use of an office in his department to interview everyone, including you and Margaux. If Marsh and Morales are willing to cut a deal, we can hold them in protective custody in isolated cells within the county jail until this thing is buttoned up."

"Good. Let's move on."

***

I drove Margaux in my Jeep to the police department where Special Agent Ramirez and two senior agents were waiting to question us after they videotaped interviews with Hank Marsh and Miguel Morales. On the way, I told Margaux how we could take down the two principles with Glacier Artesian Springs—Roger Heller and Clifford Price—and added, "If we can get Price out of his New York office and entice him to come here, we can nail him."

"How do we entice him to come here?"

"By waving a hundred-million-dollar payout in his face. Like a bull, he won't be able to resist the red cape if that kind of money is written across it."

"Who is going to be the matador with the cape?"

"Gideon. We'll need to coach him to help plant the seeds that will sprout the responses we need. We could have you join him, but chances are that Heller and Price think you're dead."

We will have Gideon make the phone call to Heller. Gideon can say that he's ready to acquiesce and is considering selling exclusive water rights to Glacier, but he wants to meet in person with both Heller and Price. He'd insist on meeting the top dog, Price, and hearing how he'd respect the spring and guarantee to only pump a limited amount of water from it."

"Where will they meet Gideon?"

"The Wagon Wheel—the same diner where Heller first met Gideon. I've eaten there a few times. There are plastic flowers in vases on each table, right next to the salt and pepper shakers. The floral arrangements have a small plastic butterfly or bee on each one. Since Gideon is a beekeeper, it seems appropriate that one of the bees on those flowers will have a sharp sting."

She smiled. "So, you're setting up a sting operation."

"Yeah. You, me, Gideon, and our friends with the FBI. I hear they're pretty good at that kind of thing."

"How about Percy King? Will he be there?"

"Maybe. That depends on how his delivery goes when he stops by *Miss Marla Jean.*"

NINETY-ONE

The following day, we did a dress rehearsal. I sat with Margaux and Gideon on the porch of his cabin, going through scenarios that could lead to the results we needed. "We need to set a trap for Roger Heller and Clifton Price with what you say to them. Then you'll take a restroom break, leaving them alone at the table. What they say while you're gone could be all we need to prove their complicity in the murder-for-hires."

Gideon nodded. "After what you and Margaux shared with me, I'm ready to set a bear trap. No one kidnaps my granddaughter and walks around as a free man. How do you propose we set the trap?"

"By steering the meeting. What you say should motivate Heller and Price to speak freely when they think their conversation is private. The FBI will have planted a bug—a concealed microphone and transmitter inside the flower vase—at a designated table in the Wagon Wheel. The FBI agents will be outside in a van, listening and recording their conversation."

Margaux looked toward the spring, concentrating momentarily on a weeping willow tree swaying in the breeze and a great white heron standing statue-like at the water's edge. "What if Clifford Price refuses to come? If Heller is the only one there, he won't be talking to himself when Gideon gets up to go to the restroom."

"If Price refuses to show, we'll have to deal with it. But with this kind of money on the table, I'm betting he'll be there. Gideon, are you ready to make the call?"

"Yes. I have Roger Heller's number in my phone."

"Good. Let's call him. Put the phone on speaker."

Gideon made the call. Heller answered. "Mr. Wright, what a pleasant surprise. I've been hoping to hear from you. Has anything changed with your situation that we should know about?"

"Well, I'm sure you know about the court proceedings. My attorney thinks the prosecutor might drop the charges at the arraignment due to things I can't reveal at this time."

"I understand. I wish you the very best."

"I'm getting a little anxious, though. I haven't heard from my attorney. She hasn't returned my phone calls or text messages. I hope she didn't go back to Seattle."

"I'm sure she has the best intentions, but she's probably just swamped in paperwork."

"I know she's swamped. Look, Mr. Heller, I've had a lot of time to think recently. I never thought I'd hear myself say this …." Gideon paused and looked at us.

"What is it, Mr. Wright? What did you think you'd never hear yourself say?"

"Well, because I have so much going on in my life, I'm now considering selling exclusive water rights to Glacier if I can get a genuine assurance that the company's powers-that-be will treat the spring with the respect it deserves. Also, I need to be assured that they will pump only an agreed-upon daily water quantity."

"Yes, sir. I know exactly where you're coming from, and I'm sorry your life has been so chaotic lately." Heller's insincere voice had a tenor of glee. "I can speak with our CEO, Clifton Price, and we would work through an agreement that I assure you will be mutually satisfying."

"I want to hear it from Mr. Price."

"I'm sure we can work it out in a phone call as the contract parameters proceed."

"No, sir. I don't operate that way. I want to negotiate with you and Mr. Price. We need to sit down at a table and see eye-to-eye on this before your corporate attorneys start to finalize what we all agree to do. I want Mr. Price to meet us for lunch in that same diner where I first met you. That way he'll understand the sense of community we have in the South. We can work out the details on a napkin and go from there."

"Mr. Wright, I'm not sure Clifton Price would be available. His calendar is booked for several weeks, and …."

"Mr. Heller, before you go on making excuses for him, maybe you ought to call the man and run it by him. I will add that, Glacier Artesian

Springs isn't the only water company that's interested in my spring. I'll meet you and Mr. Price at the Wagon Wheel diner at noon on Friday, at the end of the week. I hope this will work out for everyone concerned. Please call to let me know what you folks want to do."

"I'll do my best. No guarantees."

"I suppose it will boil down to how badly you want the rights to the world's best water. The closest thing on earth to the Fountain of Youth. Goodbye, Mr. Heller." Gideon clicked off.

Margaux shot to her feet. "Wow! Oh, my God, you were fantastic. Perhaps it was your genes that led me to study law. You certainly know how to get people to come to a meeting. So persuasive."

Gideon smiled. "I've been doing that all my adult life. After you and Sean told me what happened to that reporter and to you, this isn't so much a meeting as it is the art of a winning strategy. They drew a line in the sand too close to my family."

***

I was driving back to the marina when I got a call from Margaux. "Sean, I just spoke with Gideon. He said that Roger Heller and the CEO of Glacier Artesian Springs agreed to the meeting. Clifton Price is taking one of the company's jets to fly in for the meeting. It's happening."

"I'll call FBI Special Agent Claudia Ramirez and set up the arrangements. She'll work with the diner management and handle the covert logistics."

"Where will you be?"

"Wherever I'm needed. That might be coming to the crossroads with Percy King."

"What if Price and Heller don't say anything that will incriminate them while Gideon is away from the table?"

"That's the gamble we're taking. When giving your final summation before a jury, do you think, *what if* they come back deadlocked?"

"I see your point."

"Your great-grandfather may be up there in years, but that gives him a lifetime of wisdom to use at a table with two men not even half his age."

"You're right. I'm just nervous for him. Right now, we obviously have more than enough evidence to have the prosecution drop all charges

347

against Gideon. We're only doing this charade to elicit the responses that will shift the evidence to the two corporate criminals who sanctioned everything. Thank you for keeping me focused and for staying the course."

"We can all thank each other after the course leads to a win. I need to call the FBI." I clicked off and called Special Agent Ramirez.

NINETY-TWO

The next day, at 11:30 a.m., I had an odd feeling sitting in a van outside the diner. The sides of the van were painted with the words: *Mid-Florida Electric.* Inside was some of the most advanced audio and video recording equipment in the world. The unusual feeling in my gut had more to do with me than the FBI. I was used to working alone. And now I was embedded with federal agents as we were hoping to take down Roger Heller and his high-profile boss, Clifton Price.

Inside the diner, Gideon Wright was waiting. I knew this was the only way to protect him, Margaux, and his land and spring.

The trap was set.

Gideon had taken a seat at a round table in the corner of the diner. The FBI had arranged the table so it would be out of earshot, giving the players a feeling of privacy as they started their meeting. Gideon sat alone, looking at his watch. He took a deep breath and watched the front entrance.

There were a dozen other customers, some sitting at the counter, in booths, and at tables. He glanced down at the plastic flower arrangement in the vase at the center of the table. He stared at the plastic honeybee; a tiny audio microphone was hidden just below the bee.

Outside in the van, along with the FBI team leader, Claudia Ramirez, and a male agent, I watched the video and audio feeds on monitors. A technician sat at a small console, adjusting controls at a keyboard, the audio signal visible in a squiggly horizontal line on a computer screen.

The FBI was tapping into the diner's four security cameras, giving them a view of the parking lot, inside the diner, and the rear door. The tech removed his earphones, glancing over at Ramirez. "The audio and video signals are fine. They'll record well."

"Good." She looked up at the video monitors. "It's about to be showtime."

In another area of the parking lot, four more members of Ramirez's team were staked out in a black Ford Explorer, watching and waiting for the two men to arrive. I looked at one of the video monitors and could see Gideon sitting with his arms resting on the table, his large hands folded, and a cup of coffee in front of him. I could not detect even the slightest bit of nervousness from him.

Back at his cabin, Margaux was waiting for us to call her. When we did make the call, I hoped it would be the good news that they both needed to hear. Ramirez pointed to a monitor on the left side of the audio and video console. "That may be them. That Mercedes looks like it's from a luxury car service. There are two men in the back seat." She spoke into a small microphone on her sleeve. "Standby, team. The Mercedes pulling up in front of the restaurant may be our delivery service."

We watched as two men got out of the car. One was dressed in a dark suit, light blue shirt, and maroon tie. The other wore a navy blue sports coat and khaki pants. Even from the distance and through the surveillance cameras, I knew who was in charge. Clifton Price wore the suit and the corporate pants. He opened the front passenger door and said something to the driver. When he closed the door, the driver parked the Mercedes in an area of the lot that was shaded by moss-draped oaks.

Price stood erect near the diner's entrance. He touched one of his French cuffs, the cufflink flashing in the sunlight. It looked like Price had come from a hair and makeup trailer on a film set. His brown hair was perfectly cut and sprayed. Nothing moved on his head in the breeze. His face radiated confidence, like a man used to giving orders and having people jump to fulfill them.

Roger Heller's grin was almost as bright as Price's cufflinks. Heller gestured to the entrance, letting Price walk in front of him. I glanced up at the interior surveillance cameras as the two men walked inside. Heller pointed to Gideon in the back of the dining room. The men approached him. They made introductions, shook hands, and sat.

Price set the tone of the meeting. "Mr. Wright, may I call you Gideon?"

"Yes, of course."

"Gideon, I am truly honored to meet you. Roger has shared some of your background. Your history as a hydrogeologist is most impressive. At Glacier Artesian Springs, we could use men with your experience."

Gideon smiled. "Are you offering me a job?"

There was laughter, and Price responded. "If you want one, of course. Who knows, maybe we'll use your expertise from time to time as a consultant on our projects."

"I'll keep that in mind. Thanks for the vote of confidence."

"Absolutely. Roger tells me that the food in this place is excellent. What do you recommend?"

"It's all good. The blackened trio is one of my favorites."

Heller chuckled. "I had that. It's very good. You get gator tail, blackened shrimp, and white fish over something called swamp grits."

Price nodded. "When in Rome ...."

After a server came and took their orders, Price leaned forward, both hands and fingers splayed on the table.

I watched the exchange closely, hoping Gideon would remember what I suggested, depending on how the conversation went. Price smiled. "Gideon, I mentioned some of Glacier's projects earlier. There is no project in our entire worldwide portfolio that is more important than yours. From the water tests, which we've been privileged to assess, your spring can't be duplicated anywhere on earth."

Gideon nodded. "Yes, it is the world's best water because it delivers everything the body needs, not only to satisfy thirst but to rejuvenate every organ and cell."

Heller glanced around the diner before saying, "I truly believe it has near magical properties. They're almost unearthly in their power to renew the human body."

Gideon looked at both men. "Not only the human body, but also that of plants and animals. I have a bullfrog—the fella's missing his left foot—that's lived in the spring for more than twenty years. Some herons, egrets, and other wildlife have stalked its waters for years."

Price steepled his fingers. "So, in effect, it is the legendary Fountain of Youth. Sip the water and stay forever young."

"No, only change is forever. Like a car battery, this water helps keep it charged."

"Gideon, we are about to make you an offer that I truly think you cannot refuse. I'm glad you are sitting down to hear it."

"Okay, what is your offer?"

NINETY-THREE

Inside the van, you could have heard a pin drop. We looked at the monitors as Clifton Price gestured at Heller. "Roger, the proposed contract is in that file we carried in here. But right now, I want to sweeten the offer."

Heller smiled. "All right."

Price looked at Gideon. "After the deal is complete, maybe our graphic arts department can create labels that illustrate what's in the bottle—water from the fabled Fountain of Youth."

Gideon didn't respond immediately. "I wouldn't call the spring a fountain of youth, as in the legend of what Ponce de Leon sought. But it does have restorative elements."

Price and Heller exchanged glances. Price took the lead. "Gideon, for the exclusive rights to pump water from your spring, we will compensate you two million dollars a month for the rest of your life. And we hope you live a long life. After your death, the payments could go to the charities you designate or toward any other person or foundation you want it to go."

"That's very generous of you, Clifton. I would like for that to go to my great-granddaughter, Margaux Brennon. She's also my attorney, but I haven't heard from her in a couple days. That's worrisome since my arraignment is approaching. I need her to defend me in court. I know she's never handled a criminal case quite like mine, but she's smart. If something, God forbid, happened to her, I might need legal help."

Price nodded. "We understand."

"After my death, I would like for the monthly payments to go to Margaux. If that can happen, you have yourself a deal. If not, it's a dealbreaker. Your money, then, will be of no interest, only the health and wellbeing of my spring. And to achieve that, I might donate everything—the land and the spring—to the Nature Conservancy. The one major stipulation of that agreement is that under no circumstances would the Conservancy be permitted to allow any company to pump water from the spring."

Price and Heller looked dumbfounded.

***

Inside the van, Ramirez shook her head. "Would you look at that. Even the infamous Clifton Price is losing his cool.

I watched them through the monitors. I knew what was about to happen, at least in terms of what Gideon was going to do. How Price and Heller would react in his absence was unknown.

***

Price inhaled a deep breath, angling his head as if he were listening to a voice inside. He chose his words carefully. "So, you are telling us that the reason for your change of mind in agreeing to sell the water rights to us is contingent on your great-granddaughter, Margaux, becoming the beneficiary of the monthly financial allotments for the rest of her life."

"Exactly. If you gentlemen would excuse me. I need to head to the restroom. When you get my age, you relish a healthy bladder. Mine is healthy. It just has a lot of mileage on it."

He got up and left the dining room.

Price looked across the table at Heller. "What the shit is wrong with this scenario? I'll tell you what's wrong, Roger. You wanted to get the great-granddaughter out of the picture to ensure that there would be no heir to the land and spring."

"Wait a minute. I ran every detail past you. And you signed off on everything."

"No, you were hired to run this operation here from ground zero—start to finish. You hired that local lawyer, Percy King, and he was supposed to make the opposition go away."

"He did. Every person that became a fly in the ointment was taken out. And by that, I mean literally taken out to sea for disposal. But you knew that. There is no body count because there are no bodies."

"Is Margaux Brennon still alive?"

"I doubt it."

"You *doubt* it? Why don't you know?

"Why do you ask a rhetorical question? I told you what the plans were from the kidnapping up until the trip to sea. You not only agreed, but you approved the budget to do it."

"I never mentioned the word murder."

"You didn't have to. It was implied when we spoke about eliminating problem people. Having them gone for good and doing whatever it takes to secure the water rights to a billion-dollar spring—the original Fountain of Youth. Those were your words, Clifton. Not mine."

"Listen to me, Roger. If you want to keep your job and earn your bonus, which is contingent on Glacier obtaining exclusive water rights, you better get your ass in gear. Call that lawyer, King, and see if the woman is still alive."

"And then do what? If she's alive, she'll talk."

"If she's dead, so is this deal and your career. And if push comes to shove, I promise you that you will take the fall for this shit show. Not me. I was in New York all the time while you were down here working with that twisted lawyer and his southern knuckle-dragging Neanderthals. Call King now."

Heller took out his phone and made the call. "Percy, it's Roger. What's the status on the last cargo?"

King was driving his Cadillac. "All ought to have been delivered on time and within budget. We're more reliable than the post office." He chuckled.

"If the woman is still present, keep her that way. But we must make damn sure if or when she goes to the police, they can't track her kidnapping back to Glacier."

"Understand. The crew members weren't supposed to say anything at all to her. Nothing. One problem, Roger."

"What is that?"

"That shrimp boat is way beyond cell phone reach."

"Try a satellite phone or text. Whatever it takes. Call me when you hear." He clicked off.

Gideon came back to the table and sat in his chair. "Our food ought to be served soon."

***

Inside the van, Ramirez was about to pull the switch. She looked at me. "We have more than we need. We have enough to bust that crooked lawyer, King. I wish he were here with them."

I nodded. "We'll get him."

She spoke into her radio microphone. "Okay everyone. Let's go in there."

***

The food was just being served when federal agents, with FBI letters on their jackets, walked into the diner. Three of the agents had their guns drawn. They followed Ramirez as she approached the table, two agents moving to each side of the table. "Clifton Price and Roger Heller, I'm Special Agent Claudia Ramirez, FBI. You are under arrest for murder, conspiracy to commit murder, kidnapping, and the unlawful dumping of bodies at sea. Please stand and put your hands behind your backs."

Price shot up from his chair. Heller slowly stood. Price shook his head, palms out. "Wait just a second. Under arrest? For what? Is it against the law for a New Yorker to eat this kind of food?" He made a lame attempt at humor.

"Hands behind your back and turn around."

Price's face was flushed, his jawline hard, and his eyes darting around the diner. Heller was stoic. He looked down at Gideon with contempt. The agents cuffed the men and read them their rights.

Price looked over his shoulder at Gideon. "This is bullshit. We made you a good-faith offer and did it through your original attorney. What may or may not have transpired on a local level afterwards was not anything we condoned or elicited."

Ramirez held up one hand. "Enough. Get these two out of here."

After the agents hustled Price and Heller out of the diner, Ramirez and I sat down near Gideon. She looked across the table at him. "Mr. Wright, you did a fabulous job. We have everything that was said and done at this table captured on video and audio. After you went to the restroom, Price and Heller began the blame game, blaming each other for what they believed was the murder of Margaux, in addition to the other people who were killed. Price and Heller will go to prison for life."

Gideon pursed his lips, eyes thoughtful in the light from the windows. "Good. That's where they belong. I feel so bad for the people who lost their lives in this mess. I hope one man, who is in the middle of it all, Percy King, doesn't vanish to some other country."

I looked at Gideon. "He won't vanish. He might be in the shadows at this moment, but that's about to change."

NINETY-FOUR

Captain Hank Marsh no longer had the grin of a shark. Later that afternoon, he was in one of the police interrogation rooms, sitting in a hard plastic chair behind a table. Special Agent Ramirez and I sat across from him. She had a file folder in front of her. "Mr. Marsh, we do appreciate your cooperation in all of this. You will be in a much better position to strike a deal with the prosecutor."

He gave his Sharky smirk, a nerve under his left eye twitching. "It's all relative now. I don't have a lot to bargain for, not no more."

"You have your life."

He looked at her with contempt in his bloodshot eyes. I leaned closer. "Marsh, having gone on a short cruise to nowhere with you, I think we understand each other."

He shook his head. "What I understand about you, O'Brien, is that I might be an outlaw, but you're out of your freakin' mind. Your mama must have dropped you on your head when you were a baby."

"Here's the deal, Marsh. We're video recording you. The prosecutor will see this video. And he will hear what Special Agent Ramirez has to say about how cooperative you were or were not. Right now, you and Mutt are looking at death by lethal injection. And they don't waste time in Florida doing that. But the death penalty can be set aside if you help us bring down Percy King."

"Can you guarantee I won't get the needle?"

Ramirez nodded. "If you turn state's witness, yes. If not, we'll go have a chat with Mutt, and your chances are off the table. So, it depends on what you say and do."

"Do?"

He sat back and eyed me. "What she means by *do*, Marsh, is you're going to call King and tell him that *Miss Marla Jean* is back at the docks,

358

and you want your money delivered this afternoon. Tell King you want to have a drink with him on your boat."

"Why would I wanna do that?"

"Because I believe, if King comes to the docks, he'll be carrying a gun with a silencer. Why? Simply put, he will want to eliminate his last witnesses. That includes you and your crew, and he'll make it look like you shot and killed each other."

Marsh stared at nothing, his mind trying to grasp what I said. "Are you ready to make the call and turn the tables on a man who would put a bullet through your head and kill your crew?"

He nodded. I took Marsh's phone out of the small plastic box and handed it to him. "Call Percy King."

***

Three hours later, there were two FBI snipers with rifles on the marina rooftops. Three other agents, including Ramirez, were secluded in two moored boats very near *Miss Marla Jean*. I was on the shrimp boat and wearing a wire. Our conversation would be recorded inside the van at the edge of the parking lot.

The appointment was for five o'clock in the afternoon. I sat in the boat's pilothouse with a full view of the docks and marina. Percy King was strolling down the commercial dock, right on time. He wore a powder blue seersucker suit, carrying a briefcase in his left hand. On his head was a white Panama hat.

He came up to the shrimp boat as if he'd been on it a few times. "Hank, I'm here." His head slowly turned from left to right like an owl, with his shoulders remaining stationary, and only his head rotating. "I'm coming aboard."

I watched him climb up and over the metal ladder on the port side of the gunwale. He stood in the middle of the work deck. "Hank! It's happy hour. Let's pull the cork."

I came out of the wheelhouse and down the step to the deck. King's eyes grew wide. He blinked slowly, as if I might go away when he opened his eyes. "Where's Captain Marsh?"

"Sharky's rather indisposed now. He asked me to step in for him."

"Bullshit! What's going on here, O'Brien? What'd you do with Captain Marsh and his crew."

"The same thing that you did with Darnell Reid, Ken Chandler, Margaux Brennon, and what you tried to do to Gideon Wright. You caused the deaths of the first three, and then you wanted to have Gideon die in prison."

"What are you smoking, O'Brien? That's nonsense."

"I know you are more than complicit, King. You are much more than the simple country lawyer that you pretend to be. You are a ruthless killer with an appetite for money and power that is up there with some of the worst of the worst. Marsh and Mutt are turning state's evidence against you. They may have pulled the trigger, but you hired them. I have proof—eyewitnesses, surveillance footage, and audio and video confessions. Even your own secretary, Gladys Nelson, is talking. You shouldn't leave your office door open when you are cutting criminal deals with Roger Heller. Glady's has a keen sense of hearing."

King stared at me with a blank look on his round, pink face. "You can't prove any of these frivolous accusations."

"Are you calling murder-for-hire frivolous? Not only can I prove it, but I also have more than enough to put you on death row. You won't be able to turn to your wealthy pals, Roger Heller or Clifton Price. They're both in FBI custody, facing the rest of their greedy lives in prison. And they're pointing their manicured fingers at a crooked, local lawyer—you."

"If you thought this garbage that you're saying had any teeth in it, the cops would be here and not you. Who are you, O'Brien, a crazy Lone Ranger? You'll soon be taken off your high horse."

"Answer this for me, will you, King? Were you born bad, or was it an acquired trait? Was evil the hand that rocked your cradle? If it was acquired, when did you sell your soul, and did you sell it for the kind of money that you hoped to reap by stealing Gideon's spring? By the way, you won't be tried in a local court. There will be a change of venue, and you'll be tried and convicted in federal court. Marsh and Mutt will testify against you. Add Price and Heller, and you're going down, way down."

"Then you're going with me." He reached into his seersucker suit. I pulled my Glock from under my shirt. "No! Don't pull on me, King. There are FBI agents with guns on you."

He hesitated, his hand still under his jacket, his eyes looking around.

I took one step closer. "Slowly take your hand out of your jacket, drop the briefcase, and turn around."

I watched his eyes. Somewhere inside them, like in the dark recesses of a cave, bats fluttered. Something switched in his brain, and his face twisted into something snarling and demonic, spittle flying from his mouth. He pulled out his gun.

Before I could get off a shot, his head exploded. The first round went through his Panama hat and skull. Four more shots hit his body and the briefcase. As he went down, the briefcase was blown open, sending money flying into the air and fluttering down on the bloody deck and marina water like green confetti.

Less than thirty seconds later, Ramirez and her team were running to the boat. I lowered my Glock, putting it back under my shirt and belt. Ramirez came over the marine ladder first, followed by two of the other agents. I looked toward the rooftops; the snipers were standing there in silhouette.

"O'Brien, are you okay?" Ramirez asked.

"I'm all right."

Two more agents boarded the boat. Some of the agents checked out the rest of the boat's interiors. I looked at the marina water, where hundred-dollar bills were floating away with the outgoing tide.

Ramirez and her team surveyed King's body. One agent, wearing latex gloves, squatted to pick up the pistol. King had fallen face down, blood still pooling around what was left of his skull, and loose money was spattered with blood and brain matter.

Ramirez holstered her gun. "Did King really think you were alone after you told him there were federal agents all around and that he was in the crosshairs? Did he have a death wish? Suicide by cop?"

Adrenaline shot through my system. I stood by the port side, watching hundred-dollar bills floating, the tide pulling them toward the inlet. "That money will make someone's day."

***

As the scene was being processed by federal agents, I stood on the dock near *Miss Marla Jean,* called Wynona, and told her what happened. "I'm leaving here soon. We can go back home to the river tonight."

361

"Good. I love *Jupiter*, but I'm ready for our big shower. Thank God you're okay. I'm so glad that Claudia and her team were there as your backup. With Percy King gone, it looks like the two big fish, Clifton Price and Roger Heller, will have their day in court. I'm sure the news media will be all over it—every salacious detail in the Fountain of Youth trial."

"No doubt. Kiss Angela for me. I'll see you both soon." I clicked off and called Dave, giving him an update.

"Well Sean, who could have predicted this outcome? It's not often that the criminal elite, in this case Price, Heller, and King, are brought down, along with the grunts they hired to do their dirty work. But it happened. Congratulations."

"Save that until after the federal trial. In the meantime, thank you for all your help."

"You're welcome."

I clicked off and watched as the coroner's staff put Percy King into a body bag and onto a metal gurney. They lifted the gurney off the boat, locked the wheel extensions in place, and rolled King's body down the dock. The agents wore latex gloves to pick up the blood-soaked money from the deck. I started walking down the dock, thinking about one of the last things King said to me. *Who are you, O'Brien, a crazy Lone Ranger? You'll soon be taken off your high horse.*

NINETY-FIVE

Three months later, the criminal prosecutions of Clifton Price and Roger Heller were gaining attention, and the mob boss courtroom drama was about to begin. The charges against Gideon were dropped, and he and Margaux were spending time with each other often. I thought about that as I left our house on the river to drive to Gideon's cabin. He and I would be called as witnesses in the two separate trials, both held in federal court after Price and Heller were indicted by federal grand juries.

Although the two weren't heading organized crime families, there were parallels. The public's fascination and misguided admiration with mafia bosses dates back to the Prohibition era, when the mafia thumbed its noses at the law and sold bootlegged liquor. The mob bosses thought they were above the law and adhered only to their own chain-of-command rules.

Today, in the cases of Price and Heller, it wasn't liquor in bottles but rather earth's purest water, almost taken by force from an elder caretaker—"the custodian of the springs," as the news media were labeling Gideon. It was the exposure and downfall of a white-collar criminal enterprise that had gained vast wealth by using a hook-or-crook method to finesse and strong-arm water rights from municipal or privately owned springs across the nation. In Gideon's case, it was the classic David and Goliath scenario. As the giants stumbled and fell, Price was trying to shift the blame and guilt to Heller. In corporate cannibalism, they eat their own.

Driving to Gideon's cabin, I thought about the last three months. He and Margaux had become very close. Now bonded by blood and ideology, they would do as much as possible to cushion nature from destructive forces while enjoying the benefits of the land and spring. They had plans to open the spring to the public on a limited basis each month.

They were working with a family-owned bottling company to capture a small portion of the water discharge. That arrangement was to come with the caveat that the company would ship a portion of its water, without charge, to drought areas around the globe and to victims of natural disasters, such as hurricanes. As an attorney, Margaux was drawing up the paperwork.

Twice in the last few months, I had taken Wynona, Angela, and Max up to swim and play around the spring. Max had developed a friendship with Margaux's dog, Lily. Nick Cronus was going to visit the spring because Margaux wanted to learn how to SCUBA dive. Nick had volunteered to teach her. I smiled thinking about that.

Gideon called me earlier in the day with an offer. "Sean, I'm putting up a few dozen bottles of honey. It'll be the last harvest of the season. I have some kept aside for you and Wynona. Can you stop by to get the honey?"

"I can't turn down that offer."

"Bring your family."

"Wynona and Angela are at the Seminole res today visiting Wynona's mother, but I can be there in a couple of hours. It'd be good to see you again, Gideon."

"Likewise. Margaux and Lily should be here, too. Margaux tells me that she is as close as humanly possible to becoming addicted to this honey. I tell her that between the water and the honey, she's consuming nature's best offerings for good health. See you soon."

***

I unlocked Gideon's gate and drove slowly by the spring up toward his cabin. Margaux's car wasn't parked there yet. I hoped I would see her while visiting with him. Each time I came here and spent time with Gideon, I left learning something from him. As I got closer, I could see Gideon sitting on the wrought-iron bench at the base of his favorite tree, Seth. I parked near his car, got out, and walked toward the big tree, where squirrels were scampering about on the grass and leaves.

I smiled. "Those squirrels are going to give up acorns if you feed them too many peanuts."

Gideon didn't respond. His back was partially turned to me. I thought he didn't hear what I'd said. His head was resting against the trunk of the old tree, a cardinal in the limbs, its feathers like a red flame flickering between the green leaves. I watched the three squirrels near Gideon. "It looks like your furry friends are hungry."

No response.

I walked around to face Gideon. His eyes were closed, a peanut between his right hand's fingers. For a moment, I thought he was asleep or maybe saying a silent prayer. I stepped closer. His chest wasn't moving. "Gideon!" I ran up to him. I used two fingers to touch the left side of his neck. There was no heartbeat, and his skin was cool. I felt for a pulse in his wrists. There was nothing.

I took a deep breath. The sounds of nature—the cardinal in the boughs, the squirrels in the grass, and the bees in the flowers—all became silent as I looked at his kind face. The birdsong and buzzing around me were replaced with the sound of his voice, something he'd told me while I'd sat under the tree with him weeks ago.

This spring, the land here, and for that matter, everything on earth, are all in a constant state of rebirth and renewal. Death is a new beginning. Life begins as a march toward an end, but since there is really no end, it is a circle. If we take care of our bodies, the water from this spring just lets us recharge a little bit longer. But we, and even this old tree, Seth, are temporary. You only rent your body. One day it will be repossessed. You keep the relationships you build together. They are not fleeting. Instead, they pass through time and space to enter heaven's door.

I saw Margaux's car coming up the gravel driveway. I knew finding her great-grandfather dead on the bench under the old tree would be traumatic and painful. I wanted to run to her car, stop her, and have her turn back. But that would have violated everything Gideon believed about the cycle of life. He died peacefully under the oak. That was the way Margaux would have found him had I not arrived first. Sitting here with his animal friends would be a good way for her to remember his physical body. His spirit already lived in her heart.

I stood back a few feet as she came closer. "His, Sean. Are you guys feeding the squirrels?"

"Sort of. I think that Gideon wanted to hand the baton off to us—there's a peanut in his hand, and it looks like there are some in his shirt pocket."

"Wanted? What do you mean? She walked faster, now running up to her great-grandfather. She stopped and looked at his face. The peanut in one hand, the song of the cardinal in the tree limbs. She walked slowly over to his body, reaching out and touching his face, her eyes filling with tears.

"Grandpa, you saved us a place beside you." She sat to his right, her hand on his sleeve. She looked up at me, tears running down her cheeks, her lower lip quivering. "I wish I'd had more time with him. I cherish the days we did have together. The last few months were the best of my life. I learned so much just by being around him. I so loved his laugh, his wisdom and his kindness. Sean, please sit beside us."

I took a seat on the other side. Margaux sniffled, blowing out a deep breath and slowly regaining her composure. We sat there in silence for a few minutes, listening to the breeze rustle the leaves. She leaned forward and took the peanut from Gideon's hand. "Come here, little fellow." A squirrel ran to within ten feet of us, sitting up on its haunches. Margaux tossed the peanut to the squirrel. Another hop, and the squirrel used his mouth to pick it up.

"Sean, did you know that grandpa was just shy of his hundredth birthday? I don't know if death is ever beautiful, but for my grandfather, he led such a fulfilled life, making friends wherever he went and always helping others. So, in his case, death is fitting or perhaps fulfills the end of a life well lived because he didn't leave any loose ends."

"Gideon once told me that he believed the concept of death made us feel more alive. But in the same breath, he didn't want anyone to dwell on the inevitable but rather the here and now—the present, because he said that was the only point in time that we could choose the possibilities in life."

"He liked to recite a poem by Tennyson. It went something like this: 'All things must die … the stream will cease to flow, the wind will cease to blow, the clouds will cease to fleet, the heart will cease to beat, for all things must die." She smiled and looked over at me. "Grandpa told me what Tennyson didn't mention was that death also reminds us of what's important in life: the human relationships we form, the bonds of friendship we share, and the love we give, for they are the only forever gifts."

NINETY-SIX

Two months later, Clifford Price and Roger Heller were both sentenced to life in prison for their crimes. Gideon, of course, never got the opportunity to testify, but I think I felt his spirit the day I testified in front of a packed courtroom. I thought about that as I walked down my backyard toward the dock. Max followed me for the first fifty feet before setting off to take the lead. The morning air was cool and carried the sweet scent of honeysuckles in the breeze. The river was as flat as a billiard table and reflected the deep blue of an autumn sky.

We walked out to the end of the dock. I sat on one of the benches. It reminded me of the bench under Gideon's tree, Seth, and the first day I had met Gideon at the farmers' market. I remembered how tender he was when he sprinkled his spring water on Angela's skinned knee and the trust she felt in the old man's face. Before his death, he wrote a new will, leaving the land, cabin, and spring to Margaux. She was leaving her rented condo to move into the cabin.

Gideon was now buried in a grave next to his beloved wife, Heather. In his written will, he requested that his birth or death not be engraved on the old marble headstone we removed from his barn. The final inscription simply read:

Gideon Wright
Husband, Father, and Grandfather
He tried to leave the world a little better.

From my dock, I watched bees darting in and out of the purple trumpet flowers and jasmine on the riverbank, remembering how Gideon chatted with the bees as he removed honey from the hives. *Hi, my winged friends. I know you've been busy bees. Did you fellas make it out to the purple heather near the river? I hope so. It's sweet, like you.*

My thoughts were interrupted when I heard a diesel engine in front of my property. The engine stopped for a few minutes before starting again. I stood, looking to the left of the cabin, toward the end of the driveway. A UPS delivery truck moved on, vanishing around the bend in the road.

I sat back on the bench, picked Max up, setting her on my lap, and wondered if a delivery had been made. I watched an alligator slowly swim from the shoreline of the Ocala National Forest to my side of the river. I could see the gator's nostrils, knotty eyes, and the top of his broad back just above the surface. Its tail created a light ripple as it swam in our direction. An osprey dropped straight down from the sky, snatching a fish less than thirty feet from the gator's mouth.

"Max, what a window we have to the natural world up here on our dock. Gideon had Seth to talk to every day. But I have you, kiddo. And you're such a darn good listener." Max watched the gator swim. She lifted her bent ears as high as a dachshund could lift them.

I heard the back porch screen door close. Wynona and Angela were coming from the cabin down to the dock. Angela was carrying her favorite plush friend, a teddy bear she called Snuffles. Wynona also was carrying something in a brown paper bag.

When they got to the dock's entrance, I set Max down so she could run and greet them. In seconds, she and Angela would sprint back to me. "Daddy, Mama has a surprise for you. She said there are two surprises, but only one is in the bag."

"Really?"

"Yep. It didn't come in the bag. She put it in there."

"Okay."

Wynona approached, with a wide smile on her face. "We just got a delivery."

"What is it, and who sent it?"

"It was sent by Margaux Brennon. All together there are twenty-four—a whole case. I brought one down to you, gift wrapped in a small grocery sack, so it would be more of a surprise as we did the great reveal."

"Do we need a drum roll?"

"Maybe." She handed the paper bag to me. "Open it, or at least reach in and take the gift out."

I did, lifting out a bottle of water. The bottle was a pale shade of blue. The label had an image of a beautiful tropical spring, a shimmering pool of water in the shadows of palms and moss-draped oaks. The lettering read: *Gideon Springs – Water for the Soul.* I held up the bottle, looking at the water in the morning light.

Wynona smiled. "In Margaux's note, she said she wanted us to be the first to receive what will always and forever be a limited quantity of water."

I examined the label and thought of Gideon, remembering the first time I saw him swim in the spring, coming to the surface with wet air and a beard, a grin on his face, and a small bottle of water in one hand. I looked up at Wynona. "This is great, and exactly the way Gideon would have done it. Gideon Springs is in good hands with the next generation."

"Well, speaking of the next generation, Angela said I had two surprises. I do indeed. Sean O'Brien, my love, you are going to be a father once again. And you, Angela O'Brien, are going to have a baby sister or brother."

Angela squealed, clapping her small hands. Max barked and pranced on the dock. I stood and gave Wynona a big hug, gently lifting her feet off the planks. "A baby. I think I'm the only member of my family that's speechless now." I leaned down and kissed Wynona, then took Angela's hand and twirled her around.

After a moment, Wynona looked at the label on the bottle. "When I sip from Gideon Springs, I know I'm getting the best prenatal water in the world for our baby."

I unscrewed the cap and handed the bottle to her. She took a sip, closing her eyes as a breeze came across the old river. When she opened her eyes, a shadow moved over the dock. We looked up at an eagle soaring high above the cypress trees. The eagle flapped its wings once and rode the air current past the oxbow, sailing into the abyss between the water and sky.

The End

Made in United States
Orlando, FL
11 January 2024